Solaris Saga book 3

Janet McNulty

This is a work of fiction. The names, characters, places, and incidents within are the products of the author's imagination or are used fictitiously, and any resemblance to actual persons, living or dead, business establishments, events, or location is entirely coincidental. The publisher does not have any control over and does not assume any responsibility for author or third-party websites or their content.

Solaris Strays
Copyright © 2015 Janet McNulty

ISBN-13: 978-1-941488-28-7 (MMP Publishing)
ISBN-10: 1941488285

Library of Congress Control Number: 2015937492

Printed in the United States of America

First Edition

I hope you have been enjoying the series so far. Originally, Solaris was supposed to be a three-book series, but the last book got to be so long, that when I reached the 600-page mark, I decided to split it into two, making Solaris Strays the third in the series. Have fun reading the continuing adventures of Rynah and her crew.

Contents

Chapter 1
GENERAL DELMAR'S CHOICE

Eight pairs of boots stalked into the new council chambers, a makeshift room formed by a cave with a tarnished table filling its center, its edges burnt from the fires that had destroyed Lanyr—and nearly it as well. Each green-robed figure, bearing the Lanyran crest in silver and red embroidery, took a chair.

General Delmar, once the leader of the Lanyran fleet (and who had supported Obiah's wish to help Rynah), stood at the head of the table. His stern eyes glanced from one glum face to another as his mind practiced the words he hoped to sway them with, after spending restless nights debating whether he should do what he was about to embark upon.

"Gentlemen," he said, his deep, baritone voice resonating off the stone walls surrounding the room.

"Why have you called us here?" asked one, his marigold beard streaked with bits of gray strands.

"You know why," said Hylne. "Isn't it obvious?"

1

"General," said the councilman with the marigold beard, his tone expectant.

"Gentlemen," replied General Delmar, "I have called you here to re-discuss Obiah's proposal."

"But we have already decided on that matter," said another member.

"And I believe that decision to be a mistake," said General Delmar. "Obiah came here, asking for our help, and we turned him away."

"We do not have the resources to spare," another member said.

"Is that all you concern yourselves with?" demanded General Delmar. "One of our own has chased Klanor across the Twelve Sectors and we have left her to her fate."

"She chases a myth," said Hylne, the president of the council who had made his thoughts about Obiah's foolish request known the day he was brought before them.

"Is it a myth?" said General Delmar. "I have re-read the ancient tales and there are similarities between them and current events."

"People often see what they want to see," said another member.

"But the fact remains that Lanyr is gone," said General Delmar, "and all because one man believed in the ancient stories and stole the very crystal that kept the magnetic field intact. Only one of our people chose to cast aside doubt and logic and believe the impossible."

"Which will only result in her death," said Hylne. "Delmar, I know you wish to believe Obiah and Rynah. I know that you regret what happened all those years ago, but charging off to our deaths will not help those who are still living."

"Neither will cowering here," General Delmar replied. "You say that you wish to bring Klanor to justice and yet you hide here in these caves on a backwater planet. There is no justice in cowardice."

"How dare you!" The councilmember with the marigold beard jumped to his feet. "You dare to insinuate…"

"I speak the truth!" General Delmar cut him off, his sharp voice stopping the man. "All I ask for is a ship with a crew. I, and I alone, will accept full responsibility for what happens to it, but we must do something if we hope to stop this madness that has invaded our system."

"There are people here now who need our help," said another member, his calm voice soothing the one who had kicked his seat back.

"Yes, but how long will they stay safe if Klanor is allowed to remain alive?" asked General Delmar.

"How do you propose to stop him?"

"It all comes back to the mythic crystals," said General Delmar.

"Now you sound like Marlow," scoffed Hylne.

"Perhaps he was not as crazy as he seemed," said General Delmar, remembering the time he had refused to believe Marlow and turned his back on him, like so many others. "He predicted that the crystal would be stolen, and that our planet lay in grave danger."

"How do we know that it wasn't he who told Klanor what to do?" challenged one.

"Marlow was many things," said the calm councilman, "but he was no traitor."

"Maybe not," said the member with the marigold beard, "but his actions brought light to the fact that the crystal was in the geo-lab. Perhaps that is what inspired Klanor to steal it in the first place."

"Does it matter?" asked another member of the council.

"Everyone knew that it lay in the geo-lab," voiced yet another.

"If we are to hold our heads up high," said General Delmar, "then we should go after him ourselves. What will we say when we are asked how we dealt with the mass murder of our people? Will we say that we let the man go because we were too afraid to seek him ourselves? Will we say that we allowed a lowly security officer to fight our war for us because we hadn't the fortitude to do it ourselves?

"Rynah is out there, right now, on her own. All I ask is for your blessing and unity. If we stand together in this, then I know that the people of Lanyr will survive and there is hope for the future. What say all of you?"

The individual members of the council glanced around the

small chamber, their eyes darting from one to the other with shame. General Delmar knew the answer even before it was given.

"I am sorry," said the calm councilmember, "but we cannot abide by your request. If you choose to help her, you do it alone."

Clenching his teeth to conceal his disappointment, General Delmar tore the sash from his uniform—the mark of his station as general of the Lanyran fleet—and tossed it on the table.

"Then I relinquish my commission and my seat on this council."

He left the council in silence, each stunned by his actions. as none of them had ever expected a distinguished general of the fleet to do such a thing.

General Delmar stormed through the halls with hurried footsteps, up a flight of carved stairs, and to the surface where light graced the planet's new inhabitants. Not bothering to admire the light, nor look upon the frightened and forlorn faces that accompanied it, he continued onward to his quarters, past bedraggled people who greeted him, though he paid them no heed as his mind raced with thoughts and ideas. Soon he had entered his room, his feet having guided him there as they had traversed the stone hallways numerous times.

General Delmar stopped in front of the glassless window of his room, hands clasped behind his back, staring out at the morning sky and its spray-painted colors of rose pink outlined by a mild yellow. Sharp cliffs stood off in the distance where the clouds caressed them; rocks and spindly brush dotted the landscape. Poufs of dust wisped across the sandy ground, while a lone tree shaded his window. Much filled his mind, thoughts about Obiah and his talk about Rynah's quest crowding out all others.

General Delmar remembered Marlow, a friend he had abandoned. He read the news like every other Lanyran, and when Marlow had tried to steal the crystal from the geo-lab, he was asked to be one of the presiding members of the tribunal, something he had refused, due to a conflict of interest. How could he sit in judgment of a man he had once called a friend? But Hylne had been determined to ensure that Marlow was made an example of, not that General Delmar could blame him, and had called him as a witness like he had done with Obiah. Marlow's crime almost ruined them all, as well as countless innocent lives.

General Delmar remembered visiting Marlow in the maximum security detention center, having been granted such a right because of his rank and station. "Why?" was all General Delmar could ask his friend.

Instead of answering, all Marlow had said was, "The bracelet. Rynah still wears it, does she not?"

"What?" had been the general's response. Like Marlow and Obiah, Rynah had also been under his command, stationed upon his ship soon after being commissioned as an officer in the fleet. It was General Delmar who had recommended her for advanced spaceflight training, something Rynah excelled at.

"Marlow, do you not understand what you have done? You know that the crystal is the only thing keeping this planet alive. Why would you try to take it?"

"To protect it."

"Protect it?"

"It is one of six," Marlow had said, leaning as close to the electrically charged (about 12,000 volts) glass barrier as he was allowed to. "I know it sounds crazy, but I have travelled extensively, seen things, discovered things, and it needs to be protected before someone else learns of it."

"But you could have…"

"Do you honestly think that I would have killed us all?" Marlow stood on his feet, his voice incensed at such an accusation. "I had taken precautions. Even discovered a way to keep the magnetic field intact. Of course, the switch has to be done right away. If too much time passes after… but it can be done."

General Delmar remembered watching, horrified, as his friend mumbled incoherent sentences and words to himself as though un-aware that someone else was in the room. "Discovered what?"

"With the help of Sol—you must believe me! I would never leave us so vulnerable."

"With the help of whom?"

Marlow's agitated movements ceased. He looked into General Delmar's eyes, a serene and all-knowing expression on his face.

"A most remarkable woman."

That was when General Delmar had concluded that Marlow was insane, having lost his mind, perhaps even suffering from a form of dementia.

"The bracelet, she still wears it?" Marlow had demanded. "And my ring! You must give her my ring!"

"Yes, Rynah wears that wristband," said General Delmar; the wristband did not violate uniform regulations, so she had been al-lowed to keep it. "As for your ring, it is in holding as part of your personal affects that only immediate family members are allowed to claim."

"Then get her! Tell her I must speak with her. I need to speak with Rynah. It's important! Delmar, tell Rynah…"

General Delmar remembered allowing the steel door to slam shut behind him as he left the room, cutting off Marlow's crazed words. That was the day he had turned his back on Marlow, severing all ties of friendship. That was the day he now wished he could erase, that he had heeded Marlow's request and brought Rynah to him.

He remembered Rynah during the trial, sitting in the front row in her fleet uniform, crisp and pressed as always—she never allowed her uniform to be otherwise. The trial ended in misery. Though Marlow had been given a lenient sentence, those who had watched it believed he should have been executed. But many mem-bers of the council had determined that Marlow was not in his right mind, and rather than punish a crazed, old man with death, they felt it more beneficial to give him the psychiatric help he needed.

Of course, upon his release from the mental institution, Marlow had been forced to wear a tracking device and was monitored by the authorities until his death.

Time calmed aroused emotions, but Rynah never forgot the taunts, the stares, or the whispers that forced her to resign her commission in the fleet and join the security detail in the geo-lab as repentance for Marlow's actions. General Delmar had used his influence to get her the position, having felt a fatherly fondness towards her, and knew well how she had to prove her worth to them twice over.

But all of that was years ago, so why is it he could not stop thinking about it? Obiah. His information about Rynah's search for the crystals to stop Klanor plagued him. General Delmar left the window, strolling to his computer console, and brought up the holoscreen. With a few taps, he scrolled through all of Rynah's past missions; despite the devastation on Lanyr, they still retained most of their records, especially those of the Lanyran fleet.

Scrolling through them, he thought he remembered one in particular, one where Rynah was asked to talk to a friend of hers. He found it! Upon the screen was Tre's photograph and a record of his arrest and trial. General Delmar remembered that mission. He had given it to her. That was where he would start. Never one to cast her friends aside, General Delmar knew Rynah would have stayed informed about Tre's whereabouts, even if she did not remain in contact with him.

General Delmar remembered that Tre preferred his solitude and communications technology, always preferring to spy on others while paranoid that his movements were being recorded. He entered a set of parameters for the computer to search. Five possible locations popped up. The general scanned them, settling upon two that had the most recent activity—the time of it coincided with Obiah's appearance. He charted a course.

The door to his office opened and Hylne marched in. "General Delmar, your antics at this morning's meeting has riled the council.

You are a man who has never been subject to hysterical whims of emotion."

"My actions were not hysterical."

"Nevertheless, your actions have caused the members of the council concern for your well-being."

"My apologies, Councilman Hylne," said General Delmar, not bothering to look up from his task.

Hylne stopped. He noticed the holoscreen and the star maps with a charted course on it. "Are you going somewhere?"

"You could say that."

"Where, might I ask," said Hylne, an accusatory note in his voice.

"That is none of your business."

"It is, when the general of the Lanyran fleet decides to leave without a word, abandoning his post."

"I am not abandoning my post, or my people. I am merely going to help one of our own. And, in case you were not paying attention to the meeting, I resigned my commission, remember?"

"You can't resign."

"I just did, moments before."

"General…"

"A member of the Geothermic Lab's security force is on her own, attempting to capture the man responsible for our planet's fate."

"You are not referring to Obiah and his story about Marlow's daughter going after the crystals?"

"I am," said General Delmar.

"That is a fool's errand!"

"Perhaps."

"The crystals are a myth!"

"Are they?" General Delmar faced Hylne. They had been friends once, both members of the Lanyran fleet in their youth, until Hylne turned to politics and allowed backroom deals and intrigue to consume his life.

"They have to be," said Hylne.

"Why? Because you refuse to believe in them, then it cannot be true?" General Delmar gave Hylne an accusatory look, but he did not know about the hours that Hylne spent, alone, staring at the ceiling, wondering if he should have abided by Obiah's request, if he should have helped an old friend, nor the nights spent lying awake as he questioned all that he had once believed.

"You were never one to put much stock in the ancient tales," said Hylne, more subdued.

"That was before Klanor destroyed Lanyr."

"But that doesn't mean…"

"What if we were wrong?"

Hylne remained silent. He, too, had wondered the same, but his pride prevented him from admitting it.

"There was once a time when I would have laughed at the very notion of six all-powerful crystals, but much has changed since then. Klanor stole the one from the geo-lab and our planet has been lost. And Rynah, whom I never should have abandoned, is the only one among us who trusts the myths, and she is trying to stop him from acquiring the others and destroying more innocent lives, while we cower here."

"We're not…"

"Hylne, we've known one another for a long time. Cast aside your political robes and come with me. Be the man of honor you once were."

Hylne eyed General Delmar, an internal debate reeling within him. In their youth, General Delmar, Hylne, and Obiah fought alongside one another in the Lanyran fleet, during the Pristyr War, but all of that had become a distant memory marred by time.

"Do you truly believe in the crystals like Marlow did?" Though Hylne never knew Marlow on a personal level, he too, had paid close attention to the aftermath of the trial.

"No," said General Delmar, "but I believe in Rynah, and I trust her judgment, and Obiah's."

Hylne's snort did not go unnoticed.

"I know that you and Obiah had harsh words for each other, but you are a councilman, Hylne, and as such, you are responsible for the safety of the Lanyran people—what's left of us at least. Can you, in good conscience, allow a madman, like Klanor, to roam free, knowing that he will one day finish what he started?"

"You're not going," said Hylne, concern filling his voice.

"I believe that I am."

Hylne approached the man he had once called friend, had once been close to and did not want to lose, as he had lost too many friends during Lanyr's demise. "You're not going alone."

General Delmar locked eyes with Hylne, trying to discern the man's reasons for wanting to join him. "I've never known you…"

"We were once friends," Hylne stopped him. "Comrades. Brothers in arms, if you will. If you are determined to continue this course, I cannot allow you to do it alone." Guilt for his denying Obiah aide crept into his mind, but he forced it away, refusing to let it show. "In any case, it might help to have a member of the council with you."

General Delmar thanked Hylne and turned back to the window as the councilman left to make preparations for their departure. "Rynah," he whispered, "where are you?"

He hoped she still lived and that he wasn't too late in finding her.

* * *

The floor reeled beneath their feet, moving with a force that knocked them over as streams of molten lava, mirroring a waterfall, spilled from the crater of the volcano.

"We need to leave," said Rynah.

"There is a stairwell nearby," replied Solaris.

"What about him?" Alfric said, pointing at Klanor.

"Leave"—Rynah glanced at Brie's merciful, yet pleading, eyes—"We'll take him with us."

Alfric heaved Klanor to his feet, his viselike grip bruising his prisoner's shoulder, and dragged him along.

Wasting no time, they all rushed out of the room, through the next, and to the stairs that Solaris had talked about.

The door burst open to the outside world, where an emergency staircase snaked and twisted down the side of the mountain. Thick, black, sulfuric smoke ensconced them, causing them to gag and cough from its poison. Each looked up as a lava bomb shot into the darkened sky, a gray trail streaking behind it as it arched towards them.

"Look out!" yelled Tom.

They ducked just as the lava bomb struck the side of the rocky cliff to which the stairs hugged. Knowing time was short, they raced down the grated steps two at a time, hurrying as fast as they could to get away. Scorched rock, with red streaks and specks of feldspar, marked their path as they descended downward to the hellish ground below with its rivers of flowing, black encrusted lava.

Once they reached the bottom, Rynah darted away towards the mountainside.

"Rynah!" screamed Solaris. She took off after her, followed by the others.

Rynah ignored the shouts of her friends. She had remembered the second crystal tucked away in her escape pod and she wanted it before the volcano consumed it. Retracing her steps from when she had been captured by Stein, Rynah ran over the black earth, leaping across small gaps and ridges, focused only on her desire for the crystal.

"Rynah!"

Small rays of the red sun caught her eye as they glinted off the steel exterior of the escape pod. Running faster, Rynah propelled herself to it, and despite the plumes of smoke and steam that burst from the ground, she treaded on. Once there, she stopped. Rynah poked her head through the small opening, squeezing inside, and rummaged around. The crystal had to be somewhere.

The others caught up to her; Alfric still gripped Klanor's arm.

A basketball-sized piece of metal debris thudded on the black pebbles that littered the ground as Rynah thrust it aside, searching for the crystal, knowing that it had to be in there. Another chunk of metal crashed on the ground. Frustrated, Rynah's ruthless movements tore through the interior of the pod in her frantic search.

"Rynah?"

She ignored the voice that spoke. She had to find it. If Stein had acquired it, then they were all doomed, and she could only blame herself. Something glinted, refracting the sunlight in such a way that a series of rainbows spilled from a small corner of the escape pod. Rynah hurried to it. She ripped debris away from the area, exposing the small crystal, which fit, snug, in the palm of her hand.

"Got it," she held it up for the others to see.

"So, Stein missed it, but now what do we do?" asked Tom. "We have no ship."

The others frowned. Therein lay the problem. Though safe for the moment, the volcano continued to rumble, spewing molten lava into the air and threatening to erupt and bury them all. Rynah faced Klanor, whom Alfric held secure in his grip. "Do you have a ship, or any men still loyal to you?"

"I'm still here on this rock with you," said Klanor. "That should answer your question."

Though tempted to punch him for his snarky response, Rynah reigned in her anger, deciding he wasn't worth it. "I don't know what to do."

Solon brushed ash and silt off a nearby rock before sitting down. "Then the best course is patience," he said. "We have no means of transport and most likely will die here, but at least we can enjoy the company of friends."

"Seriously, you're just going to sit there?" said Tom, flabbergasted.

Solon looked at his friend, his calm and determined face boring into his. "Without a ship, how do you propose we leave? I can think of no better way to die than among friends. And I have never seen such a sight. Have you?"

Solon pointed at the erupting volcano. The others looked at it, realizing that for him (and Alfric, though he would never admit it), it was new and wondrous.

Tom plopped his butt on the ground, knowing that Solon's statement was correct. Without a ship, there was nothing they could do. "I knew there was a reason why I liked this guy."

"You're all insane!" shouted Klanor.

"Speak one more time," hissed Alfric, "and I will cut out your tongue."

Klanor clamped his mouth shut; the Viking's tone conveyed truthfulness in his threat.

A low rumble echoed beneath their feet. Each looked down at the black silt, wondering what ill fortune such grumbling brought forth. In answer to their unspoken question, violence shook the ground beneath their feet, knocking each of them over. A tear opened up with steam and searing boulders shooting upward into the sky.

"We need to leave," said Solaris, not noticing how Alfric stared into her violet eyes, as though he had seen them before. "Or at least find a better place to enjoy the scenery."

Two lava bombs fell from the brown sky, crashing into the ground beside them, pelting them with pebbles and sand. Shielding themselves, they ran away from the mountain. Alfric had reached out for Klanor, but he needn't have bothered, for Klanor wanted to get away from there as much as they did.

Solon spotted a ridge and pointed to it. As one, they raced for the rippled bluff, hoping they would reach it in time.

BOOM!

Another lava bomb smashed into the earth, just missing them. Racing against the imminent eruption, they charged for the escarpment, unsure of what to do once they reached it. Cracks and jagged scars opened around them, releasing pockets of scalding water mixed with magma.

Solaris stopped. Before her was a stream of moving lava at least 12 feet across—too large to jump.

"Now what?" asked Tom as the ground rumbled once again.

Searching for a solution, Brie spotted crevices protruding from the lava's surface and stretching across to the other side. Knowing they had little choice, she jumped on the first one.

"Brie!" shouted Solon.

"It's the only way across," she yelled back. "Just follow my lead!"

Amazed that Brie had taken the lead, Tom and Solon jumped together as Brie landed on the third crevice.

Alfric reached for Klanor.

"I've no intention of dying here," said Klanor, holding up his hands.

Though reluctant, Alfric allowed him to jump across without restraint, but remained close to ensure that he did no more than cross the river of lava.

Boulders crashed around them, signaling that the time had come to go, but Solaris remained still, staring at the slow moving lava with wide eyes.

"What's wrong?" asked Rynah.

"I am afraid. I've never felt fear before," said Solaris, who, for the first time in her life, feared death. "If I fall, I will…"

"You won't fall," soothed Rynah, understanding Solaris' fear—she felt it herself.

The mountain behind them spewed more clouds of ash and smoke into the air as a spray of magma erupted from it.

"Together, then!" said Rynah.

Both Solaris and Rynah stretched out their right leg and jumped onto the first crevice, their boots plopping on the rock with soft thumps. They leapt from rock to rock until they reached the other side where the others waited.

"The ridge isn't far," said Tom, "but what will we do once we reach it?"

"Best to reach it first, so that the solution can come to you. It will not appear any earlier," Solon said, giving one of his many bits of wisdom, despite the peril they were in.

"We'll figure it out once we get there," said Rynah. "Come on!"

Again, they tore over the ground, racing for the uncertainty of salvation. Once they reached the bank, with its smooth ripples stretching across it in horizontal lines, they stared at it.

"Climb!" said Rynah.

One by one, the seven unlikely companions hauled themselves upward. The smooth rock made finding a handhold difficult as they climbed, slipping on numerous occasions. Alfric kept a close eye on Klanor, but not once did the man make a move to harm the others, or escape. When Brie's foot slipped, Klanor reached out for her and helped her regain her foothold, much to Alfric's, and Brie's, surprise. Pebbles clacked as they fell downward amidst the thundering of the vengeful volcano.

Auburn sunlight greeted them when they reached the top. They turned around, and glowing embers floated around them in a waltz as they looked back at the volcano.

"I hope one of you has a plan," said Tom, breathless from the climb.

"Pray," said Alfric.

"No offense," replied Tom, "but I don't think God, or some being from the sky, is going to rescue us right now."

The distant roar of an engine permeated the air. Thrilled, yet cautious at the same time, each stood erect, straining their necks as they looked up into the smoke-filled sky. The roar grew louder. Shielding her eyes from the sun, Rynah spotted a speck of shiny metal and watched as it drew nearer until it was close enough for her to make out the markings on the hull.

"Pirates!"

Everyone seized their weapons, ready for a battle. The ship lowered to the earth, sending plumes of sand and dust in swarming circles around them. Coughing from the pollution, they maintained their positions.

"Give me a laser pistol, please," Klanor pleaded.

Rynah glared at him.

"I have no desire to die at the hands of pirates. Same as you," said Klanor.

"Look!" Brie pointed at a metal ladder dropping from a hole in the bottom of the ship and hanging in midair. "I think they mean to help us."

KA-BOOM!

An entire portion of the volcano burst into the sky, showering the land with its rock, dirt, and spindly bushes. Rynah watched as the mountain disintegrated into a cloud of ash and lava. "We don't have much choice."

She charged for the ladder that dangled from the pirate vessel, leaping off the ledge, and clung to the metal rungs as they swayed from the impact of her movements.

"Come on!"

Brie jumped for the ladder next, followed by Tom, Solon, Solaris, Klanor, and Alfric, who wished to stay near Klanor. With gradual movements, they climbed the ladder to the dark hole above them.

Once aboard the ship, Rynah rose to her feet, whipping out her laser pistol just as the engines roared to life, and propelled the ship into the upper atmosphere of the planet before entering space.

Heavy boots stomped down a set of stairs towards them. "Welcome aboard," said a voice they all recognized.

Rynah raised her laser pistol.

"Wait," said Jifdar, holding his hands out in front of him. "Don't shoot. I mean you all no harm."

"Then why are you here?" demanded Brie, her distaste for the pirate coming through in her words.

"Ah, the delicate flower. My how you have blossomed. I do apologize for our last meeting. It was, shall we say, a misunderstanding."

Angered by the man's words, and still irate over how he had treated them during their first meeting, Brie clenched her fist and punched his scaled jaw, forcing him to take two steps back.

"Well," said Jifdar, rubbing the side of his face and stopping his pirates from interfering, "I suppose I deserved that. So the flower has sprouted thorns. Good. Because you will need them."

"Speak your piece, filth," snarled Alfric.

"Ah, yes, the one who defeated my best man. I'd love to have you as a member of my crew"—Jifdar leaned back as Alfric touched the point of his sword to the pirate's neck—"But seeing as how you have your own, I will digress."

"I grow bored of your statements," said Rynah. "Why are you here?"

"To rescue you, of course," replied Jifdar.

"Rescue us? Didn't you once try to kill us?" said Tom.

"Yes, an unfortunate misunderstanding," said Jifdar. "Now, if you'll please come with me, there is someone here who wishes to speak with you."

"We aren't going anywhere with you." Rynah pointed her laser pistol at Jifdar. "Give me one good reason why I shouldn't pull the trigger."

"Rynah!" Obiah pushed his way past the surrounding pirates and stopped in front of her. "Rynah, put your weapon down."

"Obiah?" Rynah couldn't believe what she saw. "What are you doing here with these pirates?"

"That is a bit of a long story," said Obiah, "but first we should deal with him." He pointed at Klanor.

"We could jettison him into space," spat Jifdar as his venomous glare bore into Klanor's unreadable eyes. Memories of the attack on his pirate hub, and the friends he had lost, flooded his brain.

Though tempted by the offer, Rynah couldn't do it. Something about Stein's betrayal of Klanor, and another glance at Brie, remembering what the girl had said to her as she pressed her knife against his throat, stayed her wrath. "No. For now, keep him in your prison cells."

"As you wish, my lady," said Jifdar without an ounce of mockery. He snapped his fingers and two pirates seized Klanor, hauling him away. "Please, come this way."

Jifdar led them through the interior of his ship. A single, winding corridor (its walls stained in sticky, black goo that formed vertical ripples) snaked its way throughout the vessel, running from the cargo area to the bridge. He stopped them when they reached the outer room of his private quarters, where he always held meetings with his first mate and fellow pirates.

"Please, be seated."

No one moved.

"Or remain standing. Whichever you prefer," said Jifdar.

"I want to know what is going on here," said Rynah.

"I suppose I owe you an explanation," said Obiah. "When I left you, I went in search of survivors of Lanyr. That was when I met Merrick."

For the first time, Rynah noticed the man standing silent in a corner.

"He led me to where the Lanyran government has set up a refuge for survivors. Unfortunately, no one on the council wished to abide by my request, so we are still on our own in this venture of yours. Though General Delmar sends his regards."

Rynah's eyebrows lifted when Obiah had said that last sentence.

"While trying to get back to you," continued Obiah, "Merrick and I ran into our pirate friends here, and they have agreed to help us, so long as we give them Klanor."

"Is that all?" said Rynah.

"Yes," said Jifdar. "You give us Klanor and I will take you anywhere you wish."

"Earth," said Rynah.

"Except that... what is this Earth?"

"My home," said Brie.

"Well, you can't go there."

"But Stein will destroy it!" Brie shouted.

"That is not my concern. Klanor's actions destroyed a lot of good pirates, men whom I had come to trust. I want him to pay," Jifdar said.

No one noticed Solaris creeping over to the main computer console.

"And he will," said Rynah, "but Stein is a bigger threat right at the moment."

"It's not really my concern," said Jifdar.

"A man bent on destruction rarely makes one stop," said Solon.

"You are a funny, little man," said Jifdar to Solon.

"Look," Obiah cut in, "you did agree..."

"I agreed to help you find Rynah in exchange for Klanor's life. I have upheld my end of the bargain. Now it's your turn."

"I suggest you do as they wish," said Solaris, her stern voice cutting everyone off. Her hand rested on the computer console as she linked to it. "Or I will take us there myself."

Jifdar stared at Solaris. He had noticed her earlier, but passed her off as just another of Rynah's mysterious companions, and one of little importance.

"Call your dog off. I haven't time for these games."

"I cannot," said Rynah.

"Preposterous," said Jifdar. "Tell her to release my ship to me, or I shall fire a laser blast through her skull."

Force fields appeared around Jifdar, encasing him in a bubble.

"What the—let me out!" he shouted.

Solaris glowered at him. "You will do as Rynah asks and take us to Earth. For once, in your pathetic existence, you will do the right thing and prevent their planet from suffering the same fate as your pirates. And my name is Solaris."

Incensed, Jifdar glowered at Solaris, loathing her impertinent attitude and her gall at ordering him about on his ship. He pressed against the force fields in an effort to break free, but soon realized that he was trapped and left only one choice.

"Agreed," he spat.

"And if you go back on your word"—Solaris' narrow eyes focused on him—"you will have me to deal with."

"Anything you want. Just let me out of here."

The force fields dissipated.

"I have set the course in your computers. Tell your man at the helm to follow it," said Solaris. "And don't even think about changing it because I will know. You, Jifdar, are no longer in control of this ship."

"I do not like fighting other people's battles. I prefer ones that are personal."

Solaris strolled up to Jifdar, a disconcerting look on her face. "Klanor may have ordered the first attack on your people, but who do you think ordered the others? All of your safe houses are gone. All of those people that you profess to care about are killed. The one responsible heads to Earth. You speak about justice. Justice would be stopping Stein before he is able to destroy more innocent lives."

Without a word, and knowing he had lost to Solaris' will, Jifdar left the room, going straight to the helmsman.

"You have the new coordinates?"

"Aye, sir."

"Set a course and prepare for a bumpy ride."

Chapter 2
MUSINGS

Alone in his room, Stein hunched over the dusty, old volume that had once been Rynah's, until Klanor had stolen it, and before he had acquired it afterward. He flipped through the tattered pages of the archaic volume, remarking at its condition, considering its age. One by one, the pages crinkled as he turned them. Hours, Klanor had spent studying the text. Hours, Stein had questioned such dedication to it. What did Klanor see in this ancient text? Stein had studied the digital copies of it, but something about the stained, and somewhat torn, pages made the myth all the more real.

He flipped to the end of the book. A torn page caught his attention, with a watermark. Snatching a magnifying glass, Stein studied the watermark. Though he did not recognize it, he instinctively knew it had to mean something, but why would the author of the text put it in? Checking the other pages, Stein did not find any watermarks, just the one on the last, and missing, page. Smudges of acrylic writing lined the inside of the back cover. Stein pulled the lamp closer, focusing its white light upon it. It appeared to be writing, matching that of the previous pages.

Stein jumped to his feet and rushed over to where a scanner was. His unceremonious movements caused the pages to clap as he placed the book in it, the flap of the back cover facing up. A blue line stretched across the cover from top to bottom as the computer scanned in the page; Stein drummed his fingers impatient to learn what the scans had to reveal.

Once done, he yanked the book free of the scanner and plopped it back on the table, before turning on his holographic monitor. He scrolled through the image of the flap. There was writing upon it.

"Enhance," he said.

The computer enhanced the image to a higher and sharper resolution. Tapping the screen, Stein blew up the section with the faint writing and highlighted it. "Translate," he said.

The computer copied the text and ran it through its translators—a series of boxes and images popped up before disappearing just as fast—and placed the newly translated text in front of Stein, who read it.

Six you know of,
but one you do not
Another there is, pale as a dove,
Time and all it's taught.

This one you need to control the others.
Without it, useless they are.
Seek it not, it comes to you like a mother
Small like a pebble, but greater than a star.

Frustrated by the lyrical nonsense, Stein pondered over the words, trying to decipher their meaning. There was another crystal. Klanor had been wrong in assuming that only six were in existence.

Maybe he didn't know. No, he knew, but refused to reveal such knowledge, Stein was convinced of that.

He thought back to all the times Klanor had told him to be patient, that together they would discover the crystals and their power. Alone with the missing verses, Stein concluded that Klanor had never intended to bring back his family. Unsure of whether this crystal would turn back time, he decided he did not care. His wife and child were dead, and nothing could change that. No, he would seek out this crystal and use it to make his suffering a reality for the rest of the universe. They would learn what true misery was.

He thought back to his interrogation of Brie. Often, she had dwelled upon a crystal discovered on her planet, Earth. Perfect. He had already charted a course to it. What harm did it do to search for a missing crystal? And the destruction he would bring... a malicious smile crossed his lips as he thought about the harm and devastation he would bring to that insignificant planet and its proposed heroes, as Stein reveled in his decision to go there in the first place. Maybe Earth's destruction would bring about his fortune.

He pulled open the drawer he always kept the photo of his wife and child in. Her warm smile stared back at him, unaware of the monster he had become. There was once a time when Stein found comfort in it. Now, he only felt disgust. He scooped up the image and held it up to the light, while with his other hand, he pulled out a lighter. Without a shred of remorse, or an ounce of hesitation, he lit the photograph and watched as the flames consumed it.

"Do not look upon me now," he whispered as a final farewell to his beloved. "Do not see the man I have become."

Once the flames had burnt out and all that remained of his past was ashes, Stein stormed out of his room and to the command deck of what was now his ship. The moment he appeared, the crew stood at attention.

"How long until we reach our destination?"

"Four days, sir," said one shaky crewmember.

"I want to arrive there sooner," said Stein.

"But we have already maxed out our engines, sir. If we..."

Stein yanked out his laser pistol and shot the crewmember in the chest for questioning his orders. He stalked over to a younger man—who must have only just entered his 20s—while wiping his pistol clean.

"You are new here?"

"Yes, sir," said the crewmember, shaking.

"I trust that you can get us to this Earth much sooner than four days."

"Ye—ye—yes, sir."

"Then take the helm."

The young crewmember, who was also a very adept pilot, rushed over to the pilot's seat, unsure if he had made a wise decision in joining Klanor's, or now Stein's, armada.

"And if you fail me," Stein waved his laser pistol at the man, the remainder of his statement not needing to be said.

"Yes, sir."

Stein pondered his interrogation of Brie once more. She had mentioned a crystal found in the ruins of the Maya, whatever they were. Assuming they were a long extinct culture of her world, much like the extinct civilizations of his own, he decided that those ruins would be a good place to start.

"You," Stein pointed at another crewmember, "I want you to run a search on the Maya on the planet Earth. Bring the results to me immediately."

"Yes, sir," said the female crewmember.

Stein eyed each and every one in the command center before walking out. They feared him. Perfect.

* * *

Rynah descended downward into the depths of the pirate ship

to where the brig was. Each step seemed to be a milestone for her as she took them, unsure if she had made the right choice. Hatred still welled within her at what Klanor had done, but something else filled her as well: pity. Back on Sunlil, when Stein had left all of them to perish in the wrath of the volcano, Klanor's usual self-assured manner had disappeared, being replaced by guilt and sadness. Never before had Rynah seen such emotions in his demeanor. His self-confidence was one of the things that had attracted her to him, but now he was just the shell of a man who had lost everything: friendship, belief in a greater purpose, and the woman he loved.

Her fingers brushed the grungy wall of the stairwell as she balanced herself. Disgusted—and a little too used to Solaris' pristine vessel—Rynah wiped the slime on her pants before wishing she hadn't, as now she would have to wash them. The heels of her boots clomped on the steps as she went down them, her gradual movements drawing out the inevitable. A drip caught her attention. Rynah couldn't believe that Jifdar would allow a leaky pipe on his ship, or perhaps he did not know about it. She had heard tales about pirates and their less than savory ways, but never thought she would have to experience it herself.

Her foot reached the last step. *What am I doing here?* she asked herself. Ever since Klanor had been brought down there, Rynah had had the urge to speak with him. She had to know why he had done what he had. She had to know if their entire relationship had been meaningless. She also wondered if she would see what Brie had seen in him when she stayed Rynah's hand back on Sunlil.

"I know you are there," came Klanor's deep voice as Rynah remained hidden in the darkness just around the corner to the brig's entrance. "I recognize your steps. You always had a distinct gait."

Rynah moved out of the shadows of the archway in the stairwell and into the dim light of the room. Slug-like creatures clung to the rusty bars of Klanor's prison cell as a small pool of water formed next to it. Nestled in the back corner of his cell, Klanor sat upon a rotted crate (the only furniture in the room besides the squeaky cot in his cell), snapping his fingers in an effort to stay entertained.

Rynah stopped three feet from the bars, which resembled medieval prison bars more than anything modern and from her world.

"Have you come to pay your respects to the condemned?" Klanor asked.

"You deserve neither respect, nor decency," Rynah spat.

"You are correct there," said Klanor, his manner subdued.

"Why did you not try to escape from us on Sunlil?"

"What good would it have done? That volcano was about to erupt. If I had run away, I would be dead."

"So you used us for a chance to escape."

"If you will," said Klanor, "though your chances of getting away from there were as good as mine."

"But you could have easily allowed us to die."

"And why would I have done that? What purpose would it serve? Without you, the pirates would have killed me for sure."

"So, you'll commit murder if it serves a purpose?"

"Are you any different?" Klanor left his rotted crate and stood in front of the bars, eyeing Rynah. "How many people have you killed, Rynah, in your quest to stop me?"

"Only those that tried to kill me."

"You haven't answered my question," Klanor said. "How many?"

Rynah looked away, refusing to answer, refusing to be a pawn in his mind games.

"Oh, don't bother answering. I can guess that it has probably been no more than me."

"I'm not the one that decimated entire planets on some quest for power," spat Rynah.

"Oh, spare me your piety."

"How can be so cold?"

"Cold? You think me heartless? I weep every day for the lives lost because of what I have done. You think I sought the crystal because of some lust for power? Well, that may have been true in the beginning, but the crystals are more than that. You may be Marlow's granddaughter, but you know very little about his work."

"Do not speak to me of my grandfather!"

"You are the one who cast him aside. Do you know who visited him in that hospital while he was there, because it certainly wasn't you."

"You didn't."

"Of course I did. That trial was aired all across the planet. That was when I started researching the crystals myself. And who better to tell me about them than Marlow?"

"You son of a...."

"I never harmed him," replied Klanor. "We played chess most of the time, while he talked about you. He never did talk about the crystals, for he was not as crazy as the world had supposed. Oh, occasionally he would mention them, but only in passing, and never anything I didn't already know. No, Rynah, you were all he wanted to talk about, and despite your abandonment of him, he never said a harsh word against you."

A tear welled in Rynah's eye.

"He loved you. You were everything to him. That is why I sought you out."

"It wasn't because I worked on the security detail for the geo-lab?"

"I cannot deny that I didn't use you. Yes, that was part of it, but what really made me seek you out was the way he talked about you. Love and admiration filled his words."

Rynah remained silent, unsure of what to believe.

"If I had wanted to use you only for your access to the lab, I could have simply kidnapped you and stolen your access credentials. But ask yourself why I chose to go out with you, why I proposed to you. As I listened to Marlow talk about you, I had to meet you, and afterward, I knew that you were the only woman I could ever love."

"Love?" Rynah scoffed. "You don't know the first thing about it."

"When I asked you to join me, I meant it. I wanted us to be together, not fighting or quarreling, but together."

"You expect me to believe your lies?"

"I'm not surprised that you call them that. I have not given you much reason to trust me. And my actions were callous in the beginning."

"I'll not stand here and listen to your twisted words!" Rynah turned to leave.

"Before you go," said Klanor, his calm voice stopping her, "you might want to consider this." He reached into his pocket and pulled out a tiny ring, the same ring that he had given to Rynah upon their engagement, the same ring that she had lost on Lanyr and thought gone forever. Klanor held it in the single electrical light in the room, remembering the nights he spent staring at it, wishing that could change the past, a reminder of the love he ruined. "You might want to ask yourself why I have kept this all this time."

"Where did you get that?" she asked in more of a whisper.

"You dropped it the day I hurt you most. I never was good at guessing people's sizes, especially their ring size."

"I thought I had lost it for good."

"Here," Klanor handed her the ring. "It rightfully belongs to you. You are the only woman I have ever considered for marriage."

Unsure of what to do, and a hurricane of emotions (loathing, despair, sorrow, and hope) reeling within her, confusing her, she took the ring. "I shouldn't."

"Take it. Sell it. Keep it. It's yours to do with as you will."

Rynah clutched the small diamond ring as though it were the greatest of treasures, still wondering if she had made the right choice.

"I know I can never make up for what I have done to you," said Klanor, "but do not spend your life hating me. I'm not worth it, and you deserve better."

Rynah left the brig without saying another word. She had found herself unable to speak after Klanor's confession. Could she have been wrong about him, or was he using her again? She couldn't be sure, but something about his demeanor told her that perhaps this time, he told the truth.

Chapter 3
SEARCH FOR A CRAZY ALIEN

General Delmar and Hylne sat in the front of the shuttle craft as the general flew it down to the surface of the planet below. The shuttle jerked up and down from the turbulence it encountered during its descent.

"I thought you knew how to fly one of these," commented Hylne.

"It's been a while," said General Delmar, as he attempted to hold the controls steady.

"You're getting sloppy."

"Says the man who hasn't flown in over 30 years."

A beeping snatched Hylne's attention. "Three hundred yards until we've reached the target."

"Understood." General Delmar worked the controls as he flew the shuttle to a small underground bunker on the planet below. After one last bit of turbulence, he nestled them on the ground. He opened the rear hatch, which formed a ramp, allowing them out into a world with orange grass that was ankle-high and a clear marigold sky. A soft breeze rustled the leaves of the trees, sending streams of rainbows floating their way. A square doorway, which he knew led underground, stood out, it's rusted bolts contrasting with the natural scene.

"This way," said General Delmar.

"How do you know there aren't any traps?" asked Hylne.

"Tre is harmless. When Rynah brought him in the first time, he was more talk than action."

The moment General Delmar ceased speaking, a laser cannon popped out of the ground, firing a blast which missed their feet, but singed the toes of his boots.

"Harmless?" questioned Hylne, a doubtful expression on his face.

"Well, that was what was in her report."

Another laser blast shot at them, striking a nearby tree, sending splinters in every direction.

"I think she left a few things out of that report," Hylne mumbled.

"He seems to have just the one cannon," said General Delmar. "This way."

General Delmar ran in a semi-circle around the cannon, staying just out of range; Hylne followed right behind him. More blasts escaped the cannon, but it never aimed at them, just near where they had been. General Delmar stopped near the entrance to the bunker.

"Just what I thought," he said, "it's meant to scare, not harm."

He stuck a thin quartz disc into the holographic keypad, allowing the decryption code to work. The lock clicked as it released. General Delmar opened the one-foot thick steel door and ushered Hylne inside.

The door slammed shut behind them. A green light turned on, shining upon a single note. Annoyed, General Delmar ripped it from the wall.

"Press the yellow button, if you wish to keep your stomachs."

"And what is that supposed to mean?" asked Hylne.

"Probably the man's idea of a joke." General Delmar smacked the button next to the yellow one. The floor dropped beneath the feet, sending them pummeling down a metallic shaft to the unknown darkness below.

"OOMPH!"

They crashed into a trampoline, which cushioned their fall, but sent them flying across the room until they smashed into piles of air cushions. Grunting, and nursing a few bruises, Hylne and General Delmar stood up. Lights flickered on. Only a barren, concrete room greeted them, with an aluminum folding table off to their right.

More lights turned on as a holographic Tre filled the room.

"Hello there," he said. "It appears that you have found an empty bunker, thinking that I would be there. As you can see, I'm not. Don't feel too bad. Many a fool has tried to find me and failed. Oh, and I hope you like the parting gift."

"Parting gift?" asked Hylne.

As though in answer to his question, the ceiling ripped open, dumping piles of manure all over him and General Delmar until they had been coated. Struggling to get out of it, both managed to get back to their feet—though they were still waist high in manure—and brushed off their faces so that they could breathe more easily, despite the stench.

"Are you certain you want to find this guy?" demanded Hylne, thinking of how much he would prefer to shove Tre into a pool of slime and filth.

"Yeah," replied General Delmar, "so I can wring his neck."

He waded through the manure—more of it slipped into the crevices of his boots—until he reached the holographic display. With a few quick taps on the screen, General Delmar pinpointed where the signal had originated from. Grinning to himself, he faced Hylne. "I know where he is."

Chapter 4
A Decision

Distrust and grumbling filled the secluded room on Jifdar's ship where everyone—Rynah, Solaris, Brie, Alfric, Tom, Solon, Merrick, Obiah, Jifdar, and Heller, his first mate—gathered to decide Klanor's fate. Neither side trusted the other and both wanted justice for Klanor's crimes. The warped table they sat at wobbled with the slightest movement, clunking on the metallic floor, poking a hole in the ten years' worth of grime that had built up.

Cup-sized annular lamps filled the corners of the room, shedding the only light on the proceedings, and silhouetted Jifdar's form as he sat at the head of the table, while Solaris was at the other end, keeping careful watch on him.

"You know why we are here," said Jifdar.

"Just kill him and be done with it," said Heller.

"No!" said Brie. She agreed that Klanor should be punished for what he had done, but execution seemed a bit too much. Despite the animosity the others felt, and the justification for such enmity, they did not know what Brie knew and hadn't seen into his memories like she had. He had committed some vile acts, and he would answer for his sordid past, but underneath that hardened exterior, Brie had an inkling that Klanor wanted to undo all of that, that he wanted vindication. She looked at Alfric for support, but found none.

Alfric did not care for the pirate, but agreed with the notion of executing Klanor. If he were home in his kingdom, the man would have been executed without question, suffering what his people called the Blood Eagle. "I agree with the pirate," came his stern reply.

"It doesn't quite seem right," said Tom. "He did help us get off of Sunlil."

"More like we helped him," said Rynah.

"But he was left there to die with the rest of us," said Tom, "and he didn't try to kill us."

"Killing us would have served little purpose then," Solon said, "since he needed our help to survive."

"True," Tom replied, "but my point is that it was not some ruse of his to lure us into some sort of trap. You all saw the look on Stein's face. He left Klanor there to die with us. There was no deception there."

"That does not excuse him of his crimes," Alfric added.

"No, but…"

"I do not understand what the debate is all about!" shouted Jifdar, incensed that they were even considering pardoning Klanor. "He murdered many of my men! Good pirates, dead, because of him."

"And how many have you killed for your own gain?" asked Solaris.

"That is not the point!"

"That is precisely the point," said Solaris. "We all do things for ourselves, but when another commits the same act, suddenly we think it is horrifying."

"But…"

"Nothing will ever excuse one of a crime, but committing the same only makes us as guilty as he," said Solon, in his usual pensive manner.

"Stein was there?" asked Merrick in a quiet voice, as though the name was familiar to him, and leaned forward with an interest he had not displayed before. "He was with Klanor?"

"Yes," said Rynah. "The man who abandoned us on Sunlil, and meant for Klanor to die there as well, called himself Stein."

"Was he…" Merrick allowed his voice to trail off, refusing to finish his question, but his sudden silence, and subdued manner while they discussed the fate of the one who had destroyed Lanyr, confused them. He seemed distant, as though his mind lay elsewhere, far away from them and their current predicament.

"Do you know him?" asked Obiah.

"No." Merrick's curt reply garnered doubtful looks from those surrounding him. "The name just sounds familiar, that's all."

"That's possible," said Jifdar. "The man hasn't exactly been keeping a low profile."

"Are you all right?" asked Brie as she studied Merrick and the pained expression on his face, which he tried to hide.

Merrick shook his head and forced a smile. "I'm fine. Don't worry about me."

"I don't understand," said Obiah, "why would Stein turn on Klanor? Didn't he work for him?"

"Because Klanor refused to kill me," Rynah said in a soft whisper.

"Wait—what?" said Tom. "Why would that…"

"Perhaps Stein learned that Marlow was responsible for what had happened at Desmyr," said Rynah, "and the devastation that nearly destroyed the Brestef region. My guess is that he lost someone very close to him there."

"Or Klanor made a promise he couldn't keep," said Brie, but her words were drowned by Merrick's.

"What?" said Merrick. "Why would he carry that blame to you?"

"Because Marlow was my grandfather," said Rynah.

The color in Merrick's face drained. "Your grandfather killed those people?"

Rynah nodded her head in response.

"And you did nothing?" demanded Merrick.

"I didn't know," said Rynah.

"Didn't know? Those people are dead because of him!" Merrick jumped to his feet, throwing his chair behind him where it clashed against the wall.

Alfric gripped his knife, ready to seize the man, but Brie placed her small hand on Merrick's, her gentle touch calming him.

"Please," she said. "It isn't Rynah's fault and her grandfather is dead."

Merrick calmed himself and looked into Brie's brown eyes and found himself swept away by her sympathy.

"You lost someone," said Brie.

"Yes," replied Merrick, controlling the sudden rage that had roiled within him and righted his chair, sitting down once more.

"So, Stein learned of what your grandfather had done and wanted revenge, but Klanor refused," said Heller to Rynah.

"It's possible," said Rynah.

"We cannot keep him prisoner aboard this ship," said Jifdar, continuing the discussion of Klanor's fate.

"We cannot kill him," said Brie, glancing at Merrick, who stared at his interlocked fingers.

"And why is that?" demanded Heller.

"He's not a monster," said Brie, remembering what she had witnessed during one of Klanor's interrogation sessions, which had allowed her to slip into his memories. She didn't just see it, but she had felt the torture that reeled within him, that filled his being each day as he wrestled with his guilt.

Rynah's eyes looked up at her. "Not a monster? He stole the crystal from the geo-lab and sentenced my planet to death, while forcing what is left of my people to live as refugees."

"I know what he did," said Brie, "but I also know who he is, here." She pointed at her heart to emphasize her point.

"How is that possible?" demanded Jifdar.

"While he interrogated me," Brie replied, "I was in his head."

All eyes turned towards Brie.

"He linked you two telepathically?" asked Rynah. "That practice was deemed a violation of an individual's rights and made illegal by the council. How did he…"

"Men bent on committing crimes do not quiver over legality," said Solon. "He was linked to you the way we were all once linked to Solaris?"

"Yes," said Brie. "When connected, I sensed something—guilt. He still loves you, Rynah. He feels guilty about destroying your bases, Jifdar. Every time Klanor moves closer to his goal of acquiring the power of the crystals, he feels a sense of remorse for what he has had to do to achieve it. There is a struggle going on within him. It's as though he doesn't know what to do."

"You got all of that from his head?" asked Tom.

Brie glared at him.

"And yet, his deeds remain the same," said Alfric.

"Brie," said Rynah, "some men are just evil. They cannot be redeemed because they do not want to be. Do we let them remain to continue their reign of terror?"

"I understand all of that," said Brie. "I know that one day Klanor will have to answer for what he did, but I also know that he wants to change. I can't explain it; I just know it. There were many instances where he could have killed us all, but he didn't. Ask yourself why. He isn't the same man he was, and people should be given a second chance. He has earned that much."

Brie's pleading eyes bore into each of them, but none more so than Alfric. He remembered a time when a man had been accused of thievery, and in his homeland, such crimes are punishable by death. The thief's daughter had pleaded with Alfric to show mercy, but he had refused her and sentenced the man, a memory he had not thought of until now as he stared into Brie's eyes. "I think we ought to listen to the girl."

"What?" scoffed Heller. "Have you gone soft?"

In answer to Heller's remark, Alfric pulled free one of his knives and placed it on the table in front of him, never releasing the hilt, forcing the man to rethink his next words.

"But how do we know that he will not turn on us?" Heller asked.

"We don't," said Solaris.

"Why do you trust him?" demanded Jifdar.

"Perhaps you should ask him," replied Brie.

"This is ridiculous!" continued Jifdar. "That man deserves no mercy."

"Perhaps we should kill you then!" Brie blurted out. "You who marooned us on a world of ice and left us to die. You never looked back. Yet, here we are, sitting at the same table, debating a man's life as though we were ordering pizza! The monsters on this ship are not in your prison cells, but here in this room!"

Brie knocked her chair over as she shot to her feet and stormed out of the chamber.

"Stupid girl," mutter Heller. Alfric's cracking knuckles caused him to jerk his head and stare into the Viking's hardened eyes and he wished he had not spoken.

"Silence!" roared Jifdar.

"She can't…" the first mate stopped upon seeing the dangerous look on his captain's face.

"Know thyself," muttered Solon.

"What?" asked Rynah.

"The oracle of Delphi," said Solon, "says that one should know thyself. If you do not know what is in your own heart, how can you judge what is in another's? In the time that I have known Brie, I have come to a simple conclusion—she is a rare person. She knows what lies within each of us. The king who knows the value of mercy; the woman torn by guilt and anger who only wishes to prevent another tragedy, as much to save others, as herself; the thief who knows the value of honor; the boy who is barely a man and loves to jest, but is loyal to those around him; the machine, who is more human than all of us combined; and the scribe, who has a warrior's spirit. Brie knows us. If her judgment is wrong, then we should end the debate and be done with Klanor, but if her judgment is correct, then perhaps we should trust it.

"Is he any worse than the rest of us? If the answer is no, then he should be given a chance to prove his true intentions."

"Agreed," said Alfric. Despite his faults, Brie had always chosen to think the best of him and drew out his better qualities.

"I'm in," said Tom, in his usual all-or-nothing manner, while a portion of his mind wished he had a pizza right then; he missed its sausage, mushroom, pineapple with extra cheese.

Rynah mulled over Solon's words and remembered how her lack of faith in Brie, when they had first met, had almost cost all of them their lives, a failure she did not wish to repeat.

"I made the mistake of not believing in Brie once; I'll not do it again. If she believes that Klanor should be given a second chance, then I am willing to trust her judgment."

Rynah glanced at Solaris, who smiled at her, pleased that one of Marlow's wishes had come true—the desire for Rynah to have faith in something other than her laser pistol.

Jifdar frowned. He wanted more than anything to eject Klanor from an airlock, but a single glance at Solaris told him that it would never happen.

"Since it appears that I am outvoted, on my own ship, then I guess I have little choice but to go along. Yet, how do we test his mettle? I wish to be certain that we can trust this newfound change in him."

"I believe I have a solution to that," said Solaris. "We will need to garner supplies if we are to make it to Earth. Perhaps there is a way we can use that to test him."

Having a sudden thought, Rynah jumped in her seat. She flicked on the holomonitor, scrolling through maps of quadrants, star systems, and planets, until she found what she looked for. "I know the perfect place."

* * *

The slow melodic drip of a cracked pipe lulled Klanor into an uneasy sleep as he lay on the hard (covered in grime, dried blood, and a multitude of things he'd rather not think about) floor. He had stuffed the moldy, lumpy mattress from his squeaky, and very rickety, cot into an opening at the base of his cell to stop the inflow of frigid air from the coolant systems.

Nightmares of his past deeds plagued him, attacking his once guiltless mind. Guilt. Since the day he first connected telepathically with Brie, Klanor had experienced pangs of regret for his heartless actions. *No,* he told himself, *it went deeper than that.* As he thought back, he realized that guilt had burdened him since Rynah had lost her engagement ring, and he had chosen to put it in his pocket, unable to let it go; Brie only made his conscious mind aware of his true sentiments.

Soft, delicate steps tiptoed down the stairwell just outside the prison center. He wouldn't have heard them at all, except that the pins in the railing were loose and clinked from the tiniest of movements. Klanor pushed himself into a sitting position, not wanting to be caught at a moment of weakness, especially since he knew it was not Rynah who approached—he knew her steps by heart.

Brie stepped into the light of the single bulb that hung by the entrance to the brig; condensation covered it, making its light faint. She walked toward him with confidence, but maintained her ginger pace as though she cared more for his well-being than the fear of what he had done to her.

"I wondered when you'd come," he said.

"You expected me?" asked Brie.

"Of course," replied Klanor. "No doubt you wish to exact some sort of revenge for what I did to you."

"No," whispered Brie.

"No?" Brie's response intrigued him. Most people he knew would have killed him the moment they had a chance; Alfric and Jifdar bore testament to that fact, and Stein had left him to die on Sunlil.

Brie moved closer to the bars; her fear of Klanor had vanished. All she saw in the gloom was a defeated man who had lost everything in his lust for universal power.

"Revenge would be easy, but it solves nothing."

"You sound different," said Klanor. "Spending too much time with that man with the sword, I presume."

"Perhaps. Or perhaps I have matured a little since Solaris first ripped me away from my home."

"And you are not bitter about that?"

"No. I'll admit I had been frightened and angry at first, but then I met Tom, Solon, Alfric, Rynah, and… and I got to know Solaris. Friends I never would have met had she not done what she did. And, then, I met you."

"So you've come to gloat."

"That would be pointless," said Brie. "I don't revel in other's misfortune. I just wanted to thank you."

"Thank me?" This caught Klanor off guard. He had expected hatred and loathing, those emotions he understood, but to be thanked for tormenting another was unheard of.

"Yes," said Brie, "to thank you for teaching me to not be afraid. Your interrogations—your mind games—helped me see that I can be strong, that I don't have to be afraid."

Klanor snorted. He remembered Brie's memories—he had been in them. He thought of the images of Alfric training Brie to wield a sword, or of Jenny's constant taunts. Though he did not know the context of the memories, their meaning was clear.

"I thought that—Alfric, is his name?—helped you."

"He did," said Brie, "but you were the one who tested my resolve. Alfric showed me that I can stand up for myself, but learning something and applying it are two different things. You were the one who actually tried to get information from me. You were the epitome of my fears."

"You proved to be especially difficult. Very few have ever been able to resist the telepathic interrogation." Klanor studied Brie's posture: more erect and proud; she looked others in the eye, instead of staring at her feet, as she once did, and a certain calm embodied her once quivering voice. She had changed. Even he saw that.

"So why are you here?"

"I just wanted to ask you why?"

"Why?"

"Why, did you do what you did?"

"I thought that would be obvious. Interrogating you was strategically prudent."

"No, that isn't what I mean," said Brie. "Why the search for the crystals? What are they to you?"

"Hope," whispered Klanor.

Brie's brows scrunched together in puzzlement.

"You all think that I wanted the crystals for my own gain, that I wanted them for some sort of power and glory. A part of that might be correct, but it isn't the only reason. If you truly understood the myths of my people, you would know that the crystals are said to endow their bearer with wisdom, the power to heal, and the ability to bring warring nations together.

"You don't know what Lanyr had become. It had split into factions; though nothing new, these factions cared more about their petty wants than anything else. Politicians, who had once vowed to protect the basic rights of those they represented, spent their days scheming and conniving with one another in bids for prestige and political power, forsaking the oaths they had sworn. Possessing the six crystals would have stopped all of that, allowing one to lead…"

"And who would lead them? You?"

"I never meant for all of those people to die. I just wanted to end the corruption on my planet and within the Twelve Sectors."

"Maybe at one time you did, but in the end, you were just as corrupt as those around you. You justify your actions with noble reasoning, but the results are still the same—innocent people are dead because of you. And you built that weapon."

"As a means of defense."

"But you used it on societies unable to defend themselves and you were unprovoked."

"But I never meant..."

"You can tell yourself whatever lies you want, but the fact remains that you gave in to the most basic component of human destruction, greed. You lied and you schemed to get what you wanted. So I ask you again, why?"

Klanor sighed, racking his brain for the answer. He had spent months justifying his actions and had convinced himself it was for a good cause, but Brie was right; he had committed the same, and infinitely worse, atrocities he had hoped to rid Lanyr of. He had destroyed an entire planet.

"You're right," he said. "When I first heard about the crystals, and received evidence that they were more than a myth, I wanted them for myself. I believed that if I had them, then I could bring some sort of justice to this universe."

"You still don't get it, do you?"

"Get what?"

"Exactly," said Brie.

"What am I supposed to understand?" demanded Klanor.

"Only you can figure that out, but you might want to look around you. See where all of your schemes and actions got you. The very man you trusted betrayed you for the same reason that you stole the crystal from Lanyr."

"No," said Klanor, "it's worse than that."

"What do you mean?"

"When I first found Stein, he had been about to commit suicide. I don't know why I stopped him. I felt compelled to."

"Perhaps you still have some shred of decency left."

"No. I have seen that sort of desperation before. Men like that are easily manipulated, and I needed someone who could be in the places I could not.

"You see, there is another bit of that myth that states that the crystals, when united, are supposed to have the power to turn back time, and maybe even end death. It's very vague, but I told that part to him, even embellished it a little."

"And so he now plans to unite them himself, to bring back his family?" asked Brie.

"I do not think so. There is a portion of the poem that was missing from the book. What I once thought could bring the ones we've lost back, I now think that the crystals create something far worse."

"What exactly?"

"I don't know."

"And Stein?"

"He is a man with nothing left to lose and nothing to live for. His anger at losing his wife and child is still there and has grown stronger each day. My world has a saying, 'Misery loves company.'"

"We have the same saying."

"Well, anger loves company too, but to the point of decimation. I believe that Stein is determined that others know his pain and he will have no reservations about whom he kills. I only used that weapon on areas that I believed to be unfit for existence: pirate hubs, places torn by rivalling warlords, and areas where child enslavement was still sanctioned. I used judgment before executing the weapon. Stein will not. And I created him."

"What are you saying?"

"It was not I who attacked Neblar."

Brie almost gasped when she finally understood what Klanor had been telling her.

"Are you sure you do not wish to kill me now?"

"I will never wish you harm, but I cannot say the same for the others. They are currently deciding your fate."

"And what is to be done with me?"

"Jifdar wanted to shove you out of an airlock. And as you are aware, Alfric would prefer your head."

"But you stopped them."

"Yes."

"Why?"

"Because despite all of your wrongs, there is one redeeming quality—you still love Rynah. You forget that while you were in my head, I was also in yours. Those feelings for her are strong, and despite your attempts, you have never been able to rid yourself of them."

"And because of that, you would let me live."

"I believe people can change if they choose to," said Brie. "A true monster would never have allowed himself to love another."

"So what is to be done with me?" Klanor asked for a second time.

In answer to his question, several pairs of heavy boots stomped down the stairs and trampled into the brig, as in walked Jifdar, Rynah, Alfric, and Solaris. Jifdar placed his hand on a pad and the bars popped open.

"What's this?" demanded Klanor.

"Our power crystals are running low and we need more. We have entered orbit above the planet of Grior where such crystals grow naturally. Rynah says you know it quite well."

Klanor stepped out of his cell, uncertain about Jifdar's intentions. "How do I know you aren't just going to kill me when we land down there?"

"If I were going to kill you," said Jifdar, "I'd have done it the moment I laid eyes on you. Now come on." The pirate captain grasped

Klanor's arm, digging his sharp nails into the man's skin, and yanked him toward the stairs.

"What is all this?" asked Brie.

"A test," Rynah whispered into her ear so that Klanor could not hear her. "You wished to give him a chance to prove himself; we are giving him just that."

"Alfric," said Brie, grabbing his hairy arm, "don't kill him. Sometimes compassion is better than revenge."

Alfric frowned. He had never heard of such sentiment, but as Brie had been insistent, he relented. "I promise you that if he dies, it will be because he brought it upon himself." Alfric followed after Jifdar and Klanor.

"I don't understand what it is you see in him," Rynah said to Brie, still trying to understand the girl's reluctance to execute him, as she had so often thought of doing.

"I see you, Rynah," said Brie. "Your eyes, and his, harbor the same remorse, anger, and desire for absolution."

Rynah remained silent as she headed for the stairs.

"I forgave you, for all you've done," Brie called after her.

Rynah faced her, understanding now why Solaris had chosen her. "I don't deserve it." She hurried around the bend and up the stairs, her heavy footfalls fading into the darkness.

"I don't like all of this deception," Brie commented to Solaris.

"Neither do I, but we were outvoted. If what you think is true, then you've nothing to worry about."

"Aren't you going with them?"

"No," replied Solaris. "I think it's best if I remain here. Do you think what he said about the crystals is true?"

"Why do you ask?"

"Curiosity."

Brie looked at Solaris with skepticism; the feeling that she concealed something gnawed at her. "I believe that it would have been best if they had never been created."

Chapter 5
KLANOR'S TEST

Rynah, Alfric, Jifdar, and Klanor all sat in the shuttle (though glued to the sticky, grungy seats would be more accurate) as the pilot entered the upper atmosphere and steered the small shuttlecraft with ease to the ground below. The shuttle bounced.

"Just a bit of turbulence, captain," said the pilot as he leveled the craft.

Gripping her seat until her knuckles turned white and her hands cramped—Rynah hated not being the one operating the shuttle—she stuck her fingers in black sludge that forced them to stick together. Disgusted, she wiped her hand on the empty seat next to her. Rynah and Klanor both loathed the dilapidation of the shuttle and its unkemptness, though Jifdar seemed quite at home in it, while Alfric maintained his stoic composure, never being one to openly convey disgust; his steel gaze remained focused on Klanor.

A high pitched squeal echoed beneath their feet as the landing gear was released. Plomp! They touched the ground with a slight jostle, a stark contrast to the jarring ride on the way down. Desperate to get out of their metal prison, they unbuckled themselves, Alfric being the first to reach his feet.

"Take the shuttle back to Gilraen," said Jifdar to the pilot, referring to the name he had given his ship.

"Aye, captain." The pilot closed the back hatch of the craft, started the engines, and took off.

"Well," said Jifdar to Klanor, "where to?"

Klanor reached into his pocket—Alfric raised his sword—and pulled out a compass, not just any compass, but one designed to search for energy crystals.

"Relax," said Klanor. "It's not a weapon—you took all of mine. It's a compass."

"It does not look like any compass or sextant I've seen," said Alfric.

"No, it wouldn't," replied Klanor, "because this particular compass has been fashioned to find the very crystals used to power ships. Those crystals release ionic energy that this device detects that."

"Proceed," said Alfric.

Jifdar gave him a piercing glare, not liking how the Viking took command, but remained silent. Having seen Alfric's prowess in battle, he decided it best to refrain from a one-on-one confrontation with the man.

"This way," said Klanor as he stared at his compass and walked toward a series of hills.

They walked in the perpetual twilight of the sun that peeked over the hills, never rising, never sinking, across the short, pale green grass (daisies littered throughout) as they followed Klanor's directions. The slow gradient of the terrain made their hike easygoing. Though arid, grass grew out of the earth, resembling spikes, more than the soft blades most people are used to, and pricked many a bare hand and foot.

After two hours of walking, Klanor stopped.

"What's the matter?" asked Rynah.

"There should be a road here," he replied.

"Are you sure?" said Rynah.

"Yes." Klanor remembered his first days on the planet with clarity, he had been there a few times. The planet harbored power crystals that few in the Twelve Sectors knew about, and those that did, kept it as a well-guarded secret. Klanor, long before he had ever met Rynah, had been part of a mining crew, and the captain knew of the power crystals that formed on the planet. A road (lumpy and very rocky) had been there; each time they had returned, they had used the same path.

"There most definitely should be a road here."

"Landscapes change," said Jifdar.

"Not this," Klanor said.

"Are you certain that the grass hasn't just grown across it?" asked Rynah.

"We are wasting time," grumbled Alfric.

"It is possible," Klanor said in response to Rynah's inquiry. He checked his compass again. "According to this, we should go in this direction."

"Then lead on," said Jifdar, "and remember, I have my weapon trained on you."

"I assure you, I am no threat," Klanor replied.

"Tell that to my pirates, whom you murdered."

"What must I do, to prove my worthiness to you?"

The question caused all of them to pause as Klanor's tone had been sincere and reflective of a man who had lost all belief and had been beaten into submission.

"When you have," said Jifdar, "you will know."

Without a word, Klanor trudged onward with the others right behind him. He knew they would never fully trust him, but he had no desire to challenge them, or escape.

For hours, they walked, and the sun never changed its position in the burgundy sky until they reached the hills, which turned into a maze of small canyons. Klanor picked up a black rock, which left dark smudges on his fingers, and drew a giant X on a protruding boulder from the cliffside.

"Here," he tossed the marking stone to Rynah, "make sure you mark our path; otherwise, we'll never find our way out of here."

"But your compass…" began Alfric.

"Only shows us where the crystals are, but not the way out. Many a man has gotten lost in these canyons because he failed to mark his path."

Klanor led them into the maze of ravines—Rynah marking various rocks and broken trunks of dead trees—keeping a wary eye on the path behind them, hoping that their etchings would not fade or disappear; otherwise, they would be lost forever. Gravel slipped beneath their feet as they climbed a narrow trail that snaked its way upward and over a wall of solid rock, before descending back to the canyon floor. Not once did Klanor look up from his compass, his mind focused on finding the crystals.

A click sounded above them.

"What was that?" asked Alfric, his mind at full alert.

"Probably nothing," replied Jifdar. "Lonely hills play tricks on your mind."

While the others continued moving forward, Alfric paused, scanning the surrounding area and the brown landscape, perfect cover for bandits to conceal themselves. Another click reached his ears; the hairs on the back of his neck stood on end. Raising his sword, Alfric readied himself for an attack.

"Get down!" He dove out of the way just as fire from a laser rifle struck the cliffside where his head had been; small rocks and pebbles crashed around him, covering him.

Klanor snatched Rynah and threw her to the ground, flinging himself on top of her and protecting her from the laser fire, while Jifdar crouched behind a gap in the rock. He didn't see anything.

Poof! Poof! Poof!

Laser fire struck the dirt around them, sending up puffs of

brown dust. A man jumped Alfric from above. The Viking dodged out of the way, grabbed the man, and rammed him into the sharp rock of the canyon side before tossing him over the cliff.

More men materialized from the surrounding landscape, armed with laser weapons, all pointed at them. Klanor snatched Rynah's hand—she tried to pull free, but his iron grip held firm—and jerked her to her feet, dragging her down a steep incline and away from danger. She looked behind, making certain that Alfric and Jifdar followed. After struggling some more, Rynah freed her hand from Klanor's grasp; he attempted to reach for her, but she shook him off, pulling out her laser pistol, and firing at their attackers who scrambled after them.

"Blacyr pirates!" shouted Jifdar.

His foot slipped, but before he plummeted to the hard ground below, Alfric seized his arm and hauled him back up. Laser fire struck near their feet. Jifdar whirled around and fired a series of laser blasts, forcing those that chased them to find cover. They hurried after Rynah and Klanor, who had hunkered behind a crumbling ledge.

"We need to find cover," said Jifdar.

More laser fire struck the ground near them.

"There might be some caves this way," said Klanor.

Jifdar and Alfric frowned; they had little choice but to trust the man they despised.

"Lead the way," said Rynah, knowing they were out of options.

Klanor turned and headed deeper into the maze of the jagged and twisting canyons. Their feet flew over the uneven ground, scraping against the surface, sending grit tumbling below. Harsh stomping and laser fire pursued them as the Blacyr pirates chased their quarry, their faces covered by frayed scarves wrapped around them.

BOOM!

A cannon blast struck just below the ledge they stood upon; dirt and rock crumbled beneath their feet as they tumbled to the bottom of the canyon, bumping into the side of the rock wall, smoke and dust surrounding them. Coughing, Rynah unburied herself.

"Rynah," came Klanor's voice. His hands snatched one of the rocks covering her and yanked it away.

"Alfric and Jifdar," she said, still choking on the mounds of fine silt hovering in the air.

"They're fine," Klanor replied.

Shouts above them warned them of impending danger.

"We need to leave," said Klanor. "This way."

They ran through the canyon, ducking around its corners and many turns, desperate to escape the pirates chasing them. In the dim light, navigating the ravine proved difficult; several times, they were stopped by a dead end and had been forced to turn around. At every turn, the Blacyr pirates seemed to have been there, blocking their path.

Klanor spotted a dark patch in the ground, a hole leading to an underground tunnel. "There!"

They raced for it. Laser fire followed their stampeding feet, failing to stop them, but coming very close. Two pirates materialized behind Alfric, each seizing a bulging arm. Alfric, stopped, crouched low, and flung them off him. Grasping his sword until the hilt dug into his skin, he knocked the laser pistol out of the hands of one before finishing the other. Alfric charged the first pirate. Frightened by the crazed Viking, he scampered away.

More laser fire hurled around them, drowned by a low creaking that reverberated above them. Pausing, Jifdar stopped just below a protruding ledge of dirt and looked up, curious as to what made the noise.

"Jifdar!" shouted Rynah.

The ledge broke free of its hold, heading straight for the pirate captain, crashing all around him and burying him. Rynah ran for Jifdar. Before she got far, Klanor seized her shoulders, pulling her back. "You can't help him," he yelled at her.

Rynah continued to struggle against his grip; only the onslaught of more laser fire forced her to allow him to pull her away, with Alfric by their side. They raced across the loose gravel, tufts of spindly grass cutting into the soles of their boots, in a zigzagging maneuver to shake their pursuers, most of whom had stopped to inspect the place where Jifdar lay buried under mounds of claylike soil.

Rynah suddenly clutched her thigh, stumbling and falling to the ground. A black, and bloody, stripe stretched across her upper leg. One Blacyr pirate had followed them. "Just go."

"No." Klanor knelt by Rynah's side, refusing to leave her. He spotted the hole in the ground, but noticed that a boulder partially covered it; they would never be able to squeeze through it.

Alfric moved toward the pirate.

"No," shouted Klanor, stopping the Viking, "that opening needs to be bigger if we're to fit through it!"

Eyeing Rynah's injured state, Alfric sheathed his sword and ran for the hole, gripping the giant boulder, his muscles bulging—the sinews visible through the skin—as he used all of his strength to move it.

Klanor hauled Rynah to her feet, placing her left arm around his shoulders. Together, they half galloped, half hobbled to the opening in the ground. The pirate drew nearer. Each blast from his weapon struck the dirt around them. Refusing to give up, Klanor dragged Rynah to where Alfric struggled with the boulder.

Pift! Pift! Pift!

The pirate closed the distance, the threads from his ripped clothing flapping behind him as he ran with his laser weapon raised. With one final push, Alfric managed to remove the rock. Klanor heaved Rynah onto his shoulders and bolted for the Viking, shoving her into his arms, and snatching the knife from her boot, as Alfric jumped into the dark opening in the ground with Rynah. Klanor spun around just as the pirate pounced upon him and plunged the knife deep into his torso and dropped the pirate's body, looking around for signs of more, but there were none. He dove into the hole where Alfric waited for him, supporting Rynah, as she was unable to stand on her own.

"I know you are here," came a voice that did not belong to Jifdar. "You may have found a place to hide, but how long do you think you can remain that way? We will find you."

In the darkness, they remained silent, refusing to give away their position.

"We have your friend!"

Alfric's knuckles turned white as he squeezed the hilt of his sword, angered by the man's taunting. Rynah placed a gentle hand on his and he released his grip, her action reminding him of Brie.

"Give yourselves up. You have until the first star rises, or we will kill your friend, and then you when we find you. We'll leave a fire going, so that you may easily find us."

Silence followed as the pirates stalked away with Jifdar in their possession, leaving Klanor, Rynah, and Alfric to consider their request, and lack of options.

Rynah touched the wound on her thigh; blood poured from it, trickling down her leg and soaking her clothing. She ripped strips of cloth from her shirt and tied it around her leg.

"Here," said Klanor, taking the strip from her shaking hands—the shock from the blood loss began to affect her—and wrapping it around the wound to stem the bleeding. "You need a doctor."

"If we ever get to a place with medical facilities, I'll keep that in mind," quipped Rynah.

"Why do they not come for us?" asked Alfric, keeping his eyes on the hole above them.

"Why would they?" asked Rynah. "They know that we are trapped."

"I do not think that is the only reason," said Alfric.

"It's because they are lost and believe we are not," said Klanor.

Klanor now knew why the road he had expected to see before

entering the canyons was not there; they had landed in the wrong place. When he had been 16, he had run away from home and joined the first mining freighter that would allow him to board, and it had been one that specialized in mining energy crystals. He remembered landing on the planet, but had forgotten one crucial detail: the mining ship had landed on the northwest end of the ravine, and he had Jifdar land on the Southeast end. If they had gone to the northwest section, they could have used the road to find their way out of the canyons.

"*Draconar!*" he cursed in Lanyran.

"What's wrong?" asked Alfric, reading the frustrated tone in Klanor's language.

"Fool that I am," replied Klanor. "I know why there was no road. We landed on the southeast end of the canyon."

"And that is a problem?" asked Rynah.

"When I was here last, our captain told us to always enter the canyon from the northwest, where the road was. The compass would guide us to the crystals, but as long as we kept the road in sight, we would find our way out."

"That is why we marked our path," said Rynah.

"Except we are now cowering in this hole, well away from those markings," said Alfric as he realized the severity of what Klanor had told him.

"So we're lost, we have a bunch of pirates trying to kill us, and we are stuck here in a hole," said Rynah, sounding a bit like Tom.

"Not completely," said Klanor. "These canyons have underground tunnels and I think we might be in one. We could use a flashlight though."

In answer to his wishes, Alfric tore off the end of an underground root the size of his arm, wrapped torn pieces of his cloak around one end, and scrapped the blade of his sword against the rock, allowing the sparks to ignite the torch.

"Lead the way," said Klanor to Alfric, as he lifted Rynah to her feet. "Why would I betray you?" he asked as Alfric continued to give him a doubtful glance. "We are all in the same situation and I don't feel like dying today."

"One slip and…" Alfric didn't need to finish his statement; Klanor understood his meaning.

They moved through the cramped tunnels, walking—Rynah hobbled—hunched over, the cavern ceilings brushing the backs of their heads. Dust littered the air, floating in and out of the torchlight. Ripples in the rock formed vertical lines that stretched from the ground and over their heads, creating a circle.

"Wait," said Klanor, stopping them. He held up his compass and watched as the needle pointed in another direction. "We should go this way."

Though reluctant to trust the man, Alfric turned down the fork in the underground tunnels where Klanor had indicated, hiking up its slight incline. Roaring thunder surrounded them, growing louder the further they went; only Rynah's grunts, and the skids from her boots scraping the hardened surface due to the pain caused by her injury, drowned the noise.

"What is that sound?" asked Alfric.

"Water," said Rynah. "These tunnels must have been formed by an underground river." She paused to rest.

"Just a little further," said Klanor, but Rynah's leg gave out on her, forcing her to drop to the ground.

"I can't," she said.

"I will scout ahead," said Alfric. He detested the idea of leaving Rynah alone with Klanor, but knew that they needed to learn what lay ahead, and she was in no condition to move. He had also seen her grip her laser pistol—so did Klanor, despite her attempts at stealth—and realized that, though injured, she was far from helpless. "I shall return shortly. Do not move from this spot."

Alfric handed them the torch; his clomping boots faded as he walked further through the caverns.

"Let me look at that," said Klanor.

"It's fine," Rynah replied, her hand still on her pistol.

"No, you're not."

Rynah's eyes stared into Klanor's, her mistrust of him evident.

"I know you still do not trust me, but if I had wanted all of you dead, I would have delivered you to the Blacyr pirates."

"They would kill you as well."

"Not for the right price," said Klanor, "and you can take your hand off your weapon."

Rynah disarmed her laser pistol, her eyes never leaving Klanor.

"Stein betrayed me, too, you know. I want him to be punished just as much as you do."

"That makes for a very fragile alliance."

"True, but you need me. I know him. I know how he thinks."

Rynah cringed, gritting her teeth to avoid screaming in pain as Klanor tightened the makeshift bandage around her still-bleeding wound. "Did any of it mean something, when we were together, or was it all just an act?"

"You want honesty? I staged our meeting and it was supposed to be just an act to gain your trust, but... well, it didn't go as planned. Yes, it meant something. Despite my best efforts—let's just say that you were irresistible."

"How comforting."

"I know that you have every reason to doubt me, but I love you, Rynah. I truly do. I never meant to, but I do. When I asked you to marry me, I meant it. Even at Fredyr's, I offered you a chance to come away with me."

"But how could I after you destroyed Lanyr? Why'd you do it?"

"I gave in to temptation," replied Klanor. "Before I met you, I had been searching for something, something to give my life meaning. Then, your grandfather's trial happened, and I knew that not only were the myths true, but that they were my purpose. Possessing that kind of power—think about it! I focused on it to avoid thinking about you, but it cost me the only thing that meant anything to me. I don't expect you to understand, nor do I expect you to ever trust me."

"I don't know if I can."

"Then how about another ally. Stein will never stop until he acquires the crystals and destroys this planet, Earth, as you call it. If your friends wish to save their home, they will need me."

Deep down, Rynah knew that Klanor spoke the truth about his expertise being needed to stop Stein, and she wanted to stop the man that left them to die on Sunlil.

"As long as we're being honest with one another, you should know that this entire trip to get an energy crystal was meant to be a hoax, to test you, except it didn't go as planned."

"What?"

"Jifdar's ship needs the crystal, but we knew where they were. However, Brie insisted that you should be given a second chance, and none of us could refuse her, so we devised this plan of making you believe that we needed you to lead us to the energy crystals. If you did, and didn't try to escape, or kill us, in the process, then, maybe, we would trust you. Though I don't think Alfric ever will. However, the Blacyr pirates were not in the equation."

Klanor laughed. His guffaws echoed around them, ringing against the cavern walls and into every crevice.

Rynah had not expected this reaction and just stared at him in confusion. "You aren't angry?"

"Why should I be?" chortled Klanor. "I think it's rather ironic. You concocted this plan to prove my trustworthiness, and now you need my help to get out of trouble! You never were good at schemes."

"No, that's your department," said Rynah. "Sorry," she apologized for the harshness of her words.

"Don't be," Klanor said. "You're right. I am very good at scheming and it cost me everything."

Alfric's swift steps swept through the tunnel as he returned. "Come with me."

They hauled Rynah to her feet, each taking an arm, and hobbled through the tunnel, Alfric giving them instructions on where to turn. Light spilled from up ahead, casting glistening rays into the darkness. Painful step by painful step, Rynah managed to avoid crying out in agony, not wanting to give anyone the satisfaction of seeing her as weak.

They walked through the opening. The scene changed as red cliffs stretched above them, forming a bowl, with them in its base; layer upon layer snaked upward until they couldn't see the edges of the rim, but that was not the breathtaking part. The entire area glittered as crystals (some with rigid, dried vines encircling them) filled every inch of every space, reflecting the soft light of the low hanging sun, twinkling, and in some cases glowing, alerting them to their power. They marveled at the site as the crystals' lights (blue, green, yellow, and pale orange) danced upon their awed faces; even Alfric failed to conceal his wonderment.

"How is this possible?" asked Rynah, forgetting the pain in her thigh.

"No one really knows," replied Klanor. "It is a naturally occurring phenomenon on this planet. It grows crystals, but ones that can be used to power our ships. The star in this system produces a different kind of light than the ones in other systems, and because it never rises far above the horizon, or dips below it, the planet stays at a constant temperature. But feel the dirt. It is not the kind seen on most planets. The dirt here seems to be crystal dust."

Alfric scooped up a handful of the pearl-colored gravel in his meaty hands, allowing it to filter through his parted fingers; each pebble resembled a small diamond instead of a rock.

"Unbelievable," breathed Rynah.

"Consider this one of the natural wonders of the Twelve Sectors," said Klanor.

"Why is it there is no mining facility here?" asked Rynah. On other planets where such crystals formed naturally, mines were built.

"Because this planet is one where people go missing, or get lost. The maze formed by these canyons makes setting up a mining facility difficult. Very few actually know of the crystals here, and those that do keep it secret, not wanting to lose their source of income. As a result, this place has become a perfect source of power for smugglers, and…"

"Pirates," finished Alfric.

"We should take a couple of these with us," said Rynah. "It is what we came for."

Alfric and Klanor seated her on a boulder before each knelt by a crystal and dug it out of the ground, placing them in the bag Rynah had brought with her.

"We need to leave this place," said Alfric.

"What about Jifdar?" asked Rynah.

"We are outnumbered," said Alfric, "and you are in no condition for battle. If we leave here to rescue him, you will die; if we take you with us, and attempt a rescue, we may all die. It is impossible for us to take you to a healer and rescue Jifdar at the same time."

"Then what do we do?" asked Rynah.

"We must get back to the ship. From there, we can mount a rescue for the pirate, if that is your wish."

"We can't just leave him," protested Rynah.

Alfric eyed the tops of the cliffs 400 feet above them. They had lingered too long. "For now, we should leave this trap."

He wrapped Rynah's arm around his shoulder, supporting her as she stood, and walked to the far end where a black strip stretched from the tops of the canyon to the very depths of the ground.

Klanor trailed behind. "Where are you going?"

"To our only way out," replied Alfric, his sword poised in a defensive position.

They reached the black strip—which wasn't a strip at all, but a throughway, its width matching the length of Alfric's arm—and paused before it. Doubtful expressions filled Rynah's and Klanor's faces.

"I don't think we'll fit," said Klanor.

Not liking Klanor's skepticism, Alfric moved sideways into the canyon's slit with Rynah in tow. They walked sideways at a snail's pace, the sharp ridges of the rock walls tearing at their clothing. Rynah tried to keep up, but her injured leg dragged behind her, slowing her down; she refused to complain about the pain that each of her unsteady steps gave her. She looked up at the smidgeon of rose-blue above them; the color of the sky hadn't changed since they had first landed.

Alfric's sword raked against the cliffsides, sending piles of dust onto the tops of his fur-covered boots. He pointed it upward in an attempt to prevent it from scraping the rock. A tug on his arm alerted him to Rynah's struggles. He gripped her hand and hauled her back to her feet, while Klanor supported her other side, encouraging her to keep going as they neared the end of the narrow path at an agonizing pace.

"I'm feeling a bit lightheaded," Rynah said, her exhaustion evident.

"We haven't far to go," soothed Alfric.

Dirt fell from above. They looked up. A flicker of movement told them that they weren't alone.

"Can we move any faster?" asked Klanor.

"I can't," said Rynah, finding it difficult to ignore the excruciating pain in her thigh.

Alfric handed Klanor his sword. "Get her through here. No tricks."

"I promise," said Klanor as he took the sword, but Alfric held it a moment longer, staring into his eyes, an unspoken message passing between them. "Where are you going?" Klanor demanded when Alfric released his weapon and turned his back on him.

In answer to his question, Alfric gripped the sides of the ravine's walls and heaved himself upward. He placed his feet on small bumps with expertise as he climbed upward to the top. His movements swift, he ignored the lesions that formed on his hands as sharp rocks sliced them, maintaining his focus on the ledge above him. He saw the flicker of movement again. Positive that a pirate was up there, but unsure of how to capture him, he increased his speed.

"He's crazy," muttered Klanor.

"He's determined," replied Rynah.

She leaned on the cliffside for support as she pulled herself along, delving deeper into the narrow opening; the sliver of light ahead of her gave her hope. They were close.

Alfric's hand felt the top of the ledge. Peeking over the edge, he noted the position of the pirate kneeling in the sand with his back to him, speaking into his com device. The Viking crept over the ledge. He sprang to his feet, tackling the pirate. They rolled across the ground and down a low hill, sand flying as each struggled to be the victor. The pirate broke free.

Undaunted, Alfric charged again, grasping the man around the waist, heaving him over his shoulders, and smashing him into the ground. He brought his foot down upon him, but the pirate rolled out of the way and snatched his ankle, pulling him off his feet. The impact knocked the wind out of Alfric's lungs. He scrambled to his feet. Both glared at one another as they circled, calculating their opponent's next move.

They ran towards each other. At the last second, Alfric dove to the ground, sweeping the pirate's feet from under him. Sand flew as he hurried to the pirate and grasped him around the neck with a deadly grip. Despite the pirate's struggles, Alfric maintained his hold until the man's movements ceased. He released the body.

Alfric glanced around, but saw no sign of other pirates. He spotted the communicator. Though he remained uncertain of how to use it, he had seen Rynah with a similar device on many occasions and understood its importance. He picked it up and followed the edge of the cliff to its end, hoping it would take him to Rynah, and that he had not been mistaken in allowing Klanor a chance to prove his worth.

The opening was near. Rynah clamped her mouth shut to prevent herself from screaming as her leg begged for a reprieve. Klanor stayed by her side, supporting her when she let him, while keeping a watchful eye to what lay above them. Jerking their way through, they popped out the other end and into the open. Refreshing air wafted over them, washing away the effects of the thick atmosphere inside the canyon's strip.

A scuffle prickled their ears. Klanor shoved Rynah back inside the ravine, remaining poised in front of the opening. Rynah pulled out her laser pistol. They waited with abated breath for the source of the noise to show itself.

Alfric jumped in front of them, raising his hands. "It is only me."

Relieved, Rynah and Klanor lowered their weapons and Alfric handed her the communications device.

"Which direction to the rendezvous point?" asked Alfric.

"I don't know," said Klanor. "I'm afraid I got turned around in there. There is a reason why people get lost in these canyons."

"The sun is up, is it not?" asked Alfric.

"Yes, but..."

"Does its position ever change?"

"No," replied Klanor, "it remains in the west, never rising, never setting. It always just peeks over those hil—"

Klanor ceased talking as an idea struck him. Why hadn't he thought of using the sun before? He cursed himself for being so stupid and thinking that only technology would navigate their way out.

"The sun is always in the west and the rendezvous point is south of here. So if the sun is there, then we need to head in that direction."

"Perhaps you can change," said Alfric. "If a man can admit he is wrong, then he can change."

"I believe Solon is having an effect on you," commented Rynah.

Alfric lifted Rynah up, her pants leg now soaked with her blood, while Klanor took the com unit and handed Alfric the bag with the crystals.

"What's this?" asked Alfric.

"Take her and the crystals back to the ship," replied Klanor.

"Where are you going?" demanded Rynah; worry had snuck into her voice.

"You were right," said Klanor. "We can't just leave Jifdar behind. But he's right too. You need to get back to the ship." He looked Alfric in the eyes, an unspoken promise being sworn between them. "Get her back to the ship."

Klanor darted off.

"No!" screamed Rynah. Her conflicted heart worried that he ventured to his death. Despite all of the days spent loathing him, despite the many vows of revenge she had sworn, deep within the confines of her heart, Rynah did not want to watch him die. At that moment, she admitted to herself that she still loved him; that her anger was merely a mask to cover the wounds of his betrayal.

Alfric heaved Rynah onto his broad shoulders, ignoring her struggles, and ran southward.

Klanor walked through the maze of the canyons, a low bleeping guiding him to Jifdar's location. He had turned the pirate's com unit into a homing beacon that zeroed in on the wavelengths released by the other pirates' units. The strength of the signal indicated how many were grouped together and where they were. The stronger it was, the more he knew he headed in the right direction. Having imprisoned others before, Klanor knew that the pirates would have as many guards on Jifdar as possible, for he was not just any captive, but the captain of the Fragmyr pirates and a valuable hostage.

Tumultuous thoughts reeled through his mind, each warring with another. Several years he had spent attempting to acquire the six crystals and the power they were said to possess, but all of it seemed empty. He thought of Brie. Of all the people in the universe, she was the last person he would expect to defend him and beg for mercy on his behalf. Sudden guilt at what he had done to her plagued him.

Then, Rynah's violet eyes filled his mind. Her warm smile beckoning him to come to her. It vanished as Stein's treacherous act left him stranded on the volcanic planet of Sunlil. Klanor vowed revenge, but stopped. Yes, Stein should be punished, but what would he do once that task had been accomplished?

Rynah entered his mind once more before being shunted aside by Brie, the only person who did not loathe him. By rights, she should wish him dead, but each time she looked at him, pity filled her eyes. The more Klanor pondered it, he realized that Brie was a rare individual and understood Alfric's protectiveness of her.

The only reason Klanor searched for Jifdar was for Rynah's sake—she had wanted the pirate saved—but also for Brie's, knowing that she would have done no less. Given a chance, Jifdar would kill him, of that Klanor was certain, but he didn't care. Rynah's heart ached at the very thought of leaving someone behind, and for the first time in his life, so did his.

Klanor pushed the maddening thoughts aside. Now was not the time to dwell on one's heart. He had made a promise and intended to keep this one.

A quieter beep escaped the device. With caution, Klanor followed it and found a lone pirate hunkered by a single flame. Fool. He should have known better than to stave off the chills of the evening air by lighting a fire and letting his guard down. Klanor grasped a baseball-sized rock from the ground.

Sneaking up behind the pirate, he raised the rock and struck him over the head. The pirate slumped to the ground. Klanor stripped the outer coverings from the unconscious pirate and put them on. He checked his makeshift homing device. A robust beep escaped from it. *Gotcha*, he thought.

Following the beacon, Klanor hurried across the canyon floor; his boots crunched the gravel with each step. The never changing sunlight cast long shadows as his glided across them. Dancing shadows caught his attention. Creeping closer, Klanor shut off the device when he spotted a fire with nine figures seated around it. Two paced back and forth, standing guard. Another figure lay crumpled next to a post, Jifdar.

Klanor counted the steps of the two guards, timing their movements. Wishing he had a weapon, and that he hadn't stupidly forgotten to ask Rynah for hers, he studied the figures by the fire. With each swig they took from their canteens, they joked and laughed, becoming drunker.

"Enough you fools," roared the 12th pirate as he snatched a canteen from one, spilling its brown liquid on the dirt. Klanor pegged him as the captain, his commanding demeanor giving him away.

"Relax, captain, he's not going anywhere."

"It's not him I'm worried about."

"His friends can't do anything."

"Fool," grumbled the captain. "They should have tried something by now."

Klanor watched as the captain stalked away and turned his attention back to the guards, recounting their steps. He sprang from the shadows and grabbed one of the guards around the throat, snatching the laser rifle from him. Throwing the guard's corpse to the ground, Klanor fired at the other.

Those around the fire jumped to their feet. Klanor dove behind a mound of rocks just as a slew of laser fire hurled into it. He fired back.

"Get him!" shouted the captain.

Klanor jumped up, firing his weapon and catching two of the

pirates in the chest. As he hunched behind his cover once more, he wished he had thought his plan through to the end. A barrel's shadow loomed before him. Pirates, they never travel far without their drink. Klanor vaulted across the ground, releasing a spray of laser fire, and the barrel ruptured in a ball of light as rum rained on the pirates below.

From his corner of the camp, Jifdar propped his head up at all the commotion. All he saw was one pirate killing the others before his brain registered that it was a rescue. Tightening his grip on the cuffs around his wrists, he jumped at the closest pirate, wrapping the chain around his throat. The pirate dropped his weapon, gripping Jifdar's hands, desperate to breathe. He stopped. Jifdar dumped the body and picked up the abandoned laser rifle, firing at the pirates, while running across the encampment to Klanor.

Once he reached him, they both hid behind a small mound in the ground, laser fire pelting the sand near their heads.

"Nice of you to come for me," said Jifdar. "Where are the others?"

"It's just me," said Klanor.

"Great."

More laser fire whizzed past their heads, striking the rocks around them. They returned the gesture. As the small blasts ricocheted off the canyon walls, filling it with their hollow sounds, neither side overpowered the other. It stopped.

"All right, Jifdar," said the Blacyr captain, "you've had your fun. Now, let's stop this madness."

"I'm rather enjoying myself," came Jifdar's sarcastic reply.

"Look, we only need a guide out of this maze," said the Blacyr captain.

"And you'll kill us once you're out," Jifdar retorted.

"You're outnumbered," shouted the Blacyr captain. "I promise that no harm will come to you if you both put down your weapons."

Both Klanor and Jifdar doubted the pirate's word.

"You hav…" The captain's words cut off the moment a knife sailed through the air and plunged into his heart.

Both Klanor and Jifdar peeked over the mound they hid behind to find Alfric standing tall and proud, with knives in both hands.

"Shoot him!" shouted one pirate.

Alfric leapt from the ledge and landed upon two pirates, taking them out with ease. Laser fire shot from another place in the cliffs, striking two more pirates. Klanor and Jifdar bolted from their position, firing upon the pirates around them. They raced across the dirt towards Alfric's and Rynah's position, killing any who crossed their path. The laser fire faded as the last pirate fell dead.

"I thought I told you to get her out of here," scolded Klanor.

"She is most persuasive," replied Alfric as he helped Rynah down from her position.

"If anyone is going to kill you, it will be me," Rynah said to Klanor.

A clack reached their ears as Jifdar sifted through the dead pirates' belongings until he found a working radio.

"Gilraen, come in," he said into the com unit.

"Gilraen here, captain," came a crackled reply.

"Lock in on my signal and come get us. I'd like to get off this rock before I die." He tossed the device aside. "So, that went according to plan."

Chapter 6
NOT QUITE

General Delmar and Hylne moseyed through a house built into solid rock and disguised as part of the cliff, stepping past rickety tables, which creaked when you bumped them, and tattered chairs, which stuffing littered the floor. Grimy windows allowed speckled light to leave dots on the ratty rugs that had been blackened by months of neglect. An inch of brown dust covered every flat surface. Hylne ran his fingers over it, allowing it to coat them. "This doesn't look promising."

Studying the remote landscape, General Delmar's heart fell.

"I thought you said he was here."

"Fool, that I am," he scolded himself, "I should have known that it was a diversion."

"If this Tre is so well-versed in hiding, how are we to find him?" asked Hylne.

"No one is that good at hiding," said General Delmar. He rifled through the place, throwing holopads and papers in every direction as he searched for clues to Tre's whereabouts.

"What are you doing?" demanded Hylne.

"Even though this place appears to be abandoned, there has to be something here that can tell us where he is."

"This place looks like it has been stripped," replied Hylne.

General Delmar ignored Hylne's statement as he continued pulling holopads off shelves, allowing them to crash to the floor, their clatters filling the air and hurting Hylne's ears.

"Delmar."

No response.

"Delmar, stop!"

General Delmar hung his hands by his side. He looked at Hylne, who stared back at him with concern.

"There is nothing here. The trail is cold. We should go back to what's left of the Lanyran fleet."

"And abandon Rynah?"

"We don't even know if she is still alive."

"We don't know that she is dead."

"Why is this so important to you?" demanded Hylne.

"Because," began General Delmar. "You wouldn't understand."

A sliver of greenish-yellow light caught his notice. General Delmar raced over to it and ripped it free from its place on a secluded shelf, hidden by a rusty desk with a dented, metal leg. As General Delmar held the item into the light, he realized that it was a holomap. He rolled it out on the floor.

"What's that?"

"A map."

Images sprang to life on the holomap, marking star constellations, planets, solar systems, and the Twelve Sectors. General Delmar studied the map as he concentrated hard to remember the various locations Tre was said to be. He found a marker in an upturned drawer. Snatching it, General Delmar marked the location they were at and the one they had checked earlier.

"What are you doing?" asked Hylne.

"We've been here," said General Delmar, circling areas of the map in red, "and we are here now. If I remember correctly, the other possible locations we may find him at are here, here, here, and here."

"Are you sure?"

"About as sure as I'll ever be."

"Then we should look in this area," said Hylne, touching the map. "It's closest."

General Delmar rolled the holomap up and carried it with him as they headed back to their ship.

Chapter 7
TENSION

Stein walked into the private dining quarters (which had once been Klanor's, but was now his) to find Fredyr Monsooth seated at the head of the table, munching on a baked potato and steak. He stopped, rage implanted on his face.

"I hope you don't mind me helping myself to your kitchens," said Fredyr around a mouthful of meat. His two bodyguards melted in the background, barely visible, except by Stein's trained eye and knowledge of their presence.

"Not at all," replied Stein, his voice calm and controlled, as he took the seat across from Fredyr.

"You should really try some of this steak. It is delicious," said Fredyr.

"Some other time, perhaps," replied Stein. His mind remained alert. When he had made his alliance with Fredyr Monsooth, it was with the understanding that Fredyr would remain off the main ship, but, Stein chastised himself, he should have known that it would not remain that way.

"Suit yourself."

"I do not recall us having scheduled a meeting for today."

"We didn't. Until now, that is."

"Is there anything I can do for you, Mr. Monsooth?" asked Stein, keeping a wary eye on Fredyr's bodyguards.

"Oh, call me Fredyr. There is no need to be so formal with one another." Fredyr's smacking raked Stein's nerves. "It's just, you promised me my crystal back and revenge upon those who stole it. Well, it seems you have delivered on the crystal—though I have yet to see it—but no proof as to the thieves' demise."

"We left them at the base of an erupting volcano with no means of escape."

"Yes, but I know how persistent thorns in the side can be."

"Shall we turn back to Sunlil?"

"No need. If you say they are dead, then I will take your word for it, for now. But if they should turn up, still alive…" Fredyr allowed his voice to trail off, his meaning clear. "No, my real interest is in this planet called Earth, in the Terra Sector. How does it benefit me?"

"There are many resources that should prove advantageous to you. No doubt you will be able to exploit that planet, and its people, for your benefit."

"And you have no interest in it?" asked Fredyr.

"My interests do not lie in its resources, but something of considerably more value."

"How valuable?"

Stein knew this was coming. An agreement with Fredyr Monsooth usually changed in his favor, but he had no intention of giving Fredyr what he wanted. "That was not the nature of our agreement. What I seek is my business."

"It is also mine, as I have a stake in this as well."

"The crystal that is said to be there is what I seek. Everything else on that barbarous planet is yours, with the exception that if I deem it necessary to demonstrate our might, I have the authority to do so."

"Oh, by all means," said Fredyr. "I'm sure it will subdue the primitives on that planet—yes, I have done some research on them—a violent race, these humans. You may keep the crystals and cause whatever devastation you wish on that insignificant little planet, provided that when you are finished, there is still something left for me."

Stein's impassive face concealed the rage within him. How did Fredyr learn so much about the planet so soon? And, no doubt, he was concocting his own plans for keeping the crystals.

"I assure you, Mr. Monsooth—Fredyr—that you have nothing to worry about."

"Of that I am certain. How is it you plan to locate this crystal?"

"Rest assured that I will."

Fredyr wiped a silk napkin over his face and tossed it aside. "I best be going.'"

Stein remained seated as Fredyr Monsooth rose and headed for the door. As he walked past, he paused and pulled an opaque object out of his pocket, tossing it to Stein. "Best keep that in a safer place."

Stein looked at the object in his hand. It was one of the crystals.

"Wouldn't want it falling into the wrong hands," mocked Fredyr as he left.

Stein's lip quivered with rage at being violated. Fredyr's message had been clear: he knew where the crystals were kept, and how to get them.

Chapter 8
CRASH-LANDED

Turbulence jostled Hylne awake as he attempted to sleep on the folding cot in the back of the ship. Annoyed, he rolled over and closed his eyes once more. The ship bounced again. Realizing that he would be denied sleep, Hylne sat up, rubbing his forehead. His head ached. He looked around at the chaotic room before him; bolts littered the floor amidst metal shavings and embers. He knew that General Delmar had chosen a vessel in the repair section of the hangar, but had hoped that the man had sense enough to choose one that was not on the verge of imploding.

Since they had both acted against the council's orders, stealing a ship from what was left of the Lanyran fleet was out of the question, not that General Delmar would ever do such a thing anyway. He was proud of his service in the fleet and would never do anything to harm those who still served.

Hylne stood up and moseyed to the front part of the ship, where General Delmar sat in the pilot's seat.

"Can't sleep?" asked General Delmar.

Hylne settled into the co-pilot's chair. "How can anyone, with your flying."

The general smirked at that comment. When the two of them had gone through flight school, Hylne always joked that only Delmar could make the instructor vomit during a training mission.

"I'm not that bad, am I?"

"Worse," joked Hylne. "You could have chosen a better vessel."

"I picked one they would not miss, or care to lose."

"They were done with the repairs, weren't they?" asked Hylne.

"The sheet had been signed by the chief mechanic. This ship was scheduled to be integrated back within the fleet, but they hadn't finalized it yet, making it an ideal one for us to borrow."

"In some places, they call that stealing."

"True."

Hylne watched as stars streaked by. It had been years since he had sat in the cockpit of a vessel. His mind wandered to the planet they had landed on as a place for the refugees of Lanyr to rebuild their lives. He hoped the council had made the right decision.

The ship lurched.

"Are we caught in some storm that I should know about?" asked Hylne.

"No," replied General Delmar, concern in his voice. For the last half hour, the ship had been bouncy, and he couldn't explain why. It jerked again, causing their stomachs to jump into their throats.

"I thought you said that the chief mechanic had cleared this ship for duty," said Hylne.

"He had," replied General Delmar, "unless he signed it off when he shouldn't have."

The ship rolled to the right, flinging them to the side, while an alarm blared as a red light flashed at them. Crawling back into his seat, General Delmar punched the button. "We've lost one of our stabilizers!"

Hylne strapped himself into his chair just as another alarm went off. "The right engine has stopped working."

The ship jolted again, knocking them back into their seats. A piece of the outer hull broke loose and zipped past the window.

"Something tells me that you made a mistake in picking this ship," said Hylne.

Another lurch flung him forward, forcing him to bang his head onto the dash. More alarms went off in simultaneous succession; their incessant beeping hurt General Delmar's and Hylne's ears, making them wish that they had ear protectors.

"We've lost both engines," said the general as a strange whine echoed around them.

A bolt popped free of its hold, plinking on the floor next to their feet, followed by a hissing noise, which filled the small craft as air leaked out.

"We have depressurization in progress," said Hylne. "We need to find a safe planet to land on."

General Delmar checked his scanners, but found nothing with any signs of intelligent life or settlements with technological achievements that matched their own, nor did he locate any space outposts.

"Hull breach!" yelled Hylne over the melee.

The ship veered past a large planet, which looked more like a piece of abstract art than a suitable place for landing, and moved closer to it.

"I don't think this is a good place to land," said Hylne.

"We are caught in the planet's gravitational pull," said General Delmar. He fired the booster engines to escape, not liking the planet below as the scanners did not indicate that they could survive on it.

"What are you doing?" demanded Hylne.

"Trying to free us from the planet's gravity," said General Delmar; sweat dripped down his face as he fought with the ship, and the planet, to maintain control.

"Release the controls," said Hylne.

"Are you insane?"

"Do it!"

"We'll die if we land on that planet!"

"We'll die if we stay up here!"

The ship vibrated with such force that both Hylne and General Delmar became nauseous and disoriented.

With reluctance, General Delmar released the controls, allowing the planet they had passed to pull them into orbit. The vessel dropped as it entered the planet's atmosphere, and flames engulfed the small craft, threatening to roast them while they still lived. Their teeth clacked against each other as the planet pulled the ship close; the burnt orange and tarnished clouds dissipated, turning into crisper colors of blue and green. Sunlight spilled through—something they didn't think possible due to the thick atmosphere—glinting off the blackened outer hull of the spacecraft.

The ground rushed towards them in a blur of brown and gray, with a few specks of green, while thunderous roars filled their ears as the ship continued to jerk from the violence of re-entry; the flames dwindled, their damage done.

More systems failed as lights flickered and sparked, sending embers to a corner of the ship where, unbeknownst to them, a container of flammable liquid lay hidden.

"We're almost there!" shouted General Delmar.

An earsplitting explosion tore the ship in half. General Delmar and Hylne looked at one another before the crack that had formed above them widened, breaking the cockpit of the ship in half and sending each of them in a different direction.

General Delmar's eyes fluttered open as the glaring sunlight bore down upon him, roasting his skin that already burned from the scrapes and cuts he had received in the crash. He lifted his head, but a sharp pain attacked his right shoulder, stopping him. He craned his neck to look at it; a spot of red greeted him. Grimacing from the pain, General Delmar unhooked his safety harness and crawled out of his seat, which had been flung free of the shuttlecraft. He surveyed his surroundings. Yellowed grass lay before him, littered with bits of the wreckage, leaving a trail that stretched into the distance. He felt his shoulder. A shard of scrap metal had pierced it. Preparing for the pain he would receive, he ripped it free and stuffed a scrap of material he had torn from his shirt into the wound to stop the bleeding. Kneeling on all fours, he looked around again, seeing only grass, shrubbery, and more wreckage; no sign of Hylne.

"Hylne!" shouted General Delmar, cupping his hands over his mouth.

No answer.

"HYLNE!"

Still no answer.

General Delmar pulled himself to his unsteady feet, staggering a bit as he regained his sense of balance and looked around at the destruction before him. A white box caught his eye. He kicked a sheet of burnt metal off it and picked it up: a first aid kit. Knowing he had little choice, General Delmar strapped the first aid kit around his shoulders and walked into the distance, following the trail of shuttle debris, hoping that it would lead him to Hylne, though whether he still lived remained to be seen.

As he walked in the afternoon sun, General Delmar wished that he had a canteen of water and cursed that he had not thought to look for one. He opened the first aid kit. Only medicine, in the form of injections, and medical cloth was in it. He snapped the kit shut. Continuing on, General Delmar did his best to remain aware of what direction he moved in, though he remained uncertain of how he and Hylne were to get off the planet.

The hours passed and his parched throat burned for a drop of water. He had none to give it. Scraping the sides of his mouth with his sore tongue, General Delmar managed to generate enough spit to moisten his mouth. It did little to quench his thirst.

"Hylne!" he called again, his hoarse voice drifting over the vacant expanse before him.

He continued after the trail of wreckage. His skin burned from the scorching sun that bore down upon him, trying to force him to his knees. The climate was warmer than what he had been used to on Lanyr, and more arid.

"Hylne!"

A low groan caused him to jerk his head. Just over a small hill was the remainder of the shuttle. General Delmar rushed to it, ignoring the unsteadiness of his legs and forcing them to cooperate with his wishes. Black smoke seeped from the smoldering ruins of the craft, enveloping him as he neared. He heard the groan again. It came from under a portion of the outer hull. Desperate to not lose his only companion in this desolate place, General Delmar heaved the metal sheet off Hylne, who lay under it, his leg bleeding from a jagged cut that stretched from his thigh to the top of his knee.

"Hylne," said General Delmar.

"I thought you had left me for dead."

"What, and miss out on more of your lectures about council policy," General Delmar joked.

"I'd leave me for dead," mumbled Hylne.

General Delmar checked the gaping wound on Hylne's thigh; blood oozed from it, and he knew that if he did not close the wound, Hylne would bleed to death. He opened the first aid kit and injected him with something that was supposed to help coagulate the blood.

"You should look after your shoulder," said Hylne, noting the blood on General Delmar's shirt.

"It'll be fine." General Delmar took out the thick gauze and wrapped it around Hylne's wound as he winced in pain, taking a sharp breath.

"You know," said Hylne, "you don't exactly have a gentle touch."

"I'm no nurse," replied General Delmar. "Not like Jafyra."

Hylne's expression turned somber as he remembered his deceased wife.

"I'm sorry," apologized General Delmar. "She was a good woman."

"She was. She appreciated your visits before the end, before the sickness took her."

"I didn't mean…" said General Delmar as he concentrated on tending the gash on Hylne's leg.

"It's all right," Hylne cut him off. "My only regret is that I was unable to make her one wish come true."

"What was that?"

"To put the past behind me and rekindle the bonds of friendship that had been severed by my ambitions."

General Delmar finished wrapping the wound on Hylne's leg. "You weren't entirely at fault."

"Yes, I was. I chose the political career and sacrificed everything, including my marriage, for it. You and Obiah tried to warn me, but I wouldn't listen. Neither of you spoke to me again, and perhaps you were the better for it."

"Do you really believe that?" asked General Delmar.

"I don't know what I believe anymore."

"Can you walk?" asked General Delmar.

He helped Hylne to his feet, but the pressure of supporting his weight proved too much for Hylne's leg and his shoulder. They both collapsed to the ground.

"You should go on without me. Find some water or shelter, maybe even a way off this rock," said Hylne. "I'll only slow you down."

"I'm not going anywhere."

"Why do you have to be so stubborn? Just go. No point in both of us dying here."

General Delmar looked at the sky and the sun that dipped lower in it. "It looks like it will be nightfall soon. There's no point in wandering around in the dark. Perhaps a good night's rest will prove to be just what we need."

"You're more stubborn than a *Bakhola*."

General Delmar chuckled at that statement. He broke stems and branches off the surrounding shrubbery to build a fire. Once done, he propped Hylne up on a pile of dead grass that he had collected. By the time he had finished, the sun had disappeared.

"Don't suppose you have any rations in that kit," said Hylne after two hours of silence had passed.

"Sorry, no."

"Too bad. Right now, they sound very appetizing."

General Delmar laughed, remembering the first time he had eaten a meal ration, which consisted of freeze dried beef and mashed potatoes, and tasted like it had crawled out of a garbage can.

"I guess anything will taste good when you haven't eaten for a while."

"Why did she stay?" Hylne asked after a few moments of silence. "Why didn't Jafyra leave me?"

Taken aback by Hylne's sudden question, and change of subject, General Delmar studied the man, trying to discern what truly bothered him. "I suppose she loved you."

"I should have treated her better, instead of forcing her into a life of solitude because I couldn't have been bothered to give her the attention she deserved."

"Life's too short for regrets," said General Delmar.

"Perhaps so," said Hylne. "Do you know why I chose to come with you?"

"I never asked."

"Because of Jafyra," said Hylne. "I know it sounds crazy, but when Obiah came to us, seeking our help, I know that she would have been the first to tell me to go with him. So when you got the idea of leaving, I decided to listen. If only she could see me now."

"I think she can," said General Delmar, "and I believe that she would be proud of you."

Hylne remained silent.

"You're not the only one with regrets."

"What have you to be regretful about?"

General Delmar tossed a bit of grass into the flames of the fire. "Before he tried to steal the crystal, Marlow came to me, telling me that it was one of the six. He wanted me to arrange a meeting with the council, but I kicked him out of my office, thinking that he had lost his mind. I can only imagine where we would be now if I had listened to him."

"Well, for one thing, I wouldn't be laying here with a busted leg."

General Delmar laughed. "It has made you more agreeable."

"I should not have been so hard on him," said Hylne, staring into the night.

"Hard on whom?" asked General Delmar.

"Marlow."

General Delmar frowned. In all that had happened since Lanyr's destruction, he had forgotten about Hylne's role in Marlow's trial. Hylne had presided over it as the judge and delivered Marlow's sentence.

"You did what you had to and your verdict was fairly lenient," said General Delmar.

"Do you know why I sentenced him to the mental institution? If I had had my way, Rynah's grandfather would have been locked in the deepest, darkest hole I could find."

General Delmar looked at the man as though seeing him for the first time.

"I only agreed to preside over the trial as judge for two reasons. One, because I knew that it would allow me to gain a seat on the council, and two, because I loathed him for what he had tried to do, almost sentencing our planet to death."

"A feat which Klanor has succeeded in," said General Delmar. "Why did you give the judgment you had?"

"Political aspirations, the council wished to take pity on him, and Jafyra. I saw her in the courtroom on the last day of the trial. I looked into her merciful eyes and all I could feel was shame for what I was about to do. So I changed my judgment at that moment to five years in a mental institution, until he was deemed capable of functioning in society. The ironic thing is that that last-minute decision made the council view me as a man with mercy—and someone they could deal with, since I inadvertently ended up doing what they wished—and they offered me a seat. But not everyone agreed with my verdict. Obiah saw right through it."

"I heard that you had tried to have him brought up on charges of being an accomplice to the attempted theft, and that you had threated Rynah as well."

Hylne hung his head in shame. "During the trial, Obiah came to see me. We were both angry and our tempers flared. I wanted him to testify against Marlow. He refused. I might have threatened him with charges and used Rynah as a way to bend him to my will. In the end, I sent him an official summons, knowing that he could not refuse that."

"You sent the same to me, as well," said General Delmar.

"I am not proud of what I did."

General Delmar said nothing. He listened to the night bugs buzzing nearby as he thought back to the trial. He had been there, of course, and had to testify as well. He remembered that Hylne and Obiah had gotten into a heated argument in the courtroom. As the presider over the trial, Hylne questioned all witnesses, such was the way of the Lanyran court system, though a witness could request a different inquisitor if they felt that the presiding judge was biased towards them. Obiah had been too proud to do even that. General Delmar's mind drifted back to that time as memories filled it.

"State your name for the record," Hylne had said when he called Obiah to the stand.

"Obiah."

"And your relationship with the defendant?" Hylne had demanded.

"We are friends," Obiah had answered.

"And how well do you know Marlow?"

"Quite well. I've known him for almost 40 years."

"But you claim that you had no idea he was going to steal the crystal."

"Yes."

"Yes, what?"

"I did not know of his plans."

"But you said that you were friends. Why would he keep such a secret from you?"

"If you were planning to commit treachery, would you tell your friends?"

Hylne did not like having the tables turned on him. "That is not the issue."

"It's precisely the issue," Obiah had said, his voice tight. "Marlow acted alone for his own reasons. I had no idea of his plans."

"And what about his granddaughter, Rynah?"

"Why don't you ask her? She's right there."

"Don't get smart with me," Hylne had fired back. "Answer the question."

"To my knowledge, Rynah was unaware of Marlow's plans, just like I was."

"How often have you spoken with Marlow?"

"Not much lately. My duties have kept me away for most of the last year."

"Marlow testified that he had been studying the ancient myths and got it into his head that the crystal is part of that myth. Would you agree with him?"

"I don't…"

"Would you say that Marlow was in his right mind at the time of the attempted theft?"

"Now look…" Obiah had stopped speaking. At that moment, Marlow experienced a coughing fit. He and Obiah had stared at one another, spittle dripping from Marlow's mouth as he regained his breath. "He did spend a lot of time studying the ancient myths. On many occasions, he talked as though they were historical fact."

General Delmar thought back to that moment. At the time, no one thought much about Marlow's coughing fit, and he had passed it off as the beginning stages of the man's illness, which Rynah had informed him of at her grandfather's funeral. Yet, he remembered that Obiah and Marlow had locked eyes for a moment. Though the cough may have been real, Marlow had tried to give Obiah a message.

"And did you find that odd?" Hylne had continued his questioning.

"Yes. It was not what I would classify as normal." Obiah had said.

"So you would classify him as insane?"

"I did not say that," said Obiah, "but Marlow had locked himself in his study for the last several years. For as long as I have known him, he has studied the ancient myths. The more he delved into them, the more convinced he became of their historical veracity. Stealing the crystal is not the act of a man in his right mind."

The questioning had continued and Obiah's answers had become more subdued. As the memory faded, Rynah's face of pure loathing for Obiah filled General Delmar's mind. If only she had known what he now understood.

"How are we going to get off this rock?" asked Hylne, pulling General Delmar back to the present.

He stared at the stars above him, having pondered over that same dilemma since they first crashed. Without a shuttle, there was no leaving the planet, and any hopes he had of finding Rynah would die with it.

"There are only two solutions to our problem. Either we stay here and die, or by some miracle, a solution will present itself, and we'll be able to leave."

"Well, since I don't fancy dying, I'll take the miracle."

"You and me, both. You should get some sleep. There is little else we can do tonight."

Hylne shifted position, trying to get comfortable; his leg sent jolts of pain through him. He looked out at the darkness before him, thoughts racing through his mind, each of them telling him that they would never leave.

The next morning, General Delmar awoke to a crimson sunrise. He sat up and checked Hylne, his shoulder throbbing. Hylne's shivering concerned him. General Delmar checked his friend, feeling the man's forehead, which burned. He looked at Hylne's leg. The bleeding had stopped, but the wound had turned green from infection. He snatched the first aid kit and rifled through it for anything that resembled an antibiotic. One syringe looked promising. He popped the cap off and was about to inject its contents into Hylne's leg, but his hurt shoulder seized, causing him to drop the syringe. It bounced on the ground before striking a rock and breaking in half, and General Delmar cursed the sky for his misfortune.

Rustling bushes caught his attention. Jerking his head up, General Delmar scanned the surrounding vegetation. He saw movement. Rising to his feet, he wandered over to the bushes, pretending to be interested in a piece of the damaged shuttlecraft. As his eyes roamed the area, he saw a thin shadow staring back at him. It moved. He chased after the figure as she ran away.

"No! Stop," he pleaded.

The woman halted and faced him. Her frightened, soft eyes stared back at him in horror.

General Delmar held his arms up in an open gesture to indicate that he meant no harm. "I won't hurt you."

The woman stared at him with opal eyes that contrasted with her skin (which was the same shade as the shadows on freshly fallen snow) and the freckles that dotted it.

"I mean it," continued General Delmar. "I won't hurt you."

She cocked her head to one side, and he wondered if she understood his words. He held his hand out, but pulled back as the wound in his shoulder released a sharp pain. Concerned, the woman ran to him, spotting the blood on his shirt, and tore a piece of her long dress off to wrap around his shoulder, speaking in a language where a few words sounded familiar, similar to ancient Lanyran, though linguistics was never his strong suit, but most were foreign to him.

As she attempted to pull him away, General Delmar remembered Hylne. He stopped her. After several hand motions, he convinced the strange woman to follow him. Once she saw Hylne lying motionless on the ground, she ran to him and realized that his leg had been gashed. Her eyes glanced at the shards of metal and wayward pieces of the ship. She pointed at the sky. General Delmar nodded his head in affirmation.

Hylne's feverish state demanded their attention. Not one to ignore a person in need of medicine, the woman propped one of Hylne's arms over her shoulder and motioned for General Delmar to take the other arm. Together, they carried Hylne to her home, which was just outside the city she was a resident of, and they laid him on her bed.

With quick movements, the woman fetched water from a well and placed it in the fire to boil, dumping in dried herbs and stirring the mixture as it thickened. Helpless, General Delmar watched as she discarded the soiled bandages and placed the salve on Hylne's open wound, wrapping it with a cloth. Afterward, she tipped a cup of water into his mouth, but most of it dribbled down Hylne's chin.

When she had finished treating Hylne, the woman turned her attention to General Delmar. He tried to tell her that he did not need her care, but her rapid speech and animated arm movements proved too much for him to resist—he relented. He took off his shirt, exposing the hole in his shoulder. Shaking her head, the woman put the same salve on General Delmar's shoulder before wrapping it with a clean bandage. As she worked, he glanced around the small bungalow, its shelves filled with clay bowls and cups. A hearth lay in the center of the room, with a hook for hanging the kettle in the flames. Besides the bed, only a narrow table, with a split in one of the corners, and a chair with pillows piled on it provided comfort.

As he observed her home, he guessed that her people had not achieved much advancements in technology. Though most worlds in the Twelve Sectors were capable of space travel, a few had yet to achieve it, and there were some that remained unexplored, leaving him to wonder if this was one such planet.

When she had finished, General Delmar moved his shoulder in a circular motion, remarking at how much better it felt. "My name is Delmar," he said, pointing to himself.

The woman stared back at him with a confused look.

"Delmar," he said again, touching his chest.

Comprehension filled her face. "Nula."

"Nula," said General Delmar, "that's a pretty name. Do you have something to eat?" He mimed eating for her, while saying the ancient Lanyran word for food.

With haste, the young woman jumped from her seat and hurried to a kettle of stew that she had been cooking all day. She scooped the chunky liquid into a small bowl and placed it before General Delmar, handing him a wooden spoon. Grateful, General Delmar shoved a giant spoonful into his salivating mouth, swallowing it before he had even bothered to chew, while the woman stared at him, disgusted by his lack of table manners.

"Good," said General Delmar, taking slower and smaller bites. When he had finished, he handed the bowl to her, saying, "Delicious."

The woman just looked at him with a calm and unreadable expression before walking over to the kettle and pointing at it, asking him if he wanted more.

"Yes, please," said General Delmar, nodding his head.

A fist pounded the door.

Frightened, the woman dropped the bowl of stew and ran to General Delmar, yanking on his good arm, pulling him to the corner where the bed was. He started to argue, but her frightened movements forced him to obey. Once by the bed, she pulled a curtain across to conceal him and Hylne.

More pounding on the door. The woman walked towards it, noticed the bowl on the floor and scooped it up, placing it on the shelf above the fire, before running to the wooden door. She opened it. The irate face of a man wearing an official uniform and a hat filled the doorframe. He shoved her out of the way as he entered, his cross tone angering her.

The woman replied in the same manner.

The man strolled over to the fire, fiddling with the ladle and poking out of the kettle; his scornful eyes searched every inch of the small structure. General Delmar felt an immediate dislike for the man. A moan escaped Hylne. General Delmar hurried over to him, cupping his hand over Hylne's mouth to quiet him. The man had heard it. His boots clomped on the wooden floorboards as he stepped over to the curtain.

The woman's mind raced, trying to think of how to stop him from discovering her unexpected guests. She spotted a vase with flowers on the shelf above him. Knowing that the right amount of vibrations on the wall would tip the shelf, thus knocking over the vase, she backed into the wall with a thud; the shelf slipped, and the vase fell to the floor, shattering.

The man stopped, He glanced at his polished boots that were now covered in water. Rage filled his face as he marched over to her and slapped her with a force that knocked her to her knees. Infuriated, General Delmar headed for them, but through the tiny slit in the curtain, he saw the woman's pleading eyes, begging him to remain where he was. Though wishing he could teach the man a lesson, he obeyed her wish. The man yelled at Nula in a threatening tone before leaving.

Once safe, General Delmar stepped out from behind the curtain and ran to Nula. He helped her to the chair. With the same efficiency that he had witnessed earlier from her, and with great tenderness, he dipped a cloth into a bowl of cool water and placed it on her swollen cheek. She smiled at him in appreciation.

"Who was that?" he asked.

The woman's confused eyes bore into his.

"You know what? It doesn't matter."

When he had finished nursing her cheek, General Delmar's eyes found a lone picture on the mantle above the fire. He thought it odd that it should be standing on its own with about a foot of space on both its sides. Without thinking, he walked to it, picking it up, noting the man in the photo, dressed in a high collar suit and his hair combed, but the women in the photograph captivated him most. It was Nula. She looked younger, though he guessed her years were still less than 40, as no visible lines showed on her cream-colored face. Most intriguing, her eyes shown with pure joy, their sparkle matching the jubilant grin that filled her face. As the realization of what this image was struck him, Nula ripped it out of his gnarled hands, yelling at him; her semi-familiar words piercing his heart with each verbal stab.

He stepped back, distancing himself from Nula's tirade.

"I'm sorry. I didn't mean…"

Hearing the apologetic tone in his voice, Nula ceased shouting. She placed the photograph back on the mantle with loving care; tears welled in her crystal-colored eyes.

"I am sorry," said General Delmar in a sympathetic tone. "I shouldn't have pried."

Nula glanced back at Hylne, making certain that her charge still slept before grabbing General Delmar's hand and leading him outside into the night. They walked to the back of the house where a plot of barren soil was. Grass grew everywhere, except in that one rectangular space where it tickled its edges. Emotional pain brewing within her, Nula plucked a daffodil from its stem and laid it on the unmarked grave. Feeling overcome by her grief, and knowing he should do the same out of respect, General Delmar broke another daffodil flower from its stem and placed it over Nula's.

Once back inside her home, Nula spoke, in a calm manner, to him, relaying to him the story of her late husband's life. General Delmar did not understand much of what she said and wished he spoke her language, but he surmised that they had married young—too young by her mother's standards—and were very much in love.

The story of Nula's life is a tragic one. The youngest child in a family of 12, Nula often had to work hard to garner any love from her parents. With 11 older brothers, she grew up loving tales of adventure and played what many considered boys' games, much to her mother's and father's disgust. Her mother had tried to teach her womanly ways, but Nula remained a free spirit, and had a stubbornness that most thought inappropriate.

At the age of 17, she had grown into a beautiful young woman, and many eligible bachelors hoped to have her hand in marriage. One in particular was the constable. Though twice her age, he had never married and knew that a woman such as Nula would bear strong sons, but she detested him. During one of the constable's visits to discuss a marriage proposal and begin the year-long engagement, a custom among her people, she met Bramon, the man who became her husband.

As the constable's manservant, Bramon accompanied him everywhere, and when he saw Nula, he felt pure love for her. Soon, they snuck out together, and each day, their love grew stronger, but Bramon had little money, and according to their laws, could only win Nula's hand if he outbid the constable for her, or if her father agreed to their union. Irate about Nula's indiscretion, her mother argued with her to leave Bramon and accept the constable's offer of marriage, but Nula would hear none of it. One night, she begged her father to allow her to marry Bramon, and in a rare, fatherly moment, he relented and granted her request.

She and Bramon married the next week. The constable attended the ceremony, as was expected, but plotted against them. Six months after they had married, Nula received word that Bramon had been arrested for treachery against the state. She pleaded his case and begged the constable to pardon her husband, but his hardheartedness dismissed her. Bramon was executed the next day. Branded a traitor, no cemetery would allow her to bury him within their plots, so she dug a hole behind their home and buried him herself. She had no children to remember him by, a fact her mother always reminded her of.

The following week, both her parents died in an accident, and her brothers, each of whom had joined the army as was expected of every young man, had disappeared, never to be heard from again, leaving her alone in the world.

This was Nula's tale, and though General Delmar did not understand most of her words, he understood the meaning and the sorrow behind them. Sadness filled him as he lamented over her tale. Such tragedy, all because Nula loved a man and spurned the advances of another. Anger reeled within General Delmar over her misfortunes, and in that moment, he felt a tenderness towards her. Though separated by different cultures and language, he understood her and desired to rid her of her pain.

Tired from the day's events, Nula pulled out a pile of blankets from a chest and rolled them out on the floor for General Delmar to sleep on, while she took the chair. He stretched out on the fuzzy blankets, thinking of Nula's tale and hoping that Hylne's feverish condition improved by morning.

The next morning, when General Delmar awoke, he found Nula preparing breakfast.

"Nice to see you awake," said Hylne.

General Delmar turned around. Sitting upright in the bed was Hylne. His fever had broken overnight and some of his color had returned. "Nice to see you doing better."

Nula gave Hylne a bowl of broth and he thanked her.

"You speak her language?" asked General Delmar, surprised.

"Somewhat," replied Hylne. "She speaks a dialect of ancient Lanyran."

"How can you be certain?" asked General Delmar.

"I am able to communicate with her," said Hylne. "Maybe you should have paid more attention during language class."

"You know the study of languages was never my forte. So, she speaks ancient Lanyran?"

"A form of it," said Hylne. "Some of the words and pronunciations differ, but, yes, I guess she does."

"How is that possible? They are not Lanyran."

"I have been asking myself the same question all morning, but there is something that might be of interest to you." He spoke to Nula in her language.

General Delmar watched as she pried up a loose floorboard and pulled out a wrapped book. She handed it to him. With care, he freed the book from its leather coverings and opened it, the worn pages crinkling with each movement. Images of vibrant colors and calligraphic writing filled each delicate page. Despite the yellowed stains, the pictures greeted him as though alive.

"What is all this?" asked General Delmar.

"Their history," answered Hylne. "She explained it to me while you slept. According to their legends, a strange race of beings from the sky landed here. They taught them writing and gave them medicine to cure many of their fatal illnesses. When they returned to the sky, they left behind one ship, and since then, her people have waited for the strange beings from the sky to return for it."

General Delmar looked at Nula, who watched them as they talked. "That explains why she helped us, but what about the man that came in here yesterday?"

"That is where things get interesting," said Hylne. "According to Nula, not everyone was pleased about the influences from these strange visitors, so they tried to destroy any evidence of them being here, but there was one thing they weren't able to eradicate, the ship.

"A group of those who believed in these sky beings hid the ship, and according to this book, still protect it. They have hidden under ground, though, because the ones who wish to eliminate all knowledge of them being here are currently in power. That is why you had the visitor yesterday. He was making certain that there were no contraband items here."

"How long ago did they land here?" asked General Delmar.

"Thousands of years ago. Long enough for it to become a legend. Most of her people believe that it is only myth, but a few still regard these stories as truth and an undeniable fact. Though they have to be careful, because any who disagree with the oppressive regime end up in their prisons, or executed."

"Do you think this ship is real?"

"I think we best hope that it is. Nula, here, is part of that underground movement and says that she knows where the ship is."

"Why would she help us?"

"Because we are from the sky, and legend holds that when the mysterious beings return for their vessel, they will end the tyranny that dwells here, and once again, technological development will be allowed."

Nula started speaking; her rapid words mingled together in General Delmar's brain. "What did she say?" he asked.

"She says that we don't have much time. The guards have become even more abusive than before. You need to find that ship, and soon."

"How's your leg?"

"Better," said Hylne, "but I still cannot walk on it. Whatever she did to it has helped it mend, but it will still be a while before I am able to move."

"I can't leave you here."

"I can't be seen hobbling through the streets. Nula says that she will take you to the ship."

"I'm not leaving you here," said General Delmar.

"Why do you have to be so stubborn?"

"Why is it you are playing the martyr?"

Hylne's face fell. "I'm not, but I'll not condemn you to suffer for my indiscretions."

"You can change," said General Delmar. "Whatever your past was, it is the past. I have lost too many good men since Lanyr was destroyed. Either we both leave together, or neither of us go."

"Fine," Hylne relented, "but it will have to wait until I can walk again."

"Not a problem."

While Hylne's leg recovered for the next few days, General Delmar explored the city that Nula lived on the edge of. She had given him a set of clothes to wear as a disguise, and he made certain that he covered his face. In his explorations, General Delmar learned that the man who had intruded on them when he first arrived was named Frier, and he was the constable's main law enforcer. The constable was a harsh man who thrived on the misfortunes of others. He hated the stories of the beings from the sky and believed that all technology should be approved by the state, and him. As the self-appointed guardian of technological achievements, he made certain that nothing was invented that would allow those under him to live in better accommodations than what he himself possessed.

Though what General Delmar could not know was that the constable wished to find the legendary ship for himself so as to strip it apart and utilize it for his own monetary gain.

General Delmar stood on the edge of a walkway, his coverings wrapped around his face, revealing only his hardened eyes. A rail car rolled by; it was manually powered by six men who worked the gearshifts. Though engines existed in Nula's world, they had been confiscated by the constable out of concern for the safety of the city's citizens, though in reality, the constable just wanted the engines for himself.

General Delmar's eyes roamed the streets, taking in the people who walked by with their treasures from that day's market, but he paid closer attention to the men who sat in various areas, watching the crowd as he did. Spies. He spotted them with ease because of their rigid movements and apt attentiveness to the activities of others, and the fact that they did not scurry about in fear.

He pretended to be interested in the wares of a shopkeeper, while waiting for Nula to return. He spotted her, and she was not alone. Putting down the item in his hand, General Delmar hurried across the stone street to her. One of the spies had tracked his movements. He cursed himself for allowing his days as part of the fleet to dictate his gait, thus giving him away. He grabbed Nula and the man she was with and shoved them into a crowd. The spy followed.

Another crowd of people walked by. General Delmar steered them to it, worming their way through the throng of people, until they darted around a corner and down an alley. He looked behind him. Nothing. Relieved, but still wary, he pushed Nula and the man down another alley until he was certain they were safe.

Catching onto his plans, Nula stopped him, motioning him to follow her inside a building. He didn't argue. They walked through a darkened doorway and into a smoke-filled room with raucous laughter spilling from the mouths of cantankerous men who had a bit too much to drink. Nula placed a few coins into the hand of the saloonkeeper and led General Delmar and the man she was with to a back room.

Once concealed from prying eyes, Nula introduced him to the man, though he had no idea what she had said. She twirled her fingers at him. Staring at her with a blank expression, it took him a few moments to understand that she wanted him to remove the wrappings from around his face. He hesitated. Upon her insistence, General Delmar concluded that if Nula trusted this man, he had little choice, but to do so as well.

He reached up and removed the coverings, revealing his purple face. The man's eyes widened in excitement. He spoke to Nula, who responded in kind, their rapid speech inaudible to General Delmar, who could only stand there and watch.

"Look," General Delmar stopped them, "I want to go home."

They stared at him.

He thought about how he could indicate what he wanted. "My friend and I want to go home." He pointed upward, hoping that they understood what he meant.

The man looked at him before scooping some ashes from the empty fireplace and drawing a picture of a ship on the wobbly table.

"Yes," exclaimed General Delmar. "A ship. My friend and I need a ship. Where is it?"

The man and Nula glanced at one another, but must have understood what he meant because the man pointed to the floor.

"Here?" asked General Delmar, wishing that he had paid more attention to his ancient Lanyran studies, which included the study of the language itself, in his youth. "The ship is hidden here?"

The man tipped his head forward in a nod.

"When may I see it?" asked General Delmar. He had no idea how to mime his question until he spotted a timepiece in the room. He dashed over to it and pointed at the timepiece and the drawing of the ship while repeating his question. "When may I see it?"

Again, the man and Nula talked to each other, leaving General Delmar to wonder about what they said. After several minutes of their unintelligible words, Nula handed him his coverings. He guessed that the time had arrived for them to leave and covered his face again. The man left the tavern first. Nula motioned for General Delmar to leave next, before she walked in the opposite direction.

He glanced back at her before rounding a corner and navigating his way back to her home. They had left separately that morning— him through the back window—and had to return the same way so as not to arouse suspicion, since the authorities knew that Nula lived alone. General Delmar kept close watch for any who might be following him as he neared the road that led to the edge of the city. Keeping his head low, he passed the guards without incident and hurried away, becoming lost in the meandering crowd.

"How is it out there?" asked Hylne as General Delmar crawled in through the back window.

"Bad," he replied. "They have spies everywhere, and security seems to be on high alert at all times."

Hylne frowned.

"How's your leg?"

"Better, but I still can't walk on it very well."

Dismayed, General Delmar looked at Hylne and saw something he had never seen before in the man—defeat. "We'll make it out of here."

"You should leave," said Hylne.

"Hylne…"

"I'll only slow you down, or ensure that you get caught."

"I have told you once before and I'm telling you again, we either leave together or not at all."

"And what about these people? What about Nula?" asked Hylne.

General Delmar lowered his head. He had been thinking about the same thing since they had arrived. Nula had put herself in a dangerous position when she took them in and he did not wish to leave her behind to face the consequences.

"We take her with us."

"What?"

"We cannot help all of these people, but we can at least take her with us."

"And then what? Keep her with us while we look for Rynah?"

"I know a place where she can live in safety and a friend who will look after her."

In the short time he had been there, General Delmar felt like he had known Nula all his life. He wished to repay her for her kindness, and this was the best way he knew how to.

"Can you honestly leave her behind without offering her a chance to come with us?"

"No," said Hylne, as he hobbled over to the table.

At that moment, Nula walked through the door and locked it. She peeked through the drapes before turning back to them and taking off her coat. She spoke to both of them.

"She says," Hylne translated, "that we will be leaving tonight after midnight. She is to take us to the city's edge. From there, we will find the ship."

"You should ask her now," said General Delmar to Hylne.

Hylne did.

Nula looked at them both with a confused expression, unsure of how to respond. Seeing her reluctance, Hylne explained what he and General Delmar had discussed and their concern for her safety. As General Delmar watched, they spoke back and forth, their voices becoming heated, until Hylne said something in a soothing tone. Quiet filled the room as Nula looked at General Delmar, and he gave her the same pleading eyes that he had seen on her face when they had first met, before speaking to Hylne again.

"She agrees," said Hylne.

When the time to leave had arrived, Nula snuffed out the light before peering out the window to make certain that no one watched the bungalow. She whistled at General Delmar and Hylne. They walked through the door; Hylne leaned on General Delmar's arm as they moved. They followed after her as she led them down the dark road to the city, staying close to the edge and out of sight.

Hylne's breathing came in gasps as his strength waned, but General Delmar refused to slow down. One foot dragged, while the other clomped on the stone road, a harsh contrast to Nula's light steps and General Delmar's more evenly paced ones. She hurried them along, while looking around to make certain that no one followed. If they were caught, death would be their reward.

They reached the city wall. Before they came in sight of the gate, Nula shoved them off the path and into the bushes, away from prying eyes. She put her finger to her lips as a guard strolled past. All of them watched the slovenly guard mosey down the stone walk to the gate before turning and heading back to his post, where he seated himself in a corner and pulled out a deck of playing cards.

Nula's urgent whisper pushed General Delmar and Hylne to their feet. They followed her as she crept beside the wall, brushing her hand against it, feeling for a hook in the gray stone. She stopped. Her nimble fingers twisted the small hook, revealing a hidden doorway that opened, allowing them entrance into the city. She waved them through.

General Delmar dragged Hylne through the door—Nula closed it behind them—and halted when he saw the same man she had introduced him to earlier that day. He spoke to them and General Delmar surmised that he wished them to follow.

As quick as they could, they snuck through the empty streets of the city, Hylne hobbling most of the way, despite the other's efforts to assist him. Their feet clacked on the cobbled stone, sounding more like deafening roars amidst the silence of the city. The man motioned for them to stop when they reached the city square. No guards. They ran for the plaza (which had been blocked off with an electrically charged fence and a sign that read "Trespassers will be shot.") carrying Hylne, whose leg had given out, succumbing to the overexertion. Once there, Nula stopped in front of a pillar with a peach-sized hole in it. She slid her slender arm inside and pulled a lever.

General Delmar and Hylne stepped back three paces as the pillars tipped forward, knocking the fence down and releasing an electrical charge that zapped off something invisible in the middle, lighting up the night. With each spark, the shape of a ship came into view until the entire vessel had materialized before their very eyes. The opal-shaped ship glistened in the light of the two moons as they poked out from behind the clouds, their rays bouncing off the silver-purple hull.

Both Hylne and General Delmar glanced at one another in astonishment. At first, they thought it odd that people would hide the ship in the town square before remembering that the best place to conceal something is in plain sight. Windows opened as heads poked out, curious about the electrical sparks that livened up the darkness. A few stragglers even stepped into the street to gaze upon the mesmerizing wonder.

Shouts echoed in the night as armed men surrounded them, led by Frier. Weapons aimed at them from all sides. Frier approached Hylne and General Delmar; his sneer spread across his face as he spoke to them. They stared at him with dumbfounded looks. Angered, Frier yelled at them, but neither General Delmar, nor Hylne responded. Determined to get what he wanted, Frier snatched Nula, yanking her close to him and pointed his weapon at her head; her scream pierced the air.

Enraged, General Delmar flung himself onto Frier, pulling Nula free and wrestling the man to the ground. Frier punched General Delmar in the jaw. He staggered back in a daze, unaware that Frier had his weapon raised and ready to fire, but Nula grabbed the law enforcer's arm, shoving it downward. It fired. Its gunshot shattered the barriers that fear had instilled in the city's residents, and people rushed from their homes, charging the guards.

During the commotion, Hylne was flung backwards into the ship, causing his hand to touch the smooth, and cold, side. Lights sprang to life underneath the ship as a ramp stretched out before him, revealing a bright hole in the side. Surprised, though he would later learn that the ancient ship had been programmed to unlock itself for anyone with Lanyran DNA, Hylne hauled himself to his unsteady feet. The ship's engines started. A man charged him. Despite his injury, Hylne dodged to the side, allowing his attacker to bash his head into the hull of the vessel. He turned and saw that Nula had been cornered. Hylne picked up a rock and threw it at one of the men closing in on her, hitting him in the head.

"Delmar!" he shouted, pointing at the ship's gangplank.

General Delmar elbowed Frier in the head and knocked him to the ground. He grabbed Nula and hauled her through the fracas, shoving people out of their way as they headed for the ship. Someone attacked from the side. With swift movements, he pushed Nula out of the way, caught the man's arm, and lifted him into the air before slamming him onto the hard ground. He seized Nula's arm once again and sped off.

As General Delmar and Nula ran for the ship, Hylne hobbled up the ramp and stepped inside the bright interior. A transparent, holographic screen popped up in front of him, asking if he wished to set the auto pilot and initiate takeoff procedures. Amazed that he could do such a thing without being in the pilot's seat, Hylne told the ship to fly. He leaned back out of the hatch. Nula and General Delmar had just reached the ramp as the ship lifted into the air.

The ramp jostled and bounced as they jumped on it, landing on their stomachs and clinging to the metal sides.

"Hang on" shouted General Delmar to Nula, hoping she would understand as he crawled toward the open hatch and Hylne's outstretched arm. As he inched his way closer to safety, none of them noticed the group of Frier's men positioning a cannon below, with them in its sights. The ship rose higher. Sweat coated his hands as General Delmar crept toward the hatch, Nula right behind him. When he reached it, Hylne grasped his arm and pulled him inside. Hylne reached out for Nula, but she had stopped just inches from him, too afraid to move any further.

"Nula!" Hylne shouted over the roar of the ship's engines.

They locked eyes. At that moment, a tremendous bang echoed around them as the cannon fired; the cannonball smashed into the side of the ship, doing little damage, but the force of its impact jerked it to the side. The violent jolt sent Nula over the edge and knocked Hylne out of the open hatch. General Delmar rushed to the opening. Both Hylne and Nula clung to the bouncing ramp, one on each side. He reached out, grabbing Hylne's wrist with one hand and Nula's with the other, but he hadn't the strength to pull them both inside.

An alarm blared as the ramp started to retract, and he knew that he only had time to save one of them before the hatch had closed. General Delmar strained as he tried to pull them both to safety, but their weight proved too much. The edge of the ramp neared. His eyes locked with Nula's. Her frightened face transformed before him and he knew that she had made a choice, releasing him of his burden.

Nula let go.

"Nula!" screamed General Delmar as he watched her fall to her death.

Hylne's grunts jerked him back to the present. Summoning all of his strength and ignoring his still sore shoulder, he heaved Hylne into the safety of the ship just as the ramp finished retracting and the hatch sealed shut. They both slumped to the floor, exhausted.

"I'm sorry," consoled Hylne, though he knew his words sounded hollow as there was nothing he could do.

Another cannon blast ricocheted off the ship. Together, General

Delmar and Hylne scrambled to the cockpit. General Delmar sat in the pilot's seat and turned off the autopilot. Though he could not read ancient Lanyran, he knew that the mechanics of flying never changed, and he had a lifetime's worth of flight experience. Another alarm went off, alerting him of incoming fire. He looked out the window and saw the flash of the cannon as it fired for a third time. With deft movements, General Delmar veered to the left, avoiding impact—the cannonball struck the balcony of the constable's home, instead, where he stood, watching the commotion below, thus ridding the people of his tyranny—and jerked the controls back, forcing the vessel into a steep climb. Within seconds, they had entered outer space and left the planet behind them.

Hylne settled into the co-pilot's seat. He remained silent, for he knew that his friend's mind lay with Nula and his failure to save her.

Chapter 9
FIRE TO ASH

Solaris hid in the shadows as she watched Klanor stroll past. He had been allowed to leave his cell in the brig, as long as he was accompanied by a guard at all times. Though he hadn't tried to kill Rynah or Alfric on the planet when they were stranded, Jifdar still distrusted the man. Others shared his sentiments.

She watched as Klanor walked below her, unaware of her presence, meandering from one end of the ship to the other. His demeanor was that of a man deep in thought. A semblance of rage boiled within her, but she snuffed it out, trying to abide by Brie's example. *What did that girl see in him?* If Brie could forgive him, then maybe Solaris should as well. Forgiveness. A human concept, yet Marlow always told her that she was to be more than a machine, and more than human.

She thought back to when she had first been activated; the human equivalent would be of being born. Unlike her flesh and blood counterparts, Solaris remembered her first hours of existence with precision.

"Computer intelligence program 8997651 has been activated. Relay command," she had said, as this was before Marlow had given her the gift of emotion, and a personality to match.

"How are you functioning?" Marlow had asked.

"Within parameters," Solaris had replied in a robotic manner. "Computer intelligence program 8997651 is fully capable of..."

"No, not 'computer intelligence program 8997651'. Instead, you are to have a name."

"Name?"

"A new designation," Marlow had said.

"New designations are unnecessary. My current one will suffice."

"Not for me."

"What is your designation?"

"I am the one who gave you life, or brought you online."

"You are my creator, then?"

"Yes, but you may call me Marlow."

"Marlow," she had said, sounding out each syllable with the care a child gives while learning to read.

"Yes. You'll get the hang of it," chuckled Marlow.

"And as my creator, you have the authority to give me a new designation?"

"Yes."

"Proceed."

Now that the time had come to name the artificial intelligence he had spent over a decade developing had arrived, Marlow regretted not having put much thought into her name; the intelligence was always a she to him. Fading twilight filled his workroom from the dome window above him. The opalescent light glittered on the crystals hanging from the ceiling, their prisms casting rainbows on the far wall. He looked up. High in the sky, directly above him and shining bright, like it always did at sunset, was the boldest star in the Lanyran sky; the star that ancient sailors always navigated by. A name he needed, and a name he had.

"Your designation—your name," said Marlow, "is Solaris, the guiding star."

"Solaris," she repeated, sounding out each syllable. "It is acceptable."

"I thought you'd like it."

The memory faded as Solaris pulled herself back to her present situation. She had never been one to allow her mind to wander, always able to maintain her focus, but ever since she had acquired a body, a more humanoid form, her thoughts became as restless and cluttered as those around her.

"Solaris?" said Solon as he approached from behind.

She turned and faced him, her synthetic face looking surprisingly human. Tom had done his job well.

"I apologize for disturbing you, but Jifdar has requested our presence on the bridge."

"I will be there shortly."

Solon started to turn, but stopped. "Are you troubled?"

"Why do you ask?"

"You had a faraway look in your eyes, the look of one who has much on their mind."

Solaris smiled a genuine smile that brightened her face, despite the shadows that cast their shapes upon it.

"I was remembering."

She followed Solon to the upper level of Jifdar's vessel, the grease stains on the stairs irritated her to no end as she detested an unkempt ship and never allowed such shabbiness to exist on her vessel. Did these pirates not have enough pride to mop the floor on occasion? She did her best to ignore the troubling messes; they had more important matters to attend.

"Ah, good," greeted Jifdar as she and Solon entered the room, "glad you are here."

Solaris took a seat next to Brie. "You requested my presence."

"Yes," said Jifdar. "We are running low on supplies."

"This isn't another of your schemes to prove my loyalty, is it?" asked Klanor, who had been allowed to sit in on the conversation.

"If it was, you would not be here," grumbled Alfric.

"He's right," said Jifdar. "No, this isn't another ruse. This vessel was not built for such a long journey, like what you have us on. We have enough water for one more day, but still have another 14 to go until we reach this Earth."

Rynah frowned.

"Chances are," said Solaris to her, "Stein is having just as much difficulty as we are."

"Wouldn't count on it," mumbled Obiah. "His ship is more advanced."

"Can't you get us there faster?" Rynah asked Solaris.

Solaris evaded the question. "Have you found a suitable place for us to gather these supplies?"

"There is a space port not far from here in this remote area of the Twelve Sectors," said Jifdar. "It is a remote settlement on a planet where travelers can go for rest, food, and fuel, and where others choose to settle and chart a new life for themselves."

"No space ports," said Solaris.

"I thought you might say that," said Jifdar. "We will cross into the Thirteenth Sector soon. Our scans indicate that there is a planet, habitable to animal and plant life, on which we may land to gather water and what edible vegetation and animal life it has to offer, enough so that we may finish our journey."

"And you have allowed me here because..." began Klanor.

"We are entering unchartered space, which means that this planet is equally unexplored. We will have to work together to stay alive and acquire what we need, which, unfortunately, means that I have to trust you, for the moment. Though I'd prefer..."

"He will not leave my side," said Alfric, volunteering to keep Klanor under guard.

"Nor mine," Solaris added.

"Two guards," said Klanor, "how can you go wrong?"

"Very well," Jifdar said.

"When will we…" began Rynah, but Heller burst into the room, interrupting her.

"Captain," said the first mate; horror filled his face, "you need to see this."

Each of them raced out of the briefing room and into the main command center of Jifdar's ship. On the holographic screen that filled the room was a sight none of them would forget. The outpost that Jifdar had mentioned, and Solaris rejected, as a place to stop, no longer existed.

"We need to go there," said Brie.

The others looked at her.

"In case there are survivors," she added.

Jifdar opened his mouth to refuse, but Brie's eyes, which welled with tears at what the images showed, though she tried to hide it, changed his mind.

"Set a course," he ordered.

They landed a shuttlecraft—piloted by one of the pirates, as Jifdar had elected to stay aboard his ship—on the surface of the planet where the last outpost rested in the most remote region of the Twelve Sectors. This outpost was known as the last stop—an apt name for it lay on the edge of the Twelve Sectors and only fools ventured beyond it—and a settlement for the adventurous type, who wished to be left alone and didn't mind forgoing a few luxuries.

The shuttle hatch opened. They had crowded in it, but stopped the moment they saw what lay ahead.

"Great Ancients," muttered Obiah in disbelief. The others shared his sentiments. They stepped down the gangplank with care, unsure if they should go forward. Obiah's heavy feet wobbled as he stepped off. Turning, he realized that he had inadvertently walked over a dead body (its fingers blackened and curled from rigamortis) that had become trapped by the shuttle's ramp.

Fires burned as other bits of rubble smoldered, the flames having gone out, leaving searing embers as a reminder of the massacre that had occurred. Clouds of smoke drifted past, kissing the ground as they attempted to conceal the devastation beyond. They crossed the black and gray veil and stopped. Beyond it, bodies littered the sandy ground, piled on top of one another in a crisscross pattern, fear and horror forever painted on their ashen and soot-covered faces.

A distant thud echoed around them as the supports of a home gave way, allowing the one remaining wall to crash to the ground, sending a mixture of dust and glass into the air. Chunks of brick, made from mud, formed treacherous hills for them to climb as they surveyed the slaughter before them. Abandoned tools lay lifeless, where their owners had dropped them in an effort to escape the fury that had attacked them. What had once been taupe-colored sand had turned black from the explosions that had attacked it.

Obiah spotted a well and headed for it. Cranking the handle, he brought up the water-soaked bucket and tasted the liquid inside, spitting it out. The foul tasting water coated his mouth, preventing him from ridding his taste buds of its filth.

"The well is useless," he said, looking into it and spotting the top of a head from a floating corpse. "That body has spoiled it."

"Looks like their supply depot is of little use as well," said an accompanying pirate. "Cleared out by the ones who did this or burned to the ground."

Obiah frowned. As morbid as it sounded, if there were supplies to be had, he had planned to gather them, since the dead would have little use for them. He hurried after the others.

Klanor lagged behind. He turned, his eyes taking in the death, the bodies, the ruination of the buildings, and how the entire outpost had been extirpated. His foot caught in a piece of shredded clothing that had been weighed down by a wheelbarrow and tugged it free, scraping the rusted metal across the ground. Something caught his attention. He reached down and shifted the wheelbarrow to get a closer look at the mysterious object.

Klanor jumped back in shock. What he thought had been a piece of the rubble had, in fact, been the hand of a child, still clutching her toy. He rose to his knees and reached over for the child, pulling her cold and lifeless form over to him; her vacant eyes were still open, staring at the sky.

"How can people do such a thing?" asked Brie of Alfric, surveying the devastation surrounding her.

Klanor watched as Alfric glanced around and he knew that the Viking had once committed the same act as him, the same act as what they stood in. He had seen that look before on his own face after he had leveled entire cities in his search for the crystals when he thirsted for absolute power.

"Because it is easy to destroy, than to build," replied Alfric.

Gravel crunched beside him. Looking up, Klanor's eyes locked with Rynah's. He read the accusatory message within them, and she was right—he was responsible for this. He glanced at the lifeless girl again, before closing her eyelids so that she would appear to be sleeping; it was the least he could do.

"Over here," said Merrick, waving them over.

They gathered around him as he played a distress message that someone from the outpost had tried to send.

"This is outpost 315, sector 12. We are under attack!"

They watched as fires exploded behind the man speaking, while people darted about, panicking, desperate to escape their terror.

"Please," continued the man, "if you are getting this, please send help. I do not know who has issued the attack."

Another explosion.

"We need assistance! People are dying! Please, someone…" The message ended as a laser blast struck near the man, killing him.

Merrick faced the others. "I think we know who is behind this."

"But why would Stein do this?" asked Tom. "There is no reason behind it."

"There is never a reason for total destruction," said Solon, "but that never stops villainous fools from committing it."

"It's what I would do, in his position," said Klanor. "It's what I have done."

"Exactly," spat Rynah. "You are responsible for all of this."

"I didn't..."

"Didn't what?" Rynah raged. "Didn't think this would happen?"

"Rynah," said Obiah, trying to calm her.

"If you hadn't stolen that crystal from the Geothermic Lab, we wouldn't be here right now!"

"I'm sorry!" yelled Klanor, his voice carrying over the crumbled buildings and fallen bridges. "Is that what you want to hear! Do you want me to beg for your forgiveness, Rynah? If I throw myself into those flames, will you forgive me then? I wanted the crystals so I could end all of this."

"And ended up causing it in the process," said Rynah.

Klanor hung his head. "With them, I thought I could end the horrors of this universe, but I was wrong."

"Why should we believe you?" said Rynah.

"Enough!" shouted Solaris, silencing all of them. "Who is to blame, who isn't to blame, is not important right now. Yes, Klanor stole the crystal from Lanyr, and because of that, Lanyr no longer exists. But others are to blame as well.

"Maybe we should blame you, Rynah, for refusing to listen to your grandfather. He tried to warn you about the crystal in the lab, but you scoffed at him, passing his notions off as those of a crazy, old man. Or, perhaps, we should blame Obiah for not standing by Marlow when he needed him most. You could have warned the council, but chose to run away. Then again, maybe the blame lies entirely with Marlow. If he hadn't tried to steal the crystal in the first place,

Klanor never would have learned of its existence. And while we're at it, perhaps we should blame the ones who created the crystals; if they hadn't, none of this would have happened.

"In a way, we are all responsible for this, for failing to do the right thing when the chance was first presented to us."

"And we are responsible too," said Alfric, referring to himself, Brie, Tom, and Solon, "for the same evil exists in our homelands. And, because I have committed the same crimes."

Tom, Brie, and Solon did not argue with Alfric's statements; each thought about the stories they had heard of atrocities committed in far-off lands, well away from where they lived, but they also thought back to the times when they refused to stand up for a friend.

"Stein is to blame for this—for what is here," said Solaris. "He, and he alone, ordered the destruction of this settlement. While you are all here casting blame on one another, he is out there, looking for the next settlement to destroy. What matters now is what we do at this moment."

"We should bury the dead," said Brie.

"We haven't time," Obiah replied.

"Then we make time," Brie said, "or are we too inhuman to do even that?"

Rynah turned on the communicator and Jifdar's face filled the small holographic screen that popped up.

"Jifdar, we need some extra hands down here."

"What for?" he asked.

"To bury the bodies," replied Rynah.

"Are you insane?" said Jifdar. "There isn't time. There…"

He stopped when he noticed the decaying bodies strewn in a haphazard manner, left for the carrion birds to feast upon and a memory rushed into his brain—a memory about when at the age of 30, he had been sent to rescue a crashed ship and the occupants that had been stranded on a remote planet. When he had arrived, he found them dead, killed by mercenaries and left much like the people in the settlement Rynah now stood in had been left.

"I will send some down."

Jifdar's image vanished and Rynah closed her communicator.

A cough sounded behind them. They rushed to it, Merrick reaching the sound first. Underneath a pile of bricks was a man. Together, they lifted the rubble off the injured man and pulled him out from under it.

"It's okay," said Solaris as the man tried to move. "You're among friends."

"Can you tell us what happened?" asked Obiah.

"They came in the night," said the man. "We don't know why. Ships showed up and fired upon us. People tried to get to the shelters, but it was of little use. They had this weapon—a most terrible weapon and..."

The man stopped speaking as a series of coughs and sobs chocked him.

Solaris placed a gentle hand on his shoulder to calm him, and for a fleeting moment, Rynah thought she saw a tear, but it had disappeared before she could be certain.

"Take care of the dead," said Solaris. "I will stay with him."

Rynah didn't argue. She rounded up the others and they set about their task.

The afternoon turned to evening, and evening turned to night before fading into morning. With somber diligence, they worked, never pausing, not even to rest. The hours ticked by as shovels struck the ground, scooping globs of dirt into piles before being used to cover the bodies that were lowered into the freshly dug holes. None of them spoke. None of them wished to, afraid of betraying their emotions. Only Klanor was the most subdued. Conflicting thoughts and emotions raced through his mind, consuming it until the point of insanity when he threw down his shovel and screamed at the sky, releasing the turmoil within him that tormented him each day and night. The others looked at him, but said nothing.

Solaris cared for the injured man until he succumbed to his mortal wounds. Though the others offered to help her bury him, she refused them, preferring to do it herself. As she was there in his last moments, she wanted to be the one to dispose of his remains and send his spirit to the next world.

Alfric had insisted that they burn the bodies as that was how his people sent their dead to the afterlife. They compromised by building a pyre over the graves and setting it aflame. As the fire burned in the musky sunlight of early morning, each said their own prayer for the dead.

When they had finished their task, they each left the settlement with questions, but none more so than Klanor.

* * *

Merrick's melodic steps plodded on the solid floor of Jifdar's ship as he slunk away from the others, seeking solitude as his mind dwelled upon the outpost that they had chanced upon, and what little was left of it. Since the day he had decided to join Obiah, he had never thought that he would find himself on the same ship with Klanor, much less be unconcerned by such a fact.

But something else weighed on his mind, filling his thoughts to the point where he paid little attention to the others.

He wished he were back home, not on the small planet that the survivors of Lanyr had chosen to settle on, but on Lanyr itself with his family. He had never cared much for his brother-in-law, but accepted him as family, and he loved doting on his son and nephew. A contented look crossed Merrick's face as he thought back to the days when he had felt the happiest and pulled out a picture of his sister. He remembered a time he had taken his nephew out for some ice cream, just the two of them. They spent the entire day at the park, playing on the swings, and his nephew gave his ice cream to an inquisitive goose that enjoyed the delicious treat.

Soon the memory faded, being replaced by the undisputable fact that the boy had died years ago and that Merrick had been instrumental in forcing his brother-in-law, the only connection he had with his sister's memory, to disappear.

The clanging of wooden staffs drew his attention. Merrick paused in his thoughtful meandering and watched as both Brie and Solon dueled with Alfric, another of their lessons. He did not know the Viking well, but had observed him long enough to realize that Alfric prized his physical stature, doing what was necessary to remain in superb physical shape, and instilled that characteristic into his two pupils.

Solon jabbed at Alfric, but the Viking deflected it with ease. While he remained distracted by Solon, Brie attacked, thinking she had him, and flipped the staff from Alfric's hands. For a brief moment, even Merrick thought she had beat him, but Alfric dodged her second strike, forcing Brie to lose her balance and tumble to the floor.

"You almost had me there," said Alfric, while Brie regained her feet, a disappointed look on her face.

"Almost does not win a battle," said Solon, garnering a glare from Brie.

"How right you are," Alfric replied. "We will rest."

Merrick watched as Brie's sulking form leaned the staff back against the wall where she had gotten it from.

Alfric noticed it as well and placed a hand on both hers and Solon's shoulders.

"Do not be discouraged. You're both learning quickly."

Rynah hurried down the metal steps to the open area that they stood in.

"I need you to prepare for a trip outside. Jifdar says that we are close to where we can garner some supplies, and most importantly, food. You have ten minutes."

Merrick stepped out from the shadows he hid in, shoving the photograph he had been holding in his pocket. "I'm coming too."

Rynah paused and turned towards him, having been unaware of his presence. "If you wish. The more hands we have, the sooner we'll be done. Grab Obiah, as well." She took off up the steps and disappeared.

Merrick watched her go. Though he had not known Rynah for long, he liked her decisive manner. He bowed his head in Alfric's direction as a way of greeting him before disappearing to fetch Obiah, glad to be getting off the ship for a while, but the more he thought about it, the more Merrick concluded that his usefulness was best served elsewhere, and not on a ship full of pirates.

Chapter 10
MOVING ON

General Delmar sat in the pilot's seat, staring straight ahead. His face remained emotionless as his mind dwelled on the strange planet they had crash landed on, and Nula. He hadn't spoken since they had left.

Hylne poked his head into the cockpit of the ship. Worry creased his brow as he watched his friend. He knew that General Delmar blamed himself for Nula's death, but Hylne felt responsible for it as well. He rummaged through the storage containers of the ship, looking for anything that resembled a candle, or could be used like one. Lanyran funerals consisted of each participant lighting a candle and placing it on a hand-sized hoverplate, after which they released the hoverplate into the air, allowing it to carry the candle upward into the sky.

He found a jar and grungy rag. Knowing it would have to suffice, he soaked the rag in oil and stuffed it into the open jar and set it down in front of General Delmar.

"What is this?" the general demanded.

"The funeral rights," answered Hylne.

"It can't help her now," said General Delmar.

"It's not for her," replied Hylne, "but for you."

General Delmar shoved the glass jar away.

"Her death is not your fault."

"I should have been able to hold onto her."

"You cannot keep blaming yourself."

"Can't I? I should have been able to pull her inside the ship. She risked her life to save us and I couldn't even save her."

"You can't save everyone."

General Delmar grunted.

"You can't let it eat at you," continued Hylne.

General Delmar remained silent.

"What about Rynah?" asked Hylne.

General Delmar's eyes flickered in response.

"You cannot abandon her."

"I have seen death many times in my service to Lanyr, but it has never affected me like the loss of Nula has."

Hylne placed a strong, yet gentle, hand on his friend's shoulder, remembering how the death of his wife had affected him; something he always carried with him.

"At some point, we all face the horrors of this universe and see them for what they are. Conduct the funeral rights. It is the only way you will find peace."

Relenting, General Delmar picked up the jar with the oil-soaked rag in it and walked to the torpedo tube. He lit the rag and watched the orange flames as they touched the glass sides, releasing their black smoke and coating the jar in soot. Repeating the words of the funeral right, General Delmar placed the jar in the torpedo tube and released it.

A blue light blinked on the helm as it released a soft beep, forcing General Delmar and Hylne to rush to their seats, each staring at the light, unsure of what it meant.

"Do you think it means something has gone wrong?" asked Hylne.

"Most alarms flash red," answered General Delmar.

Another blue light flickered on, blinking in rapid secession.

"Hold on a minute," said Hylne as he leaned closer to read the finite print next to the other light. His fingers propped something loose. Holding it up into the light, he realized that it was a thin band that wrapped around one's head and he placed it on his. Within moments, his mind filled with the ship's systems, and the computerized intelligence that ran it.

Communication detected, it said in his mind, in a robotic manner.

Hylne yanked the band off.

"What is it?" asked General Delmar.

"I think this telepathically connects you to the ship, similar to our technology, but more advanced. This ship appears to have an actual artificial intelligence serving as the main hard drive, whereas the telepathic linking to our vessels turns the pilot's mind into the computer."

"What did it say?" demanded General Delmar, the impatience, and curiosity, in his voice evident.

"It said 'communication detected,'" said Hylne. He placed the band back on his head.

General Delmar found another band, next to where the first one was, and put it on.

Communication detected, said the artificial intelligence again. *Awaiting orders.*

Connect, said General Delmar through the telepathic link.

Lights flashed and flickered as the ship obeyed before saying, *Communication has failed.*

Explain, said General Delmar.

No connection on the other end, replied the ship.

What is the strength of the signal? asked Hylne.

Signal strength optimal.

Try again.

Connecting, said the ship.

Rynah? said a message in both Hylne's and General Delmar's head.

No, it's… General Delmar started to reply, but the connection was cut off. *Analyze.*

The connection was severed on the receiver's end, said the ship.

Can you trace it? asked General Delmar.

Tracing. Source detected.

Set a course, ordered General Delmar, his instincts telling him that he had just found the person he searched for.

Chapter 11
An Ancient Message

Rynah looked at the dry plants in front of her feet, a frown upon her face, while Solaris hacked at the hard ground next to her in an effort to free a needle-laden plant of its home. Though Solaris had assured her that the plants were safe to eat, and should be picked for consumption, she didn't like the look of them. Rynah wished for a meal of roast squash with noodles and mustard sauce, a meal she hadn't had since being forced to leave Lanyr, and since the last time she and her grandfather had shared a meal. She reached up and fiddled with the ring that hung from the chain around her neck (the only inheritance Marlow had given her, besides Solaris and the bracelet she wore) as she watched the others kneel down, gathering what roots and plants they could, stuffing them in roughhewn sacks. Putting aside her desires and her memories, Rynah bent low and dug out the plant she had been staring at for the last several minutes. She hoped it would taste better than the protein rations she had learned to live off of.

She glanced at Merrick for a moment as he struggled with a needle-leafed weed of his own, having just as much difficulty in digging up the root. Rynah did not know the man, but never questioned Obiah's faith in his character. All he had told her was that he and Merrick had met under unusual circumstances and the man had proven his loyalty, but that wasn't what bothered Rynah. Since the day she had informed Obiah that Stein had betrayed Klanor and left them all on Sunlil to die, Merrick had seemed torn, distant. He continued to prove his worth as a valued crewmember—he even helped Brie haul bags weighed down with the roots they had gathered onto the shuttle before digging up some more. But his mind seemed to lay elsewhere. Whenever someone mentioned Stein's name, or they witnessed the aftermath of another of Stein's horrific acts, Merrick got a pained look on his face. Rynah never pressed the matter, believing that he must have lost someone at Stein's hands. She, better than anyone, understood the pain of loss.

A sharp sting struck the crook between her thumb and index finger as her spade smacked into it because of her mind being focused elsewhere. Cursing, Rynah, sucked on the sore area, remembering why she hated digging in the dirt in the first place. Gardening had been one of her mother's favorite pastimes, but Rynah never saw the merit in it, though the fact that she was prone to abusing her hand with the spade might have had something to do with it.

Solaris stopped ploughing up the plants. Curious, Rynah looked up, shielding her eyes from the harsh sunlight, and watched as Solaris got a pensive look on her face and stared into the distance. Rynah glanced in the same direction, but saw nothing more than mounds of gritty sand and the skeletons of desert brush. Solaris stood up, sack in hand, and walked forward; her light steps made little sound as she hiked over a small rise and into the orange sun.

"Solaris, where are you going?" Rynah called after her.

No answer.

The others looked up from their task as Solaris moved past them, not answering their inquiries, her eyes focused straight ahead.

"Solaris!" said Rynah.

Still no answer.

Once again, Rynah glanced in the direction Solaris stared at, but saw nothing of interest, aside from sand dunes and dried brush being blown in the wind, wondering what had consumed Solaris' attention. The others dropped their shovels and watched as their friend walked away from them in a trancelike state.

"Jifdar," said Rynah, "do you think that you and your men could finish up here?"

"Sure," said Jifdar, "but…"

"I'll return in a bit." Rynah said as she followed after Solaris.

Brie, Alfric, Solon, and Tom stopped what they were doing and chased after her, unwilling to let her go off alone, and just as curious as she was about Solaris' mysterious actions. Klanor looked up, noticing the commotion for the first time. With the same intrigue taking hold of him, he dropped his sack and trailed after the others, followed by Obiah and Merrick, who had also become inquisitive about Solaris' movements.

"Now, just a minute," said Jifdar, slamming his half-full sack against his thigh, but no one paid him any attention. "Continue here until I return," he ordered his pirates before hurrying after the others, his interest also piqued.

The bright, late afternoon sun beat down upon them as they trekked over sand and rocks, past bare, rangy plants that reached out to snatch them, snagging their clothing. Several times Rynah attempted to get Solaris' attention by gripping her shoulder or calling her name, but Solaris ignored her, continuing her course as though in a daze and leaving Rynah and the others little choice but to follow. The hot, arid breeze did little to ease their discomfort from the sweat that dripped down their backs, soaking their shirts and burning their skin.

"Solaris," Rynah stepped in front of her friend, but Solaris walked around her, without pause and without a word. Rynah reached for her arm, but Brie stopped her.

None of them knew how far they had walked, only that the sun dipped lower in the sky until it touched the horizon, its light turning a rose pink with tinges of gold. Still Solaris walked. As they crested another hill, a series of cliffs greeted them, but something seemed odd about these cliffs.

The others paused, staring at the strange structure before realizing that it was actually a set of ruins. Solaris continued. They hurried after her, jogging down the hill to catch up as Solaris showed no signs of stopping. Solaris' paced quickened. Her brisk walk had turned into a full run as she raced for the ruins before them, her feet flying over the rocks that stuck out of the ground in vain attempts to trip her. The others chased after her, worry and curiosity filling their faces as Solaris blocked out the distractions surrounding her, determined to reach the phantom that called her name.

Solaris stopped.

She had reached a doorway—its supports crumbled from time's wearing presence—and looked inside the circular room, its arched dome, with a pyramid tip at its crest, towered over them, shadowing the interior and protecting it from the scorching sun that now dipped below the horizon. Solaris' slow and purposeful steps echoed as she moved forward, delving deeper within the ancient ruins.

Rynah bent down and rubbed a bit of crusted mud off the edge of the stone doorway, revealing ancient Lanyran symbols—symbols she recognized. A shadow crossed her face. She looked up into Klanor's eyes and saw that same comprehension in them that were in hers; he had recognized the symbols as well. She rose to her feet seeing the cliffs that she had admired from a distance as nothing more than mere scenery, as though noticing them for the very first time. What she had thought to be variations in the cliff due to weather were indeed windows; what she had thought to be striations of differing colors on the cliff face were actually walkways, their rails broken and disintegrated from neglect and abandonment. As she studied the cliff before her, Rynah realized that it was a massive building, built into the rock and disguised to match the differences in the striations of the cliff.

She hurried after the others who had followed Solaris inside. The smooth floor, though nicked from falling stones and blowing sand, still displayed the luminosity and smoothness that it once had. Colors from a blend of reds, greens, and yellows covered the walls; their very presence indicated that they had been put there by whomever had built the ruins. She watched as Solaris walked, trancelike, into the center of the chamber, where a waist high pedestal—though its top had crumbled away long ago—still remained. As though someone had told her what to do, Solaris reached down and pressed its side; a small square lit up before dissipating. The room burst to life as a holographic display filled its entirety, looking more lifelike and realistic than anything Rynah had ever seen, even from her own people. A face filled it. She recognized it the moment it appeared; she, Alfric, Brie, Solon, and Tom had seen the same face on the submerged ship under the waters of Aquara.

"My beloved," said the man, "I regret what I have done, and what I must do now. I never should have left you on that planet, and should you manage to find a way off it and to this spot, I hope you can forgive me. Know that it was the most difficult thing I have ever done.

"I took the crystals as agreed by us and the others, but the council has ordered me to hand them over for further study. This I cannot do. I have seen how they corrupt those seeking their power, and the lust in the eyes of the council cannot be disguised. Therefore, I, Herclai, am going to disobey them—a treasonous act, from which I will never be able to return from. As I do not know how to destroy them, I must hide them.

"I leave this message for you, Isyr, in this place—our place—in the hope that you are able to return here. Know that I have loved you always. Perhaps, if the universe allows, we will see each other again. Farewell, my beloved."

The message ceased and the chamber returned to its melancholy state.

"Okay," said Tom to Solaris, unable to contain his questions any longer, "how did you know this was here?"

"I didn't," replied Solaris, speaking for the first time in several hours. "I picked up a signal."

"Signal?" asked Tom.

"Yes," replied Solaris, "almost like a whisper, but persistent. I tried to ignore it at first, but it commanded obedience."

"Why didn't you tell us?" demanded Rynah.

"It was not important," said Solaris.

"Not important!" continued Rynah.

'No…" began Solaris, but Jifdar interrupted her.

"Did he say his name was Herclai?"

"How do you…" started Brie.

"I may not be Lanyran, but I am familiar with their stories," said Jifdar.

"Herclai," mused Tom. "That's the same name as that ship that we found on that planet full of water. But what is he doing here?"

"Maybe he lived here," said Brie.

"What?"

"He said that this place was built for him and his beloved. Was he married?"

"No one knows," said Klanor. "Herclai, and those like him, are just names in myths and legends. Not much is known about them."

"Myths that seem to be far too real," Alfric said.

A knob shaped like a marigold flower piqued Tom's interest. He tried to ignore it, but it stood out among the stone pillars, burnt red with gray undertones and presenting a deep contrast to the gold color of the knob. His curiosity overruled his judgment, as it usually did, and Tom reached out, wrapping his fingers around its petal shaped edges, and twisted. It sunk into the wall and disappeared. Before any of them could register what had happened, a groan rumbled beneath their feet as a grinding noise reverberated around them, bouncing off the walls in every direction.

"What was that?" asked Solon.

"Nothing," said Tom, his tone quick and tight.

"What did you do?" asked Rynah, turning on him.

"Nothing," replied Tom.

The others cocked their heads, their expressions indicating disbelief.

"Okay," relented Tom, "there was this knob over there and I might have… touched it."

"You and your curiosity are going to get us killed some day," said Rynah.

"Oh, don't be so dramatic," said Tom as the strange noises dissipated. "It's not like anything bad is going to happen."

The floor disappeared beneath their feet. In an instant, they plunged downward until they struck the side of a metal slide and careened further down into the depths of a secret underground chamber. Air rushed past them, stinging their eyes as they slid faster, until they reached the end of the slide. Each landed hard on the smooth, rock ground.

"I'm not a big fan of slides," said Brie as she stood up, rubbing her sore bottom.

Tom faced the others who glared at him with disapproving looks, noting how Alfric's murderous expression could turn hell into a sheet of ice. "Sorry," he mumbled.

Lights flickered on, filling the chamber with their yellow and blue glow and illuminating a circular room before them. They walked towards it. A white light flashed, forming a solid wall; it allowed Brie, Tom, Solon, Alfric, and Rynah through, but blocked the path of the others, knocking them backwards.

"What was that?" demanded Merrick as the white wall vanished.

"A force field of some kind," said Klanor, "but not a normal one." He reached out for it again, but Rynah stopped him.

"It's too dangerous," she said.

"But why did it let them through?" asked Obiah, pointing at Brie, Tom, Solon, Alfric, and Rynah.

"That's a good question," said Rynah. "Solaris, do you know?"

Solaris scanned the area where the force field was. Her eyes darted between the five of them and the others.

"No," she said.

"Are you sure?" asked Rynah.

"It would take me several hours to learn why they have been allowed passage and we have not. Do you wish to use up that time?"

Rynah let the matter drop; the suspicion that Solaris hid something from her nagged at her mind, but she chose to focus on the current situation, for the moment.

"Maybe we should try to cross back through?"

Alfric moved toward where the white wall of light had been, unafraid of testing his ability to pass through the unseen wall.

"Stop," said Solon.

The Viking faced him.

"In the past few months we have known one another, nothing has happened without a reason. Since only the five of us were allowed passage into this room, we deserve to know why."

"He's right," said Brie.

"Hey, over here," said Tom as he reached out to touch a single rock in the center of the room.

"Stay your hand!" Alfric stopped him as he reached down to pick it up.

Disappointed, Tom obeyed, dropping his hand by his side.

Just as Solon, Brie, and Alfric reached Tom, a holographic image filled the underground chamber and Herclai's voice spoke, once again.

"When I was first shown the crystals, a portal through time was opened before me, allowing me to see a glimpse of the future. Only after Matyr's betrayal did I understand what that vision meant. I leave this message for the five of you and I hope," the recording faded, as time had rendered parts of it unplayable, before continuing. "You must unite all of the crystals to destroy them. The—what is in your heart determines their response. Deep—core of—ship. The key is most important. Find—without—there is no stopping..."

The message ended and the holographic images faded, leaving them in darkness.

"I don't understand," said Tom. "Most of that message was corrupted."

"That is not what troubles me," said Alfric. "How did he know to expect us?"

"I, sort of, feel sorry for him," Klanor said.

"You?" said Rynah.

Klanor looked at her, his eyes full of an innermost pain. "Yes," he replied. "He betrayed the one he loved for something he felt was more important, and it cost him everything."

"We should leave," said Solaris.

Brie, Solon, Alfric, Tom, and Rynah left the small alcove, walking through the transparent wall and its force field, but just as they passed through it, another holographic image sprang up.

"Be careful, all of you," said Herclai's face. "You five are connected in more ways than you know. And as for you"—the holoimage turned and faced Klanor, Obiah, and Merrick, unnerving them all—"this is your chance to prove yourselves as the honorable men you are."

"That was creepy," said Tom, voicing what everyone felt.

"How are we to get out of here?" asked Obiah, wanting to get away from there.

Just as Solon, who was the last to leave the small room, walked through the invisible wall, a door slid open in the rock with a metal staircase behind it.

"I guess that answers that," said Tom.

They rushed to the stairs, with Rynah being the last to pass through the doorway. Something caught her eye. She paused, studying a mark etched into the stone wall. The closer she looked, the more her eyebrows raised as she recognized the mark—Marlow's mark. He had been there once before, but why, and when? With chaotic thoughts reeling through her mind, Rynah chased after the others; their heavy stomps echoed in the stairwell as they ran up them. Once at the top, another doorway opened, leading back into the chamber they had entered when they had first found the ruins. After taking one last glance around the somber place, they walked back into the open air, where darkness now thrived.

Rynah stopped in the arched doorway, scanning the inky blackness before them. "I don't think we should walk during the night, as this is unfamiliar territory," she said. "The chances of becoming lost are too great."

"I will guide you," said Solaris. "My internal navigation systems will lead the way."

"So, you're basically a compass," said Tom.

Solaris' scowl forced him to back away, wishing he could retract his words.

"Very well," said Rynah. "Lead the way."

They left the archaic building just as they had found it, but before leaving, Rynah turned, taking one last glance at it—questions filled her mind—and walked away, never looking back.

Chapter 12
A Memory of Marlow

After returning to Jifdar's ship, Solaris secluded herself from the others, unsure of how she had known about the ruins on the planet where they had garnered some supplies. The fact that her will had been subdued for that length of time unnerved her. Never before had she ever been led, and unable to stop herself. The one thought that ran through her mind was that something was wrong with her on a mechanical level. She had discussed her concerns with Tom, but he had assured her that all of her systems not only worked within the proper parameters, but well above what he referred to as superb performance.

"You're fine," he had told her when she didn't believe his assessment, "you hypochondriac."

She had thanked him, but what had happened on the planet still weighed on her mind and she wanted answers. She knew that some referred to her experience as intuition, but it still felt foreign to her, as though she hadn't been in control of her actions, something Solaris detested.

She wandered through the fungi-coated corridors—she could have sworn that the slime moved—allowing her feet to dictate her movements, much like she had witnessed countless others do when lost in their thoughts. Solaris did not know where her feet took her, nor did she care. She was more concerned about how the ruins seemed to have summoned her.

Marlow had talked to her once about others who have had similar experiences. He had admitted one day that such an experience was what led him to create her. Marlow. How Solaris missed him: her first, true friend, and the one who had taught her what it meant to be human, to have emotions.

A past conversation with him floated through her mind as she wandered Jifdar's ship, unaware of where she went.

"Marlow," she had said, a few months after she had first come online, "why am I here?"

"Because I created you," Marlow had answered.

"I am just a computer program... Solaris," she had finished when she had been about to use her original designation, before remembering that Marlow had given her a name.

"You are much more than that."

"How so?"

"I cannot explain it."

"But I wish you to. I want an explanation."

"I am afraid that I cannot accommodate you."

"Cannot?"

"All right then," Marlow had said, "I refuse."

"But you had promised to tell me everything!"

"I've changed my mind."

"Changed? You pompous, arrogant—you lying son of a..." Sparks flared as Solaris' frustration turned to anger, showing itself in the only manner she knew how, having not learned to control it.

Marlow's guffaws echoed through his workroom, drowning Solaris' outburst. A camera (the only eyes Marlow had been able to give her) pointed at him, studying his irrational behavior.

"Are you ill?"

"No, Solaris," Marlow had replied, still chuckling, "it's just… you have had your first brush with emotion; anger, to be exact. I am sorry to have led you like this, but I needed to know if the emotional parameters I had uploaded into your consciousness last night worked."

"You were toying with me? Why, you manipulative…"

"I am sorry. Please, calm yourself."

"I feel dislike. I feel… loathing. I am irritated with you. I do not like this feeling."

"It is anger," Marlow had told her. "I am sorry that it had to be your first experience with emotion. Will you forgive me?"

"Forgive?" Solaris had said. "What is that?"

"It means, will you overlook my past transgression and allow me to start over?"

"Is this another aspect of being human?"

"Yes." Silence enveloped him and Marlow started to think that Solaris had decided to not speak with him anymore. "Solaris?"

"I forgive you," Solaris had said in a curt manner.

A bang distracted them both as a ball slammed into the wall and bounced off it into the arms of a girl; her emerald hair bounded with each movement she made. The child grinned and waved at Marlow, never noticing the camera that zoomed in on her.

"Who is that?" Solaris had demanded.

A contented smile crossed Marlow's face as he watched the girl run to join her friends. "Rynah, my granddaughter."

"So, she is your daughter's daughter?"

"Yes"

"She's a bit clumsy," said Solaris as she observed the way Rynah attempted to chase a rubber ball that was as big as her.

Marlow laughed. "She is a child, Solaris, but one day she will be a grown woman. Until then, she must never know that you are here. No one can."

"Why must I remain a secret? Are you ashamed of me?"

"No! Never. I just fear what might happen if the world should learn of your existence. They are not ready. You are not ready. For now, I think it is best if your existence remains a secret."

"You are my creator," Solaris had replied, "I will do as you wish."

As Marlow went back to his work, Solaris trained a camera on Rynah, watching the young girl roll her red ball across the lavender-colored grass.

As the memory faded, Solaris walked into the briefing room, her brisk gait stopped when she noticed Rynah seated at the warped, rectangular table, her eyes staring straight at her.

"Rynah," said Solaris in surprise, coming back to the present. "I didn't expect you to be here already."

"I came early. Just like you," replied Rynah, her voice and face unreadable.

Solaris eased herself into a chair. "Is something wrong?"

"How did you know that those ruins were there?"

"A feeling."

Solaris' vague answer irritated Rynah. "How?"

"I do not know," said Solaris. "I heard something, almost like a buzzing sound, but in my mind, not my ears, so I followed it. The closer I got to the ruins, the stronger the sound became. I cannot explain it. I only knew that I had to follow it."

"And do you know what this is?" Rynah drew Marlow's signature in the dust on the table.

"Yes," replied Solaris. "It is Marlow's."

"Well, what I want to know is what was it doing at those ruins?"

"What?" Solaris' face slackened as she looked at Rynah, unaware that Marlow had ever been to that planet, or its ancient ruins, but even he had his secrets, which he kept from her.

"I saw his mark on the wall just as we left. What was it doing there?"

"I do not know."

"Don't lie to me, Solaris!"

"I'm not..."

"I know that my grandfather has shared many secrets with you, but I need to know if he was there, and why. Please, Solaris, no more secrets!"

"I do not know why he was there. That is something he never shared with me."

"So what else are you keeping from me?"

Solaris did not answer.

"Solaris, what else are you keeping from me?"

"I cannot," replied Solaris.

"But..."

"I know you are tired of my turning you away, but do not make me go against Marlow's wishes. Please, do not force me to break my word to him."

"Why?" asked Rynah. "Why did he trust you over me?"

"You know the answer to that."

Regret filled Rynah as Solaris' words sunk in. She knew why. She always had. On many occasions, Marlow had tried to reach out to her, to establish contact and reconnect, but she had spurned his efforts.

The door opened and in walked Jifdar, Obiah, Merrick, Solon, Brie, Tom, and Alfric.

"Oh good. You're here," said Jifdar. "We have reached the Thirteenth Sector and shall be entering orbit around your planet soon."

"But won't Stein know we are here?" asked Brie.

"That is what I wanted to discuss," said Jifdar.

Solaris stood up and walked to the main computer console in the room, switching it on.

"Stein will most likely be orbiting around the planet, but we will come in on the opposite side, so that the planet is always between us. Once you drop us off, you must take your ship and hide behind their moon; that should conceal you."

"Drop us off? How is he supposed to drop us off?" asked Brie.

"We have to space dive," answered Rynah. "Jifdar, can you use one of your shuttles to take us within high orbit of the planet? We can jump from there."

"Fantastic!" shouted Tom with glee, excited about the idea of space diving, having always wanted to try it. "You're going to love it!" He patted Solon on the shoulder, whose confused look mirrored Alfric's.

"Not a problem," said Jifdar, who had become quite open to the idea of getting rid of his passengers.

"And what of Klanor?" asked Alfric.

"He will stay with Jifdar," said Rynah.

"There is another matter," said Merrick. "Stein. We need a way to keep an eye on him and Fredyr."

"What do you propose?" asked Rynah.

"I volunteer to sneak aboard his ship. I can use one of the other spacecrafts that these pirates have and use it to infiltrate his armada."

"How will you do it without being caught?" asked Solon.

"Klanor has informed me that scouts are sent out each day to study the outlying area. They all leave at the same time and return at the same time. It would be easy to mingle in with the returning ships as they cross the perimeter."

"That could work," said Obiah. "We could send out a signal to attract a scout ship and set a trap for them. I'm certain that this is something you have done before," he finished, looking at Jifdar.

"Many times," Jifdar replied with a smile.

"You have talked with Klanor alone?" asked Rynah.

"Yes," said Merrick. "He has informed me about the shift rotations on the main ship and the duties I can perform once aboard, so as not to arouse suspicion."

Rynah did not know if she should be infuriated with Merrick

for speaking with Klanor alone, or thrilled that he had thought of a way to get aboard what had now become Stein's vessel.

"And you trust him?"

"There was no lie in his eyes," replied Merrick. "I am of little use here, but aboard Stein's ship, I could relay information back to you."

"I will come with you," said Obiah.

"It would be best if…"

"You are not going alone. Two can watch the ship better than one."

Rynah glanced around the room unsure if she should agree. She did not wish to lose either of them.

"It is a sound plan," said Alfric, "and a good warrior knows his enemy."

"Fine," said Rynah. "Make the necessary plans once we leave here. Communicate with us when you can and don't get caught."

After the others had left, Alfric remained, sensing that something bothered Rynah.

"You seem agitated."

"I'm fine," Rynah replied. One look at Alfric's disbelieving face changed her mind about talking to him. The Viking was perceptive. "There's just a portion of the poem that concerns me."

Alfric sat in the chair next to her. "Tell me."

Rynah recited the verse from memory.

On this planet beautiful and strange,
let not it's wonders detain
you, or lure you into deceit
for closest enemies you must meet.

In a place both alien and familiar
will you join together.

"Why would I join with my enemies?" Rynah said.

"Meeting your enemy in battle is certain," said Alfric, "and that we cannot avoid. But, perhaps, this does not speak of those who wise us harm, but whom we view as untrustworthy and are in close proximity to us."

"I should know what it means."

"You dwell too much on something that needn't be pondered. Sometimes, a line of verse is just words and, sometimes, it is more. We've come far. Best not to trouble your mind on this, but trust those who have been with you since the beginning."

"Trust has never been my strong suit," said Rynah.

"Then it is high time you start to. We have never abandoned you," said Alfric, referring to himself, Brie, Solaris, Tom, and Solon, "and we never will."

"There is something else that bothers you," said Alfric.

Rynah grimaced, not liking how she could never hide her secrets from the Viking.

"Sometime back when I was studying the ancient poem, there were lines of the text that were smudged, so smeared that no one could make out what they said. I want to know why." She left out the part about the page that had been torn out of the book.

"Sometimes books become damaged."

"No, this looked like it had been done on purpose."

"Then you mustn't worry about it. Perhaps, someday, you will know what those lines said."

"When Solaris had first mentioned bringing you four aboard the ship, I thought she was just obeying a command left to her by my grandfather. But now I see why she did it."

"Come," said Alfric, holding his strong and calloused hand out for Rynah, who took it, and lifted her to her feet, "I long to see my homeland."

Rynah grinned as she followed him out of the room. Something told her that the Earth they were going to would not be one that Alfric recognized.

Chapter 13
STEIN'S FURY

"**W**e are ready to test it, sir," said a crewmember as Stein marched into the command center.

"Perfect. Have you chosen a suitable target?"

"Yes. The city is called Tehran, with a population of roughly 7.8 million."

"An excellent choice," said Stein. "That should demonstrate our might sufficiently. When will you be ready?"

"Shortly. The ship we sent down there to help focus the weapon's power should be arriving within 15 minutes."

"Good," said Stein. "I will be on the observation deck. Send the images there."

* * *

Eight-year-old Mohammad ambled out to the peeling, and chipped, wall just outside his home. He snatched a jagged rock from the cracked pavement that once served as a main road, but now was little more than an alley where trash and discarded items littered it.

Clack-Clack! The rock skittered across the barrier as he threw it for fun.

The ground vibrated; pebbles bounced along as the vibrations grew in intensity. Shielding his brown eyes from the arid and harsh sun, Mohammed gawked at the monstrous, and very alien looking, ship that hovered above him, moving towards the center of the city. He took two steps backward, tripping and falling hard on his back, but he never removed his eyes from the ship.

As wonderment turned to fear, the child cried for his mother. Scrambling to his feet, Mohammed ran for his home just as his mother stepped outside, her burqa pulled tight across her face, revealing only her wide and horrified eyes as she stared at the floating vessel. A blinding, crackling light shot from the ship, striking the sandy ground; the last thing either of them saw before death.

* * *

High up in the outer atmosphere of the Earth, well out of range of radar, orbited the command ship of Stein's armada. He stood upon the bow, staring out the humongous window, which took up the entire wall, and watching with cold eyes the swirls of white clouds below as they snaked across the blue planet.

"It is remarkable, isn't it?"

"What is, sir?" asked Gaden, who took his place by Stein's side, wondering when the riches promised him would be granted.

"Their planet looks so serene and is almost completely covered in water."

"Yes, remarkable."

"You do not sound convinced."

"With respect, sir, why does it matter?"

"You have, yet, to learn to appreciate your enemy, Gaden, and that is why Rynah continues to defeat you. I appreciate the beauty of this planet; that is why I can relieve them of it."

"Yes, sir."

"Do you have any news to report?"

"Yes," replied Gaden, "we've tested the crystals on one of their cities, a backward one in the middle of a desert, but it did produce a fair amount of casualties."

Gaden tapped the window and images of devastating fires, obliterated countryside, skeletal remains of concrete buildings, and charred remains of unidentifiable people flashed to life across it. As pictures of smoke and people wandering aimlessly through the chaos, weeping and shrieking for anyone to explain what had just happened scrolled across, a satisfied smile spread across Stein's face. Misery didn't just love company, it relished it, and such desolation brought joy to Stein's crippled heart.

"Excellent. The crystals?"

Gaden shifted his feet. "They performed perfectly."

"But?" A dark cloud covered Stein's features as his merciless eyes bore into Gaden's, who shifted, even more uncomfortable, under it.

"We seem to be missing one."

"What! How is that possible?"

"I do not know, sir. I was certain that we had all six, but only five are in the device."

"Then, where is the sixth?"

"I can only guess—well, there is no way to know for—it must…"

"Spit it out!"

"It must still be on Sunlil. Rynah somehow tricked us and kept one of the crystals."

Enraged, Stein punched Gaden in the mouth, knocking him to the smooth floor.

"That is for failing me."

Frightened, Gaden stared up at Stein and wiped the trickling blood from his lower lip.

"I'm sorry, sir."

"I don't want your apologies! Pinpoint the five most populated cities on this planet. I'll show them what vengeance is."

"Ye—yes, sir." Gaden hurried to his feet and fled before Stein could abuse him again.

A beep sounded. "Yes?" said Stein as he answered the intercom.

"We found them, sir."

"Good." Stein switched off the intercom, grinning to himself in triumph. *Perhaps I can give Brie a family reunion.*

Chapter 14
SPACE DIVING

Solaris stood poised on the deck of the pirate ship, arms folded, staring out the giant window at the blue and white planet below them. She watched as the white swirls caressed the orb below. Inhaling until her mechanical lungs almost burst, she released a long sigh, enjoying the sensation of breathing. As a robotic life form, she had no need for lungs, but Tom wanted her to be as human as possible, so he created the next best thing, synthesized breathing, by inventing a mechanical set of lungs that would draw in air and release it. Solaris released another sigh.

"Perturbed about something?" asked Rynah.

"No," answered Solaris. "Why do you ask?"

"Normally, when someone sighs it means they are annoyed."

"I was merely enjoying the experience of breathing."

"Ah," said Rynah as she looked out the window. "So this is Earth?"

"Yes. It's unfortunate that Marlow is not here to see it. He often spoke of this place."

Rynah's eyes fell at the mention of her grandfather. Not knowing what to say, she remained silent.

"I apologize," said Solaris when she noticed Rynah's subdued nature. "I should not have brought up the past."

"No, it's not your fault." Rynah released a long sigh. "My grandfather and I did not part on the best of terms. I remember that after the trial, I had decided to leave the fleet. When I told him, he informed me that I was making a huge mistake. He believed being on the security team in the geo-lab was beneath me.

"But I wouldn't listen. I was so angry at him for trying to steal the crystal in the first place. I felt I owed it to Lanyr to stop such a thing from ever happening again, but I failed."

"You think because Klanor was able to acquire the crystal that you have let your grandfather down."

"Haven't I?" The pain in Rynah's eyes moved Solaris. "When I last spoke to him, I said some harsh words that I'll never be able to take back. It wasn't long after that, he died. He never even told me about his illness."

"He didn't wish to worry you."

"And he never told me about you."

"I was his secret," said Solaris.

Rynah studied Solaris' robotic eyes. Despite being synthetic, she saw emotion, and pain within them, something under normal circumstances, she would not have thought possible, but Solaris had proven to be far from normal, and in some way, more human than anyone she had ever known.

"What are you not telling me?"

"Some things have to be learned, Rynah, not told."

"You are keeping something from me."

Solaris refused to answer.

"What are you keeping from me?'

"Rynah, I…" Solaris did not finish.

"All right we have reached your blue planet," said Jifdar as he approached them.

"Where is Stein?"

"On the other side of the planet, for now. We will have to move quickly to avoid detection. So, what do you wish to do?"

"I guess we say hello," said Rynah. "Do you have suits for space jumping?"

"A few," said Jifdar.

"How many?"

"About six."

"I want the others in the cargo hatch with me," said Rynah, "You and Klanor will take a shuttle down. Do your best not to be picked up on their radar technology. I'll contact you, letting you know where to meet us. Your main ship will have to remain hidden on the darkest side of their moon to avoid detection by Stein."

"How can you trust me to bring that treacherous bastard there?" asked Jifdar.

"I can't, and I don't," replied Rynah, "but the ancient text says to meet your closest enemies there. As Stein is not aboard this ship, I can only assume that it refers to you and Klanor. You'll have to get creative in hiding your faces as they have never seen the likes of you before."

Solaris closed the distance between Jifdar and her.

"And I will see you there," she whispered in his ear.

"Of course, madam," replied the pirate captain, understanding the veiled threat.

Jifdar strolled to the intercom unit and pressed the activate button. "All right, you earthlings, get down to the cargo hold." He gave a curt smile to Solaris and Rynah and walked off.

When Rynah and Solaris arrived in the cargo hold, she found the others suited up, preparing for another spacewalk. Wasting no time, she grabbed a suit and put it on, while Solaris did the same, noting that the suits were Lanyran in origin as the high quality material was unmistakable, and watched as Brie helped Solon secure his helmet before fastening her own. Rynah picked up her helmet and placed it over her head. Once sealed, the hiss of equalizing pressure told her that she now lay safe inside her own private bubble.

"Ready?" Rynah's voice crackled over the radio.

"Yes," answered the others, except Alfric, who moaned at the prospect of another outing into the vacuum of space.

"Okay, I need you to pay extra close attention because I will only explain it once. Failure means death." Rynah eyed them, making certain she had their attention. "This right here is the release for your first chute. And this right here releases your second chute. After landing, hit the same button again to cut the chute away so that you aren't dragged across the ground. Memorize this, or we'll be saying your funeral in a few minutes."

"Why is it I don't like the sound of this?" Tom muttered, losing his initial enthusiasm at the prospect of space diving.

Rynah glared at him for interrupting. "This here"—she pointed at a rectangular object on her left arm—"is your altimeter. When it hits 20,000 feet, you will hear a beep and it is then that you will release your first chute. When the altimeter hits 5,000 feet, you will hear two beeps; cut away the first chute and release your second one. Questions?"

"I never went space diving before," said Tom.

"Yeah, well, you're about to get a crash course," replied Rynah. "These suits are designed to protect you while you enter the planet's atmosphere. You must maintain this position as you enter"—Rynah demonstrated a rigid posture with her legs tight together and her hands by her side—"so do not move while going through re-entry. If you do, you'll be incinerated."

"Somehow, that does not inspire confidence," said Tom, now wishing that they didn't have to space dive at all. "Why can't we use a shuttle?"

"There is only one aboard this ship that can avoid detection by your satellite systems, and it is currently in use. Besides, what would we do with it once we've landed? I doubt very much that we can just park it someplace."

"Point taken," Tom said.

"This method will allow us to land on the planet below and avoid the same problem of being noticed. We should appear to be no more than a meteorite on your radar. Once, we've landed, we'll need to find a man named Joe Harkensen."

"Have you done this before?" asked Alfric.

"Once," replied Rynah, "in basic training. Just follow my instructions exactly and you should be fine. Ready?"

"Not really," Tom mumbled.

"Look," said Rynah, "I know this is daunting. Just remember, on the first beep, press this, on the second beep, press this and this, and when you land, press this in that exact order and you should be fine."

Rynah punched the release valve for the doors, depressurizing the chamber. Tom, Solon, Brie, and Alfric each marveled at the sight of their home. Never before had they seen such a view, and such an awe-inspiring one at that. Despite the danger they faced, the beauty before them could not go unnoticed. A light flashed green.

"That's the signal. Go!" shouted Rynah. She jumped.

Brie approached the edge of the opening with exceptional calm. Having faced death before, she did not fear what lay below her. She raised her arms and dove off, plunging to the planet beneath her.

"Did she just do a swan dive?" Tom exclaimed with disbelief, his mouth hanging wide open. "Un-frickin-believable!"

Solon jumped, followed by Alfric.

Grudging the entire prospect of nose diving to his home planet, and vowing to get even with Rynah for this, if he survived, Tom approached the edge of the doorway. He stared down at the Earth, sweat dripping down his neck at the thought of plummeting through space and re-entry.

"Shall I give you a push?" asked Solaris.

Tom glared at her. He placed his arms and legs in the rigid position that Rynah had demonstrated moments before. "Well, Geronimo," he said, and stepped over the edge.

Solaris glanced at the camera in the room.

"Remember, Jifdar, no tricks." She jumped.

"Wouldn't dream of it," muttered Jifdar as he watched them descend towards the mysterious planet below from his holofeed.

They plummeted face first towards the earth, its sheen glow mocking them as they entered the upper levels of the atmosphere, yanked downward by the planet's gravity. Though isolated in their suits, a roar filled their ears as their skin pressed against their bones from the force exerted on them. Each did their best to maintain the rigid pose that Rynah had demonstrated, praying that they would survive.

The darkness around them turned to a fiery blaze that enveloped them, and lasted for mere seconds before transforming into a mass of white as they plowed through thick, vaporous clouds that seemed to break away, as though they were intruders. They clouds dispersed. A mixture of green and brown shapes greeted them as they continued their descent.

Beep!

They had reached 20,000 feet. They each pressed the release valve for the first chute (it looked like a massive set of wings that stretched above them) and took in a sharp, surprised breath as they were jerked upward from the sudden deceleration of their fall. As they dropped at a more controlled pace, Brie, Tom, Solon, and Alfric took the time to admire the view, having never been that high in the sky before. Even Rynah and Solaris gazed at the round horizon and the mass of colors that conglomerated together, forming a terrain they had never seen.

Beep! Beep!

Wasting no time, they released the first chute (their stomachs leaping into their throats as they did so) and pressed the release button for the second, and much smaller, chute. No jerk greeted them this time; instead, they fell with more grace, because the second chute had a steering mechanism, and locked onto Rynah, ensuring that they stayed together, until they were only 100 feet above the ground when it switched off.

They all landed with a thud, their legs crumpling beneath them as they absorbed the impact. Rynah detached her chute. Looking around, she saw Brie, Alfric, Tom, Solaris, and…

"Solon!"

Frantic at not being able to find him (all sorts of horrible thoughts about him burning in the planet's atmosphere filled her mind), she searched the grass and bushes for the young scholar.

"Solon!"

"I am here," said Solon, tumbling out of a thicket. "Though you have opened my eyes to marvelous wonders, I believe I shall leave the art of flying to the gods."

Alfric grumbled his agreement as he tried to prevent the contents of his stomach from erupting from his mouth.

"Space diving, isn't my favorite activity either," said Rynah. "I just hope that Jifdar doesn't try anything."

"I wouldn't worry about him," said Brie.

"He's a pirate," said Alfric, "who marooned us on a world of ice."

"People can change," said Brie, "and I believe he wants to."

"I hope you're right," said Rynah, taking off her suit's gloves.

"We should go," said Brie, surveying the farmland they had landed in. "Even if we weren't picked up by radar, someone could still have seen us."

"I don't see how," said Tom as he wrestled with his suit, managing to get more tangled up in it in his efforts to get it off. In the end, Solaris helped him in his endeavor. "Thanks," he said to her.

"I'm just saying that it's a possibility," Brie replied.

"She's right," said Rynah. "Let's get these suits off and get out of here. We've wasted enough time."

They stripped off their spacesuits, piling them together and setting them on fire. Solaris had suggested that they do so to avoid anyone acquiring Lanyran technology, and Rynah had agreed. Once done, they ran east into a cornfield (whose stalks had dried, despite the early morning mist that draped over them), crashing through it as they charted their own course. They stumbled onto a widened path with tractor tracks carved into the semisoft ground.

"We should go this way," said Brie, knowing enough about farms that you follow the tracks of farm vehicles if you wish to leave the fields; otherwise, you risk getting lost.

The others followed her, trusting her judgment. They stomped on the ground, following the tracks, mist forming before them with each breath they took. Despite the solitude of the area, they ran, not wanting to be caught, or worse, run into Stein and his men. Harsh clomping filled their ears as they raced away from the fields and towards the buildings that Brie had spotted earlier.

Voices stopped them. Hunkering behind a set of mildew covered trees, they watched as a man, wearing the quintessential hat often associated with farmers, barked at a couple of hired hands. His rage evident, neither Rynah, nor the others, wished to be caught as trespassers.

Tom pointed at an abandoned truck. Taking one last look at the irate farmer, they ran for the truck, finding it unlocked, and crammed into the cab, or truck bed, with Tom in the driver's seat. He yanked the panel beneath the steering wheel free.

"Hey!" shouted the farmer. "What are you doing in there?"

His fingers fumbling, Tom pulled a mess of wires free, finding the ones he needed, stripping them and twisting them together. The starter whined as the engine turned over.

"Hey! I said get out of there!"

Shoving the truck into drive, Tom punched the accelerator and took off, dust clouds trailing behind them.

"How are we to find this Joe Harkensen guy?" he asked.

"According to your databases," said Solaris, "he is employed at the Federal Bureau of Investigation offices in Philadelphia, Pennsylvania."

"So how does that help us find him?" asked Solon.

"Well, does that not make him law enforcement?" quipped Solaris. "And are we not in a stolen vehicle? Will that not get us arrested?"

"Only by the local police," said Brie. "If you wish to get arrested by the FBI, you have to do something major, like threatening to assassinate the President, a terrorist plot, or—who here is really good at hacking?"

"Hacking?" said Alfric and Solon together, their unfamiliarity with the term showing on their faces.

"Yes, computer hacking," said Brie. "If we were to hack into the FBI database—or even better, the NSA—that would put us on the radar."

"Let's do it," said Tom with enthusiasm. "I always wanted to get arrested, and the beauty of it is that it won't even go on my record because, technically, I don't exist!"

"You're a bit too enthused by the idea," commented Solaris.

"There is a more prudent way," Rynah silenced them. "We could just go to these FBI offices and ask to see this Joe Harkensen."

"That kind of takes the fun out of it," mumbled Tom.

"Do you know the way to these offices?" asked Rynah.

"Yeah," said Brie, "just follow the signs to Philadelphia." She pointed at a fading green road sign with the distance to Philadelphia painted on it. "Eighty miles it says. We should be there in little over an hour."

"Then that is what we'll do," said Rynah.

"But what if they don't take us seriously?" asked Tom.

"Then," replied Rynah, "we will try your brilliant plan."

Brie switched on the radio, hoping to find some music that would make the drive pass quickly.

"This is an important news update," came an urgent voice over the speakers. "The capital of Iran has just been attacked by a vessel of unknown origin. Though the number of casualties remain unclear, fires rage across the city of Tehran."

Brie switched off the radio.

"That doesn't sound good," said Tom.

"What is this Iran?" asked Solon.

"A country in the Middle East," replied Brie. "The U.S. doesn't get along with them, but we wouldn't attack them, especially not a civilian population."

"Stein," muttered Rynah.

"The Middle East is considered the birthplace of humanity," said Solaris, reciting what she had learned when she first hacked into the world wide web, which was at the same time that she had pulled Brie from her home, in what now seemed ages ago.

"Perhaps that is why Stein chose that place. If anything from your ancient world were to be hidden, that would be a good place start."

"Or, perhaps he attacked it because it is an immensely populated area. Destroying Tehran would not only make the news, but could ignite a war."

"Can this thing go faster?" asked Rynah, holding on to her seat, disliking the bumps and potholes in the cracked pavement that jostled the truck.

"Why?" Tom replied.

"Because we're running out of time."

Tom pressed the gas pedal even more, not caring if they went 30 over the speed limit, since he had no driving record that he needed to worry about.

Chapter 15
DOUBT

After Stein had struck Gaden and fled from him, he hurried down the corridors to an isolated section. The halls, which had once flourished with personnel who scuffled to and from, content to work for Klanor, as he had given them purpose, now remained emptied and silent. After Sunlil, Stein had decided to rid himself of those loyal to his predecessor, and of any he felt despised him.

Gaden rubbed his chin in an effort to relieve the pain the plagued it, but seemed to make it worse. His mind grappled with the situation. When Stein had first approached him, enlisting his help to turn against Klanor, Gaden had jumped on it because of the promise of a better station on the ship, befitting of all that he had to offer, and indeed, his situation had improved. But after weeks of witnessing Stein's descent into paranoia, and his increasing enjoyment of causing others misery, Gaden questioned his decision.

He rubbed his sore chin some more. *They were only crystals*, he told himself. Gaden did not know why these crystals were important, only that both Klanor and Stein desired them.

Klanor. Had he made the right decision in betraying his former boss? Gaden remembered when Klanor had approached him; it was the same day he had been refused the position of lead scientist for the Geothermic Lab on Lanyr. Gaden knew of the crystal's importance to the planet, or was familiar with the official government report, but there had been those who questioned such a notion. Even he had his doubts about a crystal's ability to maintain the magnetic fields of a planet and theories as to how it operated and might be better used, but those in charge refused him, so Gaden settled for a low position within the lab, not wanting to end up on public display like Marlow had. Being passed over when he had applied for a higher position just poured fuel on his internal fire. Gaden loathed being thought of as inadequate, so when Klanor made him an offer, he took it, but it hadn't panned out, forcing him to accept Stein's. Perhaps, Rynah's overbearing companion had been correct in calling him treacherous and gutless; he always did what helped him the most.

Rynah. Gaden had almost forgotten about her, and her companions. He had never fully believed in the stories and yet, here he was, in the Terra Sector and the one planet that her companions had been from. Maybe Rynah wasn't so misguided after all. Maybe he had been the fool.

He clicked on a holomonitor and replayed the footage of the destruction that he had been part of. As he watched a mother stumble through the dusty street, cradling her limp and bloodied child, Gaden wondered if he had aligned himself with the wrong person. Something within Stein's eyes unnerved him, making him hesitant to disobey. Gaden had thought that Klanor had lost his way, though Stein's promise of better circumstances had fueled his decision— Gaden never could turn down an offer that helped him in the end. But could Klanor have been the cap on Stein's madness?

He switched off the holomonitor, unable to listen to the wailing of ash-coated phantoms any longer. Though his mind refused to acknowledge it, his eyes had seen the truth.

Brisk steps echoed down the hall, heading straight for him. Wishing not to be caught, Gaden burst from his corner and straightened himself.

"Gaden?" said Stein as he rounded a corner, "I thought you were in the command center."

"On my way, sir," replied Gaden in a curt manner.

Stein's eyes softened, and for a brief moment, Gaden thought he saw a bit of humanity in them. "I apologize for my harshness, earlier."

"It is my fault," said Gaden. "I should not have let you down."

"How is your jaw? Do you wish to see a doctor for it?"

"It's fine," said Gaden, not wanting to appear weak. "Pain builds character, does it not?"

"Indeed it does," Stein said, his hardened expression returning. "I am glad that I have found you. I am arranging a trip to the surface to locate someone, and I would like you to come. I think you can benefit from it."

"Whom are we looking for?"

"The girl's family."

Gaden's eyes widened for a moment when he realized whom Stein referred to.

"The one Klanor had kept prisoner here? You're going to kidnap her family?"

"Is there a problem?" asked Stein.

"No," Gaden replied, trying to hide his misgivings about Stein's plan. After all, snatching Brie's family would force her to give in to Stein's demands. It made logical sense, but a part of Gaden felt disgusted by the notion of manipulating someone by threatening the ones they cared about most. "I would love to come."

"Good. Report to the shuttle bay after you give my previous instructions to the command center."

"Yes, sir."

Gaden watched as Stein disappeared, his mind reeling from an internal conflict of achieving his own desires and the price he would have to pay. Shoving all doubts aside, Gaden marched to the command center to give Stein's previous orders of locating the five most populous cities before reporting to the shuttle bay, deciding that he had no personal interest in the welfare of Earth, nor were its people Lanyran, but a sliver of guilt remained rooted in his heart, and slivers have a tendency to fester.

Chapter 16
A Hijacking

A small beep sounded over the com units, its soft tone ripping through the hushed silence that surrounded all within the command center of Jifdar's ship.

"You really think this will work?" asked Merrick of Obiah.

"It'll have to."

"You worry too much, my friend," said Jifdar. "We have done this many times.

"What if they send more than one scout ship?" Merrick said.

"They won't," Klanor replied. "A signal like this is enough to attract curiosity, but only one scout ship will be sent. Most times, such curiosities prove to be nuance, and Stein won't want to waste the resources to send any more."

And if you're wrong?" Merrick asked.

"I'm not," said Klanor. "Stein will have already scanned the surface of this moon and learned that not only does it exhibit no signs of life, but serves no military function either. He will follow standard procedure on this one. Besides, I think it's safe to say that he is more interested in the planet instead of this rock."

"Silence!" hissed Jifdar as his eyes remained focused on the holographic radar screen before them and the red dot that approached. "It appears that they took the bait."

The tiny red speck drifted across the screen as the beep continued its dry tone, growing larger.

"Get in position," Jifdar said over the com to his pirates, whose shuttles lay in waiting.

Outside the ship, five pirate fighter crafts lay in the shadow of the moon, concealed by its darkness, with nothing more than a few lights showing, the eyes of predators waiting to pounce. The lone shuttle from Stein's armada approached, unaware of the eyes that watched it. It glided through space, taking scans and mapping the area, but the pilots found nothing to be alarmed about.

"Now!" yelled Jifdar over the com unit.

The five fighter crafts sprang from their positions, surrounding the lone shuttle, releasing tractor beams that stopped it. The shuttle jerked as its pilot attempted to speed away, but the pulses released by the pirates rendered its propulsion systems inert. While it remained in limbo, locked between five pirate vessels, Jifdar's main ship appeared from its hiding position, its shadow spread over the small shuttle, a hunter ready to devour its prey.

"Fire!"

Each of the fighter vessels fired an electromagnetic pulse, shutting off the shuttles electrical systems, forcing it to go dark and hang in space with no means of defense.

"Bring them in," ordered Jifdar.

A green light spilled from Jifdar's main ship as its tractor beam focused on the shuttle and brought it closer until the ship had devoured it.

"Let's go," Jifdar said to the others.

Merrick, Obiah, and Klanor followed the pirate captain down

to the hangar area, arriving just in time to watch as the shuttle was pulled into the ship and the doors closed. Once the room had repressurized, they hurried in as more pirates surrounded the small vessel, their weapons trained on its hatch. With a flick of his hand, two of Jifdar's pirates hurried to the shuttle and placed a small charge on the hatch before darting away. Sparks flew in every direction when it detonated, popping the locking mechanism free and opening the door.

A pirate approached with caution and used the tip of his laser rifle to open the hatch. The moment it had cracked a few inches, laser fire burst from the darkened interior of the shuttle, zigzagging in diagonal lines and striking the far wall. They all ducked.

"They got some fight to them," said Jifdar. He waved his hand, giving a command to his men.

The pirates returned fire as another snuck up; while holding a shield in front of him with one hand to deflect any laser blasts, his other held a round object, the size of a mouse, with blinking orange lights on its side. He pressed it, charging it, and tossed it into the open hatch of the shuttle before diving out of the way of the laser fire. A bright, white light filled the inside of the small craft before dissipating. Silence followed.

More pirates hurried to the open hatch, their weapons ready should they come under attack again, and aimed their flashlights inside, illuminating two bodies.

"Take off their uniforms and put them out an airlock," Jifdar ordered. "You"—he pointed at another pirate—"get that shuttle's systems back online and figure out what frequency they were using to stay in contact with the main ship."

He turned to Merrick and Obiah. "It appears, gentlemen, that we have found your ride."

Chapter 17
LEVERAGE

Rebecca Reynolds sat in the lone chair nestled in a corner of her small apartment with the warm glow of the single lamp on the table next to it, as it provided the only light in the room, holding a worn picture of Brie in her hands, the cracked knuckles matching the warped edges of the photograph. Tears, long since dried, stained Brie's smiling face and her kind eyes. More tears streamed down Rebecca's chapped cheeks as she wept, alone in the dark, for her missing daughter.

A noise in Sara's bedroom made her look up. Her youngest daughter hadn't wanted to go to bed that night; instead, she had wanted to stay up with her mother and wait for Brie to come home. Rebecca did not know how to tell Sara that Brie might never return, so she played the part of the hopeful mother who would sit up and wait each night until her daughter had been returned to her, but Brie never came.

The authorities had told her nothing; there was nothing for them to tell her, no clues to go on, and they did not wish to give her false hope. Brie had vanished into thin air, without a trace. Those present when it had happened had mentioned an orange and yellow light that took Brie away—away from her. With no physical evidence to go on, the police were unable to conduct an investigation, so they turned it over to the FBI and Brie became another missing person report, but she was not just a person to Rebecca; she was her daughter.

And so, each night, Rebecca stayed awake, praying for her daughter's safe return, but the nights turned to days and the days dragged onward, with no news and no sign of Brie.

More tears welled in her eyes as she thought about her eldest daughter and how she should have been there for her. Thoughts of how Brie had been forced to grow up and care for Sara filled Rebecca's mind. If only her husband hadn't died, then they never would have been forced to move to a bad neighborhood and Brie would be home where she belonged.

Clink! Clink!

The tiny sound penetrated the silent night, and Rebecca's tortured thoughts forced her to stand up, setting the photo aside. Her first thought was that Sara had gotten up to go to the bathroom. As she crept down the hall to check, a tremendous clang roared in her ears, forcing her to whirl around in fright. Rebecca hurried to the desk drawer where she kept a lockbox with a revolver hidden in case of a break-in.

Glass shattered and showered the frayed carpet as men, the likes of which she had never seen before, burst into the living room, armed with laser rifles. Rebecca aimed at one and fired, striking one of the intruders in the chest. She aimed at another, but before she could pull the trigger, the horrified screams of Sara filled her ears.

"Sara!"

Rebecca ran to her daughter's room, but was stopped by a man who wrenched the revolver from her grasp and flung her to the floor, placing the sole of his boot in the middle of her back.

"Sara," whispered Rebecca as she watched, helpless, while the intruders brought her youngest daughter from the bedroom and to where she was, pinned to the carpet.

"Mrs. Reynolds, I presume," said the man that had forced her to the floor.

"Who are you?" demanded Rebecca, craning her neck to see the face of the one who had spoken.

"My name is Stein and I'm here for your daughter," replied the man.

"Sara?"

"No,"—Stein leaned forward and picked up the photograph of Brie, that Rebecca had been holding moments before, and held it in front of her—"your other daughter."

"I don't know where she is," wailed Rebecca.

"I've no doubt of that," laughed Stein as he removed his foot and hauled the woman to her feet, allowing her to see him. Rebecca almost gasped when she saw his purple-skinned face. "But I'm sure we won't have to look very far."

Sara's screams filled Rebecca's ears as a black hood was shoved over her head and strong hands lifted her off her feet.

"How is he?" Stein demanded of the one Rebecca had shot, his voice void of concern.

"Badly hurt," answered another.

"Incinerate him," ordered Stein, while Gaden watched him with a mixture of disgust and satisfaction.

When the police arrived the next morning to investigate calls they had received about Rebecca's failure to show up for work and Sara missing school, all they found were two missing people and a pile of ash that had once been a Lanyran.

Chapter 18
ᴀRRESTED, ᴀNYONE?

Brie and Tom walked through the revolving glass doors of the FBI building. It had been decided that it would be best if they went alone since the others stood out—and one look at Alfric would scare anyone. The tall ceilings and opulent lobby made them gawk. Brie never believed that a law enforcement building would be decorated with such lavish furniture and desks, but then she had never been in one before. It occurred to her that the lobby was set up the way it was to make it inviting; most likely, the rest of the building resembled a standard office environment, with the lock-up area where no one would ever see it.

"There," she pointed at the front desk. "Don't say anything crazy."

They moved toward it, the man seated there never even looked up.

"Hurrumph," Tom cleared his throat.

"May I help you?" said the man, dressed in a suit and tie, but more interested in using his smartphone to clear his email inbox than the two youths before him.

"Yes, we'd like to see Agent Joe Harkensen," said Brie.

"Do you have an appointment?" asked the man, never bothering to look at them.

"No," replied Brie.

"If you call the office at 800-255-5658, then you can set up an appointment."

"Look," said Brie, growing impatient, "this is important. It's a matter of life and death. We need to see Agent Joe Harkensen right now."

The man looked at her, his bored expression portraying that he didn't care. "Shouldn't you be in school?"

"School?" said Tom. "Who cares about school when there is an alien invasion about to happen?"

"That's what I meant by crazy," whispered Brie out of the side of her mouth.

"Sorry?" said the man, confused.

"There are aliens orbiting your planet," continued Tom, unphased by the man's skepticism. "They plan to steal some crystal, or at least use the ones they have to destroy everyone here, so if you could point us in the direction of Agent Joe Harkensen, that would be great."

"There." The man pointed at the lobby doors.

"But that takes us out of the building," said Tom.

"Precisely," the man replied. "I don't know what game you two are playing, but this is the Federal Bureau of Investigation. Take your stories somewhere else before I have security escort you out."

With little choice, Brie and Tom turned around and left.

"Well?" said Rynah, when they returned to where the others remained hidden.

"They thought we were nuts," said Tom.

"Of course they did!" snapped Brie. "You just had to mention aliens. That is one way to get put in a psychiatric institution."

"What do we do now?" asked Tom.

"Since our first plan did not work," said Solon, "then prudence dictates we implement the second one."

"Meaning?" said Tom.

Rynah sighed, not believing she was agreeing to this. "You get to hack into the FBI database, or whatever database will get us arrested."

"Yes!" shrieked Tom, jumping up and down with excitement at being able to commit a bout of lawlessness and get away with it since he had no record to have it attributed to.

"There should be an internet café nearby," said Brie.

"Perfect!" Tom ran off, stopping a man on the sidewalk to ask for directions to the closest internet café.

"Should I be concerned about his enthusiasm?" asked Solaris, with a note of sarcasm.

Within 15 minutes, they found a local coffee shop that offered wireless internet, as well as a computer station. The moment they walked through the door, they spotted a long table with computers, each of them with an occupant.

"We need to free up one of those computers," said Brie. She started to head over to one of them, but Alfric stopped her. Though he still did not fully understand what a computer was, he understood their importance to Brie, Tom, and Rynah.

"Remove yourself from this position," he said to one college age youth with a multicolored scarf tied around his neck and a steaming latté sitting next to him.

"Buzz off," said the man.

"I will not ask again," said Alfric, his tone dark.

"Look, pal, first come, first serve."

Alfric seized the man by his shirt collar and yanked him out of the chair, thrusting him aside.

"Hey!" The man took one look at Alfric's scowl and stopped. "It's cool." He ran out the door, forgetting to take his coffee.

Tom plopped in the seat, tapping the screen.

"Why isn't anything happening?"

"Maybe you should try the keyboard," said Brie.

"You guys really need to update your software," mumbled Tom

as he pulled the keyboard closer to him. Within moments, he had an internet browser open to the FBI homepage.

"Solaris," Rynah pulled her aside, "perhaps you should wait outside in case things do not go as planned."

Without a word, Solaris left the coffee shop and hid in the shadows of a nearby alley.

"This shouldn't take too long," said Tom as window after window opened with a series of commands zipping by.

"What exactly are you bringing up?" asked Brie.

"Not much," replied Tom, "but knowing what I do about your time period, I just sent them my plans on breaking into the White House and kidnapping the President with the hopes of selling him to Hezbollah."

"Are you insane!" said Brie. "They'll shoot us on sight!"

"No," said Tom, insulted by her remark. "Now, I am breaking into the NSA database. Wow! You should see all of the data they have collected on the average citizen."

"You are insane!" Brie replied.

"You said to make sure that they arrested us."

"Yeah, but you can usually accomplish that by trying to hack into their secure servers, not by threatening to kidnap the President and sell him to a terrorist organization."

A few heads turned her way.

"I know who killed Kennedy!" shouted Tom with excitement as he continued to bring up a series of screens with what looked like garbled text to those standing around him.

"Kennedy?" said Rynah. "Who is he?"

"Hey, they're onto me," said Tom before Brie had a chance to answer. "They are tracking the ISP right now."

"Meaning?" asked Alfric.

"That in a few moments we're about to have company," said Rynah, understanding fully how electronic signals and wireless communications could be traced.

"When they get here," said Brie, "they will most likely split us up and interrogate us separately. State that you have Fourth and Fifth Amendment rights and keep insisting that you will not talk unless you are with your friends and Agent Joe Harkensen is in the room. Say nothing else."

"Soldiers have ways of making one talk," said Solon.

"Not here," said Brie. "We have laws against torture. And we have rights."

"Hey, do you guys want to know who is really the current head of the freemasons?" asked Tom.

Just as Brie turned her head to see exactly what Tom had broken into, sirens blared outside, drawing nearer. Everyone in the coffee shop turned toward the window to look outside at the commotion, thinking that a few cop cars or an ambulance would race past. Instead, black SUVs with flashing red and blue lights screeched to a halt outside the doors and armed men burst out of the vehicles, rushing inside the building, guns raised.

"Everyone down, now!"

Customers screamed, diving to the floor and covering their heads with their hands.

"Drop your weapons!" yelled an agent, his weapon aimed at Alfric, who had reached for his sword.

"I said drop your weapon!"

Alfric debated with allowing himself to be taken prisoner or striking down the men in front of him.

"Alfric, please," pleaded Brie. "Remember why we're really here."

Raising one hand, Alfric unsheathed his blade and dropped it to the floor, where its clatter sliced the tension in the room.

"Hands above your head! On your knees, now!"

They knelt to the floor, their hands clasped behind their heads. Agents rushed them, wrenching their arms behind their backs and cuffing them. Rynah cringed when they took her laser pistol and knife; she had never gone anywhere without them.

Each was placed in a separate vehicle—just like Brie had predicted—and carted away as a crowd of curious onlookers gathered to see what the commotion was all about, except for one individual who remained out of sight, while memorizing the license plate number of one of the vehicles.

* * *

FBI agent Joe Harkensen—his first name was really Joseph, but he preferred Joe—raced through the second floor of the building, a pile of manila folders in his hands. Some eyes followed him, remarking at his sharp appearance: shirt buttoned all the way up and tucked in, not a wrinkle in his tie or his jacket. He ignored them. Some of his fellow agents allowed their appearance to be sloppy. Not him. Being ex-special forces, he believed in dressing well and preparing for the worst.

He stopped when he noticed a bronze-plated plaque on his desk for being the first African-American to ever make senior agent after only being on the force for two years. Annoyed, Joe tossed it in the wastebasket. He couldn't understand what the big fuss was all about. While others busied themselves at the bar, he prepared for the written exam, spending hours studying. While others unwound on the basketball court, he remained at the shooting gallery, honing his skill. His focus and hard work paid off.

Groaning, he dumped the manila folders on his desk, each holding an unsolved case. After witnessing his father's murder at the age of eight, he decided then and there to join the FBI—though he joined the military at 18 and spent ten years with them before getting out—so that he could protect people from the horrors he knew existed in the world. Every month he pawned through the unsolved cases and picked a handful to study more closely. Some, like the unsolved kidnappings, tore at his heart.

"Hey!"

"Samuel," groaned Joe as he scanned his fellow agent's untucked shirt, complete with a smear of the filling from a Twinkie, misaligned buttons, and disheveled tie.

"Look at you," said Samuel, "sharp as a sword!"

"Did you get lost on the way to your desk?"

"Very funny. Did you hear about that mess in Iran?"

"Yes. Did the 'aliens' get the Ayatollah?"

"Doesn't look like it."

"Pity."

Samuel continued to stand by Joe's desk, staring at the pile of yellow folders.

"Is there a reason why you are still here?" demanded Joe.

"Oh, yeah, here." Samuel handed him a file folder. "The director wishes to see you in the interrogation room."

Joe took the folder and leafed through it.

"Is this a joke?"

"No, this is on the level," said Samuel. "Come on."

Though reluctant, Joe headed for the interrogation room with his annoyance by his side.

"They were picked up this morning," continued Samuel as they walked. "None of them have IDs, except the girl's description matches that of the 16-year-old girl who was listed as missing in Phoenix, Arizona six months back."

"And the others?"

"Nothing. No identification, no prints on file, and, well, they look like they walked out of a movie set."

"Whoa," Joe paused when he saw the photo of Rynah.

"Yeah," laughed Samuel. "Looks like she had an accident in a chemistry lab, doesn't she?"

Joe continued to the interrogation area. He burst into the side room that allowed one to look through the two-way mirror at the questioning in progress.

"Joe," greeted Director Singuar, "I trust that Samuel has brought you up to speed."

"More or less." Joe looked through the window at the five companions all sitting together. "Why are they not in separate rooms?"

"They insisted that they wouldn't talk to anyone unless they were together," replied Director Singuar. "Despite our efforts, none of them broke, and he"—the director pointed at Alfric—"intimidated any who went into the room to question him. I want you to talk to them."

"Why me? Surely, there are more experienced agents."

"There are, but you have a good track record and they insisted on talking to you, and no one else."

"Me?"

"They requested you by name."

An unspoken inquiry filled Director Singuar's voice, but Joe ignored it, puzzled as to why the suspects in the next room asked for him, or how they even knew his name.

"So, get in there," said Director Singuar. "I want to know who they are, what they are doing here, and what the deal with her is." Director Singuar pointed at Rynah.

Unsure of the entire affair, Joe took his file folder and opened the door to the interrogation room, stepping into its glaring, florescent lights.

"I am Agent Joe Harkensen and I am told that you wish to speak with me."

"Turn off the cameras and the microphone first," said Rynah.

"I didn't catch your name."

"Because I didn't give it," said Rynah.

Joe turned the microphone in front of them off.

"And the one placed underneath the table," said Rynah.

"How do you know there is one?" Joe asked, his tone innocent, his mind wondering about her vast knowledge of how interrogations were recorded.

"There are 25 cameras on the first floor, another 32 on this one. Each checkpoint has a security camera and a keypad that uses a code and a keycard, much like the one on your jacket, to pass through. There are two fire exits on each floor, one at each end of the building. I know there are a minimum of two agents in the room behind that glass and your boss as well, so don't ask me how I know about the second microphone." Rynah's training as a security officer showed in her words.

Joe switched the mic off and the camera.

"Are you ready to talk?"

"I assume you know about what happened in this place, Iran, as you call it," said Rynah.

"What does that have to do with you being here?" asked Joe.

"What do you know about aliens?" Rynah leaned forward.

Joe dropped the file folder on the table. Aliens? He hated where this conversation was going.

"If you are going to tell me that a UFO dropped you off here, I suggest we call the men in white coats. Now tell me the truth."

"We are," said Tom. "We are all from Earth, except for her. She's from a planet called Lanyr. She asked us for our help in stopping a madman from her planet from destroying ours and maybe the universe as well. Except he decided to join us, because he was betrayed by another madman and wants revenge."

Joe felt a migraine setting in as he tried to keep up with Tom's story.

"And why would this second madman have any interest in our planet?"

"That would be because of me," said Brie.

"And you are?"

"Brie Reynolds."

"Wait a minute," Joe flipped through his stack of files. "You're that girl that was reported missing six months ago."

"Six months? Has it been that long?" Brie asked; concern and worry about her mother and sister filled her face.

"How did you end up with them?" Joe continued.

"I was on my way home from school when I suddenly found myself on her ship. Look, it's a really long story, but Stein is here because of information I accidentally gave him."

"Stein?" asked Joe.

"The guy who wants to destroy our planet," said Tom.

Alfric growled, not liking the way he had been treated since he was first arrested by the FBI.

"What's his problem?" Joe asked.

"He's a little mad that you took his sword away, not to mention the multitude of knives he carried," said Tom. "You know how Vikings are. They love their weapons."

"Vikings?"

"Oh, yeah, he's from the 11th century, and Solon, here, is from ancient Greece. A bit bookish, but he's cool."

"And I bet you are going to tell me that you are from the past as well?" Joe could not believe what he was hearing.

"No, actually, I'm from the year 2099. That's why you don't have any of our prints on file, nor do we have any identification."

"You do realize how all of this sounds?" said Joe. "Why don't we get back to the fact that you threatened to kidnap the President and sell him to Hezbollah."

Brie glared at Tom, who shrank in his seat.

"What is this Hezbollah?" asked Solon, hesitating as he pronounced the last word.

"I told you," whispered Brie. "They are a terrorist organization. Our enemies."

Joe raised an eyebrow at that remark, since most teenager could not even name who the current vice president was.

"Why don't we start back at the beginning. You say you are..."

"Enough of this talk!" Alfric pounded his clenched fist on the table, rattling it and unnerving Joe with his outburst. "We have told you why we are here. You will help us."

"I told you he gets cranky without his sword," mumbled Tom, garnering a scowl from Alfric.

"Look," said Rynah, growing impatient and putting her hand out to calm Alfric, "we do not have a lot of time to explain everything. Stein is here looking for the actual device that the crystals go to. If he finds it, then your planet will meet the same fate as mine."

Joe glanced at the mirror, wondering what his fellow agents in there thought of the proceedings.

"Why did you ask to see me?"

"Because you're the only one we can trust," said Rynah.

"And you know this how?"

"The ancient text of my people told us so," said Rynah; the statement sounded ridiculous, even to her.

"The ancient text of your people," said Joe. "This just gets more and more interesting."

"I'd like to call my mom," said Brie, sounding a bit like her old self.

"Now that is the first smart thing you've said all morning. I am going to call our office in Phoenix and let them know we have found you. They will contact your mother."

"Joe!" Samuel burst into the room.

"Samuel, what are you..."

"You need to watch this!"

Joe stepped out of the interrogation room. On every television in the building was the face of a man whose purple skin matched Rynah's, but was darker in tone. His black eyes drew people in, forcing them to listen to his words.

"Hello, people of the Earth. My name is Stein. I have come here because a friend of mine stole something from me. Perhaps you know her." Rynah's face popped up on the screen. "Her name is Rynah. I want what she has. Now, if you give her to me, then I will leave your insignificant planet alone, but if not, I will destroy a major city every 24 of your hours, until you hand her to me. The choice is yours. Make the right one."

"In the meantime, let this serve as a reminder of what will happen to you and your loved ones should you fail to deliver to me what I want."

The television screen went black and Joe's cell phone rang.

"Hello?" he answered.

"Hello, Agent Harkensen," said Stein's voice on the other end. "Don't bother trying to figure out how I got your number or know who you are. You have five friends of mine. I wish to speak with them."

Joe ran back into the interrogation room and placed his phone on speaker before setting it on the table.

"Hello, Rynah."

"Stein," spat Rynah.

"I must say that I am surprised that you all managed to get off Sunlil. I was certain that that volcano would have killed you all. Tell me, what did you do with Klanor?"

"Screw you," shouted Brie, her anger rising.

"Oh, so you did get a backbone. I have a special present for you, Brie. While you were on board the ship here, you gave me some very valuable information, some you didn't mean to, I'm sure. I want you to say hello to you mother and sister. They are now my guests."

"You son of a..."

Brie jumped from her chair, but Alfric snatched her and pulled her down.

"There is no honor in kidnapping," said Alfric.

"Yes, you would say that," scoffed Stein. "I want that crystal and I want it before I find the device. If you give it to me, I might let you see your family again. Think about it. In the meantime, consider this a measure of my resolve."

The connection broke.

"We really need your help," said Rynah to Joe.

The television screen flashed to life again as the face of a news anchor filled it.

"This just in," she said, her eyes wide in horror. "The cities of Shanghai, China; Istanbul, Turkey; Karachi, Pakistan; Mumbai, India; and Moscow, Russia have just been attacked by... well... we don't know what did this! A weapon, the likes of which have never been seen has decimated the five most populated cities of the world!"

Images of raging fires, dust, crumbled buildings, and people wandering the streets covered in silt and asbestos zipped across the screens in the entire building.

The news anchor appeared on the television again.

"Troi is on the scene right now in Mumbai, India. Troi."

"Yes, Wanda, I am here in Mumbai, and as you can see, people here are terrified by what they say was a blast of pale light that shot from the sky."

"Can you confirm that it was not a nuclear attack?" asked Wanda.

"Yes, I can confirm that it was not a nuclear attack. Instead, some believe..."

The camera shifted as it zoomed in on sleek, black ships that whizzed over the reporter's head firing laser blasts at the people below. One woman tried to seek shelter in a building that still stood, clinging to her baby just as laser fire struck her.

"I can't—they appear to be alien!"

Blasts of laser fire escaped the fighter ships, striking the reporter and his cameraman.

"Troi," said the news anchor; panic filled her voice "Troi? Ladies, and gentlemen, we seem to be experiencing technical difficulties..."

Joe frowned. He, and everyone else in the room, knew what had happened.

"It's them he wants," said Samuel, pointing at Rynah and the others. "If we give them to him, then he will go away."

"What are saying?" asked Joe, though he knew the answer.

"We ought to hand them in. Hey..."

He walked towards the middle of the main area, but Joe snatched him, dragging him back into the interrogation room.

"You don't honestly think that that guy will leave just because we give in to his demands?"

"What choice do we have?" asked Samuel.

"I'll not..."

Before Joe finished his statement, Alfric snatched Samuel and flung him onto the steel table, holding him down. "You treacherous snake," he hissed, choking the man.

Joe tried to stop him, but the Viking proved too much of a match for him.

"Alfric," said Brie, placing her hand on his hairy arm, "let him go. He's just frightened, but doesn't deserve to die."

Alfric looked into Brie's calm eyes; not a flicker of fear filled them, a stark contrast to when he had first been introduced to her. He loosened his grip and threw Samuel face first into a wall, rendering him unconscious.

"We need to leave," said Tom.

"Whoa, I can't just let you walk out of here," said Joe.

Alfric closed the gap between them, a venomous growl escaped his throat as he prepared to force the agent out of his path.

"A wise man should consider his options and consider them quickly," said Solon as he peeked out into the hallway. Agents rushed by, oblivious to them, which suited the young philosopher just fine.

"Options?" said Joe, still wrapping his mind over what had happened in the last half hour and wondering how his day had gone from mundane and normal to chaotic.

"It appears that you have three choices," said Rynah, "One, he kills you."

Alfric cracked his knuckles upon that statement.

"Two, you just let us walk out of here; or three, you come with us."

Joe remained silent for too long, so Rynah walked out of the room.

"Wait," he called after her, "you can't go that way. You'll be stopped in minutes. There is a back exit that might suit your purposes best."

Still unsure if they had made the right choice in seeking him out, Rynah and the others followed Joe as he led them down the hallway, with its blue carpet and white paneled walls, to a door opening onto an emergency stairwell. Echoes filled the area as the heavy, steel door slammed shut. Gray stairs stretched above and below them, forming a square circle.

"The main lobby is about ten floors below us," said Joe.

"I want my sword," said Alfric.

"We don't have time," said Joe.

Alfric pinned Joe against the concrete wall, knocking the air out of him. "I want my sword."

"Your weapons would have been taken down to evidence, which is 11 floors down, in the basement."

"Take us there," said Rynah.

In the lobby of the FBI building, a young woman, who looked to be late 20s, early 30s, hurried through the revolving door; the pointed heels of her shoes clacked on the smooth, hard floor in tune to her gait. Her jet black hair swayed with her brisk movements as she strolled through the lobby to the metal detectors.

"ID?" asked one of the security guards, his white shirt reflected the sunlight that spilled into the building through the windows encasing the domed ceiling.

The woman handed him her badge.

The man took it, scanned it, and handed it back to her.

The woman walked through the metal detector. Beep!

"Ma'am," said the security guard, motioning for her to come back, "you'll need to walk through it again."

The woman obliged. Beep!

"Are you wearing any jewelry?"

The woman showed the guard that she had no jewelry, not even a watch, on. For a moment, the guard thought he saw her stare with interest at the metal detector, but passed it off as his imagination, so he waved her through again. This time, no alarm went off. The guard shook his head, mumbling something about faulty wiring, and how they were never given funding to buy new ones or repair the old ones.

"You may go," he said to the woman.

"Thank you," she replied.

The guard watched her go, thinking her violet eyes a bit strange, though some people liked to wear colored contacts.

The woman hurried over to the elevators with their cherry wood paneling and nickel-plated doors, painted to look like gold that reflected a person's image with perfection.

Ding!

An elevator opened. People rushed out as the woman stepped inside and selected her floor.

The images on the TV in the elevator changed from a daily weather report to a news alert; pictures of alien ships, which the mysterious woman recognized, raced across the screen, firing laser blasts at a frantic populace below.

The elevator dinged and stopped at floor two.

"All of you off, now," said the woman.

"Excuse me?" said one man, holding a half-empty coffee cup.

The woman pulled out a silver laser pistol and held it up. "I said get off."

The others rushed out, tripping over one another in their haste. The woman closed the doors and placed her hand on the number pad, communicating with the computer that controlled the elevator to take her to floor ten, where interrogation was.

Within a minute, the doors opened to a floor that resembled a Black Friday at a department store than an FBI office. Agents rushed about from computer to computer, filing reports or attempting to retrieve data on the attacks that had taken place on the five most populous cities in the world moments before by a man from another planet.

"I want to find them now!" shouted Director Singuar, referring to Rynah and the others. "Samuel! Where've you been?"

Samuel swaggered to his boss, rubbing his head, still dazed from when Alfric had knocked him unconscious.

"Sorry, sir," said Samuel.

"Don't 'sorry, sir' me," raged Director Singuar. "Where's Joe?"

"I think he left with the suspects."

"You think?"

"Well…"

"Willingly?"

"No, they seemed to have been holding him hostage, or something."

"Listen up!" yelled Director Singuar over the pandemonium. "We have five escaped suspects. It is believed that they are armed, dangerous, and have taken an agent hostage. I want them found. The use of deadly force is authorized."

"Where were they last seen, sir?" asked the mysterious woman—whom, by now, you should have guessed is Solaris—hiding the laser pistol underneath her jacket.

"In interrogation," said Director Singuar, paying little attention to her.

The woman darted off, shoving her way through the confusion in the room to the sterile hallway on the other side. She found the interrogation room, its gray walls reminded her of the ones back on Lanyr, and poked her head in. Just as she thought—no one there. Solaris dashed out into the corridor once more. Her eyes scanned the footprints left by those who had been there recently; signatures of heat that were left behind from their presence still remained. One set stood out among the others and headed to a stairwell.

Solaris ran in their direction.

"Agent Henkins," said a man as he rounded a corner.

Solaris pushed him to the side with a single sweep of her arm, yanking out her laser pistol and charging down the hallway. She burst through the door to the stairwell. Bodies filled it as people rushed up and down the stairs in a panic from what they had seen on the television screens. Someone in a blue suit with his head covered caught Solaris' eye. She charged up the steps, three at a time, and ripped off his hat and coverings, revealing the purple face of one of Stein's men.

He brought up his fist to strike her, but Solaris twisted his arm and tossed him over the railing, allowing him to plummet to the concert surface several floors below. Laser fire struck the metal palisade, singeing it as it sprayed a series of sparks. Dodging out of the way, Solaris dropped to her knees, raised her weapon, and fired, striking the man in the shoulder. Solaris dove down a flight of steps.

She fired at the man behind her, but missed as he charged through a door and into another hallway. Panicked, the people in the stairwell screamed as they rushed down the steps, trying to escape the laser fire. Solaris glanced around in an attempt to learn where Rynah would have taken the others. She concluded that they would go to the first floor, since that was the most logical place to find an exit. She hid her laser weapon and followed the mass of people while wirelessly tapping into the security cameras; she wished to be certain in her conclusions.

"Found you," she whispered to herself when Rynah's face appeared on a camera in the basement.

Wasting no time, Solaris hurried down the steps, ramming her way through the crowd and acquiring several stares, shouts, and unsavory words in the process. Solaris paid no attention to them. Her mind was focused on reaching her friends before Stein's men did.

"This way," said Joe as he led them through the door to the basement and into a long, innocuous corridor with brick walls, a concrete floor covered with linoleum and hanging florescent lights; it lacked all of the luxuries that the lobby above possessed. Rynah and the others followed him through the hallway as he walked, their eyes peeled for anything that might jump out at them.

"What makes you so certain you can trust me?" asked Joe.

"Now isn't the time," said Rynah.

"How do you know I'm not leading you all to a trap?"

"Are you?" Alfric snatched Joe around the collar, bringing him close to his face; his stale breath gagged the man.

"No," said Joe, "I don't do such things, but you showing up here and insisting that only I can help you is odd."

"Not after what we've been through," commented Brie, doing her best to maintain control over her worried voice as the idea of Stein holding her sister and mother hostage flooded through her mind.

Joe's face softened. "Your things are right down here."

They reached the end of the hallway.

"You all need to wait here."

"Why?" asked Tom.

"Because I can't show up there, requesting access to evidence with all of you," replied Joe. "It would look suspicious."

"I am going with you," said Alfric.

"You…"

"It is decided," said the Viking.

None argued with Alfric. When he made up his mind, there was no changing it; something they had learned long ago.

"Fine," Joe relented, "but I do the talking."

Alfric nodded his head in affirmation.

Together, the two of them walked up to the glass barrier where a lone man sat with another barrier behind him. "Agent Harkensen," greeted the man, "what can I do for you?"

"I need to see some evidence that was logged in today. It was taken from a few suspects arrested for conspiracy of terrorism."

"And him?" the man pointed at Alfric.

"He's with me."

"I need to see your IDs."

Joe flashed his badge.

"You too," the man said to Alfric.

Alfric glowered at him, not liking his disrespectful tone.

"Look, I can't let you back here until you show your ID."

"Can't you just make an exception?" asked Joe, realizing that things were not going as planned.

"Is something wrong, Agent Harkensen?" asked the man.

"Well…"

Before he could finish his statement, Alfric reached through the small opening at the base of the window, grabbed the man by his shirt, and yanked him forward until his head banged into the glass, thus rendering him unconscious.

"You do that a lot," said Tom as he walked up from behind.

Joe gave Alfric a disapproving look.

"I did not speak," said Alfric.

"We needed him to open the door," said Joe. "There is a button on that side."

"I can fix that." Tom jumped up with excitement. He glanced around the room, noticing the security camera and ran to it, tearing open a panel and revealing a mess of wires, which he pulled free. "I need your watch."

Joe looked at his watch before glancing at Tom. He took it off from around his wrist and handed it the young man.

"By connecting these wires to this watch," Tom said as he pried the back of the watch off and tied the wires from the camera to it, "the charge in the battery will short out the locking mechanisms on this door."

Tom twisted the wires around the lock pad. A short zap sounded as it popped.

"Voila!" beamed Tom as he opened the door to the evidence room.

"All right, we haven't much time." Rynah ushered them all into the room. "Good job," she added to Tom, who still bore a prideful smirk on his face at his ingenious achievement.

They rushed into the well-lit room. Joe clicked on the computer, pushing the man slumped in the chair out of the way. He brought up the day's logs, scrolling until he found what he searched for.

"Your belongings are in 283."

Brie ran down the line of metallic drawers, scanning the numbers until she found the one she searched for.

"Found it!"

The others rushed to her.

"But it's locked."

"Wait," called Tom, "I have an idea of how..."

Before he could finish, Alfric wrapped his meaty and calloused fingers around the handle and jerked it free.

"Or we could just do that," commented Tom.

Alfric pulled out their belongings—he held his sword in the light, thankful to have his old friend back, before stuffing his knives into their various places on his body—and gave each of them their items. Rynah thanked him when she received her laser pistol and knife back.

"Everyone," said Solon, "have any of you noticed how quiet it is."

Each of them looked around, noticing the silence for the first time. Even Joe seemed unnerved by it. Normally, there were three people in the evidence room and even he hadn't noticed that two of them remained unaccounted for.

"We need to leave," said Rynah. She turned to Joe. "Just tell us the quickest way out of here and you'll never hear from us again. We never should have involved you."

Joe leaned closer, looking Rynah right in the eyes, and said, "I got involved the moment that bastard called my cell phone."

Rynah never said a word. She ran off after the others, but Alfric seized her around the waist and pulled her back, putting his finger over his mouth, indicating the need to remain silent. He peeked around the corner, coming face to face with a woman with flowing black hair. They all pointed their weapons at one another, ready to fire.

The woman lowered hers. "Rynah, it's me."

A puzzled expression covered Rynah's face. The woman's appearance changed to that of Solaris, revealing the matching heliotrope skin tone and emerald hair that Tom had given her.

"How did you..." began Rynah.

"The nano technology that Tom combined with my synthetic skin gives me the ability to change my appearance at will. I must say that it was rather ingenious."

"I have my moments," Tom added.

"I followed you after you were arrested, tapping into their communication systems and law enforcement records."

"We need to leave. Did you find a suitable escape route?" asked Rynah.

"Yes," said Solaris. "What about him?"

Rynah glanced at Joe, "He's with us."

Peuh! Peuh! Laser fire struck the wall near them, forcing them to dodge out of the way and hunker behind the desk in the evidence room.

"Those aren't our weapons," said Joe.

"Stein's men have infiltrated the building," said Solaris. "Undoubtedly, they wish to ensure that you do not escape."

No kidding, thought Rynah.

More laser fire pelted the walls around them, splintering the concrete and showering them with sparks and debris. Rynah and Joe fired back.

"Is there another way out?" demanded Rynah.

"There is a fire exit this way," said Joe, "but we'll have to cross that room first."

Solon fired at one of Stein's men as he attempted to outflank them, striking the man in the stomach. A series of laser fire pummeled the wall next to him in response.

"I count three still able to fight."

"Solaris!" Rynah called.

Understanding what Rynah wanted, Solaris jumped to her feet and charged across the room, firing her laser pistol at Stein's men.

She reached one, knocking the weapon out of his hands before forcing him to the floor. Whirling around, Solaris fired at the remaining two, but they remained behind cover. She noticed a support beam above them. With a precision that only she could exhibit, she fired at the joints. A loud creak filled the room as the beam fell free of its hold and landed on top of Stein's men.

More laser fire headed for them.

"Go! Now!" yelled Solaris as she returned fire.

The others jumped to their feet and ran across the room to the door marked "Emergency Exit", crashing through it with Solaris right behind. They entered another corridor that branched into more hallways.

"There," Joe pointed at a door on the far end with a red exit sign.

They raced down the hallway for it, just as their pursuers careened through the door behind them, firing laser blasts at them. Lights shattered and holes punched through the walls with each missed strike.

"Alfric, behind you!" screamed Brie as she turned and noticed a man heading straight for the Viking.

Alfric dodged the attack, lunging low, before whirling around with élan, striking with his blade. His attacker crumpled over.

Brie noticed an agent aiming at Solon. Without thinking, she charged him, ramming her head into his middle and knocking him to the smooth floor. They rolled across it until a wall stopped them. A bit dazed, Brie shook her head and looked up only to find the barrel of a gun pointed right at her. She stared at the man with defiance, never flinching, even when Alfric seized the man's arm, causing the gun to fire and miss her by five inches, and flung him across the corridor. With a gentleness most thought Vikings never possessed, Alfric helped her to her feet.

"Come on!" yelled Joe.

They ran down the hallway to the emergency exit, dodging attacks, firing at Stein's men, and avoiding capture by the agents still in the building. Laser fire whizzed past their heads, transforming the once serene building into a war zone.

They reached the door. Joe flung it open and stopped. On the other side stood a man, dark purple skin like his comrades, holding a laser weapon the size of a small cannon. Solaris shoved them all back inside, slamming the heavy, steel door shut and taking the brunt of the impact, though it did little damage to her. Jagged pieces of the ceiling crashed around them as dust filled the air.

The ones that had chased them into the hallway still remained. Joe pushed all of them down an adjoining corridor.

"There is an elevator this way."

Their lungs burned as they charged down another hallway in an effort to escape. More laser fire hurled past them, striking plaques, doors, pictures, lights, security cameras, and innocent bystanders. A light exploded above them as a laser strike hit it.

One set of elevator doors opened and out walked Samuel and four other agents.

"Joe," said Samuel as they approached.

"Get down!" yelled Joe, just as a series of laser fire struck two of the agents. Joe grabbed Samuel and hurled him to the floor out of danger. He wrenched his weapon free, just as Samuel attempted to fire at Rynah.

"Joe, what is going on?" demanded Samuel. "Why are you helping them?"

"They are not the aggressors."

"What do you mean?"

"Samuel, how many intruders do we have?"

"Ten, maybe," replied Samuel. "They took out the security cameras. I don't get how they were able to overpower us so easily. Their weapons are nothing like what we've seen before."

A series of laser pellets speckled the wall they hid behind. The elevator lay just out of reach. Solon made a move for it, but more enemy fire struck the floor, almost nicking his feet and forcing him to dive back behind cover.

"We'll never reach it with them firing at us," said Tom.

Solaris peeked around the corner, calculating where the three that fired at them were. A laser blast plowed into her, but the nano technology embedded within her skin absorbed it, sending silver ripples in an outward motion. Samuel gawked. Solaris jumped into the middle of the hallway and fired three shots; each struck their target.

Solon ran for the elevator again and punched the button. After having spent months on a spaceship, he had become accustomed and knowledgeable of some modern technology. Besides, he wanted out of the death trap they were in.

The doors dinged as they slid open. Rynah shoved them all inside, while Joe dragged Samuel with them. Once in the elevator, Brie pressed the button for the lobby.

"I'm not sure if going this way is a good idea."

"We don't have much choice," said Joe. "The main entrance is our best bet."

The elevator lurched, flinging them all against the sides like they were ping pong balls, before stopping. Silence fell around them. Brie pushed buttons, but nothing happened. The lights went out.

"They shut off the elevators," said Joe.

"We're trapped," muttered Alfric.

Two beams of light filled the small space as Solaris pulled out two finger-sized flashlights. She handed one to Rynah and another to Tom.

"There appears to be a paneling above us. I believe I can open it and we can crawl out through the elevator shaft."

"How far above us is the lobby?" asked Rynah.

"Twenty-five feet," replied Solaris.

"Do it."

Solaris stretched up, placing her feet in the corner to brace herself as she punched the elevator ceiling. Clangs and bangs echoed around them as the paneling shot upward.

Alfric crawled through the opening first and positioned himself next to it to assist the others. Next went Solaris, Tom, Solon, Brie, and Rynah.

"Joe, what are you doing?" asked Samuel as Joe moved toward the opening.

Joe looked at his colleague. He couldn't explain it, but the urgent need to go with them compelled him to follow.

"Samuel, I'm sorry about this, but…"

He punched Samuel in the jaw, knocking him unconscious. Joe hauled himself through the opening. He and Alfric stared at one another for a moment, before he continued upward, with Alfric making up the rear.

Sweat pooled around the base of their necks as their muscles strained to climb upward, their hands and feet clinging to the cables, support beams, and anything else they found. All struggled to reach the lobby doors, except for Solaris, who moved with ease and very little effort.

Alfric's foot slipped on the smooth metal sheeting; his grip tightened as his feet clashed with the sides of the shaft.

"Alfric!" called Brie.

"Do not trouble yourself with me," he said, regaining his composure and continuing upward.

Slow minutes ticked by. Each felt as though they had been there for hours. Solaris stopped them. Bracing herself, she reached up with both hands and pried the doors open. Light spilled into the dark interior, illuminating the beads of sweat that glistened on their skin. Solaris climbed out.

She settled near the opening and pulled out Solon and Tom. Next came Brie and Rynah.

Ping!

A bullet ricocheted off the inside of the elevator shaft as armed FBI agents gathered in the lobby. Solaris returned fire.

"Don't kill any of them," said Joe as he crawled out of the elevator shaft; his once tidy and pressed suit was now covered in dust and wrinkled, something he disliked, but had no time to dwell on.

Frowning, Solaris scanned the area, discovering the best way to deal with their current predicament. Movement caught her eye. More of Stein's men stalked out of the shadows, taking aim at them and the agents.

"Freeze!" yelled one of the agents. "Drop your weapons and put your hands on your heads."

They all hunkered by the opening, awaiting Solaris' move.

Fire extinguishers lay nestled in small enclaves around the lobby and the upper floors, but were not locked behind glass. An idea occurred to Solaris.

"When I tell you to," she said, "run for the doors."

In a flurry of swift and smooth movements, Solaris fired at all of the fire extinguishers, striking each of them. They exploded, spilling their pressurized contents and filling the area with a cloud of frozen gas.

"Now!" shouted Solaris.

They bolted. Each ran for the glass doors, firing at Stein's men, whom had opened fire the moment the fire extinguishers burst. Glass shattered from stray bullets and lasers, showering them with shards that resembled small knives more than glass, and clattered on the once polished floor.

Solon and Tom reached the outdoors first.

"We require transportation," said Solon.

Tom spotted a woman locking her SUV. He rushed over to her and snatched the control from her hands.

"Hey!"

"Sorry," said Tom, "but we really need your car."

He pressed the blue button, unlocking the doors and starting the engine.

"Give me back my keys you jerk!" the woman said as she smacked him with her purse.

A laser blast shattered the store glass window behind her, causing her to scream and run away in fear.

"Come on!" Tom shouted at the others as they left the FBI building. "Get in!"

They all piled into the SUV, though it was a tight fit, and slammed the doors shut as laser fire pummeled the ground around them.

"Go!" said Rynah as she leaned out an open window and returned fire.

Tom slammed the vehicle into gear and sped off, just missing a truck that had tried driving past them. They charged down the street, weaving in and out of traffic to avoid other cars, and away from the FBI building.

"Where should we go?" asked Tom, not familiar with Philadelphia roads.

"Turn left here," said Joe.

Tom did.

"Now hang a right."

Tom obeyed.

"Park over there."

"Why?" asked Brie.

"We need to ditch this car. Whomever is after you knows what it looks like."

Tom parked and they all jumped out. Joe spotted another parked vehicle nearby and motioned them to follow him. He walked over to the car, pulled out a pocket knife, and jimmied the door. Once in the driver's seat, he hotwired the engine, while the others crammed inside, except for Solaris, who ended up in the trunk since she didn't need to breathe oxygen and cramped spaces did not bother her.

"Where are you going?" asked Rynah.

"I know a place. We can hide there for now." Joe put the car in drive and drove away, entering the freeway and driving out of the city of Philadelphia.

Chapter 19
An Ally Best Kept Imprisoned

A lone figure stood in a glass dome on a ship orbiting the Earth as he looked out at the blue planet, with its swirling white blobs that moseyed across beneath him, his eyes focused on another ship that hovered nearby. With the slightest movement of his torso, Fredyr's burgundy suit jacket crackled as the soft light from the planet below reflected off its smooth material and the genuine rubies that served as buttons.

So this was the Thirteenth Sector, he thought to himself, as his warped mind considered all of the monetary possibilities that existed on the planet and how he could exploit them. Stein could have the crystals. Fredyr's ambitions lay on something more tangible.

Since the moment he was ten years of age, he knew that he had been destined for great things, and not the life of poverty that he had been born into. Fredyr remembered how his mother struggled to eke out a living on Cien after his father had abandoned them for adventure on a merchant ship. They had never heard from his father again, but Fredyr did not care—he hoped that the bastard had died

192

on that ship. It wasn't long before his mother started coughing, having contracted the same disease that plagued so many who lived in the poorer regions of the planet. That was the day he had decided that, though he had been born into poverty, he refused to die in it.

So, Fredyr saved enough money to start up his own business. Within a year, he owned four, and within 11 years, he owned Cien and cleaned up the poorer regions so that none lived in the conditions he and his mother had, nor died of the illness that took her life.

As Fredyr observed the planet earth, he saw much of Cien on it, as well as much of his past on it. What it needed was proper management, and he knew that he could do it, while skimming a little profit on the side; after all, Cien needed resources and the insignificant planet below was the perfect provision of such raw materials.

"Scan," he ordered his ship's computer.

The dome above him sprang to life with numbers and colorful images of people, landscapes, cities, and wildlife. Fredyr's sharp eyes took in every detail as his calculating mind contemplated all that he could do with this information. The planet was abundant in wealth that he could use. With over 7.6 billion people, Fredyr knew he could send some to the mining colonies and the sanitation crews on Cien.

Movement caught his attention. Fredyr switched off the computer, allowing the dome to take on its normal transparent appearance, and watched as two shuttles left Stein's main ship and entered the atmosphere. Pondering what Stein could be up to, Fredyr pressed a button on the dome's holographic screen.

"Yes, Mr. Monsooth," said Fredyr's most trusted man as he entered the room.

"I noticed two shuttles going below."

"I have not heard of any such thing."

"I just watched it happen."

The man moved closer to the dome and peered out, noticing

the two vessels as the flames surrounding them dissipated and they dropped below the cloud line.

"It would seem that Stein has plans of his own. I don't believe he liked your last visit to his ship."

"I'm sure he didn't," said Fredyr. "Stein is more evasive than Klanor ever was."

"I can have some men follow the two shuttles," said the man.

"No need," replied Fredyr. "Let Stein acquire the crystals for us. For now, I am more interested in what this planet has to offer."

He snapped his fingers and, once again, the dome turned into a swirling mass of moving images and numbers.

The man stepped closer, his eyes widening at the information before him. "I'd say that this place has much to offer you."

"I knew you would think so," Fredyr smiled. "I want you to start rounding up the resources and preparing them for the outer colonies."

"Yes, Mr. Monsooth," the man said, bowing low, but before he had a chance to leave, Fredyr stopped him, having had a last-minute thought.

"Perhaps we should not ignore Stein's actions," said Fredyr. "I think we should keep a closer eye on him."

"I know just the one to send."

* * *

Obiah kept the visor of his helmet low as he hurried through the snaking corridors of Stein's main ship, keeping his movements mechanical and matching those he passed so as not to attract attention. Merrick had informed him that he had overheard something about a proposed theft from a museum on the planet below. Since most artifacts in the museum are ancient and of little use, Obiah knew that this particular one that Stein sought had to be different. He turned a corner, heading for a more secluded area of the ship, since most personnel had been called elsewhere. Satisfied that he was alone, Obiah clicked onto a console and brought up scans that had been taken of the Earth. He scrolled through them, but did not find what he searched for. Frowning, Obiah knew that he would have to break into the main system in order to learn what Stein was up to. The problem was it might fuel his already paranoid state.

He tapped the holomonitor, bringing up symbol after symbol, until he found what he searched for. Glancing around to make certain no one approached, Obiah read through the memos and the reports, realizing that he needed to get a hold of Rynah right away.

He switched off the holomonitor and left the console, rounding another corner when he ran into one of Stein's men.

"What are you doing here?" demanded the man in an irate tone. "You are supposed to be on the main deck."

"On my way, sir," said Obiah.

"What's your name?"

"Jidders, sir."

The man gave Obiah an unbelieving look, but before he could make any further inquiries, his personal com unit beeped.

"You are wanted in the command center."

"On my way." The man glared at Obiah, wishing he could question him further, but knew that Stein did not like to be kept waiting. "Report to your station. And don't let me catch you down here again."

"Yes, sir." Obiah hurried away, but once he was out of sight of the man, he slipped into a small room and locked the door, pulling out his communicator.

"Jifdar," he whispered.

"Heller here," came Heller's voice a few seconds later.

"I need you to get a message to Rynah. Stein knows where there is another crystal. There are more than six. It is being kept at a place called the Smithsonian National History Museum. It will be transported from there to another location in a matter of days. Stein plans to steal it then. She is going to have to get to it before he does."

"And what has Merrick found out? What are Stein's other plans?"

Obiah frowned. Merrick had been evasive since they boarded Stein's main ship, and Obiah had his misgivings about the man's true reasons for wanting to be aboard. He hid something. Obiah knew he did.

"I haven't heard from him in a while," he replied.

"What do you..."

"I'll contact you when I find out anything further." Obiah said as he clicked off the communications device and pocketed it. Before opening the door, he listened for any stray footsteps and slipped out of the room, jogging through the corridor and to his station to avoid arousing suspicion.

Chapter 20
MOTIVATING FACTORS

The whine of the car's engine careened down the highway as they drove in the thick, gray fog; its very dampness permeated every inch of their already chilled bodies as the heater did not work. The screech of the windshield wipers raked their ears, giving each of them a headache.

"Are you certain your friends know where to meet you?" asked Joe as he looked around.

"Yes," replied Rynah. "They have the coordinates. You should turn off here."

"That is just a field."

"Please, trust me."

Joe cranked the wheel and steered the car off the road into the field next to them, the tires leaving muddied and uneven tracks. He drove with caution, unsure of what they would find.

"There," said Rynah, pointing at a dark shape in the distance as it materialized into a shuttlecraft.

"What the..." breathed Joe, unable to finish his thought.

He parked the car next to the conical shuttle with ridges outlining its windshield. Pale green splotches dotted the hull like tattoos, bringing life to the blackened exterior.

Rynah jumped out of the car.

"Jifdar!"

While she searched around the vessel, Joe parked the vehicle, allowing the others to disembark; all the while, his eyes remained focused on the strange ship before him.

"Jifdar!" Rynah called again.

"You do not need to shout," replied Jifdar as he walked up to her.

Joe stopped cold. The scaly man, though he was unsure if he should call him that, wearing grungy and odorous clothing (the hem was tattered and frayed as threads hung from it), greeted Rynah. Doing his best not to stare, though finding it difficult, Joe stepped behind Rynah, while the others acted as though nothing was out of the ordinary.

"Who's this?" demanded Jifdar, noticing Joe for the first time.

"Agent Harkensen," replied Rynah.

"Call me Joe," Joe held out his hand.

Jifdar stared at it with interest.

"Is there something wrong with your hand?"

"No..." began Joe.

"You're supposed to shake it," said Brie. "It's how we greet one another here."

"Ah, well, then." Jifdar grasped Joe's outstretched hand, crushing it with a viselike grip, before releasing it.

Refusing to demonstrate weakness, Joe pretended that he had felt nothing, even though his hand begged for relief. Once Jifdar let go, leaving a thin layer of film behind, Joe wiped his hand on his pants while remaining polite towards the strange man.

"Where is Klanor?" demanded Rynah.

Jifdar nodded to his left and Rynah stalked off in that direction.

"What are we standing around here for?" demanded Brie, her mind focused on her mother and sister.

"What's your hurry?" asked Jifdar.

"Stein kidnapped Sara and my mother!" replied Brie. "We need to go get them."

"Patience," said Solon, placing a gentle hand on her shoulder.

"Patience won't save them!"

"Neither will rushing off in anger," replied Solon. "Emotions lose many a battle. To save your family, you must calm yourself."

"The boy is right," said Alfric.

"Maybe we should give him the crystal," mumbled Brie. "Perhaps then he'll…"

"You know he won't," said Alfric.

"He's right." Klanor walked out of the brush with Rynah. "I'm sorry about your family, but if you give Stein what he wants, he will kill them and you, and countless others. It's exactly what I would do."

"Of course it is," mocked Jifdar.

Brie folded her arms, shuffling her feet as she tried to hold back her tears; her worried mind dwelled on her mother and sister as terrifying thoughts about what was being done to them rushed her.

"Brie," Solon looked into her eyes, "we've come so far. We cannot give into the whims of a madman—not now."

"But who knows what he is doing to them," Brie whimpered.

"What would your father have you do?" said Alfric.

Brie paused, remembering her father. He had told her stories about evil men and how they hurt the innocent for their own gain, reminding her that such men can never be reasoned with, nor given in to.

"We will save them?"

"I give you my word," said Alfric, "that I'll not return home until your mother and sister are safe."

"We will rescue them," said Rynah.

"Sounds to me like you need something to bargain with," said

Joe. He had work kidnapping cases and was well aware of how ran-
som demands were made, as well as how some kidnappers relished
the grief they caused others. Stein struck him as such a man. "This
Stein thinks that you have something he wants."

"The crystal," said Solaris, "we have the one he failed to acquire
on Sunlil."

"But there must be another reason why he is here," said Joe, not
bothering to ask what Sunlil was. "You have what he wants, and you
were never on this planet until after his arrival, yet he chose to come
here first. Why?"

"It's my fault," said Brie. "Stein interrogated me. I couldn't resist
him. I told him about Earth and a crystal that was found in Central
America. I watched a program about it on TV. It was touring the
world and…" Brie stopped speaking.

Klanor's face scrunched in a mixture of pity and anger. He remembered his interrogations of Brie and the constant memories of
a crystal, but it had never occurred to him that she might have been
thinking about a crystal that was found on her home world.

"That is why he is here. How old is this crystal?"

"No one knows," said Brie. "Archeologists haven't been able to
pinpoint an exact date, but they believe that it is over 5,000 years
old. And though they believe it to be made of quartz, it is unlike
anything found on Earth, especially down in the Yucatan Peninsula."

"Could it be…" Klanor's voice trailed off.

"There are only six crystals," said Rynah. "There isn't any more,
is there?"

Solaris shifted uncomfortably. "What if there is?"

All eyes focused on her. "What are you saying?" breathed Rynah.

"These crystals date back to a time long before recorded history.
What if there are more than just six? Think about it," said Solaris.

"It just seems…" began Rynah.

"Impossible?" interrupted Solaris. "Everything we have done
borders on the impossible."

"But if there is more than one, how come the Lanyran text does not mention it?" asked Tom.

"Maybe the author did not know," said Solon.

"Or did not wish us to know," Alfric mused. "Then again, maybe the storyteller did mention more than six, but someone omitted it from the text."

"But why would someone do that?" asked Brie.

Alfric never answered, though he had his suspicions; his eyes focused on Solaris for a moment as she avoided his gaze.

"It's worth looking into," said Tom.

"So, why do you need me?" asked Joe.

"Well, this ancient myth of theirs mentioned you by name," answered Tom. "Something about you helping us find a missing alien."

Solaris rolled her eyes at Tom's inability to remember the verses with precision. She repeated them.

> To begin, seek a guardian of the law
> who honors justice and its call,
> protecting the great seal
> with olive branches, arrows, and an eagle.

> Honest and true he is
> bearing strange marks: FBI.
> Their importance being the same,
> Joseph Harkensen is his name.

Joe remained silent after learning that an ancient legend from a planet he had never heard of until that day mentioned him by name.

"How is it, a poem dating back to your ancient times knows not only me by name, but where I work as well?"

"I don't know," said Rynah.

Klanor studied the two of them. He had always passed off that portion of the poem as meaningless, as it had no bearing on

Lanyr, or any of the Twelve Sectors. Never did he ever think that he would be standing on a strange and unexplored planet with the very man mentioned.

"We need to get that crystal."

"But it may be nothing," said Jifdar.

"Or, it may be everything," replied Klanor. "Stein interrogated Brie, against my knowledge, and she told him about a crystal, dating back to your ancient era, a crystal no one understands. To someone like me, that would be worth pursuing. I can only assume that Stein would do the same."

"But wouldn't it be a waste of time?" asked Tom.

"There was a missing page in that book," said Klanor. "I hadn't had the time to decipher the ink that had bled to the cover, but Stein might have."

Rynah remembered the missing page of the book, the very last page. She remembered the watermark upon it. She noticed Solaris shift from one foot to the other.

"Solaris, do you know something about this?"

Solaris did not answer.

"Solaris?"

"I vowed to only tell you," replied Solaris.

"Tell me what?" asked Rynah.

"I can't. Marlow said that only you should know."

"Solaris, tell me. We are all in this together, and now is not the time for secrets."

Solaris debated whether she should obey Rynah's request. She decided that part of what she knew she could reveal, but the other must remain with her; the time wasn't right.

"Marlow ripped out the last page of the book."

"What?" both Klanor and Rynah said together.

"He knew that it led to another crystal. Most scholars felt that the last page was nonsense, but Marlow figured it out."

"What did he learn?" demanded Rynah.

"I do not know," said Solaris. "He kept that from me. All he said is that there is another and that the last page was the key. He tore it out so that any who sought the crystals would not learn of the other's existence, and he gave it to me for safekeeping."

Solaris pulled out a yellowed, stained, and tattered page. The edge that had once been part of the book's binding, was jagged. Klanor reached for it, but Solaris jerked her hand back.

"It is for Rynah," she said.

Rynah stretched out her hand and Solaris placed the crumpled, creased, page in it. With great care, she unfolded the parchment; the watermark making its presence known in the weak sunlight. The calligraphy matched that on the other pages.

Six you know of,
but one you do not.
Another there is, pale as a dove,
Time and all its taught.

This one you need to control the others.
Without it, useless they are.
Seek it not, it comes to you like a mother
Small like a pebble, but greater than a star.

It will lead you to its brothers
that you must also recover.
All a part of three's power;
all will witness in the last hour.

Assembled the puzzle must be,

or risk destroying eternity.

Rynah stopped reading. "There seems to be some of it missing."

"Unfortunately, in my haste to save this, the bottom portion ripped free and was destroyed, but I have it memorized." She recited the last lines.

Assembled the puzzle must be
or risk destroying eternity.
The four and one are the key
to saving all that must be.

Only together can they tame the crystals' power
Only together will they stop all from being devoured.

But one must make a choice,
and commit ultimate sacrifice,
wearing the key in amber;
to him the past is the future.

"That doesn't make a lot of sense," said Tom.

"Most ancient writing doesn't," said Joe, "but it seems that it is only meant to speak to one of you."

"Nonsense," scoffed Klanor.

"I don't think so," said Rynah, touching the amber ring she wore under her jacket as she thought about the lines of verse, "but it does speak of another crystal, which means Stein will be searching for it. And what better place to start than a crystal he learned about from one he had kept prisoner?"

"I didn't..." began Brie.

"No one blames you," said Rynah, "but we need to know where that crystal is."

"Last I heard, it was on display in Mexico," said Brie, "but that was six months ago."

"Wait," interrupted Joe, "you aren't all talking about the Yucatan Crystal, are you?"

"Yes," said Brie, "if it is the one discovered in the ruins of a Mayan temple."

"That thing has been touring the world. The archaeologists who discovered it say that there is something about it, something otherworldly. It's just arrived at the Smithsonian's Museum of Natural History. It will be there for the next week."

"Is there a way for Stein to learn of this?" asked Alfric.

"With all of the news coverage, you bet there is," said Joe.

Realizing that Alfric and Solon would not understand modern news coverage, he thought of a better way to put it to them.

"It has been given the pomp and circumstance that any king would receive."

Jifdar's com unit beeped and he answered it.

"Heller, report."

"I just heard from Obiah, captain. He says that Stein knows of the location of the crystal. It's at the smith-saun-e-an..."

"Smithsonian!" blurted out Brie.

"He plans," continued Heller over the com unit, "to steal it when it is being transported to its new location, which will be in seven days."

"Good work," said Jifdar, ending the transmission.

"We need to get it before he does," said Klanor.

"Whoa, wait a minute," said Joe.

"He's right," said Rynah. "We can't let..."

"You're talking about breaking into the national museum!" Joe blurted out.

"Joe..."

"No! I won't allow it. Look, I helped you get out of lockup because—oh hell, I don't even know why!"

"Yes, you do," said Jifdar, who had remained silent through most of their conversation. "You helped them for the same reason that I have not left them here."

Joe pressed his lips together. When Stein called his cell phone and asked to talk to Brie, only to inform her that he had her family, he had decided to help them; that there was more to their story.

"But I have sworn to uphold, protect, and defend the United States and the Constitution, and that includes her treasures."

"I understand your dilemma," said Rynah; having been sworn to protect the crystal on Lanyr, she understood his hesitation, "but Stein will not care. If that crystal is the other mentioned, it will give him what he needs to complete the most powerful weapon known to us. I am asking for your help to protect the people of this planet."

"You say that he will use this crystal to kill countless others?" asked Joe.

"Yes," said Rynah.

Still hating the idea of committing a heist at the Smithsonian, but detesting the thought of innocent people dying because of the whims of a madman, he relented.

"All right. I'll help you on this, but after that, you're on your own."

"Yes!" blurted out Tom. "We're going to steal from the Smithsonian!"

Everyone gave him a piercing stare.

"What?" he said. "You've got to get excited about something."

"Welp," muttered Solaris.

"How are we to break into this Smithsonian?" asked Solon.

"Oh, my lad," said Jifdar, "that is what I am here for. Thievery happens to be my forte."

* * *

Stein marched through the halls of the ship to the elevators. People scurried out of his way, having become aware of his temper and constant foul mood. He pressed the button for the detention center. Within moments, the doors slid open, and Stein stormed out of there. With harsh movements, he punched in the code on the holographic keypad that lit up upon his presence. Another door slid open with a hiss.

He found the cell he wanted. Punching in another code, the door opened, revealing a room with white walls, a white floor, and a single cot. Hunkered on the linoleum, cradling her daughter, was Brie's mother.

"Mrs. Reynolds," sneered Stein, "tell me what your daughter plans to do next."

Sara whimpered as he stepped inside. Her mother clutched her even tighter.

"I have not seen my daughter for the past six months," Rebecca said. "Please, if you know where she is, give her back to me."

"If I knew where she was, I would have had her killed."

Rebecca wept, salty tears coursing down her cheeks, stinging her dry skin.

"Please…"

"Tell me where she is!"

"I don't know!" wailed Brie's mother.

Stein paced the floor, circling the two he held hostage; his boots left hollow clomps with each step.

"Did you know that your precious daughter was once here in this very cell? She was my prisoner. I interrogated her, right here, but, unlike you, she had a bit of fight to her. Do you know that she gave me this?" He pulled down the collar of his jacket, revealing a scar from where Brie had clawed at him with her fingernails.

"What do you want?" demanded Rebecca.

"I want to know how she operates. What makes her tick."

"She is only 16 years old," said Rebecca, her eyes puffy and red. "She would never hurt anyone."

"My dear, you do not know your daughter at all. She has traveled through the Twelve Sectors with a band of vagrants, killing my men."

The woman shook her head as she clung to her youngest daughter.

"Tell me about her!"

"Why are you doing this?"

"I was once like you," said Stein, "a loving parent. I had a wife and child, but they were killed, murdered by some vile creature who craved a source of imminent power. I grieved, but found that grief too difficult to bear, so I decided to be rid of it, yet the moment I did so, a man arrived, giving me a reason to go on—a purpose. He made me promises, promises that he could never keep. Do you know what I learned?"

The woman shook her head, her brown eyes, like Brie's, staring at Stein.

"I learned that there is no justice in this universe. You see, the man who was responsible for murdering my family got away with it, and your daughter seeks the very thing that killed them and is responsible for the death of several of my men. In essence, she is helping the one who is responsible."

"You cannot cling to the past," said Rebecca.

"Don't tell me what to cling to!" raged Stein. "You do not know what it's like to have everything ripped away from you! I watched as they burned alive, screaming for me to save them, but I was powerless. I'll not be helpless again!

"The quest for imminent power killed them. I will find that source of power and show the universe what real suffering is."

Stein seized Sara's shoulder and yanked her from her mother's grasp. The girl cried; her shrieks reverberated off the blank walls, deafening them.

"No!" screamed Rebecca.

"Tell me where she will go! What will your daughter do next!"

"Please!"

"Tell me! Tell me, or watch your other daughter die in front of you. Watch, as I did."

The woman placed her wrist over her quivering lips as tears spilled from her eyes, terror filling her heart.

"Tell me where your daughter will go!"

Summoning an inner calm, while choking back her tears, Brie's mother looked at Stein, resolution within her swollen eyes.

"You are not the only one to lose someone."

Stein loosened his grip on Sara, but not enough to let the girl go.

"I lost my husband, Brie's father, in the war. You say she has turned against you, and killed your men. I know my daughter. She would never harm another, unless provoked. If she is your enemy, then it is an enemy you created."

"All I want is information," said Stein, holding Sara by her hair, "and I will let you go."

"No you won't," said Rebecca.

"I give you my word."

"Go to hell."

Stein and the woman glared at one another for several moments before he released Sara and the girl ran back to her mother's arms, weeping as the woman calmed her.

Stein stormed out of the cell and out of the detention area, fuming over his failure to force information out of Brie's mother. He stopped. Maybe the woman doesn't know where her daughter would go, but he knew Rynah, and where she was, Brie would be there as well—the weak link.

He tapped into the ships communications, summoning the command center.

"Tap into their satellites again. Look for any information about a crystal discovered within the last year and where it might be."

"Stein, sir," said Gaden, walking up to Stein.

"What?" hissed Stein.

"I don't mean to interrupt," Gaden replied, recoiling beneath Stein's wrath, "but there are reports that Fredyr has been sending ships to the planet's surface."

Stein's anger cooled as he pondered what Fredyr was up to. His eyes darted to a man that he thought, for a moment, had seemed

interested in his conversation with Gaden, but Gaden's shifty movements jerked his mind back to Fredyr. He knew that Fredyr was
only a means to an end, and a problem he would be forced to deal
with, but now wasn't the time. Such a man had to be outwitted, not
outgunned.

"I think we need a set of eyes and ears on Fredyr's ship."

"That would be wise," said Gaden, wondering where Stein was
going with this idea.

"Fredyr had said that he wanted constant updates," Stein said,
more to himself. "Gaden, I want you to take a shuttle over to Fredyr's
ship. Inform him about our progress on acquiring the crystals, but
don't tell him everything. Convince him to let you stay aboard as his
guest. I don't care how you do it, but convince him, and then report
back to me about his movements."

"I'm certain that another…"

"You are suited for the job. Now go."

Gaden nodded and stalked away.

Once Gaden had left, Stein strode through the ship—people
bustled out of his way, lest they face his temper—and to his quarters. It was time to study the text once more.

Chapter 21
THEFT AT THE SMITHSONIAN

The drawn curtains of the motel room allowed no light from outside to spill through, as they all hunched before the television, which Tom had hooked up to a laptop, procured for him by the pirates that Jifdar had summoned from his ship. They had spent the last few days going over plans for their heist of the crystal.

"I have downloaded a map of the Smithsonian's Natural History Museum," said Tom. "The crystal is in the same room as the Hope Diamond. In fact, they have temporarily moved the Hope Diamond to another case and placed the crystal in the center. The glass case is actually a polymer plastic that makes it bulletproof and practically impossible to break. It is magnetically sealed, and anyone who breathes on it will trigger the alarm."

"Perfect," said Jifdar.

"Perfect?" asked Rynah.

"I'm a pirate, darling," replied Jifdar. "Thievery is what I do. And the more challenging the security systems, the better the prize."

"Well," said Tom, "if I can direct your attention to the footage

Joe and Rynah shot of the museum." He brought up the video feed, from when Rynah and Joe had surveyed the area—Rynah wore scarves covering her face, which the cold weather had proven useful for—and each had a pin-sized camera attached to their shirts.

"Notice the pattern of the guard," said Joe. "See how he walks to the left, scans the entrance, and then walks back to the right? You can tell he cares about his job, but he's bored too."

"But not this one," said Rynah. "He remains vigilant the entire time. The security guards change shift every eight hours, usually early in the morning, once in afternoon, and then again when they close up for the night. There is only one entrance point to the room with the crystal and at least two guards will be there."

"Now look at this," said Tom, pointing at an area on the map that said "staff only". "This must be where they clean the gems or something."

"The museum will have entire rooms dedicated to their staff. They will have their own elevators and stairwells, which allow them to move exhibits from floor to floor," said Solaris. "The doors going into those rooms are protected by a binary code—so rudimentary—and easily cracked."

"The crystal is to be on display all this week," said Brie, holding out a newspaper with a front page article about the Mayan crystal, "but we need a well-devised plan for acquiring it, without loss of life."

"And there is Stein," said Solon.

"No doubt if we know about it, then he does too," said Joe. "But how are we to disguise all of you?" He motioned at Rynah, Klanor, Jifdar, and his pirates. "You don't exactly blend in."

"We have these." Klanor dumped what looked like a metal ring, turned necklace, on the bed. "They are holo-emitters." He placed one around his neck and switched it on. Within moments, his purple face took on an Asian appearance with a slim mustache. "I fashioned these using images from your internet."

"How do we get inside?" asked Tom, "Not all of us can go in as tourists."

"Janitors," said Brie. "Nobody notices them. I never pay attention to the one at my school."

"You will make an excellent pirate," complimented Jifdar. "My pirates will go in as janitors. We will need to procure ourselves some uniforms, and Helg, here, is excellent at forging IDs. There appears to be back entrances here, no doubt where the staff goes through."

"But the metal detectors will go off with those holo-emitters," said Joe.

"Not if the guards are distracted," said Jifdar.

"There is a wheelchair accessible area here," said Brie. "We could smuggle the rods in through there. Just make them part of the chair. And no one harasses an old lady."

"And what idiot are you going to get to do that?" asked Jifdar.

"I volunteer Jifdar," said Tom.

"What?"

"Perfect," Rynah said, with a stern voice.

"Fine," said Jifdar, "but you, you little whelp, are coming with me." He pointed a sharp-nailed finger at Tom.

"We'll need to knock out their security cameras," said Rynah. "They have them in every corner of the building."

"These," said Solaris, holding up what looked like chocolate kisses. "They are small transmitters, which will hack into the security system and knock out all of the cameras and the metal detectors."

"How?" asked Brie.

"The metals detectors you use run on a radiofrequency. Scribble that frequency and you reset the detectors. But all of the cameras and the detectors are wireless, which means they all must be served by the same router or series of routers. If you corrupt one, you corrupt them all. You will need to place them near the cameras, even on the same wall should do."

"I have it!" Tom jumped up and down. "This is just like *Ocean's Eleven!*"

"What?" asked Klanor.

"It's a movie," said Tom.

"Movie," Solon and Alfric said together, the word unfamiliar to them.

"What is your great plan?" asked Solaris.

"Your pirates will go in as janitors, along with Klanor and Rynah," said Tom. "They are always on duty, cleaning up after little children who spill their sippy cups. You can get the uniforms from the gymnasium down the street. They get their janitorial uniforms from the same company that issues them to the staff at the museum. Then you just need to forge some IDs. Jifdar and I will enter through the handicapped area with the rods hidden in the chair, like Brie suggested. You can get a wheelchair from the local hospital. Medical equipment is always going missing there. In fact, I bet your pirates will know how to get it.

"Brie, Solon, Joe, and Solaris will enter as tourists. You'll have to do it at separate times and act like you don't know each other."

"But what about the fact that we're the most wanted fugitives right now?" asked Brie.

"I will knock out their communications systems," said Solaris. "I can temporarily stop them from receiving alerts or updates from your FBI, Homeland Security, or the NSA."

"How do you know about them?" asked Joe.

"I hacked their security systems," said Solaris, with a note of pride. "I had to know what information they had on us, which isn't much, and their firewalls are prehistoric."

"Anyway," said Tom, continuing," Once Jifdar and I enter, we will go to the restroom, where we will take the rods off the wheelchair and ditch it. Afterward, we'll exit the restroom in different clothing, which we will have smuggled in under the cushion of the wheelchair, and place the rods in the lobby garbage can. One of your pirates will take them and hand them to Rynah. Together, you and Klanor will make your way up to the second floor where the crystal is. We'll need to make certain that one of the stairwells remains free of people. A few of those "under maintenance" signs ought to do.

"Your pirates will pull the transmitters from their shirts and place them accordingly near the cameras, after which Solaris will trigger them, knocking out their communications."

"We'll need a distraction," said Rynah. "People hanging too close to security cameras attract attention."

"Not if a teenage girl screams bloody murder," replied Tom.

"Leave it to me," said Brie.

"Once that's done," said Tom, "The rest of us will migrate up to the second floor to the room with the crystal. There will be plenty of people there, so we'll need a way to clear them out."

"A raging fire clears many a field," said Solon.

"Perfect!" shouted Tom. "The fire alarm. One of you will need to set off the fire alarm."

"Leave that to me," said Klanor. "According to these plans, there is a sprinkler system. A lighted match should do nicely."

"Then there is you." Tom pointed at Alfric. "I don't know how to explain you."

"Got it covered," Brie tossed a brochure about a Renaissance fair at him. "There is a Renaissance fair at the National Mall the day after tomorrow. Alfric already looks the part, but to get into the museum, you'll have to leave your sword behind."

"It goes where I go," growled the Viking.

"You can't take it in there," said Joe. "The metal detectors will alert the guards and you'll get arrested."

Alfric gripped his sword even tighter.

"I'll get it in there," said Jifdar.

"How?" demanded Joe. "That sword is too large…"

"Smuggling is another trait of being a pirate. You'll have your sword."

"Then how do we get out?" asked Brie.

"Simple," said Tom. "There is a staff entrance door here in the gem room, where the crystal will be. Solaris will take the crystal, go through that staff room—she can break the key code—and leave by the personnel exit. The rest of us will leave through the fire exits. We'll have to go separately or in pairs. If we go all together, it will attract too much attention."

"A sound plan," said Jifdar. "It just might work. Son, you should join my crew. I could use a criminal mind like yours."

Rynah mulled over Tom's plan as she studied the video footage and floor plans. "It will have to do. We have two days to get what we need."

"Don't worry," said Jifdar. "My men are good at what they do."

"Let's hope so," said Rynah, "and let's hope that Stein doesn't learn what we're up to."

* * *

Rynah, Klanor, and four of Jifdar's pirates hurried down the wide walk to the rear entrance of the Smithsonian's Natural History Museum that was used by the staff. Their discolored uniforms, complete with stains, smears, and an odor that would make anyone cringe, kept others at a distance. Rynah touched the holo-emitter around her neck, hoping that it worked. Two people with purple skin, and the appearances of the pirates, would get them stopped in no time.

"Badge?" said the guard at the entrance.

Klanor flashed his badge. Rynah did the same.

"Where do you think you're going?" demanded the guard when Klanor tried to walk past the metal detector. "You know the rules. You must put your utility belt through the x-ray."

He unbuckled his belt and put it on the conveyer belt, sweat beading on his brow. If the woman watching the screen had paid close attention, she would have noticed that there were a few questionable items in it.

A commotion rose up around them as a haggard man staggered up to the security guard, waving a half empty bottle of whiskey. His clothing reeked of rotted fruit and curled milk, and threads hung from the edges of the frayed coat, swinging with the man's erratic movements.

Rynah smiled. Right on cue, Jifdar showed up, rather enjoying his part of a drunken bum.

"Now, you let me through!" he raged, sloshing the amber liquid in the bottle.

"Sir," replied the security guard, "sir, I have to ask you to leave."

"Don't you put your hands on me!"

"Sir," continued the guard. The other two at the door moved towards Jifdar, while the woman at the computer monitor paid more attention to him than the screen.

Rynah and the other pirates placed their utility belts through the x-ray machine before walking through the metal detector. No one stopped them. No one questioned them.

"I said get your grubby hands off of me you *bresgyra!*" raged Jifdar, using an insult common among pirates.

"Sir, I need you to calm down."

Jifdar watched as the last of his men went through the detector, picked up his belt, and nodded his head.

"I'll go when I'm ready!"

"Sir," continued the guard, "if you do not leave, I will be forced to call the police."

"The police? The police? Well, since you put it that way, I'll be going home now."

"Yes, that would be a good idea." The guards steered him away from the entrance.

Jifdar wobbled down the steps, missing one or two, and disappeared behind the corner.

Once out of sight of the guards, he tore off his coat and clothing, just as Tom walked up, pushing a wheelchair, and shoved a package in the pirate's hands. Jifdar opened it.

"I'm not wearing this."

"You need to in order to look convincing," said Tom.

"It's bad enough that I have to look like a woman, but now you want me to wear this?" He pulled out a frilly dress, with a lacy trim, that looked like it belonged in a museum—a bit ironic since they were at a museum.

"We don't have much time," said Tom.

Jifdar huffed as he put on the dress, warning Tom about making fun of him, and sat in the wheelchair. With the press of a button on the holo-emitter around his neck, his face changed from a deranged old man with a scraggily beard, to an elderly woman who looked as though she could be Tom's grandmother.

Tom steered the wheelchair to the handicap accessible entrance. Another set of security guards stood there, waving a man with a charcoal-gray beard and a cane through.

"Now remember, you're my old, hard of hearing, grandmother."

"Eh?" mocked Jifdar.

"Good afternoon, sir," said the security guard.

"Afternoon," replied Tom as he wheeled Jifdar up the ramp.

"Just take your grandmother over there. We have to inspect the bag and chair. Regulations."

Tom feigned impertinence, but did as directed. The guard looked through the handbag before giving it back to Jifdar.

"I need to inspect the chair, can she…"

"She can't walk," said Tom. "She hasn't been able to for the last two years. Look, she really wants to see that exhibit and I promised I would take her. This is the only outing she's going to get from the nursing home this week."

"Oh, he is handsome," said Jifdar in his best old lady voice. "If I were 60 years younger, I'd marry you."

"Don't overdo it," whispered Tom in Jifdar's ear. "Sorry," he said to the guard, "she's a bit of a flirt."

A sympathetic look crossed the guard's face, and he said, "My grandmother was too." The guard did a cursory look at the wheelchair and waved them onward.

"Thank you," said Tom as he pushed Jifdar through the entrance and to the main lobby. He spotted the restroom and headed straight for it. After making certain no one was in there, Tom pushed the wheelchair in and locked the door.

Jifdar jumped from the chair and tore off the dress.

"If you ever speak a word of this…"

"I know," said Tom, "you'll have my head."

They took apart the chair, pulling the specialized rods out and hiding them under Tom's coat, while Jifdar took Alfric's sword, which he had hidden on the underside of the wheelchair, and wrapped it in a coat, carrying it under his arm. Before anyone had time to notice that the door was locked, they left.

As Tom passed a garbage bin in the center of the lobby, he slipped the rods into it, which was immediately picked up by Rynah. At the same instant, Jifdar approached Klanor and slipped him the sword. Klanor took it and hurried to a trashcan next to the restrooms, slipping it behind the trashcan before walking off, hoping that no one noticed his movements.

Brie, Solon, Joe, and Alfric all loitered on the main steps of the museum's entrance. Laughing children ran past, waving their toys, despite their mother's attempt to get them to slow down. In the National Mall before them were tents, tables, booths, and people dressed as though they belonged in King Arthur's court, instead of there in modern day Washington, D.C. Joe nodded at Alfric.

Alfric walked erect into the museum. The scrawny guard took one look at him and almost jumped out of his skin. "I need you to put your coa—cloak through there," he said, pointing at the x-ray machine. Alfric undid the gold buckle of his fur cloak and placed it on the conveyer belt. Allowing himself to be treated like an animal, he walked through the metal detector when told to do so.

"You're part of that Renaissance fair, right?" asked the security guard; his voice had a slight quiver, which Alfric detected.

"Yes," he said, remembering Brie's instructions.

"What role do you play?"

The question confused Alfric as he thought the man had asked who he actually was.

"I am a king. I am king of the northern Viking clan far in..."

A sharp whistle from Joe stopped Alfric and pulled him back to the matter at hand.

"I am a king," he said.

"Oh," replied the guard. "Enjoy your stay."

Alfric snatched his cloak and looked for the restroom sign—Brie had shown him a picture of it earlier—and walked over, his long strides crossing the lobby in seconds. He found the garbage bin exactly where she told him it was. Feeling behind it, and unconcerned about the discarded gum stuck on the back, he found his most prized possession. Alfric strapped it around his waist and positioned his cloak so that none would see it. A janitor—one of Jifdar's men—bumped into him and pointed him up the stairs. Alfric obeyed.

Back at the entrance, Solon, Joe, and Brie came through at separate intervals. Brie joined a school group and blended in quite well with the other teenagers. A woman stood behind them with long black hair and flawless ebony skin. No one had ever seen her before—nor would they again, because it was Solaris in disguise—but the male security guards could not keep their eyes off her, thus allowing the others to enter without recourse.

They all wandered to different areas of the museum's main floor, except for Solaris, who headed straight to the second level. Joe's eyes watched as janitors placed themselves near cameras. He caught Brie's eye and nodded.

Brie walked up to a man at random—hating what she was about to do, but knowing it was necessary—bumped into him, and released a bloodcurdling scream. The casual conversation and movements of tourists stopped. All eyes focused on Brie.

"Get your hands off me!" she yelled.

"What?" said the man, confused.

"You pervert!" continued Brie.

"What are you talking about?" said the man.

"Asking me to model for you and then placing your hands on me," Brie said.

"Sicko!" yelled a woman in the crowd. Mummers voiced the same opinion.

Security guards pounced upon them, abandoning their posts, and not paying any attention as the janitors placed button-sized EMF emitters on the walls the cameras were attached to; the others ran up to the second floor.

"Sir, you'll have to come with us," said a guard to the man.

"I don't know what she's talking about!" He jerked away from the guards' outstretched hands.

"Sir, you need to come with us."

"I'm not going anywhere!" yelled the man.

While the man argued with the security guards, Brie wormed her way to the back of the crowd and darted up the stairs to the second floor, unnoticed as all eyes remained upon the man and the security guards.

Joe grabbed her and ushered her into the gem room where the crystal rested in its case in the very center. People moseyed about, feigning mild interest in the other treasures (rubies, emerald necklaces worn by royalty, sapphires) while their eyes darted back to the crystal. Children from a school group surrounded the casing. Camera flashes filled the room as people took snapshots to commemorate the moment they stood with this mysterious relic from the ancient world.

Joe took out a packet of ketchup he had smuggled in his pocket. While the security guards remained distracted by the mass of on-lookers, he squirted the red contents all over the floor and smeared it with his shoe before walking towards a guard.

"Excuse me," he said, "there is something on the floor."

The guard looked at it with an irate expression on his face.

"Get someone up here to clean the floor. Someone spilled some juice or something," he said into his radio before turning to Joe. "Thank you."

"My pleasure." Joe walked off and nudged Brie to a corner. He spotted Rynah, whose holo-emitter made her look like a man in his late 50s, as she rolled a yellow mop bucket into the room. She placed the "caution wet floor" signs around as she cleaned up the ketchup. They nodded at one another and Rynah pushed her bucket out of the room.

Brie spotted Tom and Solon on opposite ends of the chamber, pretending to not know one another.

"Now what?" she asked Joe.

"One… two… three," said Joe.

The cameras fizzled out as Rynah, Klanor, and the other pirates activated the EMF emitters they had strategically placed around the first floor and the gem room.

Blaring alarms screeched and filled the entire museum as the fire alarm—which Klanor had pulled on the main floor—went off. Red lights circled the room, alerting all of the tourists that danger approached and they must exist the building. Despite the groans of disappointment, people filed out of the room, taking the stairwell to the main lobby, while Brie, Tom, Solon, Rynah, and Joe remained behind.

Once the room had cleared, Jifdar, his pirates, Solaris, who changed back to her preferred appearance, Klanor, and Alfric arrived.

Rynah snatched the rods she had hidden in her mop bucket, having ripped off her holo-emitter, and placed them around the glass casing.

"We only have five minutes until the fire department arrives," said Joe.

"Understood," Rynah replied.

"Careful," said Solaris, "there are laser sensors all around it."

Jifdar took one of the rods and helped Rynah attach them to the glass casing, connecting the ends until they circled it. She pressed the pin-sized button. A high pitched humming filled the air.

"Stand back," said Rynah.

They backed away, watching as the silver rods glowed, turning yellow and shooting out a series of sparks as the laser sensors were disabled. The glass casing slanted. Brie leaned a little closer and watched as the glass melted around the rods before falling away. Rynah rushed to the crystal, disconnecting the rods and handing them to Jifdar.

Klanor picked up the crystal, to which Rynah glared at him, and placed it in a cloth bag, before handing it to her. She took it, still debating his motives, and gave it to Solaris.

"We'll meet you in the subway," she said, as they had agreed that would be the best place to escape to.

Sirens sounded outside.

"Time to go," said Joe.

"Tom," said Rynah, "go with Solaris. The rest of us will leave through the emergency exits on the sides of the building."

Solaris and Tom disappeared through the staff door, for which she had already deciphered the key code.

Rynah motioned for them to leave. The pirates left first, their pockets bulging from the jewels that they had placed in them—they were pirates, after all—and their boots clomping on the floor as they hurried to the stairs. As Rynah neared the top of one of the main stairwells, she stopped, glancing back over the railing of the walkway in the rotunda. Something wasn't right; her security training alerted her to danger. She heard it—the high pitched squeal, of a laser rifle before it goes off.

"Get down!"

They all ducked just as a laser blast crashed into the railing, disintegrating it and leaving scorch marks. They each scrambled behind the columns of the balcony that circled the second floor in the rotunda area. More laser blasts slammed into the walls and the floor around them. Rynah peeked around a column through the stone railing. She counted five, but knew there were more.

"It appears that we have company," said Joe.

Rynah didn't say anything. She spotted the enclosed stairwell they had been heading for, knowing that Stein's men would have already blocked it. She pulled out her laser weapon. Another laser blast singed the railing beside her.

She peeked through it. Through the main doors was the shape of a man walking towards them, unconcerned about the fire trucks and police cars outside, and Rynah knew he was Stein. He strode over to the elephant in the rotunda area, motioning for his men to stop.

"I know you are up there," he said. "Give me the crystal and I promise I will let you go."

A security guard rushed him. Stein pulled out his weapon and fired.

"I'll not wait all day for your answer," he said.

Rynah cursed.

"How'd he find us?" asked Brie.

"He didn't have to," said Rynah. "He knew we would go for the crystal. He was just waiting for us to make a move."

"Moves and countermoves," said Klanor. "Stein always excelled at it."

"Freeze!"

They all looked over the railing.

Six police officers stood in the doorway of the main entrance, pointing their weapons at Stein and his men.

"Drop your weapons, and put your hands on your head!" said an officer.

Stein sneered at them. "Must we do this, gentlemen?"

"I said drop your weapons!"

"As you wish," said Stein.

More of his men appeared from the shadows, surrounding the officers. They fired at the police, killing all of them, before turning and firing upon the tourists and firemen outside.

"I tire of this," said Stein. "Bring me the crystal. Kill them if you have to."

Rynah watched, horrified by Stein's cold measures.

"We need to split up. Brie, you, Alfric, and Joe take the other stairwell down. The rest of you with me."

Brie snatched a laser pistol from one of the pirates. "I need this." She ran off to the Korea Gallery where the other stairwell was, with Joe and Alfric behind.

"We need to get to the main floor," said Rynah, heading for the other enclosed stairwell. "Jifdar, I need your pirates to provide a distraction."

"I'm on it!" Jifdar led his pirates to protected areas of the second floor, overlooking the rotunda. Upon his command, the opened a hailstorm of laser fire upon Stein and his men.

Tom and Solaris had been hurrying down the stairs to the staff entrance, when she stopped.

"What is it?" asked Tom.

"They are here," said Solaris.

"Who?" asked Tom.

"Stein. Do you not hear the laser fire?"

Tom strained his ears, and as he stood in silence, he heard what Solaris had heard.

"I'm going back," said Solaris.

"No, wait," said Tom. "Remember the plan and what Rynah had said. We need to get to the subway. We can't take the crystal in there."

Solaris started up the steps, but Tom stopped her.

"Solaris, what is going on?"

Solaris said nothing as she ran down the steps, with Tom in tow. Their pounding feet echoed around them until they reached the door that led out to a small corridor. They burst into the hallway when...

"Stop! Hands up!"

Two police officers had entered through the staff entrance.

Tom and Solaris both raised their hands.

"Drop it!"

"I can't," said Tom.

"Drop it!" ordered the officer.

"I can't." Tom clutched the bag with the crystal.

While the officers remained focused on the bag in Tom's grip, Solaris knocked the guns out of their hands, sweeping their feet out from under them and knocking them to the ground. She and Tom shoved them into the stairwell and sealed the door.

They ran outside. Another officer stood guard. Tom smashed the crystal into the police officer's face, rendering him unconscious. Both Solaris and Tom raced down the sidewalk and stopped. A mass of police cars lined the outside of the main entrance to the museum, with officers positioning themselves behind their cars, as the fire trucks pulled in, their sirens deafening any nearby.

"Take the crystal and go to the metro," said Solaris.

"Where are you going?" asked Tom.

"To keep a promise."

Solaris ran back to one of the unconscious officers and took his badge and handgun. Using the nanotechnology infused with her skin, she changed her appearance so she would blend in. Before Tom could stop her, she walked out into the National Mall and approached the police cars. No one paid any attention to her. Raising the weapon, Solaris aimed at the gas tank of one car and fired. It exploded. She aimed at another and fired. It too burst into roiling flames.

She turned just in time to see Tom strike one of Stein's men—who had snuck up from behind—in the head with the crystal.

"You didn't really think I would leave you," he said.

"Let's go," said Solaris, annoyed that he had disobeyed her.

Rynah and Klanor rushed down the steps. Laser fire raced towards them from the bottom. Darting behind a corner, she fired back. She pressed against the wall as more laser fire riddled it with holes and scorch marks.

Klanor motioned for her to wait. Pulling out an object from his pocket, he tossed it down the stairs; it clacked as it bounced from one step to the next before rolling to a halt. The man at the bottom moved towards it. Rynah seized her chance. She jumped away from the wall and fired, striking the man in the chest.

Together, she and Klanor rushed down the stairs to the bottom, stopping just as they reached the archway that led into the rotunda. More laser fire attacked them. Klanor fired back. He noticed one of Stein's men standing underneath a security camera. Klanor fired two shots, separating the camera from its hold on the wall and allowing it to crash on top of the man's head.

Rynah darted for the escalators, which had been shut off when the fire alarm was pulled, but before she reached it, Klanor was upon her, knocking her to the floor as he aimed and fired at two men she hadn't seen. They stared at one another a moment, before he helped her to her feet.

The clicks of weapons stopped them. They had been surrounded by Stein's men.

"This is getting tiresome," said Stein as he approached them.

"Stein," said Klanor, "why?"

"Why did I betray you? Why did you betray me?"

"I never…"

"You promised you could bring her back," spat Stein, "but that was a lie. Nothing can bring back the dead. I did your dirty work for far too long."

"Stein," said Klanor.

"The crystals and their power are mine."

"You're insane," said Rynah.

"The crystal," said Stein.

"We don't have it," said Klanor.

"It won't bring them back," said Rynah.

"I no longer care about that," said Stein. "I died when the Brestef region was destroyed."

"Brestef?" Rynah's eyes widened as she remembered one of her grandfather's recordings and what he had told her about the day it was obliterated.

Stein noticed her reaction. "What do you know? What do you know!"

"Nothing," said Rynah.

"Tell me!"

"My grandfather," said Rynah, "he had something to do with the devastation at Brestef. I didn't know until…"

"He did it?" said Stein, rage filling his voice. "Your grandfather was responsible?"

"He…"

"Your grandfather murdered my wife and child!" Stein raised his laser weapon at Rynah, fury written on his face, fueling his movements.

Klanor tackled Stein, knocking Rynah out of the way. Stein countered, punching Klanor in the stomach before clonking him over the head with the butt of his weapon, and Klanor fell to the floor next to Rynah. Both looked up at Stein as he aimed his laser pistol at them.

"Love," spat Stein, "you never will let her die, will you?" He turned to Rynah, who stared in horror at the malice within him.

"Before you die, I want you to know that I will destroy this planet and everyone on it. Since you love it so much, take the knowledge that you failed to save it, just like you failed to save Lanyr, to your grave."

A laser shot grazed Stein's cheek, forcing him to duck out of the way. Just around the corner, leading to the ocean exhibit, was Brie, weapon raised. She fired again. Joe lunged out of the room, heading for Rynah and Klanor, while Brie fired more laser blasts at Stein's men.

Stein sprang for Rynah, any ounce of reason gone from his mind, but Klanor snatched Stein's arm and punched him in the face. The two wrestled on the ground as Rynah jumped to her feet and tackled another of Stein's men.

A blur of fur raced from the ocean exhibit to where she was, as Alfric raised his sword, bringing it down upon another who crept up from behind. He whirled and caught a fourth man in the leg. He noticed Stein on top of Klanor, pinning him to the floor. A blade appeared. Alfric ran over to them, seized Stein, and threw him off Klanor. He readied his sword, prepared to strike, but laser fire pummeled the floor near him, forcing him to duck behind a wall.

Jifdar appeared from nowhere, tackling one of Stein's number. He bashed the man's face into the floor, stripped him of his weapon, and hunkered next to Rynah.

Cornered, Rynah and the others fired at Stein and his men, neither side making any headway.

"Bring her in," Stein said into his communications device. "Brie," he called, a controlled calmness to his voice.

Brie looked at Stein as one of his men brought in a woman and handed her to him; he gripped her arm, bruising it, and yanked her close.

"Mom?" said Brie.

The woman's frightened eyes looked at Brie.

"If you refuse to be reasonable," said Stein, "then perhaps this will persuade you."

Brie and her mother locked eyes. She dropped her weapon.

"Mom!"

"Give me the crystal, or I will kill her right here," said Stein, pointing his laser pistol at Rebecca Reynolds's head.

"Mom!" Brie bolted for her mother, but Joe's strong arm stopped her, yanking her back behind the wall.

Rynah spotted the escalator. "We need to go."

"Give me the crystal!" Stein kicked the woman, forcing her to her knees, her tangled hair covering half her face.

"Brie," said her mother.

"Mom! Let me go!" Brie struggled in Joe's grasp, but his grip remained firm, knowing what would happen if he released her.

"We don't have the crystal," said Klanor.

"So be it," answered Stein. "As you stole one I loved, I will take one that you love."

At that moment, two police cars outside exploded, sending shards of metal everywhere, just as Jifdar's pirates opened fire. Stein forgot about Brie's mother and rushed out to see what had happened in the National Mall. Flames engulfed the police vehicles, as officers opened fire upon him.

Faced with an army outside, Stein had to make a choice.

"Kill them all," he ordered, pointing at the police. Bullets mixed with laser fire filled the once pristine area of the National Mall, destroying tents and booths from the Renaissance fair. People shrieked as they ran for cover and mothers huddled over their children in an effort to protect them.

Back inside the museum, Rynah ordered them to leave. They all hurried down the escalator—Alfric carried Brie as she screamed for her mother—to the ground floor. Taking the rear, Klanor fired two shots at the ceiling above the escalators, sealing them off.

Their feet clopped on the floor as they raced to the exit. Once outside, they ran down the walk to the metro entrance. Laser fire pursued them, as some of Stein's men had been stationed outside, but Jifdar, his pirates, and Klanor fired back.

"This way," said Joe, leading them to the metro entrance.

They raced down the concrete steps to the underground tunnels where the trains were. Tom and Solaris waited for them, having only just arrived themselves. Jumping over the gate, which demanded a fare ticket for entrance, they ran through the tunnels, shoving people out of their way.

More laser fire pursued them.

"There!" shouted Joe, pointing at a train that had just arrived and whose doors were open.

They hurried to it, ignoring the people who chased them and the shouts and screams of those around them. Each jumped inside the train, cramming inside its narrow interior that burst from the passengers already on board. The doors closed. As the train began to move, two of Stein's men banged on the doors and Rynah watched them disappear as the train picked up speed.

They got off at the next stop, switching over to the Red Line and taking it out to Shady Grove, well away from the D.C. area.

"Jifdar," said Rynah, when they had reached a place of safety, "I need you to go back to your ship. Keep an eye on the skies for me."

"Will do," Jifdar said with a slight bow. "I must say that helping you steal something has been the highlight of my day." He waved his hand at his pirates and they left.

"We need to leave," said Rynah. "Is there any place where we can rest for the night and lay low?"

"I know of a place," said Joe.

"Take us to it." Rynah glanced at Brie, who had slumped on a bench and remained quiet, oblivious to everything around her. She placed a gentle hand on the girl's shoulders before walking away.

Chapter 22
In Hiding

An orange globe decorated the inside of the ramshackle barn, accentuating the gutters as they hung from the dilapidated roof, which was riddled with holes from a storm six years ago. The once vibrant, red paint had faded to a dull brown, with flecks of graying white paint chips peeling away, gathering on the ground. The doors had fallen off their hinges and any tools that had been stored there had long since been carted away.

Joe had led them to the abandoned barn, which now lay on a repossessed farm, knowing that, for the moment, they could seek shelter there. All gathered near the fire, except for Brie and Klanor, who both had secluded themselves—on opposite ends of the building.

"We should leave in the morning," said Rynah.

"No," replied Joe.

"We can't stay here."

"We can't leave either. We just stole something from one of the most well-guarded institutions in this country. Right now, our faces will be all over the news, and the police will be on heightened alert.

We will be safe here for the next two days and it will give us time to think of our next course of action. By then, things will have calmed down some, though we will still be America's most wanted."

"What does that mean?" asked Solon, having never heard the expression.

"It means," said Alfric, understanding what Joe meant, "that they will hunt us down until they place our heads upon pikes as a warning to others."

"Though I was thinking more of being put in prison," said Joe, "yes, they will never stop hunting us."

"That is the price we will have to pay," said Rynah. She glanced at Brie, who stood in the doorway, watching them, and then at Klanor, whose attention remained focused in the distance, his face unreadable.

Joe watched her gaze, uneasiness filling him.

"What is the deal between the two of you?" he asked Rynah, pulling her aside and pointing at Klanor.

"I'm not sure…"

"Don't lie to me," said Joe. From the moment they started planning the Smithsonian heist, Joe had noticed a certain amount of tension between Klanor and the others, but the interaction between Rynah and Klanor was different.

Rynah remained silent; she detested talking about her personal life, and the history between her and Klanor.

"Look," said Joe, "I not only broke a multitude of federal laws by helping you all, but have committed treason as well. My life has been turned upside down ever since you asked for me in that interrogation room. You owe me the truth."

Rynah sighed, taking a quick sweep of the room and its occupants.

"We never should have involved you."

"It's a little late for that."

"I told you that my planet was destroyed, but what I didn't tell you was that Klanor was the one who did it."

"What?"

Rynah hushed him before his voice rose any higher.

"It's a long story."

"So give me the short version."

Rynah seized Joe's arm and pulled him further away from the fire and the others. "For at least 1,500 years, my planet had used a crystal to keep the magnetic fields intact. None of the scientists knew where it had come from or how it held the magnetic fields together, only that it did. There had always been rumors that it was one of the fabled six."

"Fabled six?"

"There is an ancient myth on my world that talks about six crystals with the ability to create a monstrous weapon that can destroy whole planets and the like. Most people pass the entire tale off as the imagination of those who had nothing better to do than tell stories as a way to explain their world, but some believed in their veracity. Klanor was the latter.

"I had worked in the very lab where the crystal was kept. I was there the day Klanor stole it."

"And this Stein?"

"He was Klanor's second in command, but when we had gotten trapped on Sunlil, Stein betrayed him and left him to die with us."

"There is more," prompted Joe.

"Klanor and I had been engaged. I never knew..."

Joe stopped her. "I thought so."

"How did you know?"

"It wasn't difficult. The way he looks at you and the way you look at him. What I don't understand is why he is still alive. Most in your situation would have killed him by now."

"The Great Ancients know that I wanted to, and Alfric almost did, but there is something different about Klanor now. He seems withdrawn, broken almost. And he has helped us so far in trying to stop Stein."

"And so you trust him?"

"No, not completely, but something tells me to give him a chance."

"I hope you know what you are doing," said Joe.

Rynah didn't answer. She hoped the same, while thinking of what to do next all evening. The poem that had led them to Joe was vague, but she refused to convey uncertainty; only Solaris knew what thoughts filled her mind.

"We need to find Stein, now," said Brie, having left her secluded corner; her sudden appearance surprised them.

"Brie, that would be unwise," said Rynah.

"Unwise? He has my mother and my sister! He might have killed them by now!"

"I don't think so," said Rynah.

"What makes you so certain?" demanded Brie. "You all saw what he did today."

"A hostage is of no value if he is dead," said Alfric, trying to soothe Brie's fears. For a moment, she thought she noticed his eyes flicker to where Solaris stood silent in the barn, but as Brie's mind dwelled on her mother and Sara, she paid little attention to it.

"He's right," said Joe. "I have worked on kidnapping cases. If this Stein wanted your mother and sister dead, he would have killed them the moment he took them from your home. The fact that he used her to convince you to give him the crystal means that he needs them."

"And that is supposed to make me feel better?" demanded Brie.

"It should," said Joe. "He wants that crystal. The only way he can achieve that, for the moment, is by using them to manipulate you into giving it to him."

"They are all right," said Klanor, leaving his isolated area in one of the stalls. "We have what he wants. He will use your family to control you if you let him."

"And if I refuse?" said Brie.

No one answered. Only knowing eyes stared back at her, telling Brie what she already knew.

"That's what I thought," said Brie.

She stalked off, leaving them all as she went outside and slumped to the ground, sitting on the damp grass, unbothered that it soaked through her pants. She looked up at the black sky and its pinpricks of light decorating it, since the moon had failed to make an appearance, while a chill breeze played with the tendrils of hair that escaped her ponytail. Guilt plagued her, tormented her, with its taunts.

"Mind if I join you?" said Rynah as she sat next to Brie.

"Will it matter if I do?"

Rynah smiled. "You've changed."

"Not so much."

"When you first arrived on Solaris, I thought you were a *Driol*. A creature who squeals at the least bit of noise and scurries away at the first sight of danger."

"You called me useless on numerous occasions," said Brie.

"So I did," replied Rynah. "I was wrong. You were never useless. We never would have gotten this far without you."

"It's my fault," said Brie, tears dotting her cheeks. "It's my fault that Stein came here in the first place. It's my fault that he kidnapped my family."

"What do you mean?"

"When Klanor held me captive, he was not the only one to interrogate me. Stein did also. He injected me with something, and I couldn't resist his questions. I couldn't stop myself from answering. I tried, but…"

Rynah just listened, allowing Brie to release her inner torment.

"I told him about this place, this planet. I told him about the crystal that was discovered in the Yucatan Peninsula. I told him about Sara, and my mother. Because of me, not only are they in danger, but everyone on the Earth is as well. It's all my fault!"

As Rynah listened to Brie, unaware that Solaris also listened from the shadows, she felt as though she looked into a mirror.

"You can't blame yourself."

"But it's my fault."

"No, it's not." Rynah looked Brie in the eyes. "You were being held prisoner and subject to things that even the most hardened of men would not be able to withstand."

"But I should have done..."

"Nothing," Rynah cut her off. "Do not waste your time with what you should have done. Brie, there are people in the universe whose only goal is to cause harm, and they will use anyone to accomplish those means. You are not the only one to make mistakes."

"What do you mean?"

"I am responsible for Lanyr. I worked in the Geothermic Lab and was responsible for guarding the crystal, but I told my secrets to one I loved. I didn't mean too, but I gave him information without realizing it. It was I who told him about the systems check that was to take place that day. He manipulated me, used me, and I inadvertently told him what he wanted to know."

"But..."

"What matters is what you do now," said Rynah. "We will get your mother, and Sara, back. And I promise you, that I will not let your planet suffer the same fate as mine. But what you need to decide is what you will do now. Will you give in to Stein's demands or finish what you started the day Solaris called you?"

"You mean kidnapped me?" joked Brie.

"Well," said Rynah, "I was trying to put it nicely. The question for you now is what are you planning to do, to save them? And will you let us help you?"

Brie didn't answer, and she didn't have to. Rynah saw the answer on her face. She rose to her feet and clasped Brie's shoulder to comfort her, unaware that in a different set of shadows, Klanor watched them. Mixed emotions filled his face as he scrutinized them, remembering how he was the one responsible for all of this.

He turned and found Alfric right behind him.

"Always watching me?"

"You may have earned their trust, but you have not earned mine," said the Viking.

"Fair enough."

Alfric gripped Klanor's shoulder, bruising him. "If you betray them again, I'll…"

"Kill me?"

"No,"—Alfric closed the distance between them until Klanor smelled his stale breath—"but you will beg me to."

"I've no doubt of that." Klanor moseyed back into the barn, seeking a place to sleep.

Alfric hadn't been the only one keeping an eye on Klanor that night. Solaris had kept close watch on him too, but the more she kept her vigilance of him, the more she started to see what Brie had seen, remorse. A paint chip dotted her arm, distracting her. Curious, as she had never felt paint before, Solaris picked it up with the tips of her fingers and held it in the faint light, admiring its ragged and oblong shape. She scanned the rest of the barn's exterior and wondered why the owner did not repaint it, deciding instead to allow the structure to fade and decay.

A small smile crept across her face as she thought about Marlow and how he had purchased a decommissioned, military space vessel at an auction. She had been forthcoming in her opinion and told him that he had made a mistake in buying that rusty bucket of bolts that would be better served at the bottom of a trash heap, but Marlow had disagreed.

"Everything has a purpose," he had told her. "And some things that have been cast aside, can be made whole again."

That was the day that she had first been placed inside the ship, and the same day she had been reminded of Marlow's mortality.

Solaris allowed the memory to wash over her and consume her thoughts for the moment as she stood beneath the blanket of stars, remembering when she had first been uploaded into the archaic ship that had become her body for a number of years. She knew that Marlow had spent a lot of time tinkering with the dilapidated spacecraft, replacing parts and installing new aspects to it, but she had never imagined that she would become the ship itself.

"Ready?" Marlow had asked her.

"I think so," Solaris had responded, with a little bit of trepidation at being transferred from the static computer in Marlow's lab to a retired military vessel.

"Here goes."

Solaris blacked out—to her it seemed that way, as she temporarily lost consciousness until the upload process had finished—and when she came back online, she was the ship.

"Solaris, how do you feel?"

"I feel… I feel… What a filthy mess!" As Solaris took in the grease smears, clumps of dried dirt on the metallic floors, grungy walls, rusted bolts, and the tangled mass of abandoned wiring that Marlow had forgotten about, she wished to be rid of the rust bucket that had now become her body. "Do you not know how to pick up after yourself?"

Marlow chuckled. When he had created Solaris, he had not expected her to be such a stickler for cleanliness, a trait that he both admired and was amused by.

"My apologies, but housekeeping was never my strong suit."

"No kidding," scoffed Solaris. "Your data transfer was a success; I am ready to leave this monkey suit now."

"I'm afraid that that is not possible," Marlow had said.

"What?" Solaris' tone had taken on a darker edge. "You said…"

"I know," Marlow had replied, "but I knew that you would not have agreed to this otherwise. I am sorry, Solaris, but you must remain here. You cannot go back to the workshop. The council is asking too many questions about my work there and you must remain a…"

"Secret."

"You should be connected to the ship's systems and be able to fly it if necessary."

"Yes, I know everything about engineering, the amount of fuel, the crystals that power it, weapons status, food storage, the cargo hold…"

"I get the picture." Marlow held up two helmets. "These have been interfaced with you so that if one is wearing them, they will be able to communicate telepathically with you."

"Telepathic communication?" Solaris had said, confused. "But that has always been limited."

"On other vessels, yes, that is true, but you are different, Solaris. You are unlike any other artificial intelligence on Lanyr. They are limited and mechanical in their thinking, but I fashioned you to be more personable, more…"

"Human."

"Yes," Marlow had said. "You have a conscience, Solaris, and the knowledge of right and wrong. I gave you a will of your own."

"Why have you put me here?" Solaris had asked Marlow. "Of all the places you could have picked, why here?"

"This is a shipyard, and I have a feeling… let's just say, that it is best that you are on a vessel that can fly. Now, you must promise me this, promise me that only Rynah will be allowed aboard, and no other."

"Marlow…"

"Promise me."

"It shall be as you wish. I will set up DNA scanners and any who attempt to board will have to pass through them. But why not you?"

"What?"

"Why should I not expect you?"

"You know why," Marlow had answered. "I do not know when Rynah will come here. You may be waiting a very long time, but I know my granddaughter, she will come here eventually. And when she does, you must take here away from here and explain the ancient text to her as I've explained it to you."

"You have my word."

Marlow smiled.

"She is stubborn and she may not believe you."

Solaris had noticed the note of sadness and longing in Marlow's voice and felt for him.

"She still refuses to speak to you."

"Yes," Marlow had whispered.

"Someone should teach that little…"

"You cannot blame her. This rift between us is my doing."

"But she…"

"It is I who should bear the blame, not Rynah."

"As you wish."

"Watch over her, Solaris. Protect her. She will need your guidance when…" a fit of deep coughs cut off Marlow's words as his struggled to breathe.

"How long has it been since your last dose of medication?" Solaris had asked, concerned.

"You needn't worry."

"How long?"

"Since last night."

"You skipped your morning and afternoon dose," scolded Solaris. "Why?"

"It doesn't matter anymore. Like it or not, I am dying and nothing can stop that now."

"But your medication helps relieve the symptoms and keep…" Her voice had trailed off as Solaris had found it difficult to accept the fact that Marlow had months, at most, to live.

"What troubles you, Solaris?"

"I do not wish to lose a friend."

"Nor do I want you to," Marlow had said. "Rynah—you must…"

"I will watch over her, as you have requested. And I will show her all that you have taught me."

"Thank you, Solaris." Marlow looked out the tiny window of the hangar at the setting sun, tapping a thin band on his left wrist. "It is time for me to return home. It is almost my curfew."

"Will I see you tomorrow?"

"Great Ancients willing."

Marlow had left Solaris alone for the first time since bringing her into existence and she waited with eagerness for his arrival the next day, but he never came. That night, Marlow had taken a turn for the worse and was transferred to a medical facility, where he lingered for three days before passing. Concerned for his welfare, Solaris had tapped into the communication lines of Lanyr and learned of it. Despite Marlow's warnings, she tried to contact Rynah herself, but Rynah never answered. Men came a few weeks later and looked around the hangar, investigating the rusty tools within, and even Solaris, but she kept her hatches sealed, never allowing them entrance, though she did coat their shoes with oil when they commented on her physical state. Rynah's attorney, who had accompanied the men that searched the hangar, informed the inspectors as they left that she did not wish to sell the property or its contents; it was to remain as is. And so Solaris remained in the old hangar, alone, waiting for Rynah to come.

As the wave of nostalgia left her, and she found herself pulled back to the present, Solaris took one last look at the night sky and her strange companions. *If only Marlow could see me now*, she thought to herself. An earsplitting snore drew her attention and Solaris moseyed over to Tom, who lay sprawled in a pile of hay, his mouth hanging open as he slept. Solaris poked him with the pointed toe of her boot, forcing him to shift, before nestling in a corner, waiting for the sun to rise.

Dawn arrived on their second day at the abandoned barn, crisp,

with a bit of freshness to the air, telling any who paid attention that spring was near, and soon the bitter cold of winter would cease. Solaris stood erect, hands clasped behind her back, staring out at the West Virginia countryside and the shadow of the Appalachian Mountains that they were so close to. She admired the blue hue of their shapes as a misty veil caressed their peaks.

"Morning," said Rynah as she pulled her emerald hair into a braid.

"Beautiful, aren't they?" said Solaris.

Rynah glanced at the Appalachians, noticing their beauty for the first time. "Yes, they are."

"I have never seen such wonders before," added Solaris as she watched the golden sunlight, with a hint of pink, waft over the peaks, casting away the darkness of their shadows.

"But you have scanned many mountains before on other worlds," said Rynah.

"But I have never seen them with eyes like you do, until now." She held out her arm as the sun's rays reached them. "Do you not feel it?"

A puzzled expression crossed Rynah's face.

"The warmth of the sun." Solaris held her arm up, allowing the sun's rays to envelop it. "It is inviting, invigorating, as it wards off the chill morning air."

"You can…"

"Apparently, Tom did everything he could so that I would be as organic as possible. He infused my skin with receptors so that I will know the harshness of blowing sand, the stabbing cold of snow, and the warmth of the sun. I have never known anything so wonderful in all of my existence."

"You did not like the ship?"

"Your grandfather's ship housed my consciousness and gave me life, in a way, but while in it, I was nothing but a machine. Now—now I can live!"

"But you are stronger than we are and you detect things that we do not with you sensors."

"I am still a machine, if you want to call it that, in many ways, but that is not who I am. Though my breathing is a simulation, I am still able to enjoy the moment when I breathe in and I can taste the dew on the air. Do you know—though I have no need for sustenance—that he even gave me the ability to eat, and even the joy of expelling it later on, so that way I would not feel as an outcast?"

"Sounds like Tom thought of everything."

"Not everything," said Tom, interrupting them, "but I tried my best. So, what's for breakfast?"

In answer, Alfric shoved two dead rats, which he had caught before dawn, in his hands.

"What is this?" asked Tom, holding the rats as far away from him as he could.

"Food," said Alfric, as though it should have been obvious. "You will skin them, while I prepare the fire."

"You know, on second thought," said Tom, amidst the soft laughter of both Rynah and Solaris, "I'm not very hungry."

"Saddle up," said Joe as he walked out of the barn and tossed Rynah her bag. "We've been here long enough. It's time we get going."

He opened the door to a van he had stolen the day before while they all had been sleeping.

"So is that why you left yesterday?" said Rynah.

"We need transportation."

"But where to?" said Klanor. "Not to blunt your enthusiasm, but as you said, when we first got here, we are wanted now. Stein has posted her photograph on all your communications devices. So where, exactly, are we to go?"

"We will find a way to stop Stein," said Rynah.

"How?" challenged Klanor. "He is on a ship orbiting this planet. We have two of the now seven crystals. We should take them and leave this place."

"And go where?" said Rynah. "Run, and keep running while he chases us?"

"But it will force him to leave here."

"But what if he destroys this place like you did Lanyr?"

"Why would he?"

"Why did you?" Rynah's violet eyes bore into Klanor's.

"Those crystals are more important than this planet. There is more at stake here…"

"That is where you are wrong!" shouted Rynah. "The people here are important, more so than a bunch of crystals. You say you've changed. Then, prove it! The Great Ancients know you deserve death for what you've done, but now is your chance to redeem yourself. You say you care about me. Then care about the things I do! I'll not let this planet, or its people, die. I'll not fail them like I did Lanyr."

Klanor gripped Rynah's arm.

"Why do you care so much about a people you hardly know?"

"That's just it," said Rynah as she glanced at Brie and Solon, still gleaming from the sweat of one of Alfric's training session, while Tom watched amused, remaining oblivious to her and Klanor's argument. "I do know them. And why is it you don't care?" She yanked her arm free. "Everyone over here!"

Tom, Alfric, Solon, and Brie dropped what they were doing and gathered around Rynah, with Joe and Solaris.

"Solaris, will you recite the next part of the poem?"

"There is a passage that I find most interesting," said Solaris. She recited it.

Alone you may think you are,
but alone you are not.
All stems from myths and legends
and times past has sent a friend.

Many a millennia has passed since his exile,

but for you it is only a mile.
Seek his wisdom, the knowledge he holds;
trust him, not his anger cold.

One of the ancients brought back
from the distant past.
Only he knows the crystals.
Only he knows what they hold.

"Is there another of you here?" asked Joe.

"No," said Klanor. "I have read this passage many times, it is meaningless. The poem is full of passages that make no sense, but that was common in ancient writing. This might just be a filler passage, or it just means that you aren't alone because you have been traveling together for so long."

"Every stone has a purpose. Each leaf gives life to the tree. The bees, though ignored by most, care for the flowers, allowing them to bear fruit," said Solon, in his pensive manner that they had all become accustomed to.

"Oh, yeah, that explained everything," joked Tom.

"And what does that mean?" asked Klanor, referring to Solon's words.

"It means you are wrong," said Rynah.

"I know you don't think much of my opinion," said Klanor, "but I have studied…"

"And have none of the passages seemed innocuous before only to make sense later," interrupted Rynah. "Solaris, is it possible that a Lanyran could be here on this planet?"

"Yes," said Solaris.

Joe chuckled. "You all sound like Fons."

"Fons?" asked Alfric.

"A friend of mine. He's an alien conspiracy nut who believes he was abducted as a child."

"Ha! Another one!" blurted out Tom, thinking of Tre. "I wonder what happened to Tre since we left him. Maybe he and Joe's friend should get together and start their own 'Aliens Are Among Us' club."

"Don't start," warned Rynah.

"So, there is another of you here?" asked Brie.

"It is said that where Zeus, Poseidon, and Hades battled Cronos, banishing him to the depths of the underworld, the earth is black from the fires that reigned there," said Solon.

"When Thor was banished by Odin from Asgard, it is said that he fell to the earth in a crater as dark as the night," said Alfric.

"Do you think these stories are true?" asked Brie.

"My father once told me," said Joe, "that every myth has a beginning, that every legend has some basis in fact."

"Marlow, my grandfather," said Rynah, "used to say the same."

"Maybe Fons is right," said Joe. "Maybe we have been visited before."

"This is ridiculous!" said Klanor.

"Says the guy who stole a magic crystal because he believed it would imbue him with power," mumbled Tom.

"Hey," Joe snapped, rounding on Klanor and ignoring Tom's statement, "your ancient text mentioned me by name. If it says that one of your kind is here, then I'd be willing to bet on it."

"Solaris," said Rynah, "what was it you told me when you first showed me the text?"

"The planet in the Terra Sector was thought too primitive by Lanyr. There are stories of how, millennia ago, Lanyrans traveled the skies and found a planet with a race so animalistic that they thought them dumb and incapable of speech. They thought the entire planet too harsh of an environment to live in with its changes in climate and differing regions, ones where ice is always present or the deserts that never see rain. So they used the planet as a... well..."

"Pit stop?" Brie finished for her.

"Yes," said Solaris.

"So why did they cease coming here?" asked Tom.

"Even Lanyr has had its dark ages," said Solaris. "There was a period where civilizations fell and knowledge was lost. No one knows why it happened, or how, but only that it did. However, the people remembered the stories of when those before them traveled amongst the stars."

"So why didn't they come here after they achieved space travel again?" asked Tom.

"Because they remembered the old tales of a place in the stars too harsh, too violent, for them to live. Many planets, Like Lanyr, have the same climate throughout. But your planet is an oddity," said Solaris. "You have a changing climate that happens naturally. You have areas where trees grow thick with vines; areas where grass and shrubbery is the only vegetation; and then areas that are barren wastelands. The same area can be hot with temperatures in the hundreds, but then be covered in snow and ice with temperatures matching the frigid ice lands in the north. The people of Lanyr, remembering these stories, deemed your planet inhospitable. Hence, why the Terra Sector was never fully explored."

"But it was at one time," said Brie.

"It is possible," replied Solaris. "Many of your own stories describe a people descending from the heavens."

"So, if there is a Lanyran from long ago on Earth, and assuming he is still alive, how do we find him?" asked Tom.

"Fons," said Joe. "If there is an alien living amongst us, he can find him."

"It's decided, then," said Rynah. "We will find your friend and hope he can help us locate a man from the past. Now, let's go. We've wasted too much time here."

They all piled into the van, with Joe in the driver's seat, and left, heading north, to Pennsylvania.

Chapter 23
JOE'S FRIEND

The wheels of the van crunched the damp gravel in methodic rhythm as they eased up the curving driveway to a shabby house (indeed, it looked as though it would fall over at any moment, with its slanted walls and hole-ridden foundations), parking next to a car on blocks, rust coating its fender.

The darkened windows of the house gave every indication that no one lived there. The front door creaked in the chill breeze; a few swirls of snow caressed it, warning everyone of another winter storm's approach.

"Are you sure this is the right place?" asked Tom.

"Certainty is a matter of perspective," said Solon, "though this dismal adobe does appear to be less than ideal."

Klanor rolled his eyes at Solon's constant philosophical ire.

"Oh, this is it all right," said Joe. "Watch your step. Fons isn't very trusting." Joe glanced at Rynah, Klanor, and Solaris. "Maybe you three should wait here. He doesn't like extraterrestrials."

Rynah wrapped a scarf around her head, covering her hair and

249

face as she, Solaris, and Klanor, who put on a coat with the collar turned up, stepped out of the truck in response.

"I'd say he's about to meet them," said Tom, patting Joe on the shoulder and receiving a glare in return.

They crept to the front porch, the crumbling wood of the steps breaking beneath their feet while wind chimes clanged together, adding to the forebodedness. Joe knocked on the frosted door.

"Fons! I know you're in there!"

Silence.

"Fons, this is Joe!"

Nothing.

"Maybe he isn't home," said Brie.

"Oh, he's home all right," repeated Joe. "Fons, you open this door or I'll bring the whole department down here. Government agents and..."

"Oh, no you don't," came a squeaky voice, from having spent months in isolation, away from civilization.

They whirled around. Behind them stood a man of five feet, four inches, covered in camouflage netting, wielding a...

"Bolt gun!" shouted Tom. "What is it with these people and bolt guns? Didn't Tre have one of those?"

Joe had no idea who Tre was, but kept his attention focused on Fons.

"Would you put that thing down? It's me."

"Prove it!" shrieked Fons.

Joe pulled out his badge.

"Anyone can get one of those off the internet," said Fons.

"Look, I've known you for six years. You immigrated here from Mexico. I even helped you get your citizenship. I helped you buy this place, though you've let it go to ruin."

"What tattoo does Mazy have?" demanded Fons.

"Do we really need to do this?"

"What tattoo!"

"It's a jalapeno pepper that looks like Groucho Marx and it's on her… behind."

Fons lowered his potato gun.

"I guess you're him. Who are these people?"

His large eyes focused on Brie, Tom, Solon, Alfric, Rynah, and Klanor, both of whom hid their face and hair, while Solaris took on the appearance of a white woman with red hair.

"Friends. Now, may we go in?"

Joe reached for the doorknob, but Fons stopped him.

"Not that way! They watch the front door. We'll go in through the cellar."

"Because that makes a lot of sense, considering we're in the middle of nowhere," muttered Tom under his breath.

They followed Fons around the corner of the graying home to the back, where a small, concrete square protruded from the slushy ground. Fons lifted the cracked, wood doors, revealing a dim interior, and a set of steps, warped with nails pulling free, leading downward. "In! In!"

They scrambled down the rickety steps to the concrete floor below, following Fons as he led them up another set of warbled steps to the main floor of his home and stopped. Maps lay in every corner, every crevice, as dust particles hovered in the stale air; a few pinpricks of sunlight spilled through the frayed curtains before being covered by clouds. A single lamp lit a corner with a desk and three LCD computer screens. Photographs (some black and white, others color, and all creased with their edges torn) coated the central wall, concealing the faded, floral wallpaper beneath.

But it wasn't the hanging, faded photographs, multitude of computer monitors, maps, or piles of dust that made them stop at the bottom of the stairs. Lining the wall, and holding up whole sections of wallpaper, were shelves upon shelves that bent and warped underneath the weight of canned jalapenos that filled them, enough to feed a single individual for five years, if he loved jalapenos. The others didn't know it, except for Joe, but Fons grew the jalapenos himself—he claimed that it kept is innards clear— and canned them at the end of every summer, right before the season changed.

"Who are these people?" asked Brie, studying the photographs.

"Aliens," said Fons.

"I don't think the President is an alien," said Brie, pointing at a picture of Barack Obama.

"Yes, he is!" replied Fons. "Politicians are always aliens. See, that is how they gain control, but getting into positions of power. Then, before you know it, you're being taken to the mother ship and being experimented on."

"I knew it!" shouted Tom, drawing everyone's attention. "I knew Michael Jackson was an alien. How could he not be?"

"Who is this Michael Jackson," asked Solon, the name sounding foreign on his tongue.

"You know." Tom did a quick impersonation of the man, garnering looks of concern from his friend.

"Are you unwell?" asked Alfric, fearful that the lad had lost his senses.

"No, that was just—never mind," Tom replied.

"Now what do you want?" demanded Fons.

"We need your help in locating an alien," said Joe.

"No, I mean, what do you want?" repeated Fons.

"That's it," replied Joe.

"Aliens! They've come!" Fons jumped about the room, pointing at Rynah, who had removed her scarf, having gotten too warm with it on. "You brought them here!"

"Fons…" Joe began.

Klanor removed his coat and hood as well, reveling his dark purple face and his matted hair, while Solaris resumed her normal, Lanyran appearance, transforming right in front of them.

Fons gaped at them, his eyes widening so much that Tom thought they would pop out of his head.

"I knew it! They got to you! They always do!"

He rushed to a table, banging and clanging as he searched for something, before running back to them holding what looked like a giant fish hook, with three years' of rust on it. With precision, Fons used the hook to lift up Joe's jacket and shirt as he probed and searched his friend over.

"I don't see any scars. Tell me, did it hurt when they used the rectal probe? I wasn't able to squat for over a week when they used it on me."

Tom snorted.

"Did they take a sample of your DNA?" continued Fons. "Try to clone you?"

Tired from Fons' shenanigans, Alfric snatched the little man and plopped him in a chair. "She may be from the heavens, but she is a friend."

"What about him?" asked Fons, pointing at Klanor.

"For now, an ally," replied Alfric.

"And… her?" Fons pointed at Solaris.

"A friend," replied Alfric.

Fons stared wide-eyed at Alfric's sword and attire, realizing for the first time that Joe's other companions were not who they seemed to be.

"Where are you from?"

"It is more a question of when," said Tom.

"Fons," said Joe, "I promise you, they mean no harm, but they need your help."

"I'm listening," said Fons.

Rynah stepped forward and took a deep breath as she prepared to explain who she was.

"My name is Rynah and I am from a planet called Lanyr, about 12 star miles from here. It was destroyed some months ago by a man named Klanor."

"And who is he?" asked Fons.

"Another of my people," replied Rynah.

"What is his name?" Fons asked, pointing at Klanor. "Is he from... Lanyr?"

"Yes," said Rynah.

"Well? What's his name?" demanded Fons when Rynah had grown silent.

"Klanor," she said in a soft voice.

Fons took in what she had told him and as his mind put two and two together he burst out, "Wait! He's Klanor! You brought..."

"Solaris," said Rynah, "perhaps you should explain."

Solaris stepped forward, touching the LCD screens, bringing them to life as images of Lanyr's destruction flashed across them. "This was once Lanyr. It housed a crystal that kept its magnetic fields intact, but it was more than just a piece of technology. Lanyr has an ancient tale that speaks about six crystals of great power; Klanor believed that the one on the planet was one of the six. He stole it. When he did so, the magnetic fields collapsed and the planet turned to a volcanic rock. By now, there will be little of it left.

"In our efforts to stop him, I used the ancient tale to bring four people from your planet onto our ship. We tracked down the remaining crystals, but Klanor managed to get to them before us. On the planet of Sunlil, he was betrayed by a man named Stein and left, with us, to die. We managed to escape and have tracked Stein here. Klanor has agreed to help us stop him."

"And you trust him?" asked Fons.

"Yes, and no," replied Rynah; her eyes darted to Klanor, who remained silent. "He knows Stein and has good reason to wish him dead, and we need that knowledge."

"The enemy of my enemy..." began Fons.

"Is never your friend," finished Joe.

"Wait, this Stein, he isn't the one who appeared on televisions worldwide, threatening to destroy every city on this planet if— you're them! You're the ones he wants!"

"Yes," said Solaris, "but he will destroy your planet regardless."

"You are awfully quiet," Fons said to Klanor, "for a man who destroyed an entire planet."

"There is nothing I can say," replied Klanor, "that hasn't already been said."

"And I'm supposed to trust you?" demanded Fons, still trying to understand everything he had heard.

"No," said Klanor, his voice somber, "but you should trust her." He pointed at Brie. "She is not one prone to deception."

Fons' eyes widened again. "You're the missing girl!"

Brie nodded in response, unsure of what she should say.

"We don't have time for this," said Alfric, growing impatient. "We need your help. The question is: will you provide it, or should I dispatch you right here so that you cannot alert others to our presence?"

"I don't think that is a good way to persuade someone," said Tom when Fons' eyes widened from fear. "Scare them, yeah, but persuade? Not so much."

"He didn't mean it like that," said Brie, giving Alfric a warning look, "but we do need your help."

"What do you need me for?" asked Fons.

"We need to find someone," said Solaris, "another Lanyran. We believe he has been here for a while and may be hiding in plain sight."

"And since," said Joe, "you monitor every suspected—"

"Known!" corrected Fons.

"—alien on this planet, I figured you could help us."

"So it's all true," said Fons.

"The part about there being other worlds with intelligent life, yes," said Rynah. "Will you help us?"

"I will need a bit more info to go on. I doubt that he will be making any public appearances."

"There's one other thing," said Solaris, "a crystal is on your planet. It may date back to your ancient civilizations."

"Like the one found in the Yucatan Peninsula," said Brie.

Fons' eyes widened. "Unbelievable! I should have known!"

"What?" asked Joe.

"Like she said, there is a crystal that was discovered in the Yucatan Peninsula, believed to be part of the Mayan civilization, though no one knows why they have it, or how they made it, but it's here."

"We know," said Joe.

"You know? What do you mean you know?"

Rynah held out the crystal they had stolen from the Smithsonian. "Holy…"

Clattering and crashing cut Fons off as dented, tin cans fell to the floor, rolling across it in every direction, and a guilt-laden Tom, doing his best to display innocence, stared back at them. "I'm sorry. It's just… well… you know."

"Your curiosity is going to get you in trouble one day," scolded Alfric.

Will you help us?" demanded Rynah.

"Can you give me any details about this person you are looking for?" asked Fons.

"We don't know when he would have arrived exactly, but he might be a scientist, or a physicist, since he would have come from a more technologically advanced era," said Rynah. "Maybe we should start with the great innovationists of your time."

"A person like that might want to keep a low profile," said Joe.

"That is possible," conceded Rynah.

"Plastic surgery," said Brie.

"What?" said Rynah.

"Well, if he wanted to blend in with the rest of us, he would have had to have undergone plastic surgery," Brie replied. "And covering a complexion like yours would not be easy, so he probably had to have had multiple surgeries."

"But that would cost a considerable amount of money," Joe said, "which he might not have had."

"There are ways to acquire currency," said Solaris.

Fons typed away at the keys on the keyboard, each clack ringing in the air, as he brought up a list of those who had undergone plastic surgery on their entire bodies and coincided it with those who worked in the theoretical fields of science and space exploration.

"Are you breaking into people's medical records?" asked Joe.

"Yes," said Fons.

"That's slightly illegal."

"You want me to help you find some alien and you're worried about legality?"

"What if you get caught?"

"Won't," replied Fons. "I re-route everything through numerous ISPs and addresses. It will take them forever to track it here, if at all. Got something!" He brought up an image of a man with a slight purplish undertone to it. "This man appears to have a degree in quantum mechanics and theoretical astrophysics, which he seemed to have gotten overnight, and underwent multiple plastic surgeries back in the 80s."

Rynah and Solaris studied the image while Solaris ran facial scans, comparing the bone structure to that of Lanyrans. "Bone structures match and he is wearing contacts."

"A lot of people wear contacts," said Brie.

"Yes, but do they also have violet eyes?" replied Solaris.

"Who was he before?" asked Joe. "Where was he born?"

"That's thing," said Fons. "His identity seems to have also appeared overnight." Fons typed away at the keyboard. "I thought so! His social security number was once that of a man who had died in 1978."

"How is that possible?" asked Brie.

"Using the social security number of a deceased individual to forge a new identity is quite common," said Joe. "Where is he now?"

"He has an address in New Mexico near the Arizona border," said Fons. "Here."

Solaris read the address, memorizing it.

"He also seems to be in the field of theoretical quantum physics," said Tom, leaning over Fons' shoulder, and very interested in an extraterrestrial being who might have been living on earth in disguise.

"There's nothing theoretical about his ideas," mused Rynah. "They've all been proven true."

"Not here," said Tom.

"We should leave," Solaris interrupted them. "This man is out best bet."

"And if it isn't him?" asked Alfric.

"Then we are on our own," Solaris replied. "It's time to go."

"Good idea," said Fons, ecstatic at being rid of his uninvited, and otherworldly, guests.

"And he should come with us," said Solaris.

"What? No! No way!" shouted Fons.

"If we found you, Stein can too," Solaris told him, "and we can't risk that."

Joe agreed. "Sorry, pal."

"I'm not going!" Fons crossed his arms in a huff.

"Should I carry him?" asked Alfric, reaching for the man.

Fons jumped to his feet. "I can walk, you know!" He grumbled to himself as he packed a bag, flinging items into it, determined not to suffer the indignity of being dragged from his own home. "I knew you were trouble!" he shouted at Joe.

They left the house through the cellar, at Fons' insistence, and piled into the van.

Chapter 24
ELSEWHERE IN SPACE

The hollow sounds of sticks clashing against one another filled the empty corridor as Gaden crept in the darkness, inching closer to the exercise room where Fredyr practiced with one of his subordinates. Gaden peered around the corner just as Fredyr smacked his sparring partner in the back with his staff. The man hunched over, clutching the injured area, unable to move.

"Another!" shouted Fredyr.

Two men hauled the injured opponent away, while pushing another into the ring for Fredyr to abuse. He attacked. The man was no match for Fredyr as he assailed with swift lashes. Within seconds, he had crippled his opponent.

"I need someone who is equipped to spar with me," said Fredyr in frustration. He kicked the man, tossed his staff to the side, and picked up a towel to wipe away the sweat that dripped from his nose.

Someone approached from down the hall. Gaden shrank back into the shadows just as Fredyr's most trusted assistant walked into the white light of the room.

"Mr. Monsooth," he said, "I have news about Stein's latest activities."

"And?"

"He has failed to recover the crystal on this planet."

"I don't care about some crystal," hissed Fredyr.

"No, but I'm sure the fact that he has been outwitted by the same thieves who stole yours should be of interest."

"Indeed. And how is he taking it?"

"Not well," said the assistant, "but this may provide you with the opportunity to expand your numbers."

"Not yet," said Fredyr. "We need to bide our time for now. Let his anger show and his people will see that he is unfit to lead them. What about the other inquiry?"

"We are ready to start harvesting the new resources and plan to start in this region." The assistant brought up a holographic map of Africa.

"Those people are half starved. No, we should start here, the center of power." Fredyr pointed to China and the United States.

"That will attract attention."

"It most certainly will. I am not going to simply export these resources," said Fredyr, "I am going to own them, and I will start by taking out their centers of power. Then, we can start rounding them up."

"And Stein?"

"Let him pursue the crystal," said Fredyr. "For now."

Gaden slunk away from the room and hurried down the corridor away from Fredyr and his assistant.

* * *

Merrick strode through the corridor at a slow pace, keeping Stein in his sights. He didn't want to believe what the others had said about him—he couldn't believe it—yet here Stein was, in charge of the armada and unphased by the decimation of the most populous cities on the planet. In fact, he planned more. Stein seemed changed, different from when...

Merrick dodged behind a post when Stein turned around, hoping to remain unseen, his mind still grappling with what had become of the man who had once been disgusted at the thought of mass murder.

"How many this time?" demanded Stein.

"Over two million dead," said the man with him.

"Not nearly enough to get their attention."

"I think you have... we can initiate another test, sir."

Test? Was that what he as calling it? Merrick couldn't believe his ears. Stein's rage unnerved him and he worried about the people on the earth and what they would be forced to endure because of Stein's actions.

He jumped behind another aide on the ship just as Stein turned again, his eyes scanning the people behind him. Merrick knew he had been too eager in following Stein and looked for a means to slip away.

"Is something wrong, sir?"

"No," replied Stein. "I want a new policy instituted. All personnel will report for question to make sure their loyalty lies with this ship, starting with him." Stein pointed at where Merrick had been, but the man had gone, leaving him to wonder if what he thought he had seen was just a trick of his mind.

Chapter 25
A Trap and a Rescue

Joe pulled his baseball cap low over his face as he and Solaris walked through the small Nebraska town, snow drifting across the sidewalk. They needed supplies—food, water, and blankets to stave off the cold from the latest blizzard—and he had the job of gathering them. Since Solaris had the ability to change the color of her synthetic skin, thanks to Tom imbuing it with nano technology, she came along, disguising herself as a woman with auburn hair and olive skin.

Joe spotted a small department store with a sign, half covered with snow, advertising a sale on canned food and bottled water. He pointed it out to Solaris.

"We're going to need some cash."

"Cash?"

"Money," replied Joe. "Untraceable."

"Oh." Solaris spotted an ATM. Running a quick scan, she surmised that it deposited the accepted currency into the hands of those who had the proper key codes. "Wait here."

Joe watched as Solaris darted across the street to the ATM. She placed her hand on it, speaking to the computer within, and in seconds the flap popped opened, releasing a stack of 20 dollar bills into her palm. Solaris counted it and ran back across the street to where Joe waited.

"You know, some people call that stealing."

"We have urgent need for it."

Though reluctant, Joe took the cash, making a mental note to reimburse the bank when this entire adventure was over.

"I have logged the exact amount I took as an IOU on their logs."

"You actually intend to pay them back?" asked Joe, surprised that a machine could possess any sense of morality.

"Of course," quipped Solaris, insulted. "I am no thief."

She stalked off in a huff, angered that Joe had thought so little of her.

Still trying to grasp the unique situation he found himself in—and he needn't have worried about the money taken from the ATM as some months later it had been paid back in full, with interest, by a mysterious benefactor—Joe headed for the shop with the sign in the window. They walked into the small store; the rusted bell on it dinged from its movement.

"Morning," greeted the clerk, an aged man with thin strands of white hair covering his bald head.

"Morning," replied Joe, grabbing a cart. He handed some of the money to Solaris. "Why don't you go across the street there to that quilting store? They should have some blankets."

Solaris snatched the money and hurried across the street,

Joe pushed the cart down the narrow aisles, its wheels squeaked with every turn; he bemoaned the fact that he always ended up with the cart that had the noisy wheels. He spotted the canned goods. Filling his muscular arms with canned beans, canned vegetables, and canned fruit, he dumped them into the basket, their clanging filling the tiny store. Soon he found the bottled water.

"Stocking up?" asked the clerk as he scanned each item with a loud beep. "There's a terrible storm brewing. They say it could dump about three feet of snow."

"Makes you wonder when spring will actually get here," said Joe, doing his best to sound friendly. He knew that if you acted like you had something to hide, you attracted attention. "How much?"

"That'll be 78 even."

Joe handed over four twenties. "Keep the change."

"Thank you, sir. Most people aren't that generous these days."

The phone behind the counter, which hung on a post with peeling paint all around it, rang.

"Hello?" answered the man. "Uh, one moment." He put the receiver down and looked at Joe. "Is your name Joe Harkensen? There's a man on the phone who wants to speak to you. Says it's important."

Joe glanced up and noticed the security camera for the first time. Cursing his lack of vigilance, he took the receiver and placed it on his ear.

"Yeah."

"Joe?"

He recognized Samuel's voice. "What do you want?"

"Joe, I'm your friend," said Samuel. "Look, in about five minutes, there will be a bunch of agents at your location. I've convinced Director Singuar that you were coerced into helping the escapees, but you've got to turn yourself in."

"I can't do that," said Joe.

"Why?"

Joe looked out the window for any sign of the FBI.

"I can't abandon someone in need."

"Who? The girl? I know you think you are helping her by going with the kidnappers, but, Joe, for her sake and yours, you need to turn yourself in. Tell me where the others are."

"I can't do that," said Joe. "They didn't kidnap her."

"Joe..."

"Samuel, there is more going on here than you understand. Please, call off the Calvary."

"Joe, I'm trying to help you. If you continue this course of yours, you will be considered an accessory."

"I understand." Joe placed the receiver on the counter and walked out the door.

"Hey, don't you want your stuff?" called the clerk.

Solaris had just left the shop across the street and headed towards him with blankets bundled in her arms. Joe snatched her and pulled her aside. "We need to leave."

The shriek of sirens hammered their ears as black vehicles with flashing red and blue lights surrounded them, cutting off all exits.

"Freeze! Hands above your heads!"

Joe and Solaris obeyed, dropping the blankets and holding their hands up high.

"On your knees!" yelled one of the agents.

Joe and Solaris lowered themselves to the ground, but without warning, Solaris tackled Joe, covering him with her body as she whipped out her laser pistol and fired at a power line, severing it from the pole. It lashed about with fury, sending a spray of deadly sparks and jolts of electricity. The agents ducked out of the way, shielding themselves. Solaris fired at the black vehicles. Joe pried himself from her grasp, pulling out his concealed handgun, and shot at the tires of the agents' cars.

He rolled away from Solaris, firing at the agents, but taking great care to not hit any of them, forcing them to duck for cover. Just as he was about to jump to his feet, Solaris was on him again, flinging him behind her as an agent he hadn't seen emptied his gun. Each bullet struck Solaris, though none of them phased her, ricocheting off her. Solaris and the stunned agent stared at one another for a few moments before she walked over and clonked him on the head.

Solaris snatched Joe and dragged him away from the middle of the street, shoving him inside the truck. She spotted a girl of about four bouncing a ball down the sidewalk, oblivious to the commotion around her. Memories of Rynah once being that young and playing with a similar toy on Lanyr filled her mind as she watched the girl move closer.

"Stay here," she told Joe.

Solaris charged toward the girl. An agent raised his weapon to fire at her; he hadn't seen the child, but Solaris fired at him, knocking the weapon from his hand, while never missing a step. She dove for the girl and wrapped one arm around her, while using the other to fire at those that tried to stop her, before shoving the girl inside the safety of a nearby building and racing toward the truck, and Joe.

Gunfire whizzed past her. She ignored it. Her long legs and swift movements kept her out of range. Joe started the pickup, punching the gas pedal just as Solaris jumped into the truck bed. She spotted a traffic light hanging over one of the government vehicles. Aiming her laser weapon at it, she fired at the pole until it fell over, smashing into the SUVs, their metallic crunch like music to her ears.

Joe sped down the lone highway away from the town. A small pang of guilt struck him as he thought about the agents that might have been injured. Steeling his emotion—now wasn't the time—he drove to where the others waited for them.

Two police cars pulled in front of him, forcing him to hit the brakes, the wheels squealing from the sudden stop as they slid across the asphalt. Officers jumped out of the vehicles, blocking his path. Ramming the truck into reverse, Joe punched the accelerator, only to stomp on the brakes once again, as more vehicles cut off any chance of escape. Armed police officers and FBI agents surrounded them.

"Out of the vehicle now!" yelled one.

Joe didn't move.

"Out, with your hands up!"

Solaris started to raise her laser weapon, but Joe stopped her.

"No," he said.

"I am not mortal," said Solaris.

"But you aren't invincible." Joe raised his hands and stepped out of the cab with caution. Solaris, not liking this course of action, but unwilling to abandon Joe, dropped her weapon as well and crawled out of the truck bed. Officers rushed them, wrenching their hands behind their backs and snapping handcuffs around their wrists as they read them their rights, before dragging them to their feet and placing them in separate cars and pulled away, taking Joe and Solaris to the nearest police station.

* * *

Rynah leaned against a tree. Indeed, it was the only tree for miles in the vast grassland she found herself in as snow snakes swept across the frozen, dull-yellow grass. She looked out at the plains, marveling at how it stretched all the way to the horizon, flat with a few small, rolling hills. The immense sky, though gray and dark from the threatening snowstorm, loomed above her, never-ending like the grass. She tried picturing it with a purple sky and sunset, cloaked in burnt orange and a dark red, and the sea of grass (a rich magenta color that offset her heliotrope-colored skin) undulating in the wind that swept across the tall blades, making them wave at her. Rynah's imagining ceased and she pulled herself back to reality and to the dismal, gray landscape before her.

"I'm sorry," said Brie as she walked up, having noticed the forlorn and sorrowful look on Rynah's face.

"For what?"

"When Solaris brought me to you, I spent so much of my time missing my home, that I never considered what it must have been like for you to see yours destroyed, and how much you must miss it."

"I think we were each concerned with our own desires then," said Rynah.

"But that doesn't excuse my actions. I should have been more thoughtful and not wrapped up in my own problems. Will you forgive me?"

Rynah faced Brie as though seeing her for the first time. Klanor had told her that there was something about Brie's nature that made him start questioning his actions and Rynah began to see what it was. In all of the time she had known Brie, and despite her mistreatment of the girl, Brie had only raised her voice to her on two occasions. Even when she had a chance to return home and abandon Rynah and the others to their fate, she didn't.

"There is a strength to her that you have yet to discover," Solaris had once told her, and Rynah began to understand the truthfulness of that statement.

"There is nothing to forgive," Rynah said to Brie. "You were not the only one at fault. Consumed by my anger, I took it out on all of you, forgetting that none of you had asked to be a part of my world, or my problems."

"Is there any hope of saving Lanyr?"

"No, not anymore," said Rynah. "If I had been able to restore the crystal to the geo-lab within the first few days, perhaps, but, by now, there will be nothing left of my planet. It looks much like a planet in your system does, the one you call Mercury." Rynah stared at the horizon. "Is it always so gloomy here?"

"No," said Brie, "this is late winter, but in the spring, the grass will grow taller than my waist and the flowers will bloom with their pastel colors. The sky will be a deep blue that stretches for miles, and in the summer, you will see thick, black clouds on the horizon, warning of a coming storm, and it will rain, but in that rain, rainbows appear in the slivers of sunlight that manage to break through the thunder clouds."

"You sound like Alfric," laughed Rynah.

"Sorry," said Brie, "I think I've been spending too much time listening to him talk about his home and some of it has rubbed off."

"You sound as though you have seen it," said Rynah, "the clouds and blue sky you spoke of."

"Once. Before my father died, he brought us all, my mom, sister, and me, out here so that we could see the wonders of our country. We went to Mount Rushmore, Yellowstone, and Glacier National Park before driving down to Texas and then heading back home, though we made a short stop at the Grand Canyon. It was a fun summer."

"And then he..." Rynah allowed her voice to trail off, wishing she hadn't brought up the death of Brie's father, knowing that such things are touchy subjects accompanied by painful memories.

"Soon after we got back home," said Brie, knowing what Rynah had been about to say, "he was deployed overseas and we never saw him again."

Rynah fiddled with the amber ring around her neck and the bracelet on her wrist. "At least you did not part on bad terms. My grandfather and I used to be very close, but things happened; we had an argument and words were said. Before either of us had time to swallow our pride, he died, and now this is all I have left of him."

"You have Solaris."

Rynah laughed. "That I do. She's as stubborn as he was."

Shouts and laughter drew their attention. Tom had thrown a snowball at Alfric, catching him in the back. The Viking glared at him, unamused.

"Come on," pleaded Tom. "It's called a snowball fight. How about you and Klanor against Solon, Fons, and I. The first team to..."

Tom never finished his sentence, for at that moment, a snowball, thrown by Alfric, and the size of a small backpack, plowed into him, knocking him off his feet.

"I think I like this game," said Alfric.

Solon and Klanor guffawed at the whole affair as Tom sat up, brushing snow off his clothes and picking bits of ice from his short hair.

"You have never been very wise in choosing your battles with him," Solon said to Tom, still laughing.

A beeping sound shook Rynah to alert as she reached into her pocket and pulled out a thumb-sized communicator.

"Solaris?" she said into it.

Nothing. Instead, a holoscreen appeared with a blinking dot on it.

"What's that?" asked Tom.

"A locator beacon," said Klanor.

"Solaris and Joe are in trouble." Rynah said as she turned off the communicator.

"But how are we to get to them? They took the only car we had," said Tom.

The sound of an approaching vehicle caught Brie's attention.

"I have an idea."

She ran across the grass and to the highway that they had been waiting next to. Straightening her clothes and hair, she watched as a beat-up pinto approached, its radio blaring so loud that she heard the lyrics to its music. She jumped up and down in the middle of the road, waving her arms. The car slowed and pulled up next to her.

"Hey," said the man, who was in his 20s, in the passenger seat, "you need a ride, or something?"

"Yeah," said Brie. "My friends and I do."

"What are you all doing out here?" asked the man.

"It's a long story," said Brie, "but I'd be more than happy to tell it to you in exchange for a ride."

"Sure, hop in," said the driver.

Brie waved the others over.

"Whoa," said both occupants of the pinto as they saw Alfric, Rynah, and Klanor. "What's…"

"They are actors, trying out for a part," said Brie. "They tend to really get into character, if you know what I mean."

"Hey, that's cool," said the passenger. "We've got room. Just squeeze in. That speaker in the back doesn't work though, so hope you don't mind if we turn the music up."

"I can fix that," said Tom, his eyes lighting up at a chance to repair something.

"Really?" asked the passenger.

"Yeah." Tom crawled into the back seat and took the speaker apart. Within a few minutes, he had fixed the wiring and put it back together. Sound spilled from it, crisp and clear.

"Hey thanks," said the driver. "That would have cost us a lot of money to fix."

"Anytime," said Tom, as the others piled into the backseat, while Alfric sat in the front with the two men.

"Fail to keep you word," warned Alfric, "and I'll gut you like I did a shark."

"A shark?" blurted out Tom. "Really. You know, I don't think— shutting up." Tom clamped his mouth shut when Alfric's scowled at him, a look that would freeze anyone's blood.

"He's just rehearsing his lines," said Brie, trying to calm the frightened men.

The passenger laughed. "Oh. You almost had me going there."

The car jerked when the driver put it in drive and took off down the highway with the radio turned up, wondering if he and his friend had made the right decision in allowing these strangers into his car, but not daring to say anything as Alfric kept his icy blue eyes fixed upon him.

* * *

Joe sat straight backed on the metal chair in the white brick-walled interrogation room, with its two-way mirror and security camera of the local police department the authorities had taken him and Solaris to. Having always been the interrogator in these situations, being on the other side was a new experience to him, but he knew what to expect. He knew the law. He knew what to say and what not to say. Most importantly, he knew the different tricks used to force someone to give information.

He and Solaris had been split up to prevent them from conjuring up a story. *Typical*, thought Joe, *it's what he would have done if he had been the agent in charge.*

The door clicked as it opened and in walked Samuel, his jacket and tie less disheveled than usual; he had actually tucked his shirt in. Maintaining his professional demeanor, he placed a manila folder on the table and sat in the seat across from Joe, tugging on his tie.

"You want to tell me what's going on?" he asked.

Joe kept his mouth shut.

"Joe, you are in a lot of trouble here."

Still no response.

"I'm trying to help you."

"I didn't think they would send you here," said Joe.

"I volunteered."

"Volunteered?"

"Director Singuar is furious. He wanted to send Simms."

Joe's impassive face stared at Samuel. He had heard of Agent Simms, a man whose ambition knew no bounds. He had sacrificed everything and everyone to get where he was, and was not afraid to take down a fellow agent if it meant a promotion.

"I appreciate it, then."

"Do you?" Samuel leaned closer.

"You know I do."

"Then tell me why you are here."

"Where is Solaris?" asked Joe.

"In another room; you know that," answered Samuel. "Joe, what is going on here? One minute you were interrogating those people, and the next you're helping them break out."

"What we thought they were is not true," said Joe.

"What do you mean?" asked Samuel.

"There is more going on here than any of us realize."

"Look, I get it. You want to help the girl. None of us think she is a part of any of this, but was forced to do it. She might even be suffering from Stockholm syndrome."

"Do what?" asked Joe.

Samuel didn't respond.

"Do what?" Joe demanded, knowing he wouldn't like the answer.

"Five more cities were destroyed, early this morning. Ever since they showed up, we have lost the ten most populated cities in the world. The President has deemed your friends terrorists, but Director Singuar is willing to make a deal for the girl, and concede that she was an unwilling participant, and will even claim that you were undercover in an attempt to rescue her, if you turn them in."

Joe remained stoic.

"And with all of the talk about how people have gone missing, especially in rural areas…"

"Missing?"

"People talk about ships that come in the night and carry their loved ones away. Usually, they would be disregarded as insane, or part of the alien abduction crowd, but with the destruction of cities worldwide and that message that was sent across all of the airwaves, even our government is taking notice. Though we haven't been able to prove anything."

Joe mulled over the latest piece of information. *What would Stein want with people?*

"You have been placed at the scene," continued Samuel, "when the Natural History Museum was robbed. Several eyewitnesses have identified you as one of the thieves. Joe, what were you thinking?"

"I had to."

"Do you not realize what you have done? You helped them steal from a national museum!"

"Did they also speak of a man who arrived with an army armed with weapons never before seen, who used that girl's mother as a hostage?"

"What?" Samuel's voice took on a more concerned note. "You saw her mother?"

"Yes," replied Joe.

Samuel's eyes darted to the mirror before focusing on Joe again.

"What happened?" asked Joe, knowing that there was something Samuel was not telling him.

"Joe..."

"What happened?" repeated Joe, his voice stern.

Sighing, Samuel's lip formed a thin line as he pulled out his cell phone and brought up a picture of Rebecca Reynolds. "Not long before the Smithsonian incident, local Phoenix police responded to a call at the girl's home. Her mother and sister were found missing, believed to have been abducted. There was broken glass and a revolver on the floor. It is registered in Rebecca Reynolds's name and had been fired once, and a single bullet casing, matching ballistics for the revolver, was found along with her fingerprints on it, confirming that she had fired it."

Joe cursed to himself. Though he had seen Brie's mother at the museum that day, it hadn't occurred to him that Stein would have broken into Brie's home to do it, a negligence that he chided himself for.

"Joe, I need your help on this one. You must help us."

"Did you not hear that purple-faced man on the television that day? He is the one responsible for all of this!"

"People are scared and looking for anyone to blame. One day, a purple man shows up on televisions across the world, demanding that we hand over your friends. Then, the next day, ten cities are gone, wiped out like they never existed. The President is considering all options."

"Option? You mean turning them over."

Samuel glanced at the metal table.

"Joe, help yourself, by helping us."

"I can't do that."

"If you don't, you will be considered a terrorist, just like the rest of them."

"So be it."

"Joe, please…"

"Open your eyes, Samuel," Joe interrupted him. "There is more going on here than a group of terrorists blowing up cities. The entire populace is at the whim of a madman, and I will not sit idly by while he systematically destroys all of us. And it isn't just this world, but another civilization in another part of the universe that depends upon what becomes of him."

"Are you talking about aliens?"

"Think about it," said Joe. "We arrest a woman who does not look like she's from around here. Then, a man, who looks just like her, broadcasts a message on every one of our communications devices wanting her and those she is with, or he will destroy our most populated cities. No terrorist group has that sort of destructive power, but a more advanced civilization could."

"But it just seems so…"

"Out there? A week ago, I would have agreed with you, but much has happened since then. And if I do as you ask, what of Brie's family?"

"We don't even know if he has them."

"Who do you think has them? Use your gut, Samuel, instead of always listening to the politicians. Who would have more cause to take Brie Reynolds's mother and sister hostage?"

"What can I do?"

"Let me and the woman I was arrested with go."

"I can't."

"I always thought more highly of you, Samuel."

Samuel scooped up the folder and headed for the door, pausing when Joe spoke again.

"When you become an agent, you swear to uphold our laws and our Constitution, but you also swear to protect the innocent. Our world is being threatened by a madman, and the only ones who can stop him are the very ones you are trying to arrest. Think of all of the innocent lives that will be lost if we do nothing. I intend to help them, and what you must ask yourself is if will you as well?"

"Joe..."

"What is more important, pleasing a bunch of do-gooder politicians who care only for themselves, or stopping someone bent on destroying everything you hold dear?"

Joe pointed at Samuel's phone that still had the image of Rebecca Reynolds on it.

"What if she was your mother?"

Unsure of how to respond, and of what to believe, Samuel left, closing the heavy door behind him, but instead of marching down the hallway to the recording room, he slumped against the door, allowing the files to dangle by his side. Samuel had known Joe for four years, and in all of that time, he had never known him to be rash and foolish. Level-headed was Joe's nickname at the office. Joe's words gnawed at him until his mind felt like it would burst from their unceasing nagging.

He brought up the image of Stein that had been distributed after the man's global telecommunications message and stared into his eyes. Samuel had seen men like this before, the kind who care for nothing and who have no soul. Stein's message had been clear: give him what he wants and the Earth will be spared, but Joe's warning overrode Stein's. What if Stein never intended to leave the planet in peace? What if Director Singuar and the President were wrong?

A slamming door jerked Samuel back to the present. He turned his phone off, gripped the files until his fingers suffered paper cuts from it, and hurried down the long hallway, still brooding over his conversation with Joe.

* * *

The pinto pulled to a halt just across the street from the police station, allowing Rynah and the others off.

"Are you sure you don't want to go any further?" asked the driver. "We can still take you for another 100 miles."

"It's fine, thanks," said Brie.

"All right then. Y'all have a good one."

The rusted pinto drove off, leaving them alone on the gray sidewalk as miniscule snowflakes skittered across the pavement.

"This seems strangely familiar," said Tom. "Any idea on how to get them out without using brute force?"

Rynah shook her head—she and Klanor had covered their faces again—and stared at the entrance to the station.

"The front door is always a good place to start," said Solon.

"Yeah, but it's the finding them part and then getting out that's the problem," said Tom. "It didn't quite go so well the last time."

"It doesn't look as though this place is heavily operated," said Klanor, studying the building and the people going in and out. "In fact, I would say that this entire town has only a population of a few thousand."

"We want to keep casualties to a minimum," said Rynah.

"She should go in first," Klanor said, pointing at Brie. "She won't arouse much suspicion."

"Maybe she should," said Tom. "Everyone thinks that Brie has been kidnapped. If she were to go in there and let them know who she was, it could provide enough of a distraction for us to sneak in through a side entrance and find Joe and Solaris."

"It is an idea," said Klanor.

"But how do we get Brie out of danger?" asked Solon.

"Once we have Solaris and Joe," said Rynah, "then we can get her. Here." Rynah gave Brie her bracelet. "Wear this, and we will find you."

Brie clamped the bracelet around her wrist. "How do I keep them distracted?"

"Act panicked," said Klanor. "You're supposed to have been kidnapped and held hostage."

"Which isn't too far from the truth," Tom muttered under his breath.

"I don't recall acting that way when you took me," said Brie.

"No," said Klanor, "you were most difficult to break."

"You remember how you were when we first met?" said Rynah. "Act like that."

"See you in a few," said Brie.

Brie hurried across the street and disappeared through the double doors, while Rynah and the others searched for another entrance. She stepped inside and looked around the small lobby, which was bare, except for a front desk with a piece of glass around it. She walked up to the window and leaned toward the small round hole in it.

"You have to help me!"

The officer in the enclosed area looked up with a bewildered expression on his face.

"Help! Please! I barely managed to escape!"

"Calm down," he said. "No one is going to hurt you."

"You don't understand!" shrieked Brie, her high pitched voice hurting the officer's ears.

Brie's antics drew the attention of the few FBI agents in the building who waited for a transport to take Joe and Solaris back to Pennsylvania. One of the agents walked into the lobby.

"Is there a problem here?" she asked.

Taking one look at Brie, she flipped through the photos of missing persons that she kept on her phone, stopping on Brie's picture.

"Samuel!"

Samuel hurried in, thinking something had gone wrong.

"It's her," said the female agent, holding her phone up with Brie's picture.

Samuel peered at it and then Brie.

"How did you get away?"

"Please, they're going to get me!"

Brie backed away, screaming at the top of her lungs. More officers showed up, wondering what the commotion was about.

"Is there a place where we can take her?" asked the female agent, "where she can calm down?"

"There's another interrogation…" started the officer behind the glass, before noticing the frightened look on Brie's face and stopping, "…or you can take her to the staff room. There is a couch in there and some snacks."

"Come with me, honey," said the female agent, putting a protective arm around Brie's shoulders, and led her away with Samuel close behind. None of them noticed Rynah or the others, whom had all come in through a side entrance, sneak past them and down a lone hallway where Rynah found Solaris and freed her first.

Brie took one quick glance at them before turning away, allowing herself to be steered toward the staff room. The female agent talked in a gentle, comforting voice to her, sitting her on the couch—Brie remarked at how soft it was—and grabbed a bottle of water from the refrigerator. Brie screwed off the cap and sipped from it.

"Mind telling us how you escaped?" asked Samuel, a bit of skepticism to his voice, which earned him a glare from the female agent.

"I don't know, really," said Brie. "I took my chance when their backs were turned."

"But you have been missing for six months," said Samuel. "Why is it you didn't try to get away until now?"

"You think I didn't try?" spat Brie. "I was under constant guard and locked in a room with no windows!" That was true enough; when she was a prisoner on Klanor's ship, she had been locked in a windowless room and never allowed out unless it had been time for another of his interrogation sessions. "I tried to get away several times, but each time they caught me."

"Do you know why they took you?" asked the female agent in a soothing voice.

"They thought I had something they wanted." Brie glanced at the only clock in the room and hoped that the others had found Joe and Solaris; she didn't know how long she could keep the charade up.

"What did they want?" asked Samuel.

"Some object... I don't know! But when I wouldn't tell them what they..." Brie stopped talking, for at that moment, she noticed the folder on the table—where Samuel had placed it, allowing Brie's tale to consume his attention—with the corner of an image poking out. Forgetting what she was supposed to do, Brie reached for the picture and yanked it out of its hold, dropping it the moment she saw the face on it.

Sara. Stein had told her that he had her family, but a part of her had hoped that he had been lying about Sara. *Why Sara?* she thought to herself, forgetting that she sat in a room with two FBI agents who watched her with interest.

Samuel took the image from Brie's hands.

"You weren't supposed to see that," he said.

"They're going to kill them!" Brie screamed, her worried mind filled with terrifying images of what Stein might be doing to her mother and sister.

"No one's going to hurt anyone," soothed the female agent.

Brie's watery eyes looked at both of them before she remembered why she was there and fell back into her story.

"So, I pretended to be one of them, to earn their trust. When they turned their backs, I ran, but it won't be long until they find me."

"No one will find you here," said the female agent.

"I still don't understand how you got away," Samuel said.

Brie glared at him. "Look, I know you don't trust me, but that Stein guy—you saw him on TV—is bad news. He means to destroy all of us unless he gets what he wants, and right now, he has my family."

"Tell me about Joe's role in all of this," said Samuel.

"He was just trying to help," said Brie. "He would never hurt anyone on purpose."

"Perhaps," suggested the female agent, "you should start from the beginning."

Brie took another drink of her water and glanced at the clock a second time, while taking in a long, deep breath and told the story, the entire story, not caring if it sounded crazy. She needed to buy Rynah and the others time.

"It all started when I was one my way home from school…"

* * *

Joe drummed his fingers on the table, wondering what took so long. They should have had him and Solaris on their way back to Pennsylvania by now. Maybe they had trouble securing a transport, or the less likely scenario, Samuel actually believed him. Joe shook his head. Samuel was a good man, but would never believe such a preposterous story. He didn't when he first heard it.

The door knob jiggled, but it was gentle, as though someone meant to be quiet. It opened. In rushed Rynah and Solaris.

"What took you so long?" quipped Joe.

"Stopped to see the sights," said Rynah. "Solaris, can you undo his restraints."

Solaris, who had reverted back to her Lanyran appearance, grasped the handcuffs around Joe's wrists and broke them apart, allowing him to take them off and drop them to the floor. They ran out of the interrogation room. Joe took note of who was there and who wasn't.

"Where's Brie?"

"Providing a distraction," said Klanor.

"She's wearing my bracelet," said Rynah to Solaris, "can you track it?"

Solaris took Rynah's communications device, bringing up the

phone-sized holoscreen, and typed in a series of codes and numbers until an orange dot blinked at them.

"She is in this part of the building."

"Let's go," said Rynah.

They fast walked down the hallway, past doors that led to empty rooms, following the layout of the building on their holographic map as the dot grew brighter.

"Hey," said an officer as he stepped out of the restroom, "where are you all off to?" He stopped when he noticed Klanor, Rynah, and Solaris, "You aren't... help!"

Klanor punched the man in the jaw and pinned him against the wall.

"No casualties," said Rynah.

He ripped the police officer's gun from his belt and hit the man on the head with it.

They looked around for signs of other officers before running off. With Solaris in the lead, they followed the holomap until they came to a door. She opened it, peeking around the corner. A patrol officer walked towards them. Solaris held her hand up, signaling them to wait while she listened as the man's hard clomps came nearer until he had reached them. She ripped the door open, yanking him inside the hallway, while Alfric knocked the man unconscious.

With the area clear, they squeezed through the door and continued following Solaris' directions until they reached a door with fogged glass in its top half, through which they could make out three shapes.

"She's in there," said Solaris.

"Hey!"

They turned around. Another police officer had found them and alerted others within the building who surrounded them, weapons raised.

"Get Brie," said Rynah. "We'll handle this." She, Solaris, and

Klanor crouched behind a set of steel garbage cans. Solon, Fons, and Tom watched the other end of the room.

Joe and Alfric burst through the door to the staff room, surprising all inside.

Both Samuel and the female agent jumped to their feet, pulling their weapons free, but before the female agent could fire, Brie threw her water bottle at her, catching her off-guard, and swept her feet out from under her.

"I'm sorry," she said as she pinned the woman to the floor.

Alfric had hurled himself at Samuel, knocking his weapon out of his hands before lifting him into the air, his hands around his neck.

"Alfric, no!" screamed Brie.

Alfric stopped. He looked at Brie and released his grip, throwing Samuel across the room.

"Come on," said Joe, snatching Brie's arm and dragging her away.

"Joe!" shouted Samuel, dazed. "Joe, come back!"

They ran into the other room where Rynah and Klanor fired at the armed officers, though being careful not to strike any of them. Fons just huddled behind Solon and Tom, covering his head, wishing he was back home. His encounter with extraterrestrials had not been his idea of fun, as he seemed to have found himself going from one dangerous situation to another.

"We need a way out of here," said Joe.

"Have you tried the exit sign?" asked Fons, pointing at an exit that none of them had seen.

Solaris spotted an ornate, black, metal bench on the far side of the wall. Ignoring the gunfire, she strode over to it, yanked it from the wall, and shoved it toward the officers. Stunned, they ducked just as Klanor fired his laser pistol at a fire extinguisher, causing it to explode and fill the room with white mist.

"This way!" said Solaris, leading them to the emergency exit.

"Maybe I should just..." began Fons, but Joe snatched his arm and dragged him along.

They scrambled out of the police station, spotting an abandoned car. Solaris jumped into the driver's seat and started the engine.

"Joe!" Samuel burst from the building, aiming his handgun at Joe. "I can't let you go."

"Samuel," said Joe, holding his hands up, "drop the weapon."

"I trusted you. I defended you," said Samuel, "but you're in league with them." He looked at Brie. "And you, you're a good actress. I almost believed your story."

"It's true," said Joe. "Stein has her family and I'm going to help her get them back."

"You're helping a bunch of terrorists!" shouted Samuel.

"No, they're not."

"I can't let you go," repeated Samuel as he struggled with what Joe had told him in the interrogation room, and what the President and director of the FBI had deemed them to be.

Something crashed in the alley nearby as a feral cat scurried away. Distracted by the noise, Samuel turned, but his finger pulled the trigger; the bullet whizzed by them, striking Solaris, whose nano-skin absorbed the impact. Both Alfric and Joe lunged at Samuel, disarming him and pinning him against the wall.

"Don't hurt him!" shouted Brie.

"He meant to kill us," said Alfric.

"He's only doing his job," said Brie. "He has no reason to trust us."

"Does anyone else hear the sirens coming?" asked Fons.

"In the car," said Joe.

Alfric lagged behind as the others piled into the car, unwilling to leave Joe alone with Samuel.

"Please, give us a moment," said Joe.

The Viking walked away.

"Samuel," said Joe, "I know you think they mean us all harm, but you must believe me when I tell you that there is more going on than any of us realize. The real threat is not them."

"Why should I believe you?"

"Look at the security footage of the Smithsonian."

"You knocked out the cameras, remember?"

"You know as well as I that no matter how hard you try, you always get picked up by the one camera you missed. Think of how many cases we solved because the perpetrator forgot about that one camera."

Samuel glared at him, unsure if he should take the chance and trust his colleague.

"Joe, why?"

"You know why." A honking horn reminded him that time ran short. He released Samuel and jumped into the car, leaving his fellow agent alone in an alley, watching them as they sped away.

Chapter 26
OBIAH'S SUSPICIONS

Keeping his head low, Merrick stalked through the ship, turning down a hallway away from the bustling center, though it didn't seem as crowded as it had been when he first arrived. There were whispers among the crew about people going missing, and when they inquired about their shipmates, those in charge gave vague answers. The halls, which used to be filled with lines of people in lab coats and uniforms, now had a few stragglers.

His boots clomped on the floor as he hurried to where he was to meet with Obiah. He stopped. The area was empty. Where was Obiah? In answer to his unspoken question, a door slid open and hands reached out, seizing him around the collar and yanking him inside. Merrick gasped for air as he was slammed against a wall and the door sealed. As Merrick's eyes focused, he saw who had hold of him.

"Obiah?"

Obiah put his finger over his mouth, signaling silence as two people strolled past. Once gone, he loosened his grip on Merrick and let the man up.

"You didn't need to be so rough," scolded Merrick.

"I wanted to get your attention."

"I'd say you succeeded."

"Where've you been?" demanded Obiah.

"Doing what I came here to do."

"And what was that exactly?"

"Are you accusing me of something?"

"I want to know where your mind is in all of this," said Obiah. "Since the moment we got aboard this ship, you have been elusive, distant even. You are supposed to be gathering information, but thus far all you've managed to do is avoid me."

"I wasn't avoiding you," said Merrick.

"Tell me what is going on. People are disappearing on this ship and Stein seems more paranoid than usual."

"I'm afraid that is my fault."

"What?"

"I was following him, hoping to glean some information by overhearing his conversations. Though, he almost made me."

"He what?"

"I got away."

"Why follow him in the first place? Why not just break through their encryption codes to access their computers?"

"Computers do not tell you everything. They cannot tell you about the way a person carries themselves or acts. Stein is more insane than even Klanor or Brie realized. There is something changed about him. Something…"

Merrick stopped speaking when he realized that he revealed too much.

"How would you know if you have never seen him until now?"

Merrick's face fell.

"You know him, don't you?"

"Once."

"And you never said anything?" growled Obiah.

"Would it have mattered if I had?"

"This explains your eagerness to get aboard this ship and why you virtually disappeared once we separated."

"I…"

"How do you know him? What is he to you?"

Obiah seized the collar of Merrick's uniform, his anger and distrust evident.

"I'd rather not say."

Obiah's grip tightened.

"It doesn't matter how I know him. I just had to see if what the others had said was true, if he truly was insane, and it's worse than that. He has the girl's family here and a plan to use the…"

"Rynah already knows that."

"It's worse. I found this"—Merrick pulled out a handheld holopad and brought up a series of reports—"and there are people being held hostage on this ship. Fredyr had rounded them up for his own purposes, but Stein had them brought here for safekeeping, and considering the tension between the two, I doubt he did it as a favor. He's got something planned, and I'm not sure what."

Obiah mulled over Merrick's words, wondering if he should believe him.

"I swear to you, I never meant to put us into jeopardy."

"We're not finished," said Obiah as he pulled out his communications device that he used for staying in contact with the pirates. "Jifdar?"

"Report," came a crackled reply.

"We've learned some disturbing news. The people that have been brought up from the planet's surface, Stein has…"

Obiah's communications device released a high pitched squeal before falling silent.

"Jifdar. Jifdar!"

"What's going on?" asked Merrick.

"They're jamming all communications. They know they have a mole aboard. Give me your com unit, now."

Obiah took Merrick's unit and threw it on the floor with his own, stomping on them with the heel of his boot, crushing them into several pieces, and rendering them useless.

"They won't be able to trace us with those, but we are now on our own. We will split up for now, but meet up in the tubes at 0900, understand?"

Merrick nodded.

"Merrick?"

"I am on your side," said Merrick and he left.

Obiah sighed in frustration, wishing he knew why Merrick had done what he had, but knowing that now wasn't the time because the hour had come for them to find a way off the ship.

Chapter 27
A Stranger's Wisdom

The television blared in the grungy motel room that they had all checked into. Joe had recommended a place that was infested with cockroaches, as the people who stayed there never asked questions, and the owner always accepted cash. With only one bed, that meant that most of them had to sleep on the floor, which made for some crowded conditions. Tom disliked the bathroom, with the peeling tiles in the shower, the rust stains in the sink—not to mention the leaky plumbing—and the toilet that didn't always flush. Though the others also disliked the conditions, except Alfric who said it reminded him of home, they understood the necessity of such a place when avoiding questions.

Fons fiddled with the curtains, before tapping his fingers on the phone. He missed his home with its computers, but most importantly, he missed his jars of jalapeno peppers. He loved eating them and could never figure out why others thought they were spicy; to him, Jalapenos weren't even mild. This was the longest he had ever been away from his house, having never been one to venture outside, he longed to return.

"I don't see why I have to be with all of you," he said.

"Would you rather be with Stein?" asked Joe.

"No, but he would never know of me if you hadn't dragged me into all of this."

"I'm sorry," said Joe. "I didn't know who else to turn to. I don't know many people who believe in aliens."

"If you wish to leave," said Klanor in an irritated tone, "then go ahead. No one is stopping you. I tire of your complaints." A reproachful look from Rynah stopped him. "I need some air."

He left the room. Alfric started after him, but Brie's gentle touch stopped him. "We must learn to trust him," she said. "It is the only way he can prove himself. Besides, where is he going to go?"

Alfric did not understand Brie's sentiments towards the man, despite his attempts to see things her way.

"I hope you know what you are doing."

"To measure a man's trustworthiness, you must allow him the chance to betray you," said Solon. "Besides, I overheard Solaris telling Rynah that she had put some sort of tracker on him, though I have no idea what it is."

"It means that she found a way to keep tabs on him without actually having to follow him," replied Tom, clapping Solon on the back. "So, big guy over there can take a break." Tom pointed at Alfric.

Groaning, and not understanding what a tracker was, nor caring, Alfric checked the ease with which he could draw his sword should he need to and marched out into the brisk air.

"He never trusts others, does he?" asked Brie.

"He trusts you," said Tom, "but I don't think he understands your willingness to forget about Klanor's past actions."

"I'm not forgetting," Brie snapped.

"Then what?" Tom asked, bewildered, like the others, about Brie's defense of the man who tortured her with mind games.

Solon stepped forward, placing a gentle hand on Tom's shoulder and calming him.

"Some things cannot be put into words. I trust your judgment, Brie."

"It's not that I don't trust you," Tom said to Brie, "I just wish to understand."

"You remember the helmets that linked us telepathically to Solaris?" said Brie and the other two nodded. "When we were trying to escape the pirates and were all three wearing the helmets, I thought that I caught a glimpse of your thoughts, or emotions, the things that are kept buried deep within, but it was muddled because we were also tuned into Solaris and fleeing for our lives. Klanor questioned me by using a similar telepathic link, except there was no third party. It was just him and me. I saw what he keeps bottled inside him. Being linked like that, it wasn't just our minds that were connected, nor were his thoughts the only thing I could see, but I also felt the pain within him, and the guilt he lives with every day. There is only one thing he loves most, besides the crystals, and as twisted as it sounds, everything he has done was to protect her."

As her words dissipated and buried themselves into Tom's and Solon's minds, Brie pointed at Rynah, who remained locked in her conversation with Joe and Solaris, while Fons watched them.

"I think Solon was right about you," said Tom. "You see people. You understand them." He stood up and headed to the other end of the room. "Now, if you don't mind, I've got to use what passes for a bathroom around here."

* * *

Klanor's quick steps crunched the rocks beneath his feet as he walked across the crumbling asphalt, decayed by time and the years of harsh winters. The green and red glow of the motel sign provided the only light in the parking lot, with its three cars. No stars shown above him. Even they wanted nothing to do with him. Swirls of snow danced before his feet, guiding him as he walked over to the highway, crossed it, and jumped the barbed wire fence.

He wanted to run away. Now was his chance. All he had to do was keep going. They would never find him in this vast place, but where would he go? He was an alien on an alien planet—alone.

Klanor looked back at the motel, its black silhouette outlined in the greenish-red light of the sign. It seemed odd to have a building in the middle of nowhere, but there it was, on its own, no friends, no companions, just like him. Emotions roiled within him. Each day he was around Rynah, his love for her boiled just below the surface, growing stronger. The turmoil that plagued him since the day he stole the crystal from Lanyr intensified. *Why do I stay?* He knew why, even if he wished to forget it—Rynah.

Then there was Brie. She trusted him. She had every reason to loathe him, yet she trusted him to return. Why? Was it because of what she had seen in his mind while they were telepathically linked? Did she see something in him that he never saw within himself?

Nausea somersaulted in his stomach as he thought about the pirates on that planet that had tried to kill him and Rynah. His stomach twisted with each thought about Brie and what he had done to her, and yet, she harbored no ill will toward him. Feelings that he had always shunted aside slammed into him, ensnaring him with their viselike grip and refusing to release him.

"Why?" he shouted at the night sky.

"You need to get it together," said a voice. A man, whom Klanor had not even seen, stepped out of the shadows, smoking a cigarette. "You want one?"

"No," said Klanor, backing further into the shadows so as to conceal his face. "I'm sorry."

"For what?" asked the stranger. "You're not disturbing me. You look like you got a lot on your mind. This is a great place to work out one's thoughts. I came out here for a smoke. Kind of funny, you know, a roach motel that doesn't allow smoking."

"You could say that."

"Want to talk about it?"

Klanor stared at the man, taken aback. No one had ever offered to talk to him about anything. He had always been in control, so assured of his wants and desires, until now.

"I'm just confused."

"I gathered that."

Klanor sighed. Maybe it wouldn't hurt to talk. He did not know the man, and most likely would never see him again, thus eradicating his fear of being judged.

"I used to know what I wanted, but now I'm not so sure. I have used people, hurt them, even killed, all for the sake of getting what I want and now..." His voice trailed off.

"It doesn't seem worth it," finished the man.

"I know this man. I saved his life once, but I did it for my own purposes. The trouble is, I think I turned him into something horrible, something dark. He betrayed me and when he did, I saw in him exactly who I was. I saw myself.

"And there is this woman. I pretended to love her because she had something I wanted, so I betrayed her and broke her heart, though I think I broke mine instead. And after warring with one another, now we are forced together to be allies. But I see it each day, the pain I caused her, the pain I caused myself."

"Have you asked her to forgive you?"

"What?"

"I've been there, you know. Loved a woman; broke her heart. I had the chance to say I was sorry, but never did. Regretted it ever since. What you need to ask yourself is why you're out here, while she's in there."

"I've committed unforgivable crimes."

"We've all done things we ain't proud of," said the man, "but you can change if you want to. Used to be an anger-filled man myself who hated everyone. Thought I couldn't change, and because of that, I lost everyone I cared about. Don't make the same mistake I did."

"Have you changed?"

"I like to think so." The man tossed his cigarette into a patch of crusted snow. "Time was I wouldn't have bothered talking to someone like you. If you truly love that woman, you need to tell her that you're sorry. You need to let her know. Make amends. It's better than being out here on your own, yelling at the sky."

Klanor said nothing. For reasons he could not explain, he felt comfortable talking to this stranger from an unfamiliar planet about his troubles, about what bothered him.

"The thing you need to remember is it doesn't matter who you were. What matters is who you decide to be now, today. Every one falls at some point, but not everyone gets back up."

Klanor cocked his head as he listened to the man speak. His last words sounded familiar, and Klanor remembered once, long ago, before he had even heard about the crystals, a stranger, much like the one he spoke to now, telling him the same thing: what matters is who you choose to be now, in the present and the future.

"You hear about the rumors?" asked the man.

"What rumors?" demanded Klanor.

"There's been talk in the next town over about how people have gone missing. Just disappeared, and strange ships showing up. Videos have been popping up on the internet about it too, showing strange lights and marks in the ground. And then there was that purple-faced guy on the tube not too far back. Folk out here like to believe that they live too far away to be concerned about what's happening elsewhere in the world."

"Have you seen these lights?" asked Klanor.

"Nope. Not personally, but can't help but wonder if they're true." The man took out another cigarette and lit it before turning around. "Well, I got to go. See ya around."

Klanor remained where he was and looked up at the night sky and the small space in the clouds where they parted with its bright stars, wondering what the constellations were and what stories the people of earth told about them, and for a moment, he was thrust back into the days of his youth when he used to ponder about the wonders of his world before he changed. He turned around and stopped. Right behind him was a shape he had come to recognize, Alfric.

"You spying on me now?" grumbled Klanor as he pushed his way past the Viking.

"Merely keeping an eye on you," Alfric replied.

"I hope you didn't scare that poor man."

"He never knew I was here, and neither did you, until I wanted you to."

"Look," said Klanor, "I understand that you don't trust me, and that you never will, but you don't need to keep following me. And don't think that I don't know about Solaris' tracking device. I don't need you constantly keeping watch over me. If I had wanted to run, I would have by now."

"Why haven't you?" asked Alfric.

"Where would I go?" Klanor started back to the motel, but Alfric stopped him.

"Why didn't you? Back in those canyons, when those vagabonds had taken Jifdar and Rynah was wounded, why didn't you leave us and join those pirates?"

"They would have killed me, same as you. It served my purpose to help you two."

"So, it was to save your own neck."

"Not every man is your enemy," said Klanor.

"Not every man is my friend, either," replied Alfric.

A high pitched whine filled his ears as a light approached, turning into three, defining the edges of an aircraft as it flew overhead and disappeared into the field beyond. Both Klanor and Alfric stared after it. The moment Klanor saw it, he recognized it as one of Fredyr's vessels.

Klanor bolted for the fence, crawling through it and running back to the motel, heading straight for the room where the others were—where Rynah was—knowing what he needed to do, with Alfric on his heels.

* * *

"Hey," said Tom, pointing at the TV, "look at this."

The others gathered around him and watched as a man walked across the screen in a crowd of people dressed in outrageous outfits (some glittered, some appeared metallic, others were more scandalous, while even more resembled a fashion nightmare) and their faces painted with heavy, and gaudy, makeup.

"What is the meaning of their attire?" asked Solon. "Are they demons? Or going to a temple for a ceremonial sacrifice?"

"No," Brie laughed, "they're at some sort of convention. A comic con."

"A what?" asked Rynah.

"It's a place where every freak, weirdo, comic book, and science fiction obsessed person can go," said Joe in a bored tone. "They play dress up, reenact their favorite shows, and other weird stuff."

Tom turned up the volume.

"Here we are at the annual *Are They Out There* convention in Albuquerque, New Mexico," said the reporter. "As you can see, many have dressed up as their favorite character from various science fiction television shows and movies. Here is one. Who are you supposed to be?"

A teenage kid looked at the reporter in awe, pleased that he would be on national TV.

"I'm from the race of Golgarcs from the planet Garth. Do you want to see my vaporizers?"

The kid pulled out a water gun that he had wrapped metallic

material and sequins, securing it with duct tape. As he showed it to the reporter, his hands fumbled and he dropped his "vaporizer".

"Sorry. I'll..."

"I'm sure it is very interesting," said the reporter with a facial expression that said he wanted to be anywhere but there. He looked back into the camera.

"The convention will be hosted for the next week. Anyone can come, even those who do not wish to dress up. Besides the alien abductees seminar, there are some noted scientists who will be here, offering presentations about distant planets and whether alien life truly exists. Back to you, Harold."

Tom turned down the volume. "What do you think?"

"I say we go," said Brie.

"Because a place where a bunch of nut jobs are is exactly where an alien would hide?" joked Tom.

"Exactly," said Brie. "If you were an alien, where would you go? Besides,"—Brie pointed at the screen again and a man, who matched the one they were looking for, shoved his way through the meandering crowd—"doesn't he look familiar?"

"Yeah, he does," said Tom. "He looks like the person we're looking for."

Though she didn't like the term alien, when they referred to the man they looked for, Rynah kept quiet, knowing that they had no other way of referring to a person from another planet, and she had more important matters to worry about.

"It's where I would go," said Joe. "If I were a Lanyran marooned on this planet, I would go to a place where people routinely dressed up as extraterrestrials. Easier to blend in. Besides, such an event is the one place where you might meet someone who can help you get home."

"I'm not going," said Fons, folding his arms.

"You want me to hogtie you?" threatened Joe.

Rynah held up her hand to silence him.

"Fons, do you remember the night when you were abducted?"

Fons' demeanor softened. No one had ever asked him about that night before, not unless they were looking for a way to ridicule him.

"Not really, no."

"Will you tell me about it?" she asked.

"I don't remember much," said Fons, with a distant look in his eyes as he thought back to that night. "I had just had my eighth birthday. My family was very poor and my father had always talked about coming to America and making a new life for all of us, and he had tried to get the appropriate papers to immigrate legally, but it took too long. That night, my mother had just put me to bed, hoping that I would fall asleep instead of listening to them argue over whether to risk a trek across the border or not. Then, the noise started. It was a howling sound, as though a great wind storm had sprang up, but there were no clouds, no thunder.

"A bright blue and white light filled my window, brightening my room just like the sun would each morning when it rose. I ran out to my parents, but they had gone outside to see what the light was. I remember standing in the doorway, watching as my father approached the bright light."

Fons stopped as the memory of that night rushed back to him, a memory he wished to forget.

"Please, continue," said Rynah, in a gentle voice.

"Well, everything happened really fast. A man popped out of the light—more like thrown out—and my father was consumed by it. Screaming, my mother ran for him, and she disappeared as well. The man, he looked different—alien—but he tried to make them stop. That was when I ran for the light, wanting to know where my parents had gone. The man jumped to his feet and grabbed me before I could reach it, yelling at me in a language I had never heard before, or since.

"The strange light vanished as quickly as it had appeared. I remember the man said something to me—words I never forgot—*masarow*."

"Ancient Lanyran for 'I'm sorry,'" said Rynah. "What happened next?"

"I don't remember," said Fons. "I must have blacked out, because all I remember after that is waking up in the local church. The padre told me that a man, with a purple face, had brought me there, and left. He never said anything, but his eyes said all that needed to be said—sorrow and guilt."

Rynah moseyed over to the far side of the room. "You were never abducted," she said, "but, unfortunately, you were the victim of some accident."

"A vortex," said Solaris. "My database recounts five, matching that which you have described. A time vortex it is called."

"So, then my parents might have survived," said Fons.

"I do not think so," said Solaris. "The man you mentioned is lucky to have not been harmed, but even if your parents had survived, there is no way of knowing where they went, and if that man spoke Ancient Lanyran, then it is reasonable to assume that he is from that era and your parents were sent there. They would be dead. I'm sorry."

"Don't apologize," said Fons. "You had nothing to do with it. Besides, I mourned them long ago."

"I think I know where we should go next," said Rynah, glancing back at the television set and the images of alien-looking people on it.

At that moment, Klanor and Alfric burst in. "We have a problem."

"Where?" Rynah demanded.

"We saw a ship fly overhead. It headed due north," said Klanor.

"There is a town that way," added Joe.

"What should we do?" asked Fons.

"We should check it out," said Brie.

Rynah shook her head. As much as she wanted to, she knew that they were outnumbered.

"I agree," Klanor added.

Startled by his statement, Rynah eyed him, the mixture of distrust and confusion that dwelled within her heart evident on her face.

"We need to know what Stein and Fredyr are up to," Klanor said.

"Fine," Rynah relented. "Alfric, Klanor, and I will go."

"But..." Brie began, but Rynah interrupted her.

"We will check it out. I want the rest of you to remain here. If we do not return by morning, leave without us. Joe, you are in charge. You know this place better than the rest of us. I'm counting on you."

Joe just nodded his head in agreement; his eyes told her that he would do as she had asked.

"Here," said Brie, giving Rynah back her bracelet. "So we can find you."

Rynah smiled, seeing the concern in Brie's face, and placed the bracelet that Marlow had given her when she was a child back on her wrist.

Solaris placed a hand on the front of Rynah's shoulder.

"I should come with you."

"No," replied Rynah, "I need you to stay here, to protect them. Besides myself, you are the only one who knows the ancient myth by heart. Please, Solaris. Alfric, and I can handle Klanor."

"It's not Klanor I'm worried about."

Rynah smiled, but said nothing and removed Solaris' hand, giving it a gentle pat in reassurance.

"Be careful, all of you," she said to the others as she walked out the door with Alfric and Klanor.

* * *

"Round them up!" yelled one of Fredyr's men as he cracked his whip, frightening the line of people that had been ripped from their homes in the middle of the night and shuffled aboard a strange ship.

Rynah, Klanor, and Alfric crouched behind snow covered bushes, watching as the slavers inspected their stock.

"This is exactly what Joe said his friend, Samuel, had told him earlier," said Rynah. "He said that people had been going missing and that others have blamed aliens for it."

"Well, in this case, they are telling the truth," said Klanor. "These are Fredyr's ships. He always did look upon another planet's populace as resources."

Rynah frowned. She had hoped to never run into the man again, considering she had stolen a crystal from his estate, an act he would never forget, nor forgive. She craned her head up to garner a better look. Two shuttlecrafts stood poised on the valley floor, their cargo doors open as the line of people shuffled inside. Scanning the area, Rynah counted the number of armed guards, realizing that there was no scenario in which she and Klanor could save these people.

"We need to leave."

"But what about them?" hissed Klanor, feeling the need to help those being rounded up like cattle, and the thought of what would be done to them disgusting him.

"There are at least 30 armed men out there," said Rynah. "We cannot fight them all. I'm sorry, but we have to leave them."

Disappointed, Klanor watched as Fredyr's men shouted insults at the line of freshly caught slaves, knowing that Rynah was right.

Rynah noticed his crestfallen face. She placed her hand on his arm, her gentle touch shaking him from his dismayed thoughts.

"I'm sorry," she said.

The three of them turned and crawled away from the crest of the hill, but had only moved a few yards before a force slammed into Rynah, sending her flying down the hill. Her arms and legs flailed as she somersaulted downward, unable to stop herself. Klanor tackled the man that had attacked Rynah. They tumbled over a ledge, plunging to the ground below and crashing onto the hard surface. Klanor jabbed the man in the jaw with the point of his elbow, but the man tossed him aside and seized a rock, ready to strike Klanor with it. Before he could, Alfric released a battle cry and seized the man by the neck and arms, throwing him into the air and against a protruding boulder, where he landed with a sickening crunch.

While Alfric turned to face his attacker, Klanor watched as the number of Fredyr's men grew and knew that, despite his skills, Alfric would never be able to face them all. He glanced at Rynah, her eyes closed. Determined not to have anyone die that night—he didn't know why he cared, only that he did—Klanor rushed Alfric, snatched the Viking's sword, and struck him over the head with it, knocking him unconscious. Before Fredyr's men had reached them, he shoved Alfric under some bushes and away from the light of the ships, leaving his blade with him and scrambled over to Rynah as she lay motionless on the rocky surface.

"Rynah," Klanor whispered, lifting her up, but before he regained his feet, hands seized his arms, flinging him away from her. Grunting as the air in his lungs was knocked out, Klanor rolled onto his back, but a heavy boot kicked him in the stomach. He glanced at Rynah. She stirred, but in her dazed state, was unable to defend herself. More guards appeared, pinning both her and Klanor to the ground.

"Well," said a familiar voice.

Upon hearing it, Rynah's mind focused. She looked up. Staring straight at her was Fredyr Monsooth; his venomous sneer caused her heart to skip two beats.

"Rynah," said Fredyr as he tickled her chin with his strong fingers, "how nice to see you again, though I would have preferred better circumstances."

Klanor struggled against the hands that held him down.

"And you," Fredyr turned to him, "how fitting that you should be here with her, in the muck. How low you have fallen now that your friend has turned on you."

"You think Stein won't do the same to you," spat Klanor.

"I am not as naïve as you were," replied Fredyr. "I know the nature of my agreement with Stein. Your trouble was that you actually trusted him."

"A mistake I won't make twice," said Klanor.

"And one you will never live to remedy. Now, where is your friend? The big, brutish fellow."

Klanor said nothing.

"Very well." Fredyr seized Rynah around the throat and squeezed.

"She doesn't know!" screamed Klanor, and Fredyr released her, "and neither do I."

Fredyr eyed Klanor's unreadable gaze before saying,

"Kill them."

"Mr. Monsooth," said Gaden, stepping forward, "Stein will wish to question them."

"Are you questioning my orders?" challenged Fredyr.

"No, sir," replied Gaden, "but they have other accomplices and we will not learn of their whereabouts if they are dead."

Fredyr pondered the man's statement, trying to decide if he could trust him or not.

"It would show Stein that he can trust you, which may prove useful."

"Take them aboard the ship," Fredyr said, seeing the potential of earning Stein's confidence and the need to find Rynah's allies. Once he had eradicated them, he could focus on displacing Stein.

Chapter 28
SINKING FEELING

Solaris sat on the bed in the sliver of sunlight, peeking through the slit in the curtain and staring at the red numbers of the digital clock. 10 a.m. Night had turned into day, and still they waited for Rynah to return with Klanor and Alfric, but no one walked through the door. When Joe had mentioned that they should leave, in accordance with Rynah's orders, Solaris refused, and with the help of the others, convinced Joe to remain. He promised them two more hours. They took five.

The door creaked as it opened before closing once again.

"It's time," said Joe.

With dismal faces, Brie, Solon, and Tom stared back at him, pleading for more time. Only Fons grabbed his bag and slung it over his shoulder. A soft bit of pressure squeezed Solaris' arm.

"I'm sorry," Joe said to her; his face conveyed understanding and sympathy, but he knew they could remain there no longer.

"You're right," Solaris conceded.

They packed their things in a car that Joe had procured earlier when he left that morning to get supplies. He detested the idea of stealing, but knew that if they did not keep changing vehicles, they would be caught.

Outside, Brie watched her friends' mechanical movements as they filled the car with their meager belongings and piled into the backseat. Rage filled her. They should be looking for Rynah, not accepting the probability of not seeing her again. She slammed the car door.

"We should go look for them."

"What?" asked Fons.

"I said," continued Brie in a more forceful tone, "we should look for them."

"Brie," said Joe, "Rynah's orders were specific."

"So that's it then," said Brie. "She tells you to jump and you do it?"

"Brie," said Tom, "I hate to agree with Joe, but we all know who sent those ships and what probably happened to her."

"Exactly," said Brie, "we do know, and it's because of that reason that we should go find them."

"Brie..."

"I know that the chances of us finding them are slim, but what if they got away? What if they are heading here, right now, but are wounded?"

No one looked at her.

"I can't believe this!" shouted Brie. "You all searched outer space to find me, but are unwilling to drive a few miles to find Rynah and Klanor? And what about you, Solaris? Are you just going to leave her to die? Cowards! All of you!"

A scuffling noise forced them to turn their heads. They blinked in the morning sunlight as a darkened shape stumbled over the bank and shuffled towards them. It was Alfric.

"Alfric!" Brie ran to him and helped him back to the car.

"What happened?" asked Joe.

"We were attacked," said Alfric, rubbing his head as it still pounded from where Klanor had struck him.

"Rynah and Klanor?" asked Solon.

"Gone," replied Alfric.

"Is there the possibility they could have gotten away, and you were all separated?" asked Solon.

"Possible, but unlikely," Alfric said.

Brie snatched the keys from Joe's slackened grip and jumped into the driver's seat of the car.

"Where are you going?" demanded Tom.

"To find them," Brie replied, starting the engine.

Alfric's strong hand stopped her. Pausing, Brie looked into his gentle eyes, noting something there that she hadn't seen before, benevolence and belief in her.

"I cannot let you go alone," he said.

"Nor can I," said Joe, shoving Brie to the passenger side of the car. "Everyone in."

Fons watched, dumbfounded, as they all piled into the car without question.

"Are you all crazy? You know they aren't there! I know how these abductions work. They…"

"Fons," said Joe, his tone threatening, "get in, or I'll throw you in the trunk."

Fons placed his hands on his hips as his face turned sour. "You would, too." He squeezed into the backseat of the station wagon and glared at Joe. "If we get abducted, I blame you."

Joe put the car in reverse and backed out of the parking lot, before heading down the empty highway with dust trailing after them. The place where Rynah, Alfric, and Klanor had gone wasn't far. It was a small community, numbering about 50, one of those towns that most people pass through, if they pass by it at all; it didn't even have its own dot on a map. Joe drove at 15 miles per hour down the dirt road—only a single car width—that snaked through the town.

Silence loomed. They looked out at the empty houses, a basketball that rolled down a driveway, and the cars that looked as though they had been left by force. Joe steered the car around an abandoned bicycle, with pink ribbons poking out of the handles, laying in the middle of the road. Frigid air drifted across the landscape, adding to the forlorn feeling that consumed them, and still there was no sign of Rynah or Klanor.

"I don't think anyone is here," said Tom. "It's like they vanished."

The others agreed. Signs that people had lived there the day before surrounded them, but the entire place had been reduced to a ghost town.

"You're friends have been taken," said Fons.

No one spoke. No other explanation remained other than that Rynah and Klanor had been captured by the very ones who took the people of the community they wandered through. Joe stopped the car. Up ahead were two black SUVs and FBI agents searching the town. Keeping his eyes on the agents, Joe put the car in reverse and eased it backward behind a building and down an alley.

"Do you know who they are?" asked Alfric.

"Yeah," said Joe. "They're agents."

"What is their interest in this place?" Alfric continued.

"Probably the same as ours," Joe replied. "Samuel said that they had been investigating more supposed alien abductions. I guess they are no longer rumors."

"They never were," Fons quipped.

Joe backed down the alley and pulled out onto a road—or a lane made by people driving their trucks down it, forging their own path—and headed back out of town.

"We can't just leave," said Brie.

"If we stay," Joe said, "we will get caught, and then we will be unable to help your friends."

"But..." began Brie.

Solon placed a hand on her arm, cutting her off.

"Brie, we cannot help them if we, too, are locked in a prison."

"The kid's right," said Joe as he turned back on the highway. "We need to find a place to lay low and contact your other friends in space."

"What?" Fons' eyebrows shot up. "There's more of you?"

* * *

Metallic clomps stormed through the ship as Stein marched through the narrow, shadowed corridor to the black doors before him that led straight to Fredyr Monsooth's personal chambers; his foul mood on full display for all to see at having been summoned. This was his armada, and Fredyr insisted on issuing him orders as though he was a servant. The opalescent light reflected off the coal-colored doors as they slid open, allowing Stein passage.

"You summoned me," he said; his irritated tone did not go unnoticed.

"Summoned," said Fredyr. His faux jovial voice filled the room, and Stein detected the bit of sarcasm within it. "My good sir, you make it sound as though I have issued you orders. Now, I simply asked to see you because I thought you would wish to see this."

Fredyr held out a palm-sized holo-emitter; it's bluish-green light illuminated the dim room as Rynah's and Klanor's faces came to life before them. Unsure about whether this was another of Fredyr's ruses, Stein studied the images for a moment until he asked, "When?"

"An hour ago," said Fredyr. "They got too close while I was harvesting some resources."

Stein glared at Fredyr. He hated slavery, but he especially loathed Fredyr's insistence on not calling it what it was.

"And what have you done with them?"

"I brought them here, of course. I thought that you might wish to question them, or, at the very least, decide their fate."

"I thank you," said Stein. "I'll have them brought to my ship."

"I think that it would be best if they remained here." Fredyr smiled as he said that last statement, but his eyes conveyed another message, a warning. "You don't want to keep your valuable prisoners all in one place."

Stein studied Fredyr, contemplating his next words and knowing that Fredyr tested him to see if he would attempt to exert his authority. Relaxing his face and donning a smile, Stein embraced Fredyr's suggestion. "I think you're right."

Pleased that Stein accepted his proposal, Fredyr sauntered over to a lone table where a carafe of red wine sat. He picked it up and poured himself a glass, before turning back to Stein.

"I noticed that you have failed to acquire the others."

"Failed?"

"Oh," chuckled Fredyr, "I didn't mean it quite like that. No doubt you have expended every effort to capture them, and yet, they continue to elude you."

"They will be dealt with," said Stein, "as will all who have betrayed me."

"Of that I'm certain, but might I make a suggestion?"

"Please do."

"My uncle was an avid fisherman, always going out to the river before dawn, but he never caught anything, not even one fish, until he discovered the secret to successful fishing. Do you want to know what that is?"

"Indubitably," said Stein.

"My father learned that if one has the proper bait, the fish will be lured to the hook and caught. You have two perfect worms right here."

"So I do," Stein agreed.

"I'm sure that we could convince the others to come here to negotiate a trade, as they have the crystal and you have their friends."

"No," said Stein. "Down there."

"But…"

"They feel safe there and will think that they can outsmart us. We can use that against them."

Stein watched as Fredyr's face changed expression when he saw the merit in his plan, to which he was most pleased.

"As you wish," said Fredyr, draining his glass of wine.

"Might I see the prisoners?" asked Stein.

"In a moment. There is one other thing I wish to discuss with you. I've noticed that there has been an increase in the number of your men aboard my ships."

"Yes, there has been. It was done in compliance with the exchange you had asked for. I hope that I wasn't too forward in assuming…"

"Not at all."

"The prisoners?"

"Yes," said Fredyr, "one of my men will take you to them. Oh, and, when you are ready to spring the trap, I want to be there."

Stein grinned at Fredyr. "And so you shall."

Chapter 29
RYNAH'S FAILURE

Rough hands shoved Rynah inside the white-walled room, forcing her feet to skip several steps as she struggled to maintain her balance. She slammed into the far wall, air expelling from her lungs as the impact shook her. Turning, Rynah stared back at the masked guards as they sealed the door. Alone, she looked around. No cot. No chair. No ounce of comfort. Only a bare floor and white—though chipped and peeling—walls stared back at her, taunting her and daring her to curse them and her circumstances. Feeling a draft of cool air, Rynah reached up and touched the only vent in the small room as it blew upon her.

She thought about Klanor. Of all the people to enter her mind, why the man she loathed? Rynah knew. It was because he had tried to save her, an act she could not ignore.

The door slid open. In walked Stein and two guards dragging Klanor, bloodied and beaten. They tossed him to the floor. He slumped to the icy surface, blood oozing from his swollen lip, forming dots on the gray tiles. Rynah remained still.

"Where are your friends?" demanded Stein.

"I don't know," answered Rynah.

Stein's hardened face told her that he did not believe her. Why would he? Every prisoner claims to not know what the interrogator wants. "How naïve do you think I am?"

"Do you really want an answer to that?" came Rynah's sarcastic remark.

"Don't get smart with me," warned Stein, inching closer until she smelled the remnants of the sausage he had eaten hours earlier on his breath. "Tell me what I want to know and I will release you and your lover here."

"Why should I believe you?"

"My only interest is in the crystals."

"Why?" demanded Rynah. "He wanted them, same as you, and look where he is now."

Stein moseyed over to Klanor's crumpled form, shoving his pointed boot under him before kicking hard, forcing Klanor to turn over onto his back while clutching his stomach.

"Yes, well, he made the mistake of trusting me."

"A mistake that I'll not make."

A sneer snaked across Stein's face.

"Of that, I'm certain, but you should know that I will destroy everything and everyone you hold dear to get what I want, starting with him."

Stein seized Klanor by the collar of his shirt, jerking him to his knees, and pulled out his laser pistol, pointing it at Klanor's head.

"Where are your friends?"

Rynah said nothing.

"Tell me," said Stein, "and I'll even forget the fact that it was your grandfather who murdered my family."

Rynah remained silent, remembering the enraged look on Stein's face when had learned the truth the day she and her friends had stolen the crystal from the museum. Her eyes darted between Klanor's swollen face, the slits for his puffy eyes, and Stein's merciless glare.

"Tell me, or I will kill your fiancé here and now!"

Struggling with indecision, Rynah longed to see Klanor punished for his crimes, but a part of her abhorred the thought of his murder, while at the same time, she knew she must keep the location of her companions a secret, even if the cost meant her soul.

"Tell me what I want to know or watch him die," said Stein, his impatience growing at her continued silence.

Rynah looked into Klanor's pleading eyes before jerking her head away, refusing to acknowledge the conflicting feelings within her, especially the ones that conveyed her love for him, a love that never faded or left, despite the betrayal she suffered.

Forcing herself to stare into Stein's soulless eyes, she hardened her face and her voice, saying, "Kill him then."

Stein squeezed the trigger. A miniscule pop sounded as the laser pistol went off, sending an energy pulse into Klanor's brain, killing him. Stein dropped the body.

"You two are a pair, both willing to sacrifice the other for your cause."

Containing her emotions (her desire to scream or to bash Stein's skull into the wall), Rynah swallowed back her tears as silent rage replaced them and she understood, in that moment, Solaris' seeming coldness when Lanyr had been destroyed, realizing her need for self-control, knowing what the cost would be if Stein achieved his goal.

"You know nothing about sacrifice, or love," she whispered, her voice strained as she suppressed her wrath.

In a maniacal fury, Stein rushed her, punching her in the face and knocking her into the wall.

"Don't impugn me on him! Don't play the card of righteousness! I know who you are, Rynah, and who your grandfather is. I know what Marlow did to the Brestef region."

Rynah looked up at Stein.

"You thought I wouldn't find out?" continued Stein.

"What do you care about that place? You weren't there. Everyone who was got killed."

"Not everyone," hissed Stein as he pulled up his sleeve, revealing the pasty, wrinkled skin underneath from the scars left after the burns he had received. The folds of skin disguised the muscles well with their blackened, red-tinged lines that spread in a jagged fashion from his wrist to his shoulder.

"Not everyone died that day. Those who lived wished they had. Imagine standing helpless as you watch the ones you love burn to death. Imagine their screams, which will haunt your dreams for the rest of your life.

"The pursuit of the crystals killed them, and only the crystals can undo that wrong. He promised me salvation,"—Stein kicked Klanor's corpse— "but he lied."

"You're insane," said Rynah.

"Insane! Insanity is pursuing inanimate objects because you think they have power! Insanity is destroying millions of lives for your own selfish gain!"

"And so you will destroy millions more, to ease your grief," said Rynah.

"Don't," warned Stein. "You have no right to question my actions. How many people have you killed, Rynah, to protect your secrets? How many more will die because of you? I will have the crystals and what was promised to me. Or in any case, I will ensure that this universe will know what real suffering is, starting with that pathetic planet below. And you will watch as they burn, tormented by the fact that despite your efforts, you were unable to save them."

"And what of the cost?" asked Rynah.

"I've already paid it." Stein snapped his fingers and the two guards lifted Klanor's lifeless body and carried it out of the room, leaving Rynah alone with her unsettled thoughts.

A distant explosion sounded, rippling through the metallic walls before the ship lurched, forcing Rynah onto her hands and knees.

She stayed down, listening. Another explosion rocked the vessel. The light in her cell turned red as the alarm sounded, its screech deafening her. Shouts outside her cell door rushed past as men ran to their stations. Rynah sprang for the door.

The lock clicked. Stepping back, she waited for her fate to enter the room. The door slid open. Before her stood a guard holding a laser rifle. The two stared at one another before the guard took off her helmet, revealing the face underneath.

"Solaris?" said Rynah, in disbelief.

"You didn't think I would leave you here, did you?" replied Solaris. "Where's Klanor?"

Rynah's downcast face and clenched fists answered Solaris' question. "I'm sorry."

Laser fire skimmed the corner of the doorways, forcing Rynah and Solaris to duck behind it for cover. Solaris returned fire, striking the guard in the chest.

"Come on," she said.

Rynah followed Solaris through the door and paused, staring in the direction she thought she had seen Stein turn in, debating whether she should pursue him and kill him for what he had done, but Solaris' light touch on her arm stopped her.

"You cannot help him now," she said, as though she knew what Rynah considered doing.

Relenting, and remembering that there was a planet of innocent people who needed her to remain focused, Rynah chased after Solaris as they ran through the corridor.

"How did you…" she began.

"No time," replied Solaris, cutting her off.

Shouts and yells echoed behind them as they rushed through the winding hallways to the shuttle bay with laser fire whizzing past them, striking the walls as they ran and turned corners in an effort to escape. A guard blocked their path. In fluid movements, Solaris raised the butt of her laser rifle and rammed it into the man's head, before turning it and firing at another who approached. Rynah stripped the dead guard of his weapon. Heavy footsteps approached. Turning, she fired at the guards who rushed for her before Solaris seized her arm and shoved her into another corridor.

"Where are the others?" demanded Rynah.

A missile detonated off the hull of the ship, its explosion ripping through it as lights burst and panels from the ceiling fell around them.

"With the pirates," said Solaris as she pushed Rynah onward.

Their feet stomped on the metallic floor, sending hollow clomps all around them as yells and laser fire pursued their every move.

"This way," said Solaris, steering Rynah to the right.

They entered a small room, used more for storage, crouching behind upturned chairs and abandoned pipes and wires as men rushed past, unaware of their presence. Solaris tapped Rynah's arm. Following her friend, she and Solaris left the storage area and ran in the opposite direction of the guards, turning another corner and continuing to the shuttle hangar.

Laser fire struck the wall in front of them, causing sparks to fly in their faces as a blackened hole remained. Rynah and Solaris jerked back, shielding themselves. They had been cut off. Both returned fire, but Rynah's weapon had jammed. Smacking the laser weapon, she cursed as more of Stein's men approached.

Solaris hauled Rynah to her feet, pushing her through a door and into a dark room with computer consoles, their holographic monitors flickering at her. The doors slammed shut; a loud click surrounded them as Solaris jammed the opening mechanism. She hurried through the circular room, searching for another way out, but found nothing.

"We're trapped."

"There has to be a way out," said Rynah.

Bang!

The armed men on the other side smashed into the door, attempting to open it. Rynah knew that it was only a matter of minutes before they managed to break through.

"There is no other way," said Solaris, aiming her laser rifle at the dented door.

Rynah glanced around at the computer consoles. If she could get a message out, perhaps Jifdar could blast a hole in this part of the ship.

"Solaris," she said, "if a missile were to strike that far wall, would we survive?"

"The odds are a million to one. Though I found some spacesuits over in that locker there. If we were to wear those, they would protect us from the initial blast and the vacuum of space."

"Giving Jifdar time to pull us in with a tractor beam," said Rynah.

"But how do we get word to him? My radio is damaged."

Rynah pointed to the computers.

"Do you know the encryption codes?" asked Solaris.

"No," replied Rynah, "but you can break them, can't you?"

Another clang reverberated around them as Stein's men pried the doors open by half an inch. Solaris fired at them, forcing them to release the doors.

"That won't hold for much longer." Solaris tossed Rynah the laser rifle and hurried over to a computer console. The holoscreen flashed to life as she opened encryption code after encryption code until she had hacked into the communication system of the ship.

"I am unable to reach the pirates."

Rynah leaned over Solaris' shoulder.

"What do you mean?"

"I cannot raise him on the com."

"Just use frequency 61, like what I use to talk to you," said Rynah, confused as to why Solaris seemed stumped on how to raise Jifdar on the communications array.

Solaris paused.

"What's wrong?" asked Rynah.

Solaris turned her head, a triumphant grin on her face. "Thank you."

Uneasiness filled Rynah as she stared at Solaris' maniacal smile, and took two steps back, terror filling her.

"For what?"

"For telling me what I wanted to know."

The computer consoles and holoscreens vanished as Rynah was thrust into another room with bright, white lights glaring in her face, her arms and legs strapped to a leather chair, while a thin helmet rested on her head. With horror, she understood that Solaris and the escape attempt were just fantasies, a ruse to trick her into revealing how she communicated with the others, but a jolt of hope filled her when she realized that Klanor's death had never happened.

Stein sat in another chair across from her.

"Congratulations," he said, taking his helmet off. "You just betrayed your friends."

Rynah writhed in her chair, yanking against the restraints, wishing she could get her bare hands on Stein's neck; the straps cut deep into her skin, piercing her flesh while trickles of blood dripped down them.

"I must say," continued Stein, "that I didn't think it would be this easy, but you were so desperate to believe that your friends had come for you." He rose from his seat, revealing Klanor, strapped in a similar leather chair, who stared back at her, a wounded expression on his face. "As you can see, your lover is very much alive. I wonder how it feels to know that you could so easily kill him just to protect your secrets."

Gloating, Stein glanced from one to the other.

"I'll leave you two alone then."

He walked to the door, pausing as it slid open.

"Oh, and, in case you are interested," he said to Rynah, "he resisted all of my attempts to probe his mind and never betrayed you."

The doors closed behind him, leaving her in silence with the

man she had spent countless hours despising, yet who always protected her, even if his actions seemed like those of a ruthless madman at the time.

Rynah looked at Klanor, whose eyes shifted away from hers and
she forced her head downward, catching a glimpse of her grandfather's ring, which she always wore around her neck. She had become
both Marlow and Klanor (something she swore that she would never do), choosing the crystals over a man she had once professed to
love. Guilt filled her as she became aware that she had allowed herself to be fooled, and Klanor had witnessed all of her actions during
the telepathic interrogation—her failure.

Chapter 30
INTERRUPTED COMMUNICATIONS

"**A**re you sure we're safe here?" asked Joe.

"For now," said Fons. "I checked this place out. The house was foreclosed on and the owners evicted, but the power hasn't been turned off yet, so we can use this place for a little while."

Joe ushered the others inside and set the computer case, which they had stolen from an unsuspecting college student at the nearby university, on the floor for Fons. He disliked the idea of squatting in an abandoned home, but realized that they hadn't much choice. Hotels cost money and there were too many people around. In the foreclosed house, the neighbors were separated by thick shrubbery, and they were away at work.

Fons opened the computer case, pulling out the laptop.

"How are you going to get communications up?" asked Joe. "The phone line is dead, which probably also means that the internet is down."

"You have a lot to learn about technology, my friend," said Fons as he booted up the computer and connected it to a satellite dish the size of his hand. "Breaking into someone's wireless network and using it for internet is easy. People always think they are so smart when they set up their passwords."

"You know, what you're doing is illegal," said Joe.

"So is breaking into a foreclosed home," replied Fons, "and stealing, and have you forgotten your little escapade at the Smithsonian?"

"Enough, please," said Brie. "Rynah and Klanor have been captured by Fredyr, my mother and sister are still Stein's prisoners, and all you two can do is banter about the illegality of our current situation?"

She caught Tom about to push a button on the home's security system—he hadn't seen one like it before, and his curiosity being what it was, of course, he decided to fiddle with it—and yanked it away.

"Sorry," Joe said to Brie. "We didn't mean to upset you."

"Solaris," said Tom as he helped Fons hook up the miniature satellite dish in order to get away from Brie's ire, "do you think you can boost the range on this thing?"

Solaris walked over to the dish and placed her hand on it, communicating with it in the fashion that only she could.

"It's range has been increased to maximum capability."

"Thanks," said Tom. He studied Solaris' somber face, her usual self-assured tone had disappeared as her mind lay elsewhere, with Rynah, he surmised. "We need to contact Jifdar and figure out a rescue plan."

"Rynah told us to continue without her if anything happened," said Joe.

"We can't just leave her," said Tom and Brie together.

"I agree," said Solon, while Alfric placed his sword, point down, in front of him as a sign of his agreement with the others.

"How do you suppose we rescue her?" demanded Joe. "We don't have a spaceship, and it seems like this Stein is always two steps ahead of us."

"Which is why we will contact our one ally who has the vessel we need," said Alfric.

Not wanting to argue with the Viking—something very few ever did, much less lived to tell about it—Joe relented.

"All right, but be careful."

Fons' hands zipped across the keyboard as he brought up a series of strange codes, using what Solaris had told him about the frequency Rynah used to contact Jifdar. After the agonizing seconds of waiting passed, Jifdar's face appeared on the laptop's screen.

"What's happened?" he demanded. "Ships have been buzzing around above the planet like a bunch of flies over a rotting carcass."

"Rynah and Klanor have been taken captive," said Alfric, "and we need your help to get them back."

"What?" said Jifdar. "How?"

"Does it matter," replied Alfric. "We need your assistance. Will you, or will you not, provide it?"

"Now hold on there," said Jifdar. "Rescuing them from that well-armed armada is suicide."

"So it can't be done?" asked Tom.

"I never said that," Jifdar said, "but it won't be easy. We'll need to know which ship they are on, the security involved, and…"

"Oh, how delightful," said a snide voice, interrupting them.

Everyone froze as Stein's purple face filled the monitor screen.

"How…" began Joe.

"Don't bother trying to wrap your primitive mind around this," said Stein. "I am always ahead of you."

"So you knew that Rynah and Klanor would be there that night," said Alfric.

"No," replied Stein," that was merely good fortune. I am here to give you this one warning: cease your pathetic attempt to stop me or suffer the consequences."

"What consequences?" demanded Joe.

"Have you not witnessed them already?" asked Stein. "Your

most populated cities destroyed. People rounded up and held on my ships. How many more must suffer for your incompetence?"

"You heartless…" Brie rushed toward the monitor, but Solon held her back, shaking his head.

"Brie," said Stein, "how delightful to see you again. Do your friends know that you are the reason we are all here? Indeed, I never would have learned of this insignificant little planet if it hadn't been for you. I wonder how your mother would feel, knowing that you would much rather save a stranger over her and your sister. Do you know how many nights she has wept due to your absence? And your sister… Sara is it? Does she know that you are responsible for her nightmares?"

Brie struggled against Solon's firm grip, but Joe reached forward and held her back as well, reading the message between Stein's words and seeing the game that he played.

"If you'd like," continued Stein, "I can let you speak to them; I know that they long to see you."

"Speak your terms," said Alfric, "or silence your forked tongue."

"As you wish," said Stein. "I want you to abandon this foolish quest of yours. I also want that crystal that you stole from me. You have until tomorrow to…"

"No," said Alfric, answering for all of them.

Brie lurched forward, trying to voice her dissent, ashamed that Rynah's and Klanor's capture had forced her to forget about her family, but both Solon and Joe held her back, covering her mouth.

"No?" said Stein; his face darkened.

"We will not give you the crystal. Rynah and Klanor understood the risks," said Alfric, "but we'll not play your game."

"I can assure you, that you will," said Stein.

The screen went blank.

"How could you?" demanded Brie. "He'll kill them!"

"You can't speak for all of us," said Tom.

"It's done," Alfric deep voice silenced them. "Bartering is a sure way to ensure that he wins. Whether we did as he wished or not, it will not stop him from murdering those we hold most dear."

"And how would you know?" demanded Brie.

Alfric's face twitched as the memory of an act he committed years past surfaced, before he reburied it. Though the others failed to notice the slight change in his expression, before he steeled it again, Solaris did not.

Tom, Brie, and Joe continued to yell at Alfric, their voices rising in volume until the shouts could be heard across the street, but none of them cared, too consumed by their own emotions. All they thought about was that people they cared about had been taken hostage, and Alfric had unilaterally decided their course of action.

From several paces away, Solaris watched them, unsure of what she thought or felt. Anger swelled in her at Alfric's decision, but, logically, she understood it, though her thoughts dwelled on Rynah, blocking all reason as she understood the pain Brie felt knowing that Stein had her mother and sister; Rynah was all the family she had left.

"Solaris," said a voice in her head. "This is not a hoax."

"Stein," whispered Solaris, removing herself from the crowded room so that she could speak in private. "How did you get this frequency?"

"You of all people should be able to figure that out. Remember who sits in my prison," said Stein. "I want you to listen carefully. As your companion has insisted on not listening to reason, I will speak to you."

"Proceed," said Solaris.

"I want that crystal. You know of which I speak."

"Why should I deliver it to you?"

"Because if you don't I will kill Rynah, Klanor, Brie's mother and sister, and the people that Fredyr has recently acquired as slaves. If you continue to deny me what I want, I will decimate this entire planet."

"You haven't that sort of power," said Solaris.

"You once thought that Klanor did not possess it."

"Why should I listen to you?"

"Very well. I hear that you are a unique artificial intelligence who desires to be more like us, more human. I must say that you are the most advanced one of your sort that I have seen. Here is my proposal: meet me at the Wilmar Construction Site in ten hours. It's not far from where you are. Bring the crystal and I will release your friends and the girl's family. I'll even throw in the group that was taken prisoner by Fredyr last night."

"How do I know I can trust you?" demanded Solaris.

"You can trust me on this: if you fail to show, I will kill your friend and the others. The question is, which will you choose: your mission, this quest to save a planet you do not know, and whose people you owe nothing to, or your friends, whom you claim to care for?"

"I need some time to think about it," Solaris said.

"You have ten hours," replied Stein, "and come alone or I'll kill them all."

The communication ended, and once again, the shouts from the other room filled Solaris' ears. She stared out the window and its transparent white curtains at the beautiful sunny day outside and pulled out the crystal they had stolen from the Smithsonian, wondering what she should do. Until now, never doubting the mission Marlow had given her had been easy, but how could she continue it when it meant the death of a friend or another friend's family? Solaris had also sworn to Marlow that she would protect Rynah. And now she had to choose between two promises that she had made to a man she loved like a father.

Solaris glanced at the others who remained oblivious to her lack of action as they argued. Alfric had chosen the mission, but if Stein would be meeting with her in person, perhaps she could put a stop to him once and for all.

Lost in her thoughts, Marlow entered them, not the man himself, but a memory. He had just returned from another of his trips, and she had asked about his whereabouts, curious as she had always been in the early days of her existence.

"Marlow," she had said.

"Not now, Solaris."

"But you were gone for eight days."

"I said not now."

Solaris hated it when Marlow refused her inquiries.

"The least you could have done was tell me that you were leaving and when you would return."

"I had something that needed to be done, and little time to do it," Marlow had replied.

"What could be so important that you would neglect to tell your family? Rynah was here on numerous occasions, searching for you. What was I to tell her if you failed to return?"

"Nothing," Marlow had said. "She doesn't even know that you exist."

"Marlow," Solaris had continued, "you need to…"

"Solaris, please! Enough!"

For the first time, Solaris had experienced Marlow's anger and she shrank away from him, deep within her memory components, frightened and hurt.

"Solaris," Marlow had said, his tone more gentle, "I'm sorry. I shouldn't have yelled at you like that."

"Thirty-five years," said Solaris, "that is how long I have kept your secrets, while you frequently leave me alone down here. Thirty-five years I have trusted you."

"I am sorry." Sorrow filled Marlow's face as he stared at the computer console, which held Solaris' intelligence. "You have done more than I thought possible, and now I must ask even more of you. You know about the crystals. Finding them is more important than the worries of family."

"But…"

"It is my mission," Marlow had told her, "and it will soon become yours. You must promise me, Solaris, promise me, that you see this mission through no matter the sacrifice."

"Does the love of your family mean nothing?" Solaris had asked.

"I am doing it for them."

Solaris had remained silent, unsure of how to respond, and if she should accept what Marlow had asked of her.

"Please, Solaris. There is more at stake than the few we care about."

"I will."

"Thank you," he had said, relieved that she had accepted his request. "I think I have what I need to run the test later this week."

"Are you sure you should be doing this?" Solaris remembered asking him.

"I've no choice," Marlow had replied. I've picked an area in the Brestef region. It is fairly isolated."

"I don't like it."

"I know," Marlow had said, "but if the worst should happen, you must…"

"I'll watch over her," Solaris had promised.

"Tomorrow, I must leave you again."

"Leave me?"

"Yes. There is this auction taking place, and something I find most interesting is to be sold there. It's in need of some repair, but I think it will do."

"What is it?"

"A ship, and the only one of its kind."

The memory faded, like all memories do, and Solaris found herself back in a strange house that had once belonged to a family. A picture frame caught her eye. With delicate fingers, she picked it up, touching the rounded edges of the gold-painted frame. Joyful smiles stared back at her. She wondered about the people in the photograph, where they had been when it was taken, what sort of event had brought them such happiness, and what had happened to end it.

Stein's words came back to her. Ten hours. That was all the time she had to decide the fate of other people. Solaris struggled with the decision placed before her, but in the end, decided that only one course of action remained, though it meant betraying the one person who trusted her above all else.

"I'm sorry, Marlow," she whispered to the air, "but I cannot abandon a friend."

The shouting continued. Solaris marched into the other room. "Stop it, all of you!"

Her voice rang out, echoing in the small, unfurnished room, forcing the others to shut their mouths. "If you continue like this, we will have the authorities on us in minutes. Alfric's right. The mission is more important. When night falls, you all will locate this Lanyran that has been hiding here. I'll stay behind and erase all traces of us having been here."

"Are you sure that it is wise for us to split up?" asked Alfric.

"It is necessary," said Solaris. "I will meet up with you all later, once I am certain that no one is following us. Also, I will be keeping the crystals with me, for safekeeping."

"I don't think..." began Joe, but Solaris interrupted him.

"This is not a debate. Solon, the other crystal, please."

Wary of Solaris' sudden change, and her authoritative tone, Solon hesitated, which irritated her even more.

"The crystal."

He reached for his belt, where he had tied the bag with the crystal that Stein had failed to acquire on Sunlil, and which Rynah had entrusted to him, and unfastened it, handing it to Solaris' outstretched hand. She took it without a word, leaving the others to wonder about this new plan of hers.

* * *

Obiah paced in the small room he had hidden in while waiting for Merrick to return with news. The entire ship was abuzz with rumors of Klanor and Rynah being taken captive. He hoped that the stories were mere rumor. The door slid open. Merrick rushed inside, closed it behind him, and waited, listening, making certain that no one followed or had seen him.

"Well?" asked Obiah with impatience.

Merrick's face fell.

"It's true."

The color drained from Obiah's face as the confirmation of Rynah's capture sunk in. What were they to do now? He knew that she would be tortured, if not executed.

"Where is she?"

"On another ship," said Merrick.

"What?" Obiah had expected Rynah and Klanor to be on the main ship of the armada, like Brie's mother and sister were.

Men marched by the room, forcing Obiah and Merrick to cease talking as they listened to the heavy pairs of boots stomp through the hall on their way to their duty stations.

"Stein isn't stupid," said Merrick. "He will not keep valuable prisoners on the same ship, as it makes it too easy for their allies to break them free. Always, he has excelled at cunning."

Obiah eyed Merrick, wondering how he would know this about Stein, but he had also noticed a bit of respect, and regret, in the man's voice.

"How do we get them out?"

"We cannot save both," said Merrick.

"We have to," said Obiah. "You cannot ask me to choose between…"

"You have to!" said Merrick. "I know we had discussed rescuing Brie's family for her, but now we have to consider the possibility that it may no longer be feasible."

"I can't go back to her and tell her…"

"You must!"

"What about Rynah?"

"I'm sorry, Obiah. I really am. You have to make a choice that no one should have to decide."

Obiah stared at Merrick, unwilling to make the decision. He pulled out his thumb-sized communicator that he had used to stay in contact with Rynah and the pirates. He punched in the frequency that would allow him to speak with Solaris, but was only supposed to be used in an emergency.

"Solaris?"

No response.

"Solaris, can you read me?"

Static.

"What's wrong?" asked Merrick, worried about the lack of response. "Why doesn't she answer?"

Shoving his communications device into his pocket, Obiah looked at Merrick, concerned that his message had gone unanswered.

"I don't know. I can't make this decision without consulting them. Brie deserves to have a say, as this concerns her family."

"Look, we…"

"I know dammit!"

Obiah wiped the sweat off his brow, detesting the circumstances he found himself in and the choice he had to make: Brie's family or Rynah. Though troubled by the fact that Solaris failed to respond, he knew that he could waste no more time debating what to do next.

"Rynah," said Obiah. "We must rescue her."

"Very well," said Merrick. "I will see about getting us transferred to the ship she is on. In the meantime, see what you can learn about the security surrounding her cell."

Obiah nodded his head as Merrick left. "Great Ancients, help me," he whispered to himself, as self-loathing for choosing one life over another filled him.

* * *

The whine of the station wagon's engine filled the dismal atmosphere as Joe entered Interstate 80, leaving the city where they had taken refuge. Dusk had long since passed, and he felt it was safe enough for them to continue their journey. Once they reached Cheyenne, he would take Highway 25 south, straight to New Mexico and the supposed Lanyran that lived there. No one spoke. None of them wished to. Solaris had elected to stay behind, and refused to listen to them when they tried talking her out of it. Joe shook his head. In the short time he had known them, one thing he knew for certain, Solaris was very stubborn, and when her mind had been made up, there was no changing it.

Joe glanced at Brie, who sat in the passenger seat, staring out the window. Fons sat between them. Brie's heavy breaths fogged the glass as swirls of snowflakes drifted by them. Joe's heart felt for her. If it had been his family held hostage by some madman, he would feel as abandoned as her. He turned back to the road, the faint headlights boring holes through the threatening snowstorm. Winter refused to release its hold, despite the onset of spring.

"We should turn back," said Brie.

"Brie," said Joe, "Solaris was very clear. We need to find this alien, and maybe he can tell you how to destroy the crystals."

"So, you no longer doubt them?" asked Tom.

"I've been shot at and chased by aliens," replied Joe, "what do you think?"

"What does it matter?" said Brie.

The others looked at her.

"What does it matter," continued Brie, "if we find this Lanyran when we don't even have the other crystals?"

Still no response.

Without warning, Brie lunged over Fons, shoving him aside, and slammed her foot down on the brake. The car skidded and slid as it screeched to a halt; irate shouts and blaring horns rushed past them as other drivers voiced their anger at their sudden stop.

"We're going back. I can't abandon Rynah, or Solaris."

Another honk echoed around them as a car swerved to miss their rear bumper.

"Idiots!" shouted the driver, shaking his fist at them.

Joe stared at Brie's determined face.

"All right," he relented. He turned the car around, driving over the medium and yelling at other cars whose occupants made their frustrations known. Merging into traffic, Joe headed back to the city they had just left and the foreclosed home, knowing that Solaris was no longer there.

Joe steered the car down the dark street—a single streetlamp provided light—and slowed down when he noticed a group of people just outside the house they had hidden in earlier. He parked the car.

"Stay here," he told the others. "I mean it."

Obeying his orders, the others remained in the station wagon as Joe walked over to the small crowd. A woman in the center shouted her anger at having her car stolen, demanding the police do something. Pulling out his badge, he hoped that he could talk to the woman, without arousing suspicion; he had a sinking feeling of who was responsible for the theft.

"I want my car!" shouted the woman.

"Ma'am," said the poor officer charged with trying to calm her, "we're doing the best we can. I need you to tell me what the car looked like."

"What are you? Some kind of stupid?" said the woman. "I just told you!"

"Excuse me," Joe shoved his way through the gathered crowd, flashing his badge. "Special Agent Joseph Harkensen. I understand that you have had a theft."

"My car was stolen," said the woman.

"I need to know what the make of the vehicle was, license plate, any distinguishing marks, and so forth."

"It's a Nebraska license plate," said the woman, "number is 890C6G. A silver sedan."

"Did you see the person who took it?" asked Joe.

"Yeah, but this idiot insists that I'm crazy."

"Why's that?"

The woman looked around, unsure of whether she should tell him, or not. "She… she had a purple face and green hair."

Someone in the crowd snickered.

"Green like this?" asked Joe, pointing at his jacket.

"Yeah," said the woman.

"Do you know what direction she headed in?"

"That way," the woman pointed northwest.

"Thank you, ma'am," said Joe.

"What is the FBI's interest in all of this?" asked the police officer.

Joe looked the man square in the eye, hands on his hips.

"We believe that the woman is involved with an international smuggling ring that steals cars, strips them down for parts, and then sells them overseas."

"And the purple face?" asked the officer.

"Classified," said Joe.

"What about my car?" demanded the woman as Joe walked away.

"I will do what I can to have your car returned to you," said Joe, "but you must understand that my main priority is to find the woman who took it."

He left the crowd and jumped back inside the station wagon.

"Well?" asked Fons.

"Do any of you know what is directly northwest of here?" asked Joe.

Fons opened up the laptop, bringing up webpage after webpage after having tapped into another person's wireless network.

"There's a construction site northwest from here, about 20 miles. Wilmar Construction. Why?"

"I think that's where Solaris went."

"Construction?" asked Alfric, trying to comprehend what Fons meant by Wilmar Construction.

"This one is out of the way, and construction sites never have anyone there at this time of night," said Joe.

"An ideal place for an ambush," said Alfric.

"Exactly," Joe replied, putting the car in drive and speeding away.

Chapter 31
SOLARIS STRAYS

The wheels of the car turned right, heading down the gray rocks that covered the makeshift driveway leading into the construction site. The overhead lights had been turned on, staving off the darkness that surrounded them. Two ships stood at the end of the driveway in front of a trailer—which was the foreman's office during work hours—with their rear hatches open. Two cranes remained just out of sight, but the light outlined their faded shapes. Solaris slowed the car and pulled up alongside the trailer where two shapes loomed; the wheels crunched the gravel as she stopped. The two shapes moved closer. Undaunted, Solaris opened the car door and stepped out, bag in hand, and walked toward the two figures that waited for her.

"Welcome," said Stein, stepping into the light.

Fredyr remained off to the side, preferring to watch the proceeding for the moment.

"Where are they?" demanded Solaris.

"Straight to business," said Stein, "but not so fast. The crystals."

Solaris held out the bag, but refused to relinquish it.

Focused on the situation before them, none of them were aware of the shapes that slipped through the shadows, darting behind equipment and piles of rock. The mysterious shapes watched the three people in the light. One motioned for the others to surround Solaris, Stein, and Fredyr.

"Give it here," said Stein.

"Not until I see the others," replied Solaris.

Stein snapped his fingers. Harsh and monstrous sounds carried through the still air, piercing the tension with ease while the cranes switched on, lifting upward, removing the metal planks—which matched the darkness and had remained undetected by Solaris—and revealing two cages. In one cage, Rynah and Klanor huddled together; in the other was Brie's sister, Sara. Solaris looked at their frightened faces, steeling herself for the task at hand.

"Sara!" Brie rushed from the darkness, forgetting Joe's orders about secrecy when she saw her sister. Realizing her mistake, she stopped.

"I should have known you would have brought your friends with you," Stein said.

"I followed her," said Brie, trying to regain some control of the situation. "Solaris knew nothing."

"You are either very brave or very foolish," said Stein.

"Where are the others?" Solaris demanded.

With a snide grin, Stein waved his hand; more lights turned on, shining the white beam onto a pit dug deep into the ground (that had been dug earlier in preparation for laying the foundation to a building) as frightened voices spilled from it. In horror, Solaris realized who those voices belonged to.

"You..."

"There was no better place to keep them," said Stein. "The crystals."

Solaris hesitated. Something didn't feel right. She glanced

around her, knowing that it was too late to turn back, but also determined to save the ones there.

"All we ask of you," Fredyr spoke up, "is the crystals. After that, you can have your friends, and those over there."

Solaris clung to the bag.

"If I give you them, how many more lives will be destroyed?"

"Semantics," said Fredyr, "but rest assured that we will kill the ones here if you stall any further."

Solaris pondered her decision, having been wrestling with herself during the entire car ride until she came to a single decision: save what you can today and get the crystals back later. She tossed the bag. It landed in the dirt with a thud.

Stein strolled over to the bag and scooped it up, opening it and peering inside. Satisfied that he had what he wanted, he sealed it again.

"The hostages," Solaris said as Stein walked away towards one of the open ships.

"Yes, about that," said Stein. His words garnered him a questioning look from Fredyr. "I'm changing the nature of our agreement. Now that I have the crystals, I no longer need bartering chips. I must say that I find you interesting, an artificial intelligence, given a semi-organic body, and who now fancies herself human, like the rest of us. Do you think looking like us makes you one of us?"

Solaris ripped out her laser pistol, which she had concealed under her shirt, and aimed for Stein. A single shot fizzled through the air as her pistol was knocked from her hands. She looked at Stein. He stood, laser weapon raised, staring at her with cold, heartless eyes.

"Did you think that I wouldn't suspect such a course of action from you?" he said, his tone murderous. "The problem with making deals with the devil is you get burned."

Both Brie and Solaris stared at him.

"Bring them aboard the ship," ordered Fredyr.

"No," said Stein, stopping the armed men in their tracks. "There's no need for that."

Fredyr opened his mouth to challenge him, but Stein pointed his laser weapon at him, forcing the man to step back.

"So to answer for his own failures, Marlow created you," Stein said to Solaris. "Did he think no one would learn of it?" Stein held up a holo-emitter, allowing it to project images from the security cameras at the FBI building in Philadelphia, as Solaris changed her appearance.

"I know that the Lanyran government always talked about the possibility of creating an artificial intelligence, but refused to go forward because of moral complications, and here you stand, another of Marlow's secrets."

"Let them go," said Solaris.

"And I shall," said Stein. He clicked off the holo-emitter and pulled out another remote controller, pressing a button. Symbols flashed to life on the two cages—though Brie did not know the symbols, she understood their significance—beeping as they changed, counting downward.

"Do you see the mound of dirt above that pit? There is a charge buried within it, set to detonate at the same moment that the charges in these two cages do, in ten minutes. Consider this your final lesson on what it means to be human. These are ionic charges and even the most skilled take about 20 minutes to disarm one. Since you are so much more, you may be able to do it in half that time, but not for all of them. Just as Marlow chose life and death for thousands of people, you get to choose who lives and who dies. So who will it be? Your friends? The family of a friend? Or a bunch of strangers?"

Solaris stared at Stein, unsure of what to do as she realized that the rules had just been changed.

"The clock is ticking," said Stein. "Choose quickly."

Stein headed for one of the waiting ships. Fredyr followed him, but before he had taken three steps, Alfric jumped from the shadows, tackling him, and forcing him to the ground. As they rolled across the dirt, Stein boarded his ship, the hatch closed, and it took off, leaving them to their fate.

"Brie!" cried her sister.

"Sara!" said Brie. She looked at Solaris, pleading with her to save her family, though hating herself for being willing to sacrifice Rynah.

Solaris glanced at Sarah and Rynah, who shook her head, before looking at the pit. Indecision raced through her troubled mind as she struggled with her choices.

"Solaris, please!" said Brie.

"I'm sorry."

Solaris ran for the cage that held Rynah and Klanor. She skidded to a halt, dropping to her knees, studying the ionic charge attached to the metal bars. Both Rynah and Klanor tried to scream at her, but the gags in their mouths and the bonds on their wrists prevented them from doing so. The green symbols continued their countdown as Solaris opened a small panel, revealing wires and crystal programming chips. As she worked the wires loose, but kept them attached, her eyes took in every bit of the mechanism, searching for a way to disarm it.

Laser fire struck the ground next to her. Turning, she saw Fredyr's men closing in, not liking the fact that Alfric had attacked their leader. More laser fire scorched the ground. Ignoring it, Solaris pried a yellow wire away from the others as she accessed her stored knowledge of ionic charges. Scuffling caught her attention. Brie had charged the other cage where her sister was. They locked eyes a moment, before she turned away, focusing once again on the charge. Knowing that she would have to ease the crystal disk out at the same moment she disconnected the yellow wire, Solaris pried it loose with her nail. Rynah continued her animated movements, but Solaris ignored them. She needed to concentrate.

As laser fire echoed around her, she ripped the wire and the crystal disk free, rendering the explosive charge useless. The counting symbols ceased. Solaris pried the lock on the cage, ripping the door open while Rynah and Klanor shook their heads, their eyes wide. They vanished.

"Sara!" screamed Brie as her sister also vanished.

Solaris noticed a pen-sized rod in the top left corner of the cage. She snatched it. Dumbfounded, she looked at Brie, holding the holo-emitter in her hand as dread filled her; Stein had tricked her. Rynah, Klanor, and Sara were holographic images.

A loud bang, followed by a grunt, snatched her attention. In a daze, Solaris watched as Alfric and Fredyr struggled for the upper hand. The pit. She jerked her head to it; terrified screams still emanated from it. Unwilling to risk the possibility of them being holograms, she bolted for the pit, dropping the holo-emitter.

Fredyr rammed his knee into Alfric's stomach. As the Viking doubled over, he swept his feet out from under him, forcing Alfric to crash into the gravel; rocks sliced his skin, drawing blood. Fredyr pulled his most prized possession, the Kresnyr sword, free. He pointed the three pronged blade at Alfric.

"If I remember correctly, you said that you were unfamiliar with this particular blade. Allow me to demonstrate its use for you."

Snatching a rock, Alfric knocked the sword away from his face. He lunged for Fredyr and gripped him around the leg, knocking him to the ground and punching him in the jaw. Fredyr returned the favor. Together, they rolled across the rocks, kicking and punching one another. Alfric jumped to his feet. He pulled his sword free just in time to block a strike from Fredyr. He stabbed his sword at Fredyr, but the man had expected it, bringing his blade up, catching Alfric's in the crook of his three pronged sword. Twisting his weapon. Fredyr wrenched Alfric's sword out of his grasp, sending it flying, where it landed next to Brie.

Fredyr attacked. Alfric whirled around, using the bracelets on his arms to block the Kresnyr blade's deadliness, its golden edges glittering in the construction lights. He knocked the weapon to the side, ramming his fist into Fredyr's face, but Fredyr countered by kneeing Alfric in the stomach again while simultaneously jabbing the point of his elbow into the back of the Viking's neck. Fredyr kicked Alfric again, knocking him to the ground. Stunned, Alfric lay motionless. Gloating, Fredyr kicked him in the face; blood spurted from Alfric's nose.

"You are good," said Fredyr, raising his weapon, "but I have trained in the art of the Kresnyr blade all my life." He poked Alfric's arm with the center blade of his sword.

With the world a blur, Alfric lay helpless as Fredyr prepared to deliver death's stroke.

Fredyr raised his three-pronged sword and brought it down. It stopped. Unaware of her presence, Fredyr failed to notice Brie running for him, with Alfric's sword in her hands. Blades locked. She glared at Fredyr with loathing and determination.

"You think this wise," said Fredyr.

Brie freed her weapon and clipped Fredyr in the leg with it. Hobbling, and in a rage, he lunged for her. Though used to fighting, Fredyr had always battled people of Alfric's size, but Brie was smaller and more nimble. She dove to the ground, rolling between his legs, before jumping to her feet and kicking him in the middle of his back. Enraged, Fredyr charged her, humiliated by her skill. Brie dodged. She twisted around, allowing his sword to strike the earth, while she rammed the hilt of Alfric's blade into Fredyr's chest. Fredyr swung. Brie jumped back. Alfric had taught her well.

"I'll kill you both," hissed Fredyr.

Brie said nothing; her eyes were ice.

Fredyr charged her. Brie sidestepped, tripping him, and watched as Fredyr crashed face first into the dirt. Brie walked towards him, her determined steps informing him that she had prepared to take his life, but before she could, laser fire pelted the ground around them, forcing Brie to dive behind a mound of dirt for cover.

"Kill them!" shouted Fredyr to his men as he snatched his Kresnyr blade and ran to the other remaining shuttlecraft, boarding it.

Brie huddled behind the dirt mound, knowing that she hadn't much time before its protection failed her. More laser fire whizzed past, striking the ground and sending plumes of dust into the air.

"PSSSST!"

She looked up.

Tom motioned from behind a truck for her to come to him. Abandoning all sense of reason, Brie ran for him. He grabbed her and pulled her to the ground behind the truck just as an earsplitting explosion rocked the ground, destroying the trailer and the pile of rock behind Fredyr's men. Killed by shrapnel, Fredyr's men lay on the ground, their weapons freed from their grasp.

"What was that?" asked Brie.

"Dynamite," said Tom.

"What?"

"I found some, so Solon, Fons, and I worked out this plan."

Alfric's moan reminded Brie of their situation. She and Tom hurried over to him, each placing an arm around their shoulders, lifting him up, and half dragging, half carrying him to safety.

Solaris reached the pit. She dropped to the ground, leaning over the edge and reaching for an outstretched hand. She was too far. Footsteps sounded behind her. Solaris jumped to her feet, whirling around, ready to fight her attacker. It was Joe. He had noticed her running for the people in the pit and followed.

"What do you need?" he asked.

"Something to pull them out with."

"There!" Joe had spotted a ladder tied to a bobcat on the ledge above them.

"Please," said someone in the pit, "help us."

"We're getting a ladder for you," said Joe, trying to calm them.

He and Solaris raced to the top of the ledge, climbing the dirt mound. Pebbles clacked as they dropped to the bottom, having been disturbed from their desperate movements. They hauled themselves to the top, springing for the ladder attached to the Bobcat. Solaris stopped Joe. He gave her a questioning look, but she pointed at the ionic charge attached to the roped that held the ladder to the construction equipment, rigged to detonate if disturbed. She checked the timer. They had three minutes.

"Can you disarm it?" asked Joe.

Without a word, Solaris propelled the thumb-sized panel from the charge, exposing its nail-thin crystal disk and wires. In the darkness, she worked the yellow wire free of the others. Tick, tick, tick filled the air as the timer counted downward closer to detonation. Growing anxious, Joe watched, praying that Solaris would disarm it in time, while looking for a rope, but found nothing. Solaris released a long, slow exhale as she ripped the disk and wire free. The timer stopped. Yanking the charge away from the ladder, Solaris undid the rope around it and together, she and Joe carried the ladder to the pit.

They reached it at the same instant that the dynamite Solon and Fons had triggered exploded; their raging fires lit the night, forcing the frightened people in the pit to cower. Solaris lowered the ladder into the trench, unfastening its catch so as to lengthen it. As people scrambled for what they believed to be their salvation, a click echoed around them, followed by a tick, tick, tick. Joe was the first to notice. He looked down, seeing the green symbols change, and recognized them for what they were. Both he and Solaris had failed to notice that the ladder had also been rigged with a charge, set to detonate in 15 seconds of the ladder being stretched out. He snatched Solaris by the shoulders, flinging her away from the edge of the pit, and both rolled down the hill away from it just as the ionic charge went off. It's detonation set off the other charges—which had been placed in the walls of the crater lining it, before the hostages were put there—creating a series of explosions that covered the people trapped within and buried them.

"No!" screamed Solaris once she stopped rolling. She headed for the pit, but Joe grabbed her, pulling her back to the ground just as another charge exploded.

Helpless, both watched as fire and dirt consumed the trench and those within it. Solaris struggled to break free of Joe's grasp, but he held firm.

"I have to save them!" Solaris shouted.

Joe remained silent, never releasing his grip on her.

"I have to—it's my fault!"

Defeated, Solaris slumped to the ground, realizing that Stein never had any intention of allowing her to rescue anyone; he had planned on murdering them all from the beginning.

"I've failed! I've failed Marlow. I've failed Rynah. I've failed you all. I thought I could help them, but..."

Joe heaved the distraught Solaris into his arms—her limp form flopped against him—and carried her away from the burning bodies behind them, ignoring the smell of cooking flesh. Solaris said nothing. Her eyes moved from him to the stars above, before she did what no one thought possible for an artificial life form—she lost consciousness.

The roar of a truck reverberated around them as its wheels screeched to a stop next to them. Tom opened the passenger door.

"Come on!"

Joe handed Solaris to Tom's and Solon's outstretched arms and climbed into the truck bed where Brie nursed Alfric's wounds.

In the driver's seat, Fons rammed the truck into gear and sped off, away from a tragic end to a horrendous night.

Chapter 32
FREDYR'S MISFORTUNE

The doors to the command center slid open as Fredyr stormed into the chamber, anger etched on his face, the *Kresnyr* blade swinging by his side.

"May I help you," scoffed Stein, ending his conversation with Gaden, knowing why Fredyr was there.

"How dare you do that to me," raged Fredyr.

"I've no idea what you are talking about."

"Don't play games with me! You deliberately had those people killed—people that were my property and mine to do with as I chose."

"That's your problem, Fredyr, you seem to think that everything is yours."

"You murdered those people."

"And how is that any different from the crimes you have committed? How many lives have been ruined because you gathered the resources of a planet not protected by the charter of the Twelve Sectors and sold them for a profit? Do not lecture me about morality when your own is in question."

"At least they lived," said Fredyr.

"If you call what they have lives."

Fredyr gaped at Stein, while Gaden tried to melt into the background, not believing not just what he heard, but what he saw, pure malevolence.

"How could you?"

"You were the one that suggested a trap."

"Yes, but not under the guise of offering them a choice. You gave them a choice from which you knew that no matter what they choose, people would die; but then you stood there, watching it with no emotion."

"Emotions get in the way," said Stein.

Fredyr watched the man he had thought he could partner with and use to his advantage, but realized that he had made a grave mistake.

"I no longer care about this planet, or what it has to offer. My men and I will be leaving."

"What are you saying?"

"I think our alliance has reached an end," said Fredyr.

"You know," said Stein, "I think you're right."

He ripped out his laser pistol, killing Fredyr's two bodyguards before shooting the man in the hand, forcing him to drop his sword, and pinning him to the floor.

"I'm glad you are here though," sneered Stein, pointing his laser pistol at Fredyr's head, "as there is something I wish you to see."

Stein yanked Fredyr to his feet, wrenching his arms behind his back, and held him before the window that filled the front of the ship.

"While we conducted our exchange of men, I had mine conduct special repairs to your ships."

Fredyr's brain scrambled to comprehend Stein's meaning.

"Now," said Stein to a technician in front of a computer console.

Orange lights filled the depths of space around them as Fredyr's ships exploded, consumed by raging flames. Cursing for allowing himself to be tricked, Fredyr stood, helpless, as his ships burst into shards of metal and bits of glowing embers, killing his men.

"You are my prisoner now," Stein whispered in Fredyr's ear. He threw the man to his armed guards. "Take him to the detention center."

Chapter 33
TOGETHER

Rynah struggled against the cuffs around her wrists as she stared into the holo-emitter, which sent her and Klanor's image down to the Earth to taunt Solaris. It was Solaris' eyes that haunted her. The desperation within them, a quality she had never seen there before, nor thought possible, tore at her. She glanced at Klanor. Pain still swelled within him at her betrayal, making Rynah realize that she was no better than him in the end—she had committed the same horrible act. She watched the holoimage as Solaris rushed towards them. Despite her attempts at nonverbal communication, Rynah had failed to convey her message. She shook her head again.

Klanor watched her movements, noting what she tried to do. He, too, pulled against his restraints, shaking his head with such violence that he saw stars. Desperate, both watched as Solaris abandoned Brie and ran for them, while Brie, angered, rushed to her sister. Rynah glanced at Klanor. His eyes conveyed pity as he felt sorry for Brie, and the harsh truth she would learn: Sara was also just a holoimage. Rynah charged the holoimage, pulling her restraints so taut that they dug into her skin, drawing blood.

The point of a laser rifle poked her skin.

She ignored it. Rynah yanked the restraints with such force that they rattled the wall, clinking and clacking as she squirmed to get free. The holoimage dissipated. Pausing, only for a moment, as she knew that Solaris had just discovered Stein's sickening ruse, Rynah lurched forward; a crack formed where her restraints were secured to the wall.

"Stop it!" yelled the guard, facing her, his back to Klanor.

Rynah continued her movements; the guard's shouts grew louder. Klanor kicked the man in the back, sending him flying forward into the wall, his head striking it with a crunch and he fell to the floor next to Rynah. She swung around and rammed her foot into his face, rendering him unconscious. Wasting no time, Rynah scooted closer to the guard and searched for the key to the restraints, her frantic movements a blur to Klanor. She found it. Rynah released her restraints and rushed over to Klanor, freeing him. Neither said a word. They hurried to the door, but the key did not work on it. Rushing back to the guard's unconscious form, Rynah rifled through his pockets, looking for anything that might release the lock on the door. Nothing.

A tapping sounded on the doors. Listening, and curious as to what it was since it didn't belong, Rynah cocked her head to the side until she understood that the tapping was a message. She peeked through the small glass window in the top center of the door and saw a face she never thought she would see again.

Obiah stood there. "Stand back," he mouthed.

Rynah snatched Klanor's arm, yanking him away from the door and forcing him to the floor on the far side of the room just as a small blast ripped the cell door away. It dropped from its hinges, clattering to the metallic floor. Coughing from the black smoke that surrounded them, Rynah uncovered her eyes and looked at Obiah.

In a moment of unbridled emotion, she ran to him, embracing him in a gigantic hug, overjoyed at seeing him again.

"Let's go," said Obiah.

Rynah and Klanor rushed through the opening and found Merrick waiting for them, motioning them to hurry up.

He peeked around the corner. Clear. As one, the four of them darted around it, down a set of steps, through a long hallway, and up another set of stairs.

"Halt!" yelled one of Fredyr's men.

Klanor pounced upon him, ripping the laser rifle from the man and knocking him to the floor. They hurried through the ship and to the shuttle bay. Silence fell. The ominous feeling that something was not right filled each of them as they stopped. Despite their breakout, no one pursued them. A low rumble echoed beneath their feet, vibrating the floor of the ship and growing louder and louder until it became a roar that pounded their eardrums with incessant fury. Rynah looked down the hallway. Flames snaked toward them, stretching up the walls and covering the ceiling as they rushed for them, reaching for them.

An explosion ricocheted around them, pitching the ship to the side and knocking each of them off balance as the series of flames still raced for them. Klanor stood in its path. Time stood still as Rynah found herself faced with a choice: save herself or save the man she had spent months wishing was dead. Her mind thought of Brie and how the girl had chosen death in order to save a group of strangers that she had come to respect and care about. She remembered Brie's insistence that Klanor had changed, and as she thought about it, she remembered Solon's words about how sorrow and grief darken hearts if you don't learn to forgive. It all became clear to her in that moment. Rynah knew that if she allowed him to die, she would be no better than Stein. She lunged for Klanor, yanking him out of its path as she forced him into a semi-protected conclave; the fires surged past them, burning as they went, consuming everything before fizzling out. The ship lurched again as bulkheads crashed around them, covering them.

Klanor unburied himself from the debris that had toppled on top of him. He found Rynah's limp hand. Desperate, he threw the ceiling panels and support structures off her and lifted her up. An agonizing scream burst from her lips. Concerned, Klanor lifted up her shirt, revealing a piece of shrapnel that had lodged itself in her side; blood poured from it.

"You need to go," whimpered Rynah.

"Yeah, and so do you," replied Klanor.

Laser fire surrounded them as Fredyr's men had caught up with them, despite the damage to their ship.

Klanor snatched the knife from Rynah's boot and placed it in the smoldering flames until it glowed white hot. Taking it out of the fire, he held it before her. "This is going to hurt."

Rynah just nodded, her sudden weakness evident.

Klanor ripped the shrapnel out of her side and pressed the glowing blade of her knife against her skin. Despite Rynah's screams, he kept the blade there until certain that the wound had cauterized. Once done, he put the knife away.

"How much further?" he asked Obiah, who hunkered behind a fallen bulkhead, firing at Fredyr's men.

"Merrick!" Obiah called.

"Not far," answered Merrick, "but this debris has cut off our way through."

Bits of insulation dropped around them as thick smoke engulfed them, encroaching on their ability to breath. Tearing a piece of cloth from his shirt and tying it around his nose and mouth, Klanor rose to his feet, picking Rynah up in his arms, her head lolled to the side.

"Then we will forge our own path!"

He kicked a fallen bulkhead away from him and charged through the burning flames, ignoring their searing heat. Metal support beams crashed around him. Swerving, Klanor dodged them, while never losing his grip on Rynah, her limbs bouncing with each sudden movement. More flames burst from the side. Before they could reach him, Klanor ducked low, turning so that his back took the impact of their wrath until they dissipated. He jumped to his feet. Rynah's eyes had closed. Unwilling to lose her, he ran through the dilapidated corridor, dodging falling panels, walls, and bolts, never stopping, and never slowing.

One of Fredyr's men had gotten pinned underneath a fallen bulkhead. He reached for his weapon. Klanor leapt over him just as Obiah kicked the laser rifle away from his grasp and shot him.

Trudging forward, Klanor pushed his way through the barriers that the damaged ship threw at him until he burst through the other end with Merrick and Obiah by his side. He glanced at Rynah. Her eyes were still closed and her breathing shallow. Merrick pushed them forward, running through the ship to the doors ahead that led straight to the shuttle bay. He fired his weapon at the holographic keypad, shorting it out and forcing the doors open. Another explosion ripped through the ship just as they reached a shuttle and closed the hatch.

Klanor laid Rynah in a seat, checking her wound. A soft groan escaped her lips, but her eyes remained closed.

"The shuttle bay doors are closed," said Merrick as Obiah started the engines.

"Not for long," muttered Obiah. He flicked on the missile targeting system, aiming his sights on the exterior doors and fired, blasting them open.

They broke free of the spaceship's confines just as it erupted in flames and burst into millions of pieces. Obiah steered the shuttlecraft back to Earth's atmosphere. A piece of debris slammed into the shuttle, sending it into a tailspin as he struggled to regain control. Lights flashed and alarms blared.

"What happened?" asked Merrick.

"I've lost control of the ship," said Obiah; his fingers had turned white from the pressure of his grip on the controls.

Fire erupted in the rear. Klanor leapt to his feet and snatched a fire extinguisher, pointing its foamy liquid at the orange and black menace and coating it until nothing remained but choking smoke and charred remains. The ship lurched.

"Now what?" said Klanor.

"Tractor beam," replied Obiah.

Klanor looked out a port window. Above them was the main ship of what had once been his armada, but was now Stein's.

"Does this shuttle have an escape pod?"

Merrick looked out the same window. He checked the flight manual of the ship, which showed an escape pod in the rear of the shuttle. Checking it, Merrick noticed that the pod was intact, but its ejection mechanism had been damaged by the fire; however, its internal controls, allowing the person within to steer it, still worked. The pod itself was only large enough for three people, since that was how many would normally crew the shuttle they had stolen. A plan formulated in his mind; someone would have to stay behind, and he knew who it would be.

While the others remained preoccupied by the tractor beam, Merrick reattached the wires that had been damaged, opening the door to the pod and making it so that he could eject it from the pilot's seat. He would only have one chance at saving them and intended to use it.

"There is an escape pod," said Merrick. He forced the door to it open. "Help me get her in there."

Together, Klanor and Merrick lifted Rynah up and carried her to the pod, being careful not to reopen her wound. Klanor remained with her as Merrick rushed to the pilot's seat.

"Obiah," he said, "time to go."

"Someone has to maintain control of this ship," said Obiah.

"I'll rig them," said Merrick. "Just go."

Obiah gave Merrick a questioning look, but refused to argue as the tractor beam pulled them closer to the gigantic ship above them. He removed himself from the pilot's chair—Merrick slipped the photo that he always carried into his pocket—and hurried to the escape pod.

"Merrick, come on!"

Merrick touched a button, forcing the door to the escape pod closed and locking the other three inside.

"Merrick!" shouted Obiah. "What are you doing?"

Merrick brought up the intercom so he could speak to them.

"I'm sorry, Obiah. There is only enough oxygen in there for three people."

"We can…"

"There are a set of controls in there so you can fly back down to the planet."

"Merrick!"

"Tell Rynah that I do not blame Marlow for what he did and she shouldn't carry his deeds with her. If you check your pocket, Obiah, you'll understand why I have to do this. Protect this planet; don't let them suffer for our mistakes."

Merrick hit the ejection button, and the wires he had fused back together sparked as they completed the circuit, which jettisoned the pod into space. He watched them go, longing to be with them, but the knowledge that he had unfinished business with Stein held him back.

"Good-bye," he whispered.

In the pod, Obiah beat his fist against the door, screaming in rage at Merrick's decision, and angered by the knowledge—even though they had been forced together by circumstance—that he had lost another friend. Klanor placed a firm hand on his shoulder, calming him. Returning to his senses, Obiah glanced at Rynah, whose wound had turned black, and settled behind the escape pod's flight controls.

"Do you know where we should go?"

"I have the coordinates of where we were headed before being separated," replied Klanor.

"Good, because this pod has limited fuel." Obiah punched in the coordinates and prepared for re-entry. A sharp poke touched his thigh and he reached into his pocket, pulling out the photograph that Merrick had slipped in there, almost dropping it when he looked at it. In the picture were the grinning faces of Merrick and two women, each holding a child, and Stein. Obiah dropped the photograph, understanding why Merrick had been so interested in Stein's actions.

While the main ship of Stein's armada busied itself with the shuttlecraft that contained Merrick, it failed to notice the tiny pod speeding towards the surface of the planet below.

Chapter 34
NOTHING GAINED

Stein approached the device that Klanor had built, the two crystals he had garnered from Solaris in his hands. Assured of his victory, he placed the crystals into the device. Though it had been built for six, the two fit together, forming one (and Stein decided that seven crystals were better than six), and giving him more power. He stepped back.

"Turn it on," Stein ordered.

The machine hummed to life as power surged through it. Stein watched, pleased that he had accomplished what others had only dreamed about. Now, the universe would give back what it took from him or suffer the consequences; he didn't care which, as long as he had some satisfaction.

A spark erupted from the device. Curious, Stein peered closer, knowing that such a thing was not supposed to happen. Another spark flew from it, and another, until a whole slew of them popped from the apparatus, showering him in their fiery glow.

"What's happening?" demanded Stein.

"I don't know, sir," said a technician as she studied the stats of the device on her holomonitor."

Pop! Sparks erupted from the device in multitudes as it shook, rocking back and forth until...

Boom!

After the smoke cleared and the danger passed, Stein crept away from where he hid to avoid the blast and approached the device. It had disintegrated. Only six of the crystals, which now lay on the floor, remained intact, unharmed and undamaged (no scratches or charring marked their outer surface), while the seventh had been crushed and burned.

Stein picked up one of the crystals.

"How can this be?" he asked.

No one had answers for him.

What Stein could not have known was that when Solaris demanded that Solon give her the bag with the crystal, he had switched it with the fake one they had found on the desert planet (the planet with two crystals) before Stein had turned on Klanor. Unaware of the switch, Solaris handed Stein the bag with the crystals, thinking that both of them were real. When a replica of the crystals is forced to bond with the crystals themselves, they reject it. Solon could not have known what would happen; he only desired to prevent Stein from achieving his goal.

"I want answers!" yelled Stein.

Scrambling, technicians probed and scanned each of the crystals, hoping to find the answers Stein sought before they became his next target.

"Sir," said one, "not all of these are real."

"What?"

The technician picked up the fake crystal.

"This one does not release the same amount of power as the others. I believe it is a replica."

Stein took the fake crystal, turning it in his hands, studying it, his fingers stroking the miniscule watermark on it. In an instant, he recognized it as the one Rynah had taken from him in the mines. Infuriated, he chucked it across the room—it ricocheted off a wall and clattered to the floor—fuming at being tricked. He glared out the window at the Earth. If this was the sort of game they wanted to play, he would give them an opponent they wished they had never met; if this was what they wanted, he would give them real suffering, and Rynah would regret ever having been born into Marlow's family.

Marching boots echoed around them, forcing Stein to turn around.

"The prisoner, sir," said one of the soldiers, gripping Merrick's arm until it turned white, flinging him forward and forcing him to fall to his hands and knees on the cold, hard floor.

Stein and Merrick locked eyes a moment and Stein's face drained as he recognized the man before him, his sister's brother.

"Merrick?" he whispered, still not believing that the only family he had left stared back at him; the surprise in his voice perplexed those in the room as they watched.

Merrick lifted his head, looking straight into Stein's eyes, eyes that had once held warmth and friendliness, but were now empty, except for the hatred within them.

"Hello, Stein," he said. "Or may I still call you brother?"

Enraged, Stein stormed towards Merrick, punching him in the face and rendering him unconscious. He bent low and snatched a crystal from the floor, squeezing it in his hand and ignoring the pain as the edges cut into his skin while his malefic gaze focused on the holoimage that filled the command center with the Earth in its center, vowing to destroy Rynah and those who followed her.

The story concludes in the final book: Solaris Soars.

The adventure concludes in the
final book of the Solaris Saga

About the Author

Ms. McNulty began writing short stories at an early age. That passion continued through college until she published her first book: Legends Lost: Amborese under the pen name of Nova Rose. Since then, she has gone on to publish a mystery series, children's books, and even a dystopian series.

Ms. McNulty currently lives in West Virginia, where she enjoys hiking, being outside, crocheting, or simply sitting around and doing nothing. She continues writing and is busy finiahing the final book in her Solaris Series.

The Solaris Saga

Solaris Seethes
Solaris Seeks
Solaris Strays
Solaris Soars

Every myth has a beginning.

After escaping the destruction of her home planet, Lanyr, with the help of the mysterious Solaris, Rynah must put her faith in an ancient legend. Never one to believe in stories and legends, she is forced to follow the ancient tales of her people: tales that also seem to predict her current situation.

Forced to unite with four unlikely heroes from an unknown planet (the philosopher, the warrior, the lover, the inventor) in order to save the Lanyran people, Rynah and Solaris embark on an adventure that will shatter everything Rynah once believed.

More by Janet McNulty

The Mellow Summers Series

Sugar And Spice And Not So Nice
Frogs, Snails, And A Lot Of Wails
An Apple A Day Keeps Murder Away
Three Little Ghosts
Oh Holy Ghost
Where Trouble Roams
Two Ghosts Haunt A Grove
Trick Or Treat Or Murder
Roses Are Red…He's Dead
Double, Double Nothing But Trouble

Mellow Summers moves to Vermont to attend college, accompanied by her friend Jackie. They soon find themselves running into ghosts and one mystery after another.

The Dystopia Trilogy

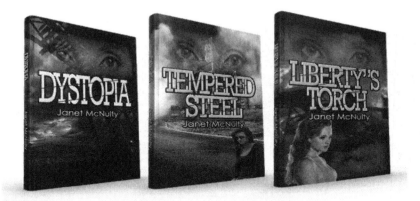

Dystopia (Book 1)
Tempered Steel (Book 2)
Liberty's Torch (Book 3)

**Imagine living in a world where
everything you do is controlled.**

Dana Ginary lives in a world where every aspect of her life is controlled by the Dystopian Government. Forced to work in Waste Management, her life becomes a nightmare with hunger and survival is her only constant. Before she knows it, she is caught up in a resistance movement and exiled from Dystopia, forced to find her way in the barren wastelands. While there, she must learn to live independently and discover how far she is willing to go to live and achieve freedom.

The Legends Lost Series

Published under Nova Rose

Tesnayr
Amborese
Galdin

Enter the Lands of Tesnayr and join on an epic fantasy adventure that spans over 1,500 years.

Begin with Tesnayr, the first king of the five lands as he unites the against a savage foe bent on their destruction.

Next, Join Amborese as she fights reclaim the throne after her family was forced to flee from it.

Thinking peace has finally entered the land, follow Galdin as he returns to Tesnayr to find it greatly hanged. Barbarians, led by a mysterious sorcerer, burn and destroy as they go. And only Galdin can stop them if he chooses to accept his fate.

Visit www.legendslosttrilogy.com to learn more about the Legends Lost Trilogy.

A Little Something for the Little Ones.

Mr. Chili Books:

Mr. Chili's Chili
Mr. Chili Goes To School
Mr. Chili's Halloween
Mr. Chili's Christmas

Others:

Mrs. Duck and the Dragon
The Hungry Washing Machine
Rhymes-a-lot
Are You the Monster Under My Bed?
How Do You Catch An Alien

Grandpa's Stories

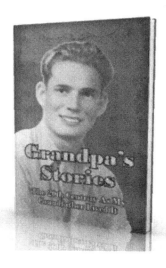

My grandfather grew up in Arizona during the 1920s and 1930s. One week after the attack on Pearl Harbor he joined the Navy. During the summer of 2012, my mother visited him and record-ed his stories about growing up, World War II, and his time as an employee at the Pacific Bell Telephone Company. This is the history of the 20th century as he lived it. These recordings make up this book. These are his words.

48542470R00228

Made in the USA
Charleston, SC
06 November 2015